A Spell

for

Trouble

A Spell for Trouble

for

Trouble

AN ENCHANTED BAY MYSTERY

Esme Addison

CROOKED LANE

NEW YORK

Published in the United States by Crooked Lane Books, an imprint of The Quick Brown Fox & Company LLC.

Crooked Lane Books and its logo are trademarks of The Quick Brown Fox & Company LLC.

Library of Congress Catalog-in-Publication data available upon request.

ISBN (hardcover): 978-1-64385-303-1
ISBN (ebook): 978-1-64385-324-6

Cover illustration by Teresa Fasolino

Printed in the United States.

www.crookedlanebooks.com

Crooked Lane Books
34 West 27th St., 10th Floor
New York, NY 10001

First Edition: May 2020

10 9 8 7 6 5 4 3 2 1

To my parents, for always knowing I was meant to be a writer and providing a lifetime of unconditional love and support.

To my in-laws, for sharing their culture, history, heritage, and hospitality—*dziękuję*.

Rodzina nie jest czymś ważnym. Jest wszystkim.

The family is not important. It is everything.

—A Polish proverb

Chapter One

The house at 136 Cypress Lane didn't look like trouble—quite the opposite. The seafoam-green Queen Anne was well kept, with rows of purple tulips blooming beside the wraparound porch and daffodils leading up to the brick walk to the front door. Alex stepped out of the SUV and onto the sidewalk. Everything about this place was lovely. So why had her father insisted for years that she not set foot within miles of Bellamy Bay?

"Miss? Do you want me to get the dog?" The taxi driver gestured uncertainly at the large German shepherd grinning at Alex through the back window.

"Oh, sorry! I'll get her." Alex understood how fierce her dog appeared to others, even if Athena was a big baby, deep down. "Come on, girl. You need to stretch your legs."

Once the dog was free from her harness, she leapt from the vehicle. Alex admired her black-and-brown fur as she sniffed the area, pausing at the base of the mailbox.

Dad. The feeling of guilt suddenly weighed her down. He would not have approved of this trip. "We're not going," he would tell her when the invitation came to visit for Christmas or Thanksgiving, his face darkening at the mere thought of seeing her aunt and cousins. Inevitably he'd produce an excuse for not heading down south and spending the holidays in Bellamy Bay. Still, the invitations came year after year, and so did his grumbling remarks. *They don't mean it. They're just being polite. They're not like us. Trust me, you don't want to go there.* Alex had the impression that, for some reason, he'd blamed her aunt for her mother's death. But that tragedy was no one's fault.

"Sorry, Dad," she whispered. She was sure he'd meant well enough, but now that she was all alone in the world and unemployed to boot, Alex lacked the fortitude to decline an invitation to visit her only relatives, no matter how estranged. Besides, clean ocean air and a break from the mayhem of Manhattan were just what she needed.

She waited while the driver popped the trunk and hurried around to the back. "Do you need help with the bags?" he asked.

"I don't want to trouble you." She struggled to lift her largest suitcase, and it fell to the road with a thud.

"It's no trouble," he replied. They'd been riding together for about an hour east since he'd picked her up at the airport in the port city of Wilmington, North Carolina, and had become friendly. He quickly emptied the trunk, piling her small suitcase, duffel bag, and an old backpack neatly on the sidewalk. "I can help you to carry it—"

Alex held up a hand. "No, I insist. You have a long drive back, and I don't want to take up any more of your time."

He gave her a nod and a smile. "I appreciate that. You take care of yourself."

"You too."

Alex lifted the strap of her duffel bag and hefted it over one shoulder. She faced the Queen Anne. How long had it been since she'd seen her *ciocia*—her aunt—Lidia and her cousins Minka and Kamila? Not since her mother died, which made it . . . at least twenty years. What would she say to them? She tried to ignore the nervous twinges in her stomach, focusing instead on maneuvering the other pieces of luggage so that she could carry everything inside in one trip. She had one suitcase in each hand, a duffel on her back, and the backpack strapped to her front as she wobbled slowly up the walkway.

Without warning, the front door swung open and a voice boomed, "Well, look at *you*."

"*Ciocia* Lidia." Alex smiled.

How was it possible that Lidia had barely aged in over two decades? She was stunning. Her ivory skin was smooth and her long, blue-black hair sparkled with threads of silver. Alex paused as her aunt turned her bright-blue eyes toward her. She swallowed a lump that had suddenly appeared in her throat. "It's so nice to see you," Alex managed, her voice weakened by unexpected longing.

"Oh honey, you don't know how many years I've waited for this. I just—look at you. Look at how gorgeous you are." Lidia gripped Alex by both shoulders. "Minka! Kamila! You've got to come out here!" Lidia paused to sigh. "Oh, Aleksandra. If you don't look just like your mother."

A pleasant warmth crept over her skin. She'd loved her father dearly, but he'd nearly banned any talk of her mother after her death. It was nice to hear her mother mentioned in conversation and not feel like she was doing something wrong.

"Alex is here!" A bright, energetic voice rang out as a woman with a head of shoulder-length chocolate-brown curls came bursting out of the house. "Why didn't you tell me?"

"I did," Lidia laughed, and stepped aside so that her daughter could pull Alex into a bear hug.

"Do you remember me?" The young woman stepped back to give Alex a full view of her round face and pretty dark-blue eyes. She was wearing a pink sweater and blue jeans. "I'm Minka."

"Of course I remember you," Alex said with fondness. Twenty-four months younger than her own twenty-eight years, Minka had been the baby of the group. "Last time I was here, you told me your doll had a fever and you made me crush herbs for her with a mortar and pestle."

Her younger cousin giggled, delighted. "I remember that. Do you still use herbal remedies?"

"What?" Alex snorted. "No, of course not. Unless Tylenol counts as herbal?"

"Bad move, mentioning Tylenol," a tall, athletic woman with a caramel-blonde ponytail said, approaching with a grin. "Mom and Minka run an herbal apothecary downtown, a few blocks from here. Modern medicine is a curse word in their house."

Alex recognized her instantly as Kamila, her cousin who was two years older than her and the former ringleader of the trio during her summers at the beach. She had the same swagger she'd always had, and she'd grown into a woman with girl-next-door beauty. Alex flushed, afraid she'd already offended her family. "I didn't mean anything—"

Minka grinned at her sister. "Don't start trouble, Kam. And don't you listen to her," she said to Alex. "She's a hard-nosed cop."

Kamila ignored her sister and leaned in to embrace Alex. She was wearing running shorts and a tank top covering an athletic bra, as if she'd come straight from the gym.

"I didn't know you were a police officer," Alex said.

"And last we heard, you were working in risk management," Kamila replied. "Is that right?"

Alex nodded. "That's correct."

Grinning, Kamila cocked an eyebrow. "I'm sure there's a joke in that somewhere."

Alex smiled. "Go ahead, I'm not offended. People who strive for risk-averse lives are statistically healthier and have a higher life expectancy. There's tons of studies to prove that."

Her cousin laughed. "In my experience, life is more exciting when you take chances. Otherwise, what's the point of living?"

Alex opened her mouth to tell her cousin that ever since her mother had died, she'd tried to live her life as cautiously as possible; how else could she avoid danger? But she changed her mind when she saw her cousin smiling down at her dog. Why ruin the mood with her prudent philosophy on life? She smiled as Kamila reached down to allow the German shepherd to smell her hand. "Is this your baby?"

"Yes. Her name is Athena. Dad raised her as a puppy. She was supposed to be a police dog."

"Supposed to be?" Minka said, and dropped to her knees to invite the dog over, but Athena remained aloof.

"Sorry about that. She's a little concerned that people keep hugging me," Alex explained, and smoothed the ridge of fur that was standing behind Athena's neck. "It's all right, they're family," she assured her, and Athena lowered her ears and crept toward Minka. "She went through a year of *Schutzhund* training, but she was much too friendly to be a K-9."

As if on cue, Athena rolled onto her back and allowed Minka and Kamila to scratch her belly. "*Schutzhund* is attack-dog

5

training," Kamila explained to Minka as Athena wriggled happily in the grass.

"Yeah, can you tell she's a trained killer?" Alex chuckled. "But that's only one component of *Schutzhund*, and the one Athena happened to fail at. Fortunately, she's pretty good at listening to basic commands. And she's just over two years old, so she's pretty calm." Alex watched the dog with fondness. She'd taken over her care after her father died, and Athena was her last link to him.

*　*　*

The house was lovingly decorated, cheery, bright, and clean. Alex admired the wide planks of the hardwood floors and the sea-glass-green vase of fresh-cut flowers decorating the entryway. Warm colors and antique nautical maps brightened the sunlit home. Lidia showed Alex to her bedroom on the second floor. "This was your room when you were a child," she said. "Do you remember?"

Alex nodded slowly as she took in the soft-yellow walls and the canopied bed. The duvet cover was a buttercream yellow sprinkled with colorful blossoms. Silk butterflies swung from the ceiling, and fresh flowers in crystal vases perfumed the air. "I felt like a princess in here."

Her aunt gazed at her thoughtfully. "Yes, this was your kingdom."

Alex walked to the window and opened the curtains, gazing at the view. In the backyard, Lidia kept a vegetable-and-herb garden and had encircled a koi pond and a fountain with an explosion of vibrantly hued flowers. Some of Alex's happiest childhood memories involved those gardens. Her family used to visit Bellamy Bay for weeks at a time, and she had passed many summer days watching the fish in the koi pond, or staring in wonder at the fountain. Fashioned from a silver metal tinged with blue was a life-size statue of a beautiful mermaid kneeling in a large shell filled with water. She held a small fish that trickled water out of its open mouth into the shell below.

The mermaid's hair, a long tangled mass of waves, covered her bare chest, and her fish tail curved seductively around her.

Sometimes a dark-haired boy from the neighborhood had joined her, and they would run through the rows of flowers, imagining they were in a magical place. He'd even woven her a crown of violets. She missed those days long after her mother died and her father stopped bringing her to Bellamy Bay.

Lidia set a hand on Alex's upper arm, pulling her out of her daydream. "Why don't you settle in and we'll make you some tea?"

"That sounds great."

Alex waited for her aunt to leave the room before she flung herself backward on the bed. The room smelled like lavender and lemongrass. Her muscles loosened from the long car ride as she took a few good, deep breaths. The last month of her life hadn't been spectacular, but Alex hadn't had time to dwell on it. Now she had nothing more to do. She was here, in her aunt's house, relaxing for the first time in ages, and it struck her that everything she'd worked for was gone. She'd never get promoted at her firm. All of her plans and all of those years of sacrifice and hard work— *poof.* She felt the heaviness of the loss.

Somewhere, a teakettle whistled.

Alex pulled herself up with a sigh. Distraction was the only answer. She changed into a pair of comfortable old jeans before heading downstairs.

Like the other spaces in the house, the kitchen was filled with sunlight and warmth. Lidia was on a step stool reaching for mugs on the high shelf of a narrow wooden cabinet while Minka lifted a steaming kettle off a stainless-steel gas stove. "Something smells good," she said, before spotting a plate of *kolaczki*—Polish cream-cheese pastry—on the wooden top of the breakfast bar. "Oh my gosh, I haven't had these in ages!"

The *kolaczki* were filled with fruit jelly, and the corners of the pastry were folded in the center so that they resembled angel wings. Kam was seated at the breakfast bar. She slid the plate toward Alex, who lifted a sugar-dusted cookie and took a bite. As the flavors of sweet apricot and creamy pastry melted on her tongue, she felt like a child again, sitting in this very kitchen, enjoying her mother's cooking. "You used to bake *kolaczki* with Mom at Christmas," she said as she settled contentedly into her seat.

"They're your favorite, as I recall," Lidia said. "Your mother had to hide them from you or else you'd eat the whole plate." She set a filter over the top of a mug and poured the tea. "This is specially made for you, my dear. A blend of lavender, chamomile, ashwagandha, and honey." She set the steaming mug in front of Alex. "This will get you feeling better in no time."

"Feeling better?"

She hadn't told her aunt anything about her trouble at work. Lidia had simply called her out of the blue one afternoon to invite her to spend some time with them at Bellamy Bay, and Alex had accepted. There had been little discussion except to share excitement about the reunion. How could she possibly know Alex's entire life was broken?

"It's written all over your face," Lidia explained, as if reading Alex's thoughts. She settled into the chair beside her niece and set a warm hand on her wrist. "Sweetheart, you're a senior consultant at an international firm taking a vacation without an end date. Something must be wrong."

Alex inhaled the faintly spicy scent of her tea and released a sigh. What was the point in hiding anymore? She was far away from everyone back in New York, and something about this place was so comforting that she longed to unburden her troubles. She wrapped her hands around the hot mug and eased her elbows onto the counter. "I sort of . . . quit."

It had all happened so fast. The director who had been supervising Alex had taken another job, and someone new had come in from the office in Chicago. "Her name was Cornelia. She didn't like me. I tried to make a great first impression. I stayed later than usual and came in earlier. I gave her my best work, but nothing I did was ever good enough for her. She rode me constantly, tried to embarrass me in front of others. It became toxic very quickly for me."

Minka wrinkled her nose. "You poor thing."

"Stuff like that happens at the police station," Kamila added. "We have this new detective, some hot shot who thinks everything we do is wrong." She rolled her eyes. "I get it."

Alex nodded and took a sip of her tea. The ashwagandha was strong but pleasant, balanced by the soothing honey and chamomile. "Delicious, *Ciocia*. Thank you."

Lidia scooted the plate of *kolaczki* closer. "You probably need another one."

She did. This time, Alex selected strawberry. "It wasn't what I'd expected," she continued. "I mean, I've done well for my clients. I'm good at what I do. Well, I was good." She shook her head. "I don't know where to go from here or if I'm even going to stay in the same field. The point is, I thought Cornelia would be happy to work with me." She picked at a few crumbs on the plate. "I thought I was on track to become the next risk management supervisor. Everyone said so, including my last boss. But during my review, Cornelia told me it was her recommendation that I remain a senior consultant."

"That sucks," Kam exclaimed.

Alex chuckled at the outburst. "Yeah, it does." She took another sip of tea. "I was angry. It felt so unfair. I still don't know what her problem was with me. But after the anger passed, I just felt tired. Burned out. I'd been working at least sixty hours a week for years, and I realized that while I was working, life was happening."

Her chin trembled as she thought of her father and his illness. She'd visited him when she could, but he'd been receiving care for his bad heart in central Connecticut while she'd been working her tail off in New York City. When he died three months ago, she'd been nearly overcome with grief and regret. "I chose my career over being with my father," she whispered. "I could have taken a leave, but I was really hoping for a promotion—"

She took a breath to stop the tears from spilling, but one slid down her cheek and landed in a pile of powdered sugar on her plate. She was human and therefore entitled to make mistakes; her father had taught her that. He'd been a police detective and then the chief of police before he died, and he'd understood bad choices and redemption. Deep down, she knew he would have forgiven her for not being at his side. But she was struggling to forgive herself.

"So anyway, after the meeting with Cornelia, I spent a couple of days feeling bad. Then I quit. And you know, it felt good to walk out." Biting her bottom lip, she glanced at her aunt. "And then you called, out of the blue, almost like you knew I needed to get away."

Lidia wrapped her arm around Alex's shoulders and pulled her closer. "Well, I'm glad you're here now. We're going to take good care of you."

"It's what we do best," added Minka as she rounded the breakfast bar to join the hug.

Even Kam added her arms. "You're safe here, Alex."

She wasn't used to being taken care of—whatever that meant. "I'm grateful to be here, but I don't want to be a burden. I'm not going to lie around the house. What can I do to help out?"

"Why don't you come to work with us?" Minka said as she untangled herself. "At Botanika."

Alex recalled Kamila's warning about modern medicine. "Is that the herbal apothecary?"

"Yes, and it's great," Minka continued, shooting her sister a warning look. Kam retreated to her seat without saying a word. "We'll teach you all about plants and flowers, and show you how to make herbal remedies and other stuff. Right, Mom?"

Lidia nodded and gently rubbed Alex's back. "You're welcome to join us. And I'll pay you, though it won't be the salary you're accustomed to—"

"That's fine," Alex said quickly. She had come to Bellamy Bay for a distraction, and Botanika sounded perfect. Besides, she'd lived as frugally as one could in New York City, dutifully saving a third of her paycheck for the past five years. She'd be okay financially, at least for a while. "When do I start?"

"Bright and early tomorrow morning," Lidia said. "Unless you want to take a few days to get settled?"

Getting settled sounded dull, and Alex feared that if she was bored, she'd begin to dwell on her recent regrets and mistakes. "Tomorrow is great," she said.

She was taking a vacation from her normal life, she reasoned. It sounded risky, but maybe it was time to live a little.

Chapter Two

The next morning, Athena was hiding under the bed with a shoe. Alex saw her tail peeking out from under the dust ruffle, wagging a half-moon across the wooden floor. This was a new game, only made possible because the big house in Bellamy Bay provided so many more hiding places than Alex's apartment in Brooklyn.

"Athena," she scolded. The German shepherd's tail swished faster. "Okay, fine. If you come out, I'll give you a cookie."

The dog scrambled out from under the bed and obediently dropped the shoe before sitting at Alex's feet, her ears at full attention, a happy grin on her face.

"This is becoming a bad habit." Alex broke off a piece of biscuit and waited for the dog to lift it from her fingers. "I need both of my shoes, you know." But then she smiled and scratched at the dog's fluffy chest. She could never stay mad at Athena. "Come on. It's time for work."

Minka was waiting by the mailbox for Alex and Athena, checking her cell. She looked up as they approached. "Alex, you're doing it again."

"Sorry. What?"

"Biting your nails." Minka gently pulled Alex's hand away from her mouth. "I've never seen a person so tense."

Alex was no good at unwinding. For years, her blood had buzzed with the energy of New York City. Each morning she'd rushed from her brownstone apartment in Brooklyn to her skyscraper office in Manhattan, where she'd put in ten-hour workdays.

"I know, biting my nails is a bad habit," Alex conceded, and placed the offending hand at her side. "I'm trying to relax." They headed down the sidewalk toward Main Street, leaving behind the neighborhood of historic homes and passing a bakery, a bookstore, an antique shop, and a diner. The sun was up, but the town was still sleepy. "Tension is just something I'm especially good at."

"Listen to you, trying to relax." Minka laughed. "Well try harder, girl. You're on vacation now. Sort of," she added, because they were technically heading to work.

The herbal apothecary was located on Main Street. A hanging wooden sign advertised *Botanika* in simple scroll, and gold lettering above the storefront window read *Apothecary*, but otherwise the shop did not draw attention. The store windows were decorated with colorful bottles and vials that recalled a time when medicine was prepared by a pharmacist rather than shipped from a factory. There was an equally picturesque retail space beside the apothecary, but the windows were dark and a *For Sale* sign was tacked to the glass door.

That morning, they arrived moments before business hours. Lidia was already inside, but she had locked the door behind her. Minka turned a key in the glass door and swung it open, sending out a warm gust of air scented with sweet orange, cinnamon, and lemongrass. Alex inhaled, and her normally tense muscles released. Even work was different in Bellamy Bay.

"Hi, Mom," Minka called out to the empty shop floor.

Lidia popped out of the back room carrying a basket of hand-made pastel-colored soaps. She had an energy about her that filled the room, or maybe it was her personality. "Good morning, *kwia-tuszki*," she smiled, using the Polish word for *flowers*. Lidia spoke perfect English, but she resorted to Polish whenever she felt like it. "Did you sleep well?" She set down the basket and came over to give them each a warm kiss on the cheek. She smelled a little like cloves.

"I slept like a baby," Alex replied. "I actually can't remember the last time I slept so soundly."

"Wonderful. Later this morning I'm going to teach you how to make one of my favorite items. Perfume."

"Sounds great. Athena, go in your spot," she said. Lidia had already prepared a little corner in the shop for the dog, who trotted over to a pillow and discovered a bone in her basket of toys.

"Come on." Minka grasped Alex lightly by the elbow. "We'll straighten up a little before we open."

Alex was pleasantly surprised by the charming character of the space. The red-brick walls were lined by live-edge wooden shelves neatly stacked with glass jars and tins. Little chalkboards explained the shop's offerings: beeswax and calendula salve to promote healing, soothing herbal milk baths to detoxify and unwind, lotions to ease insomnia and bath salts to alleviate muscle pain and soften dry skin. The air in Botanika smelled at turns like lavender, lemongrass, and rose petals, depending on where one was standing. It was all nice, even if she didn't fully understand the appeal of an herbal apothecary.

Minka showed Alex around the shop and taught her how to stack and straighten inventory. There was an order to the space.

Body and bath products lined the wall closest to the door, while medicinal products were organized against the opposing wall. Tables of candles and shelves on the floor were spaced to encourage customers to meander rather than walk up and down aisles. Glass bottles of loose-leaf teas nestled against the back wall, invitingly advertising flavors like Rose Petal Mint and Lavender Bergamot. Some teas offered more than a delicious flavor, and these had been given names like Good Luck, Calm Down, and Abundance.

Soon after opening that morning, Lidia came out of the back room carrying her purse. "Got to make a supply run. I'm out of beeswax. Hold down the fort?"

"Of course, Mom." Minka tied her Botanika apron—bubblegum pink—and then blew a kiss as Lidia headed out the door.

Alex set to work straightening bottles on the shelves. Her aunt had a *lot* of products. "Does she make all of this herself?" she asked Minka as she aligned jars of hand salve. "She's very creative."

"I help out here and there, but yeah, it's mostly Mom," Minka agreed. "She knows everything about herbal remedies. You've seen the library at home, right? It's full of textbooks on plants, folk remedies, and biology."

"Really? I had no idea." Alex paused to read a label on a short jar of ointment. "Belladonna? That can't be . . ." She looked over her shoulder. "Isn't belladonna . . . ?"

"Deadly nightshade," her cousin replied, without looking up from her work filling small linen pouches with fragrant lavender buds. "Women used to squeeze the berries into their eyes to make their pupils dilate, which they believed made them more attractive. It's extremely toxic. Deadly, even."

A Spell for Trouble

As a risk management consultant, Alex realized she was a trained pessimist. She saw nothing but danger in every patch of ice and uneven sidewalk. She realized this quality made her a buzzkill in most circles, but Alex viewed her caution as protectiveness toward others.

She lifted the jar from the shelf and turned it over in her hands. "But if it's poisonous, how come belladonna is in an ointment for arthritis? I don't understand. Every minute of my risk management training is telling me that advertising a toxic ingredient can't be a good idea."

Minka laughed and set down the pouches. "Belladonna leaves and roots can be used for pain relief. We have a few customers who swear that ointment is the only medicine that works for their joint pain." Alex must have looked unconvinced, because Minka continued, "We've sold it for years. No one has gotten sick." She took the jar from Alex and set it in its rightful place on the shelf. "Really, it's fine."

"But is this . . . ?" She didn't want to ask Minka if the shop was *legal*. Even though this shop screamed risk and potential lawsuits, voicing that observation would appear ungrateful after all the hospitality and kindness her aunt and cousins had shown her. Besides, Lidia's little shop had been in operation for decades, and she was meticulous and knowledgeable and thorough—

Minka touched Alex's arm. "You're a little bit of a worrier, aren't you? It's okay; a lot of people don't understand what Mom is doing here. They get suspicious."

Alex sighed. "I've got to loosen up. I know."

"I like you the way you are." Minka smiled. "And I'd never tell you to stop caring. But you don't need to worry."

She was a worrier. That's what she did. But Alex nodded, resolving to try. "Okay. Thanks."

"And although we have products to treat a lot of illnesses, Mom believes there's such a thing as going too far; does that make sense? It's one thing to offer an alternative cough syrup, but we don't want to offer an herbal remedy that might discourage someone from taking medicine for a serious health condition."

This sounded like a wise policy to Alex. If customers were tossing their blood pressure pills in favor of tea, that could attract the wrong kind of attention to Botanika.

The bells on the front door chimed as a woman entered. She paused to tousle her long, orange-red hair and hike the strap of her leather messenger bag up on her shoulder. Then she fixed her close-set green eyes on Minka. "Good morning," she purred.

Minka glanced at Alex before replying, "'Morning, Pepper. Can I help you find anything?"

"I think I'm all set." Pepper craned her neck around the shop before walking deliberately toward a shelf of manuka honey cough syrups. She lifted one bottle, considered its ingredients, and replaced it on the shelf. Then she lifted another one and did the same. Finally she found a bottle she liked and brought it to the back counter. She wore a long-sleeved, high-necked jade-green minidress that contrasted sharply with her freckle-covered milky complexion. She locked gazes with Minka and smiled again.

"Good Health." Pepper wiggled the blue glass bottle between her fingers. "I stock up on this tonic every few months."

"Excellent choice," Minka said. "It's perfect for those pesky spring colds."

Alex approached the register as Minka reached for the bottle. Pepper yanked it away. "Hired a new shop girl, have you?" Her thin lips curved into a smile. "No, you're not just an employee . . .

you look like family with all that lush dark hair. Except your eyes are green. You must be a Sobieski."

Alex smiled politely. "I'm Alex Daniels. But yes, my mom was a Sobieski. Minka's my cousin."

She pursed her lips. "And I'm Pepper Bellamy." She extended a soft hand, and Alex accepted. "How do you like Bellamy Bay so far?"

"It's nice. I used to come here all the time as a kid, but it's been a while."

"Well, you've come at a nice time. It's too cold to go into the water in May, but it's usually sunny and the tourists haven't flooded the area yet. It's really the perfect time for a visit." Pepper sniffed. "Unless you're prone to colds, like me. One day it's warm, one day it's cold. Without your aunt's product line of immunity builders, I would always be under the weather."

Alex looked at the bottle with interest. "What's in it?"

Pepper shrugged. "Don't know. Don't care. All I know is that it works. I swear by it."

"It's just echinacea, elderberry, lemon, and ginger," Minka said with a smile.

"Interesting," Alex murmured, giving her cousin a sidelong glance. She wondered if it wasn't just the placebo effect that made Pepper feel better, but it would be rude to ask.

Alex reached for the tissue paper as her cousin calculated the price on the register. "Want me to help, Minka?"

"Don't bother wrapping it. I'll just throw it in my bag." Pepper opened the messenger on her hip and removed a small brown leather wallet. "You know, my ancestors founded this town. My last name is Bellamy. Easy to remember, right?" She grinned as she stuck her debit card in the reader.

"Sure is."

"It's French. My people were Normans. Descended from Vikings. *Belle amie* means *good friend*." Pepper sighed. "Ironically enough, I've never had any good friends. It was weird in school. Everyone thought it was such a big deal that the town was named after my family." She shrugged. "Anyway, I'm sure you already know that."

Minka turned to Alex. "Pepper's a reporter for the *Bellamy Bay Bugler*, so she knows everyone. She also has a gossip blog."

"That's a side project," Pepper noted. "Just for fun. I've been researching the town's founding families for a feature I'm writing, and I'm trying to dig up some dirt. You'd be surprised at how colorful the town's history is."

"Interesting," Alex said, not sure how to respond. "I look forward to reading it."

"You know the Wesleys, I assume."

Alex shook her head and looked at Minka questioningly, but she only grimaced in response. "Haven't had the pleasure yet. Why?"

"Because," she grinned. "The Sobieskis and the Wesleys go waaaay back, Alex. We're talking thick as thieves." She dropped the bottle of cough syrup into her bag before flinging the flap over the top. "When I find something juicy on the Wesleys, don't be surprised if it involves the Sobieskis, too. But that might be fun for you, to learn more about your family."

Minka tilted her head in a show of mild annoyance. "That sounds really great, Pepper. Have a nice day."

"You too, Minka. So nice to meet you, Alex." Pepper paused. "Do you happen to have any of that fabulous sea-vegetable soap? I swear it does wonders for my energy levels."

"I just put out some bars," Minka said. "Come over this way."

The bells over the shop door chimed, and a man entered. He looked like he might have been quite attractive when he was younger, but now he just looked tired, bloated, and uncomfortable in his own skin. As he approached, Alex sensed a desperation about him.

"Is Lidia here?" he whispered to Alex, glancing at the door to the back room.

"No, I'm sorry, she stepped out."

To her surprise, he seemed relieved. "Good."

She smoothed her apron. "Is there something I can help you with?"

He gave Alex a once-over that made her feel dirty. "You a Sobieski?"

She folded her arms across her chest. "Yes."

"Then yeah, you can help." He kept his voice low. "I'm looking for one of Lidia's special . . . potions, you know what I mean?"

"Potions?" she echoed. His pallor was gray and he hadn't shaved in at least a day. What he needed was a nap and a good hot shower. Maybe some leafy green vegetables.

"Yeah, potions," he said. "Something with a real kick. I got some stuff going on. Real problems."

"Mr. Bennett." Minka's forehead creased in concern as she left Pepper standing near a display of bath bombs. "I didn't expect to see you here."

"Minka," he replied. He rushed to meet her and leaned his hands against the back counter. "I'm desperate. I've got some problems. Nasty divorce. My wife's taking me to the cleaners. And now my business partner wants to sell our company to the highest bidder." He cringed as if the very thought was painful.

"Everything I've worked for is about to go up in smoke. I just . . . I need a little luck. Please."

Minka studied the man, her arms folded. After a moment, she sighed. "Okay. But just this once."

She approached the jars of tea. Without hesitation, she chose a small linen bag and filled it with leaves from the Good Luck jar, emptying the contents. She smelled it before holding it under Mr. Bennett's nose. "This will do the trick."

Alex caught the spicy fragrance from where she was standing.

Mr. Bennett took a deep breath. "What's in there? Smells good."

"It's an herbal tea blended with cinnamon, bayberry, patchouli, and ginger. It's spicy, sweet, and tart all at the same time." She pulled the string tight on the bag to close it. "Make it into a tea and drink it twice a day for two days. By the third day, you'll be swimming in good luck. Be sure to drink it on an empty stomach or else it won't be as effective."

His shoulders eased as he took the bag. "Thanks, Minka. I mean it."

She nodded. "Sure. Just don't tell Mom."

"I won't. But hey, while I'm here." He took a look around the shop. "I'm also looking for a gift."

"Just a gift?" Minka asked.

Alex wondered what she meant by that question.

"Something pretty for my something pretty."

He lifted his eyebrows and Alex cringed, but Minka went to the perfume display and picked up a bottle. She spritzed a sample into the air for him to smell. "Here. This is our most popular scent. Violet."

"I'll take it."

Minka rang up the purchases, her hands deftly wrapping the tiny purple glass bottle. Other customers had entered the shop and Pepper stood off to the side, sniffing candles and watching with interest. By the time Minka had rung up Mr. Bennett's items, she was nearly pushing the bag into his hands. "Have a nice day."

He turned to leave. Then he froze.

Lidia stormed through the front door. "Randy." Her voice boomed through the space as if amplified, and her blue eyes narrowed in rage. "What are you doing here?"

"Lidia." The word escaped on his breath. "Now, don't get angry—"

She grabbed him by the lapels and pushed him to the back wall. He dropped his bag on the way, sending tea leaves scattering across the floor. Athena awoke with a start.

"I thought I told you to never set foot in my store again. Was I not clear?"

Alex's jaw dropped. Her tiny aunt had pressed Randy Bennett against the wall like a giant bug on a pin. Everyone in the shop was watching. Pepper's eyes widened as her mouth almost comically fell open.

"I was just leaving, Lidia. I promise. I'm not making trouble."

"I don't like you," she scowled. "And I don't want you in my shop."

The jars on the shelves clinked together softly. Athena jumped up from her bed and cocked her head at the clattering glass. Alex braced herself against the wall. Were they experiencing a small earthquake? Did North Carolina have earthquakes?

"I know; I understand." Bennett wriggled in her strong grip. "But I'm in bad shape, Lidia, okay? I need a little help. A little good luck. For old time's sake."

Alex could have sworn the windows were rattling. She looked at Minka, who shook her head as if to say *Keep quiet*. Alex chewed her lower lip. The air in the shop thickened, as if a storm was gathering. Two women in the shop huddled close together in alarm, but Pepper reached into her messenger and stealthily removed a notepad and pen. Athena stood directly beside Alex, her hair raised and her body on high alert.

"Good luck?" Lidia seethed. "You'll have good luck over my dead body."

Bennett's eyes enlarged as she somehow lifted him off his feet so that his toes were barely touching the floor. "Don't do this. Please. You think I'd set foot in here if I wasn't desperate?"

Alex held her breath. The three other customers in the shop each stared at Lidia. Minka covered her face and observed the drama from between her fingers. She was the one who had waited on Bennett. Now Alex understood the risk she'd taken.

Alex silently implored her aunt to stop. *Please. Just let him go.*

"Come on, Lidia," he said softly, his voice tinged with meaning. "Haven't you punished me enough?"

His plea hung in the hot air. Suddenly, Lidia dropped him. She stepped back, watching as he crumbled to the floor. "You got what you wanted. Now get out of here." She turned away.

He climbed to his feet, smoothing the lapels of his suit jacket. "Hey. I paid for those." He pointed to the spilled tea leaves.

Lidia shot him a deadly glare, and Alex feared she was about to physically launch him out onto the sidewalk. Instead, she paused to collect herself and walked calmly into the back room. When she emerged, she was holding a different bag of tea leaves. "Here." She flung it at his feet. "Don't come back."

She set her hands on her hips and watched him as he fumbled to collect his purchases. He left without a backward glance.

Once he was gone, the tropical air in the shop cooled. Pepper's fingers flew across her notebook. Lidia smiled brilliantly. "I'm so sorry about that, everyone. Long story. Water under the bridge and all that." She smoothed a hand down her long, shiny black hair. "I feel like some lavender-and-hops tea. May I get some for anyone else? Complimentary, of course."

One customer meekly raised her hand. Another followed. Pepper put away her notepad and slipped quietly out of the shop. Alex was still huddled by the cough syrups. Her aunt's anger couldn't possibly have shaken the shelves and windows—that was irrational thinking. They must have experienced a tiny earthquake. She'd have to check the news.

"Minka? Can you make some Calm Down tea, please?" Lidia hummed to herself as she swept the spilled tea into a dustpan.

"Sure." Minka seemed grateful to have escaped the skirmish and Lidia's anger. Alex had never seen her move so quickly. "I'm sorry, Mom," she whispered. "I know I should've told him to leave, but he was so pathetic—"

Lidia emptied the dustpan into the trash. "It's over. He won't come back."

"Yes, ma'am."

Sensing that the threat had passed, Athena relaxed her posture and turned her head to check on Alex. "I'm okay, Athena," she assured her with a pat on the back. The dog returned to her pillow.

Once Lidia had left the floor and gone into the back room, Alex tiptoed to Minka's side. "Um, what just happened there?"

Her cousin was holding back tears as she scooped tea leaves into a teapot. "It's all my fault. I shouldn't have waited on him. Mom's told me a hundred times." She wiped at her eye with the back of her hand. "Sorry. I hate it when she gets like that."

Alex agreed that Lidia's anger was terrifying. "You know, I think I'm going to step out for some fresh air. Is there a place around here to get some coffee?"

"Coffee O'Clock. It's right around the corner." Minka reached under the counter and found her handbag. "Can you grab one for me, too? I can run the shop while you're gone; it's fine." She pressed some bills into Alex's palm.

"No problem. What would you like?"

Minka gave her an order twice before Alex gave up and made her write it down. *Skinny half-caf latte with stevia syrup and a dusting of cinnamon on top.*

"Oh, and a biscuit," she added with a laugh. "They have *the best* biscuits in town. Strawberries and blueberries are in season—see if they have any freshly baked biscuits with either of those, please."

Alex smiled as she tucked the slip into her pocket and called Athena to join her. Minka didn't keep anything simple.

Chapter Three

The May morning was clear, but the breeze off the water was chilly. Alex spotted whitecaps in the distance, and her long hair whipped her cheeks.

"Athena, sit." The dog sat and lifted her nose in the air to catch scents as they passed. Alex paused to pull her hair back, weaving it into a quick, messy braid.

"She's lovely."

The male voice at her back startled Alex. She turned around to see a handsome man grinning at her.

"Sorry if I surprised you."

"No worries," Alex replied, and then grinned. It was hard not to smile back at a man with deep dimples accenting both cheeks.

He stood about six inches above her five-foot-five frame, with short blond hair and smiling blue eyes. His shoulders were broad, and even beneath his light-blue hoodie she could make out his muscular arms.

He gestured to Athena. "Is she friendly?"

Alex patted her dog on the back. "She's a trained attack dog," she said sweetly, enjoying the way his eyebrows jumped in surprise. "But she won't bite unless I tell her to. Her name's Athena."

"I'll be on my best behavior," he said, and reached down to scratch Athena under the jaw. "My name's Jack. Jack Frazier."

"I'm Alex . . . and I'm late. We're on a coffee run, and I should probably get going."

His face brightened. "I am, too. Want to walk together?"

Alex couldn't think of a reason why they shouldn't go together and tugged gently on Athena's restraint. "Sure."

When they reached the shop, Alex attached Athena's leash to a bike rack a few steps away from the front door. "Athena, stay." The dog flopped to the ground and looked happily at Alex, her ears pricked up at the sky.

The door to the historic brick-front building was glass and trimmed in bright teal, as were the two large picture windows on either side. The sidewalk outside was fragrant with the scents of buttered biscuits and coffee beans. Inside, Alex admired the hardwood floors, which shone like amber honey. As they neared the end of the line, Jack said, "This is my first time here. What's good?"

"I actually have no idea," she replied. "I'm not from here."

"Me neither. Where are you from?"

"Originally from Connecticut—that's where my father's family is from—but I've been living in New York City." When Jack laughed, Alex said, "What's so funny?"

"I'm from New York City, too. I grew up in Rochester, but I've spent most of my adult life in the city."

"Get out of town." Alex grinned. What were the odds?

"I swear it," he said. "There's a lot of us heading South, you know. Better weather. Better cost of living. Slower pace of life . . . Are you a transplant?"

She shook her head. "Just visiting family. My mother was born here, though she spent more time up North than not. You?"

"I'm here with family, too," he said. "But here to stay." When he unzipped his sweat shirt, she noticed he was wearing a NYPD T-shirt.

She gestured toward his chest, which she noticed looked lean and hard with muscle. "You're a policeman?" When he nodded, she couldn't help but bite her bottom lip and try not to laugh. "Well, you're not going to believe this, but my dad was also in law enforcement. He was a police detective in New Britain."

"You're right, I don't believe it," he said with a laugh.

"It's true! So, what are you going to order?"

"I'm going to try a bagel."

"Such a New Yorker. Which kind?"

"I'm a plain-bagel-with-butter kind of guy."

"No nonsense. I like that."

"Next," came a shout from the counter.

Alex approached and placed her order. The barista, a young man wearing a UNC Wilmington baseball cap, added the name *Minka* to the cardboard cup without even asking, then told her they were sold out of biscuits. Best for her to come before nine AM if she wanted one.

Jack ordered a black coffee and bagel and joined her at the end of the counter. "Wow, I guess biscuits are popular around here."

"It is the South."

He laughed. "That's true. So how are you spending your time while you visit your family?"

"Believe it or not, I'm working. Over at Botanika. On Main Street?"

His forehead creased as he tried to place the name. "I don't think I've seen it."

"It's an herbal apothecary. But we sell all sorts of things. Lotions, shower gels, teas. You should come by sometime. It's nice."

"Maybe I will. My mom loves tea."

He was going to buy a gift for his mother? How sweet. Her order was up before she had the opportunity to reply. She gathered a warm cup in each hand and gave Jack a smile, noting with some relief that he didn't wear a wedding band. "Well, maybe I'll see you tomorrow."

He nodded his head. "Looking forward to it."

*   *   *

When Alex returned to the shop, she delivered Minka her coffee and found her aunt waiting for her.

"I promised I'd show you how to make perfume. Are you ready now?"

Nervous at the thought of crossing her aunt, Alex tried not to look it. "Of course, *Ciocia* Lidia."

The back room of Botanika was bright and filled with all sizes of amber bottles and glass beakers. Lidia kept her work space tidy and organized. There were soaps curing on baker's racks in one corner beside the gallons of olive, coconut, and other oils that she used to make them. She used only natural colorants, like purple Brazilian clay, turmeric, and liquid chlorophyll, and yet Lidia's soaps were brilliantly bright. Lye was kept under lock and key, as were the essential oils, some of which were caustic.

"Alex, I'm sorry you had to see all of that earlier," Lidia began. "I have a bit of a temper. People in Bellamy Bay know it well, but it can be alarming." Her lips lifted into a wry smile. "It's another Sobieski trait, I'm afraid. We feel a deep love for our friends and family, but betrayal—well, we never forget those who hurt us."

Alex had a hundred questions about that comment. How had Randy Bennett betrayed her aunt? What had he done to get himself banished from Botanika, and why had he still returned?

"Loyalty is a double-edged sword," Lidia continued, "but I love my girls, Kamila and Minka and you, Alex. I love my friends and my customers. I love you all fiercely. Even if I could change myself, I'm not sure I would."

She took Alex's hand in her own as if to reassure a child. "You lifted him up," Alex said, laughing a little. "He must be twice your size."

Lidia's smile was pained. "I was angry, that's all. Real strength would have been resisting that rage." She gave Alex's hand a gentle squeeze before dropping it. "Well. Next time, I'll work on compassion." Lidia sighed. "Let's make perfume."

She led Alex to a corner, where she had organized delicate glass bottles into a row on the soapstone counter. As they put on gloves and protective eyewear, Lidia gave Alex a lesson on the science of scent.

"In any good perfume, there are different notes," she explained. "Top notes are what you smell first, but they disappear quickly. Never buy a fragrance based on top notes." She snapped her glove in place. "Then you smell middle notes for a bit, but eventually these will fade away to reveal the bottom notes." She smiled. "The bottom notes are the key to holding the perfume together, but you don't even sense them for hours."

She explained that scents could be assigned colors and matched together the same way shades could be combined to create a harmonious painting. "Today, we're going to mix fresh green and purple floral scents to create an intoxicating fragrance. I call it Violet. It makes a woman irresistible."

Alex clapped her hands together. "I can't wait."

Lidia had memorized her recipe. Alex watched in awe as she worked down the line of glass bottles. A drop here, ten drops there, all of them falling into a large beaker of perfume base. She instructed Alex and watched patiently while Alex added a few of the notes herself.

"When did you realize that you wanted to do this work, *Ciocia?*"

"I've always done it," her aunt replied. "For as long as I can remember, I've loved the healing energy of plants. My path was always clear."

What must that be like, to feel like a life path was clear? Two weeks ago she'd been working in New York, and today she was making perfume in North Carolina. Tomorrow—who knew? "I seem to have wandered off my path," she said.

Lidia offered a reassuring smile. "Sometimes people say that when they're moving in the wrong direction and self-correct."

When they were finished, Lidia stopped to swirl their creation. "You can smell the notes blooming. Here." She held the jar out to Alex. "First, close your eyes."

Alex did as she was told and waited. Inhaled. The colors of the fragrance swirled behind her eyelids.

"Can you pick out the notes? There are no wrong answers. It's like tasting wine."

But to Alex, the notes were distinct. "The top notes are clear and bright. Fresh and green. Grass—cucumbers, maybe? It makes me think of fresh buds on trees." She recognized Violet as the scent Bennett had just purchased for his someone special, but of course she didn't mention that.

"Violet leaves," Lidia agreed. "What else?"

Alex closed her eyes and waited for the top notes to clear. A sweet herbaceous scent revealed itself. "Lavender?" She shook her head in wonder. "*Ciocia* Lidia, it's lovely. Really."

Lidia capped the jar and moved it to one side. "You probably can't find the base notes yet, but they're violet blossom and juicy sweet raspberry. Don't worry, eventually it will all come naturally to you." She wrapped an arm around Alex's waist and pulled her closer. "It's good that you're here, Alex. I know you don't see it yet, but Bellamy Bay is a nice place to heal. It's because we're so close to the water."

Alex nodded. "I'm glad I came."

She loved New York, but Bellamy Bay was refreshingly quiet. As if reading her mind, Lidia said, "You can go ahead and relax, *moja droga*." *My dear*. "Let your guard down. This isn't like the city." She planted a kiss on her cheek. "It's peaceful as a garden here."

Chapter Four

The next morning at Botanika brought a steady stream of activity. From the minute they flipped the lights on, customers began browsing. Their first customer was a mother looking for something for her sick son. After a few more customers came and went, Minka nudged Alex. "Have you noticed? They're all buying cough syrup."

"Maybe it's the change of seasons? A spring cold?" Alex said, thinking of Pepper's complaints. "Doesn't anyone go to the doctor's office in Bellamy Bay?"

"A few." Minka grinned. "The ones who don't believe in Mom's voodoo, as some say."

Alex chuckled at that. "I'll brew some more of that peppermint tea with sweet orange and hand it out. That's good for congestion."

"We're running low, so you may have to cut some more mint."

Alex brought bundles of dried peppermint from the back room, pulled on some gloves, and began chopping the leaves.

She'd only been half joking with Minka about the town doctor. Alex did feel at times like Lidia and Minka were serving in that role, giving people the comfort they needed. And so far, Alex loved the feeling she got from helping people, too. She had to admit, working in risk management had never felt this good.

But ruminating on what had happened in New York wasn't productive, and Alex was desperate for distractions. Working helped. Drinking wine and gossiping with her cousins was fun. And the dashing Jack Frazier certainly took her mind off her failures, but she hadn't seen him that day.

The knife slipped. "Ouch." Alex yanked her left hand away and brought her finger to her mouth. She tasted blood. Athena leapt off her pillow and trotted over to nudge Alex's elbow. "It's okay, girl."

"You all right?" Minka was at her side in a flash, urging her hand out of her mouth. "Let me guess, your left hand wandered while you were cutting with your right?"

Alex winced and sucked a breath. The cut stung. "I wasn't paying attention. My own fault." She shook her hand as if to shake off the pain. Blood droplets spattered.

Minka winced. "Let me see."

Alex tried to relax while Minka took her injured hand in both of her own. Carefully, Minka removed the glove, peeling it off to prevent more blood from spilling. Then she leaned closer, peering at the cut and whispering something softly.

"What did you say?" Alex asked.

Her finger felt as if it was vibrating, and then a burning sensation engulfed her entire hand. Silently trying to bear the pain, she gritted her teeth and closed her eyes. She must have cut close to a nerve.

Minka straightened. "Wash it off. You'll be fine." She tossed the glove into the trash bin and patted Alex on the shoulder before turning and hurrying back to a customer standing at the counter. "So sorry to keep you waiting."

Alex was stunned. She had blood all over her hand, and Minka hadn't even offered a Band-Aid? She could very well need stitches. "That's okay, I'll just find the first-aid kit myself."

She turned on the small sink in the corner and braced herself for pain as water hit the wound, but it wasn't bad. Maybe she didn't need stitches after all.

Carefully she washed the wound with an herbal wound wash made with manuka honey, yarrow, and water. Once she'd cleaned up, Alex turned off the water and dried her hands with a paper towel, avoiding the injured tip of her index finger. She brought her hand closer to examine the wound, and—she frowned. She didn't see much at all. Barely a sliver of a cut, let alone the gaping wound she'd feared. Her finger was fine. It didn't even hurt. "Huh."

She glanced over a shoulder at Minka, who was chatting with a customer as she bagged her purchases. There were drops of blood on the cutting board and counter, and some of them had even hit the wall. She had definitely been bleeding. Now she poked at her finger with a paper towel, trying to locate the spot where the skin had opened. When she came up empty, she examined her entire hand. Nothing. Not a single mark.

Just to be safe, Alex wrapped a paper towel around her fingertip before cleaning and disinfecting the counter area. The peppermint she'd chopped would have to go into the trash now, but she wasn't going to chop any more today. She'd find another herbal tea to serve instead. When the counter was clean, Alex removed the paper towel on her finger to check for blood. The towel was perfectly white. "What the heck?"

She wasn't losing her mind. She wasn't. Alex dropped to her hands and knees and dug through the trash, pushing aside the peppermint leaves and paper towels as she sought her glove. "Aha."

She pulled it out and unrolled the purple glove. It was bloody, and there was an unmistakable slice where the knife had penetrated. This had been no paper cut. Alex frowned as she crumpled up the glove again and tossed it back into the trash can. She was not at all sure what to make of this.

She didn't have more time to dwell on the injury because Lidia swept out from the back room carrying blue bottles of cough syrup in a basket. "I heard we're running low. Alex, would you mind helping me with these?"

"No problem," she said, but she felt oddly disoriented, and her knees were shaky as she joined Lidia. "This is a best seller." Alex was trying to sound light, but her laugh sounded choked.

"Manuka honey cough syrup. It's a family recipe," Lidia said proudly. "You know what manuka honey is?"

"Not really."

Lidia sorted the bottles by size as she spoke. "It's honey made from bees that have pollinated tea trees. Tea tree oil has known antibacterial properties. I use it in several of my products. Works well on oily skin. Creates a lovely lather in soap." She rose up on her toes to slide the new bottles of cough syrup behind the bottles already on the shelf. "So we start with manuka honey, which is sweet and soothing. Then we add some peppermint and oregano oils. Peppermint is antibacterial, but it also helps to numb a sore throat. Oregano oil is the most effective antibacterial ingredient in nature."

"It must work very well if so many people are buying it."

"I hear good things." Lidia shelved the final bottle, brushed her hands on her apron, and picked up the empty basket. "I'm a little behind on candle production, so I'll be in the back for about an hour."

She reached up to touch a lock of Alex's hair. "There's a gentleman at the door," she whispered. "He appears lost, but I suspect he's looking for you."

"Who?" Alex moved toward the front door. Sure enough, Jack had just entered and was staring like a deer in the proverbial headlights. "Oh." She turned back to Lidia, her cheeks warming. "Yes, I kind of know him."

"I thought so. You should go see him. He looks frightened." Lidia winked before turning and walking away.

Alex approached with a friendly smile, noting that his fresh, crisp cologne of tangerine, ginger, and pine was as bright as his grin. "Hey, Jack."

"Hi, Alex." He looked relieved to see her. "I, uh . . ." He glanced around at the shelves of bottles and lotions. "You know, I've never been here before. I don't know what any of this is."

That explained his panicked expression.

"Well, there's a lot to see," she began. She was brand-new to the world of herbal remedies—could she actually explain any of this to him? "Are you looking for some aftershave? Maybe a shower gel?" She caught his amused gaze. "Not that you . . . I'm sure you're clean."

He chuckled at that. "How about some tea?"

She snapped her fingers. "Right. Tea. For your mom." She pointed to the jars against the far wall. "Is she a customer? Does she have a favorite?"

He paused to turn a bottle on top of a display pyramid. "She's never mentioned coming here, but she doesn't leave the house much. She has a difficult time getting around. It's why I moved closer."

"I'm sorry to hear that."

But Jack didn't respond. He was reading the label on the display bottle. "You busy here?"

"Yeah, really busy. Today has been hectic."

He set down a lotion for eczema and turned another one for poison ivy. "Can I be honest?"

Alex paused. "Of course."

"I don't know how a place like this stays in business. Not with so many pharmacies around."

Alex's shoulders tightened. That wasn't the kind of honesty she'd been hoping for. Still, his question was reasonable. "I didn't understand at first, either. But people seem to really like it. It's an alternative to traditional medicine, I guess."

"Medicine?" Jack had picked up a bottle of perfume called Seduction. "*Find love where you least expect it,*" he read from the label, then arched a brow at Alex. "You're selling love potions?"

"Okay, so it's not all medicine," she said.

"Sounds like snake oil to me."

Alex took a breath as her defenses began to rise. She might not know much about the products at Botanika, but she was certain she didn't like what Jack was insinuating. "It's perfume," she replied, and lifted the bottle out of his hand as politely as possible. "My aunt makes it herself, and it's very pretty."

He held up his hands in a gesture of surrender. "I don't mean to pick on your aunt." His blue eyes softened as he studied her guarded posture. "I guess skeptical guys like me aren't your demographic."

"Yeah, my aunt doesn't have a product line for hardened detectives." Alex found her smile again. "You should try some of the tea. Maybe you'll change your mind. I'll make you a cup—"

"No thanks. I'll just find something for my mother. If you could just point me in the right direction?"

"Of course."

She led him to the tea shelves and walked him through the different flavors. He steered clear of the functional teas, finally settling on a blend called Summer Garden, a combination of jasmine and rose, two of his mother's favorite flowers. "I hope this brightens her day," Alex said as she scooped the leaves into a bag.

"Thank you." His voice revealed a sadness. "It's ironic. After my parents divorced, my mother moved down here to be close to her best friend from college. But she was diagnosed with dementia about six months ago and no longer remembers her."

"Oh, Jack. I'm so sorry to hear that." Alex glanced around the shop. "I think we have a tea or tonic that could help with her—"

"No," he said, a little too firmly, then softened his voice. "She's under a doctor's care, and he's doing everything medically possible to help her. I don't want to give her false hope."

Alex sealed the bag and pressed it gently into the palm of his hand. "I'm sure she'll enjoy this tea."

She brought him to the counter and rang up his purchase. "Thanks for stopping by, Jack. It was nice to see you."

Jack looked down at the counter. "There was something else."

"Oh?"

Alex paused as he stuffed his hands into the pockets of his jeans and cleared his throat. She thought she heard him say, *Go ahead and ask her out.* But his mouth hadn't moved. At least she didn't think it had. She gave him a strange look. "What did you say?"

"I didn't say anything."

"Oh, I thought . . ." Alex's voice trailed. She could've sworn she'd heard him. "Never mind." It must have been her imagination.

Jack shifted his weight. "I was . . . actually wondering if you would like to have dinner with me."

"Oh. *Oh.*"

"Or lunch. Just as friends," he added quickly. "I mean, we're both from New York, and so I thought we might have a lot to talk about. I don't know many people in town. But if you don't want to, it's fine."

He eyed her like a hopeful puppy, and Alex didn't see the harm in having dinner with him. "Well, when did you want to have dinner?"

He smiled. "How's Saturday?"

"Hmm." She tapped her chin as she pretended to think. "And where would we go?"

Jack shrugged. "There's this place off Main, some Japanese-Southern fusion restaurant. I've been hearing rave reviews."

Alex was intrigued. "All right." And then she told him her aunt's address. "Pick me up around seven."

"Yes ma'am." His smile broadened. "Looking forward to it."

Alex returned the grin. "Me too."

* * *

After Jack left, Minka wanted all the details. Who was he? Where were they going? How had she met him?

"He is so cute." she said, nearly bouncing on her toes. "And I am so proud of you for finding a date your first week in Bellamy Bay." Minka sighed and shook her head. "You really are a Sobieski."

"What? No." Alex laughed. "It's strictly friendly. He's a nice guy."

Minka cocked her head to one side and gave her cousin a knowing smile. "Uh-huh."

The rest of the afternoon passed in a flash. Nothing could get Alex down. It wasn't until closing time that she noticed her aunt standing quietly in the back of the shop. Lidia kept looking at her watch and watching the door.

"*Ciocia*? Is everything okay?"

Lidia had been unusually quiet, but since she'd mentioned she was behind on her work, Alex reasoned that she was feeling some pressure to finish on time. "Do you need some help making candles? I'm happy to stay late."

Her aunt smiled tightly. "Thank you. I need to leave on time. Do you two mind closing tonight? I have somewhere to be." She checked her watch.

"Of course not," Minka said. She had already begun to empty the till.

Alex grabbed a broom from the closet.

Purse in hand, Lidia gave Minka and Alex a quick kiss on the cheek. "I'll be home later. Have dinner without me." With that, she stepped into the evening.

Chapter Five

A lex hadn't seen Kamila since dinner when she burst through the door of Botanika just after opening on Wednesday morning. Her eyes were wide and her usually smooth ponytail looked messy, as if she had been raking her hands through her hair.

"Did you hear? Randy Bennett is dead."

"What?" Minka gasped. "What happened?"

"They found him in his home this morning. The coroner hasn't issued an official cause of death yet. The autopsy is being completed now."

"An autopsy?" Minka winced. "Does that mean they think it was murder?"

"Shh," Kamila hissed with a furtive glance around the shop. "Don't jump to any conclusions yet. He was a middle-age man who died alone. I wouldn't say autopsies are routine, but it's not unusual under the circumstances. We won't know anything until we get the results."

Lidia came out from the back and joined the three women, her face pale. "Oh my. Randolph," she whispered.

Alex shivered. She hadn't known Randy Bennett well, but this tragedy struck a little too close to home. "He was just here. He bought that tea," she murmured. "Today was supposed to be the day he got his luck back."

She felt a nudge on her hand. Athena, sensing a change in her mood, was at Alex's side to reassure her. She patted the dog's soft back.

Kamila leaned her back against the counter. "It looks like Bennett's luck officially ran out."

Alex replayed Randy Bennett's visit to Botanika in her mind. He had definitely seemed agitated, and he'd complained about his ex-wife and his business partner. Would someone in his life have actually murdered him?

Or . . . Alex and Minka shared a glance. What if something in the tea had killed him? Perhaps a toxic ingredient had crept into the mix? As if reading her mind, Minka shook her head, and Alex could have sworn she heard her thoughts. *No way. It wasn't the tea.* Still, her skin tingled. "This is so unsettling."

"I know," Kamila agreed. "This stuff never happens in Bellamy Bay. It's usually the most boring place in the world to be a police officer."

"The coroner won't find anything," Lidia declared. "Randy was overweight and he had high blood pressure. He must have died from natural causes. Sad, but not suspicious."

"We'll know soon enough." Kamila pushed off the counter again. "Anyway, I wanted you to hear it from me first. You know how gossip can spread, especially when there's any kind of investigation." She held her mother's gaze. "And I know he was in here this week, Mom. Minka told me that you had an outburst."

Lidia raised her chin. "So what? He knows—he knew—he wasn't welcome here."

Kamila set her jaw, assuming a position of authority. "You can't behave that way. People are going to talk. If the coroner finds anything unusual, you may be questioned about Bennett's death—"

But Lidia lifted one hand, halting the lecture. "Thank you for stopping by, Kamila. I'm sure this must be a busy day for you." She rolled the sleeves of her navy sweater to her elbows. "Now, if you'll excuse me, I have a lot of work to do." And with that, she retreated to the back room.

Minka stared after her mother. "I don't—wow. Poor guy."

Kamila shrugged. "It happens."

"He wasn't a terrible man," Minka continued. "He didn't deserve to die."

Alex nodded toward the back room and lowered her voice. "What happened between Randy and your mom, anyway?"

"She won't say. And believe me, we've asked," Minka said. "Whatever it was, it happened a long, long time ago."

"It must have been very serious," Alex remarked. "From what she said to me, it sounded like he betrayed her in some way."

"By Mom's standards, that could mean he got a coffee order wrong," Kamila snorted.

"Kam," Minka warned. "That's not fair."

"Maybe not. But Mom's got to watch her temper or she's going to land herself in hot water." She narrowed her eyes at Minka. "I don't know why you continue to defend her conduct. You know as well as I do that she's got anger issues."

"No, she's just . . . passionate. Are you really so perfect?"

"See, there you go again. Rationalizing her behavior." Kamila lowered her voice so that her words were barely audible to Alex. "If you don't find another apartment soon and move out of that house, you're going to end up just like her."

Minka's blue eyes flashed. "You know I've been looking. I can't help it that my landlord sold my last apartment building."

Alex stood abruptly. "You know, I'm going to make some tea. Something to calm the nerves," she said. "Anyone else?"

Minka turned her body away from Kamila. "I'll take one," she said. "Heck, we should brew a bunch of it. Customers will be coming in, and everyone in town knew Randy Bennett."

Alex filled the teakettle at the sink. "Kam? You want tea?"

"No thanks. I've got a ton of paperwork to do." She brushed invisible dirt from the front of her uniform pants. When she spoke again, her voice was calmer. "I'll try to be around for dinner tonight, but who knows. This thing might blow up, depending on what the investigation reveals." She blew a piece of hair out of her face.

Minka set a hand on Kamila's arm. "Listen, I don't want us to fight about this."

Her sister took a moment to reply. "Okay. I don't either. Just forget it."

"I'm sure that Randy Bennett died of natural causes," Minka assured her. "But I think you're secretly hoping for some excitement. No offense. I mean, I'm sure traffic stops are great."

Kamila rolled her eyes. "And on that note." She gave them a little wave. "Love you both. See you later. Maybe."

The shop was still quiet, but they'd been open less than twenty minutes. As Alex waited for the teakettle to whistle, her thoughts turned to Randy Bennett. He'd seemed so desperate when he'd entered Botanika looking for his so-called potion. What had been happening in his life that would lead him to believe that tea leaves could actually change his fortune?

*   *   *

Of all the products her aunt created, Alex found soap the most relaxing to make. *Ciocia* Lidia had already shown her how to read recipes and use the scales, and now she expected Alex to prepare her own batch of detoxing soap using gifts from the ocean: seaweed, wild spirulina, and sea kelp.

"It's a basic recipe," Lidia explained. "Nothing fancy. And I'll be right over here if you need me." Her aunt was busy making products to stock up for the summer season.

The quiet focus that the craft demanded was a welcome change from the busy, angsty storeroom floor. All anyone wanted to talk about that day was Randy Bennett, and Kamila was right, the rumors were flying. In under an hour, Alex and Minka had heard—definitively—that Bennett had died of a heart attack. And that he'd fallen down the stairs. And that he'd been robbed and shot.

Minka had tilted her head. "Honestly, this is ridiculous. Have you ever heard of a single person dying in so many different ways?"

Alex had sighed. "He truly was unlucky." She was relieved to escape the gossip.

She was interested in the soapmaking process, particularly by how the different oils worked together to create a balanced bar. Coconut oil, so moisturizing in oil form, created a very bubbly, hard, and cleansing bar of soap that could dry out the skin. As Lidia explained while Alex worked, coconut oil must be balanced with something like olive oil, which was gently cleansing and soft. But olive-oil soaps had little lather, so adding an ingredient like palm oil would support the big bubbles from the coconut oil. The result was a hard bar of soap that lathered well and cleansed without drying the skin—all made without any detergents.

She carefully measured each ingredient the way Lidia had taught her and added a blend of essential oils that smelled fresh and clean: spearmint, orange, rosemary, and lemon. The best part of the process was mixing the lye water into the oils and stirring the batter, which went from oil to a puddinglike texture in seconds. Working quickly, she added scoops of sea kelp and spirulina to the mixture. She smiled as she poured the soap into the wooden loaf mold and created some fancy swirls on top with a rubber spatula. If only her chemistry class had been this much fun.

She was so lost in her own work that she barely noticed that Lidia had grown silent. Alex set her soaping equipment into a ten-gallon bucket. She'd clean it tomorrow after the saponification process was complete and there was no caustic lye remaining in the batter. She pulled off her gloves and removed her goggles. "Is everything okay, *Ciocia*? You've been quiet."

Lidia had arranged a selection of herb-infused oils on the counter and was weighing beeswax pastilles into a bowl. "Everything is just fine," she replied, keeping her back to the room.

Alex didn't buy it. Her family had been acting strangely ever since Kamila had come through the door that morning. "Is there—do you want to talk about Randy?" she began in an uncertain voice.

"Thank you," Lidia said over her shoulder. "But I enjoy silence."

"Okay. I'm just saying that if you wanted to talk about it—"

"I said no, Aleksandra." She turned around, and Alex was smacked with a sudden gust of air. Lidia's blue eyes were bright, and her voice was sharp. "If you're finished, I'm sure Minka could use some help."

Alex's chin quivered. "Then I'll leave you alone."

She pushed open the door to the retail floor and allowed it to shut loudly behind her. Alex told herself that her aunt's brusqueness was nothing and that grief and regret could make a person do strange things, but that brush-off had stung. She'd only been trying to comfort her.

Alex yanked a clean apron from a drawer. "Whatever." But for the first time since she'd come to Bellamy Bay, she felt like the outsider she was.

Chapter Six

For the next few days, Alex's family avoided discussion of Randy Bennett, except that Kamila mentioned in passing at dinner one night that she'd heard the coroner's report had revealed no suspicious cause of death. "And you were so worried," Lidia said, giving her oldest daughter a kiss on the cheek. "All for nothing."

The week passed quickly as Alex committed to learning more about the products at Botanika. She brought home samples of lotions and salves, and sampled all the teas. On Friday, Alex was standing at the back counter reading a book on holistic remedies when a tall figure passed in front of the front window. Her stomach tightened. It was Jack, and she hadn't seen him since they'd made plans for dinner. She ran to greet him at the door. "Hey, Jack," she gushed. "How did your mom like the tea?"

But Jack's face was pained as he gave her an incredulous look. "I'm not giving my mother anything from this store." He glanced around the shop. "Is Lidia here?"

The chilly greeting confused her. Two uniformed police officers entered the shop behind him, raising an alarm in her mind. "Yes, she's in the back. Do you need to see her?"

"Yes. Please ask her to come out."

Minka said, "I'll get her." Alex watched her cousin walk into the back room and call, "Mom? Someone's here to see you."

Athena let out a huff and hurried to Alex's side, the hair on her back at attention. When a low growl started in her throat, Alex set a hand on her head. "Hush, Athena."

She studied Jack's oddly clenched jaw. "Jack? W-what's going on?" Her eyes jumped from Jack to the two officers guarding the door. "Did something happen?" Her thoughts went to Kamila. "Is my cousin okay?"

"Your cousin?" He blinked, momentarily confused. "Oh, you mean Officer Sobieski. Yes, she's fine."

But her chest tightened as Lidia walked out, wiping her hands on a towel. Her aunt's face gave nothing away, but her posture was steely. "Hello," she said.

"Lidia Sobieski?" Jack said.

"Yes." She put the towel down on the counter and set her hands on her waist.

He took a step forward. "I'm here to arrest you for the murder of Randolph Bennett."

"What?" Alex's blood went cold. "She had nothing to do with his death."

The shop was silent. Several customers were pressed against the wall, watching the scene unfold.

Jack turned to Alex. "I'm sorry. I know this is upsetting."

"Upsetting?" Alex's voice cracked. "It's ridiculous. The coroner said he died of natural causes."

"Actually, the coroner concluded that Randolph Bennett was poisoned," Jack explained. "We've kept it quiet while we conducted an investigation."

"What?" Minka shrieked, then clapped a hand across her mouth.

Lidia's face was blank with shock.

Alex was light-headed. "I don't understand."

"His stomach was empty except for tea leaves and berries," Jack continued. "We have witnesses who have made statements saying that your aunt and Mr. Bennett were involved in an altercation on Monday. They saw her go into the back and get him a bag of tea."

"That's impossible," Minka shouted. "My mom wouldn't hurt anyone."

"Well, quite a few people may disagree," Jack replied carefully. "Ms. Sobieski is known for her, uh, fiery temper. And the witnesses in your shop that day said she pushed Mr. Bennett against the wall and threatened him."

"I was here. She never threatened him," Alex said. "*Ciocia* Lidia, say something. Tell them what happened."

But the officers were already moving to lead Lidia away.

Panic rose in Alex's chest. "*Ciocia* Lidia, you didn't kill Mr. Bennett. Tell them."

Lidia stepped forward, resigned. "Of course I didn't kill him." She looked at Jack. "I know you're just doing your job, and I know you are sincere. But you're making a mistake."

Jack frowned. "I'm following the evidence, ma'am."

Minka stood helplessly at the back register, tears streaming down her cheeks. Alex threaded her fingers through her hair. This couldn't be happening.

"Jack, you had to come into her shop to make this arrest?" she hissed. "In front of everyone? You couldn't even be decent about this?"

"Alex, please—"

She brushed his hands away. "You could have asked her to turn herself in. You didn't have to do it this way."

"I'm not sure you understand the gravity of the situation." He clenched his jaw. "We had a search warrant executed on your aunt's residence today." He pulled a folded square of paper out of his jacket pocket.

Alex's jaw dropped. "You searched the house?"

"While we weren't home?" Minka gasped.

"Standard procedure for an emergency warrant. We had to act quickly before evidence was destroyed, so the court granted permission. We didn't need anyone to let us in. We knocked, and when no one answered, we broke down the door."

Alex groaned. "You're kidding me."

He handed the paper to Alex. "We found the plants we believe your aunt used to poison Mr. Bennett: deadly nightshade. The berries were found in Mr. Bennett's stomach."

"That's not true," Minka burst out. "That plant has medicinal uses. Mom uses the leaves, not the berries."

He handed Alex the document. "Here. You can read the warrant yourself. We have probable cause to arrest Lidia. And we have reason to do so immediately, before she harms someone else."

Alex grabbed the warrant from his hand and tried to focus on the words, but her head was reeling. The cause of Mr. Bennett's death had been found to be *severe anticholinergic syndrome*—whatever that meant—and the police were claiming Lidia's tea was responsible.

"I had my suspicions when I found the bag of tea from Botanika next to the body, and fortunately the coroner's conclusion came quickly. The lab rushed the preliminary toxicology reports and confirmed that the berries in his stomach were deadly nightshade. It doesn't take many berries to kill an adult. Maybe a couple dozen. We found more than enough." Now Jack folded his arms and he lowered his voice to address her privately. "This was a brutal way to die. Mr. Bennett probably suffered hallucinations and delirium before his heart and lungs stopped."

Alex glared at him. "I thought you said *this*"—she waved her hands around the shop—"was all snake oil? Now you're a believer?"

Jack had the decency to look away. "I really am sorry about this, Alex. You have to know that I'd never do anything to intentionally hurt you or your family."

His words barely registered as she watched one of the officers lead Lidia out the door, reading her aunt her Miranda rights.

"Don't talk to anyone, *Ciocia*," she called out. "Don't say a thing. I'll find you a lawyer."

"It's all right, Aleksandra," Lidia called over her shoulder. "Call Tobias Winston. He's our family attorney."

Alex met Jack's gaze. "You're making a huge mistake. I hope you know that."

He shifted from one foot to the other. "About tomorrow night. Under the circumstances . . ."

"Don't worry. It's off." Alex's cheeks warmed with anger. "It's *so* off."

Jack nodded but didn't reply.

Alex stormed away to hug Minka, who had covered her face with her hands. "It's okay," she soothed her. "It's a terrible mistake, that's all. We'll get it sorted out."

Minka sniffled. "Mom would never hurt anyone. Her entire business is healing."

"Minka. Alex." Kamila burst through the front door. "I just heard. Oh my gosh."

"You could've warned us," Minka said, her eyes filling again. "You just let them arrest Mom."

"You think I actually knew about any of this?" Kamila said, visibly shaking. "They lied to me, said they didn't have a suspect in the case yet."

Alex moved to shield her cousins from prying eyes. As Minka covered her face with her hands, her body shuddering with sobs, Kamila's face softened.

"I didn't know," Kamila insisted. "Oh, Minka." She pulled her sister into her arms. "We'll figure it out."

"Officer Sobieski? A word?" Jack approached cautiously.

"Please, just give me a minute with my sister." Once he turned, Kamila shot him a drop-dead look. "Come on, why don't you two wait in my car." Kamila led them to the front of the shop. "We're going to meet Mom at the station. I just need to see what Detective Frazier wants first. I hope it's an apology."

"Your mom said to call Attorney Winston," Alex said.

"Good idea." Kamila was already pulling out her phone. "I'll get this cleared up if it's the last thing I do."

Alex and Minka walked out the door together, keeping their heads high despite the crowd gathering outside. Alex didn't know any of the faces in the crowd except one: Pepper Bellamy. And she was taking notes.

*　*　*

The women piled into Kamila's small white SUV and, after dropping Athena off at home, drove straight to the Bellamy Bay police station. When they arrived, local media were already standing outside, snapping pictures and recording footage.

"No comment," Kamila said when a reporter shoved a microphone in front of her. She ushered Minka and Alex inside. "Bunch of vultures," she growled. She led them to a small waiting area lined with hard plastic chairs. "You can wait here. I've got to talk to some people."

"I don't want to wait," Minka said. "I want to talk to Mom."

"Minka." Kamila squeezed her sister's shoulder. "It's going to be a little while."

Minka plopped herself into a chair and set her head on her hands. "This is terrible. Just a nightmare."

Alex turned to Kamila. "We're okay. I'll sit with her."

Her cousin gave a small nod and left the room. Alex took the chair beside Minka, who was staring at the gray linoleum floor. "The whole town will think Mom killed someone. No one's going to shop at Botanika. We're going to lose the house—"

Alex gripped her cousin's hand. "One thing at a time. We're going to focus on getting your mom out of here, okay? We'll post bail—I've got some money in the bank. We'll figure it out."

Minka's complexion was ashen. "I think I'm going to throw up."

She ran out of the room, leaving Alex alone—but not for long. A figure darkened the doorway.

"Hi, Alex." It was Pepper Bellamy.

Pepper flipped her hair over one shoulder and stepped into the waiting room. "Mind if I sit?" She took Minka's seat. "It's such a shock about Lidia, isn't it? They're saying murder, right?"

Alex's lips tightened. "I'm not sure," she lied. She eyed Pepper sidelong. "Why are you here?"

"Oh, you know. I am a reporter, after all. There's a story here, and I'm going to write it." Pepper pulled her messenger bag onto her lap and dug inside. "People are saying the police searched Lidia's house. Is that true?"

Alex massaged her forehead with her fingertips. "That's what I hear. It just seems so extreme to treat Lidia like a common criminal."

Pepper found her notepad and flipped to a clean page. "But if she poisoned someone . . ."

Alex straightened in her seat, wary of Pepper's intentions. "She didn't."

"You have proof?" Pepper leaned in, pen poised over her pad. "An alibi for the time of the murder? The police are saying it was about ten Tuesday night."

Alex wasn't sure where her aunt had been that night, but she'd definitely been out. Of course, she could tell Pepper this. "I don't have proof—or know if she has an alibi—but I know she wouldn't kill anyone."

"How do you know that? You haven't been to Bellamy Bay in forever. How well do you really know your aunt?"

Alex opened and closed her mouth, unsure how to respond. She really *didn't* know her aunt. But she was family, and who wanted to believe the worst of a family member?

"Everyone in town knows she has a temper." Pepper grinned. "And you can't deny she knows her poisons."

No, Alex couldn't deny that. But maybe she could appeal to Pepper's sense of decency, if she had any. Alex frowned when Pepper began writing something down. "You and Minka went to school together, right?"

Pepper narrowed her eyes, nodding slowly. "Yeah, so?"

"Minka's as sweet as they come. You wouldn't go out of your way to write something that would hurt her, would you?"

Pepper pursed her lips. "Not on purpose, no. But I have a job to do and my journalistic integrity to consider."

"Look, I understand that, but can't you at least wait until the police complete their investigation?"

Pepper shot her a look of regret. "Sorry, I have a responsibility to the public." Then she grinned. "Speaking of which, I'm also working on another article, one you're really going to be interested in."

Alex's stomach began to churn. "Why will I be interested in it?"

"It's a bit of town history. Here it is." She pulled a dog-eared notebook from her bag. "I'll give you a sneak peek." She leaned closer to whisper, "I know the truth about the Sobieskis."

"Which is what?"

"You're witches."

"What?" Alex burst out laughing. Witches? No one believed in witches anymore. Was she actually going to publish that? "Pepper. That's . . . the weirdest thing I've heard. Ever. Truly."

Pepper opened her notebook and flipped through the pages. "Water witches, descended from mermaids," she continued. "It's been town lore for years. Some people believe it; most think it's absurd. But I finally have proof." She looked up from her notes. "It's all in my great-grandfather's journal. Two greats, in fact. Captain John Bellamy? The great-grandson of the founder of Bellamy Bay."

"I hate to break it to you," Alex replied, "but finding something in a journal from however many hundreds of years ago doesn't make it true."

"It's all in there," she continued, as if Alex hadn't spoken at all. "The town was founded on the story of a woman who could transition between her human form and being a mermaid at will. She fell in love with a fisherman and swapped life in the water for a permanent life on land, just to be with him. They left Warsaw in search of a new life together where no one knew her secret, and landed here in Bellamy Bay. Sweet, right?"

"Yes, I read all about that in a fairy tale by Hans Christian Anderson," Alex replied. "It's called 'The Little Mermaid.'"

Pepper licked her thumb as she scanned her notes, undeterred. "Anyway, she and the fisherman married and had daughters, daughters who lost the ability to turn into mermaids but retained some of their powers. Captain Bellamy recounts this history and even gives a family tree. These women—your ancestors—were renowned for their beauty, healing powers, and prowess with men," she added, with a touch of resentment. "Take Jack Frazier, for example. He's the most eligible bachelor in town, and he hadn't shown interest in anyone. Until you arrived." She arched a brow.

"The police detective?" Now this was ridiculous. Alex sat back in her seat. "I don't know what you're implying." Besides, if she never heard the name Jack Frazier again, it would be too soon.

Pepper drew close again. "Look, there's this story that I found from way back, when one of your ancestors was rumored to have murdered someone through witchcraft. Have you heard of this?"

"Again with the witches." Alex rolled her eyes. "No one is going to actually believe this."

"But there are many in town that do." Pepper's pen hovered over her notebook. "Did you want to make an official comment for the article?"

"Yeah, I'll make a comment." She leaned closer. "You're writing about fairy tales. How's that?"

Pepper smiled slightly. "I'll make a note."

Minka returned then, clutching at her torso. "I have a knot in my chest that just won't—oh." She stopped when she saw Pepper. "What are you doing here?"

Pepper rose. "Leaving." She dropped her notebook and pen back into her messenger and slung the strap over her shoulder.

"Minka, I'm sorry about your mom. If I write about this—I hope you understand I'm just doing my job."

"Everyone's just doing their job," Minka muttered.

"'Bye, Alex." Pepper left without a backward glance.

Once she was gone, Minka took her seat back. "Sorry, I wouldn't have left if I'd known she was here. She was fixated on our family even in high school."

"Are you all right?"

"I've been better." Minka took a deep, restorative breath. "I could really use some Calm Down tea. But Attorney Winston is here, so at least we know Mom is in good hands."

Alex massaged her temples. "So, Pepper said some wild things."

"Pepper is always saying wild things. What's new?"

"She said that we're water witches, descended from mermaids." Alex laughed in disbelief. "She also said something about a murder. Does she really believe that?"

Minka waved a hand. "Honestly, we have bigger problems right now than some colonial-era gossip. And if Pepper goes and prints some story about our family being witches—well, I can't see reasonable people believing that, can you?"

"I'm glad to hear you say that. I was kind of stunned by the wackiness of it all."

"Don't worry about Pepper. She's an annoyance, that's all. We can deal with her."

Kamila poked her head through the doorway then. "Hey, girls. I got the scoop."

Minka jumped up. "What is it? When are they going to let Mom go?"

Kamila took her sister's hands in both of hers, instantly calming her. "They're suggesting a low bail and house arrest. She may even be able to go to work. Now, she's going to have to stay here until Monday—"

"What?" Minka's hands went to her cheeks. "She has to stay in jail?"

"I did my best, but the chief won't let her out until she's been arraigned, and court isn't until Monday. She's going to be right here," Kamila said, trying her best to soothe. "We have a holding cell and it's decent. She's the only one in there. Everyone knows Mom. They'll be good to her. We can even bring her meals and books."

Minka balled her fists. "It's not good enough, Kamila. Mom cannot sit in jail for the weekend. She's not a criminal."

Alex wrapped an arm around Minka's shoulders. "Of course she's not a criminal, and none of this is fair. It's frustrating, but we have to be patient. Justice can be slow."

Now Kamila stepped back. "This is serious, Minka. They think Mom killed someone. She can't just walk out of here."

Minka sat back into her chair. "What are we going to do?"

"Can you tell us what happened, Kam?" Alex asked.

"Bennett didn't show up to an important dinner meeting Tuesday night, and he wasn't returning phone calls," Kamila explained. "Edwin Kenley—that's his business partner—called the police to ask them to run a welfare check. They arrived Wednesday morning and were going to just knock on the door, but Stephanie was there. She's his soon-to-be ex-wife."

"The wife was leaving the house?" Alex said.

"No, she was just arriving," Kamila replied. "She unlocked the front door for the police and gave them permission to enter, and that's when they saw him. He was found beside a half cup of Mom's Good Luck tea. They found tea leaves and deadly night-shade berries in his stomach."

"But there's no deadly nightshade in that recipe," Minka insisted. "Those are bayberries."

"The police found deadly nightshade berries at Mom's house. They're saying she added them to Bennett's tea to poison him." She paused. "She hated him. Don't you think it's at least possible—"

"Don't even say it," Minka cried. "Mom may not have liked Bennett, but she wouldn't resort to murder."

Kamila was silent for a long stretch as she stared at the floor, looking troubled. Then she turned to Alex. "There's no reason for you to stay here tonight. Why don't you and Minka take my car home? I can get a ride."

"I'm not leaving," Minka declared. "I'll sleep here all weekend, too."

Kamila looked at Alex and opened her arms in a pleading motion. Alex got the hint. "Minka, Kam's right. We should get home and straighten up."

Slowly, she coaxed Minka to her feet and toward the door.

"I'm not going to sleep. Not until Mom is out of here."

"I know," Alex said. "And I'm not going to rest until these charges are dropped." It was a risk, her committing to finding a murderer and clearing her aunt's name. It was dangerous. She could get hurt. She understood all of that. And the little girl inside her who'd lost a mother, that believed with all her heart, that if her mother hadn't been so fierce and independent she'd be alive today begged her to step aside and let the police handle it.

But something within Alex had changed when she reunited with her aunt and cousins. She knew without hesitation that fighting for the family she'd just discovered was worth any dangers she faced.

Chapter Seven

In the course of executing the search warrant, police had moved furniture and left cabinet doors wide open. Alex was dismayed to discover that someone had even searched her dresser drawers and tossed her clothing all over the bed. She and Minka spent most of the night cleaning the house, feeling equal measures of embarrassment and anger. Athena walked through the house with her ears down, disturbed by the disruption around her. Fortunately, the owner of the local historic renovation company was able to repair the front door early on Saturday morning.

They decided to close Botanika for the weekend. There was no reason to subject themselves to any gossip that might have walked through the shop door—not that the gossip was confined to the store. Pepper Bellamy had been busy online, posting all over her personal gossip blog. Alex and Minka did their best to ignore her efforts and keep themselves busy. For Minka, that meant binge-watching rom-coms. Alex took several long runs around town and sat in the garden, thinking. Surrounding by pink hollyhocks, purple sweet peas, white peonies, and yellow rosebushes, she allowed the falling water of the mermaid fountain to lull her into an almost meditative trance as she tried to process what was happening to her family.

*   *   *

Thank goodness, her aunt was arraigned on Monday, released on bail, and placed under strict house arrest. Tobias met her at home to be certain she understood the rules. "You cannot leave your home, not even to visit your gardens."

"What?" Her face lost its color. "So, I'm not even allowed to have sunshine and fresh air?"

He cringed. "There's a concern you may have access to more poisons, since you're known to be so handy with herbs and such. And you cannot work at Botanika," he explained. "That means you cannot prepare any products that will be sold. Is that understood?"

"They're determined to bore me to death," she grumped as she flung herself onto the overstuffed chair in the living room. "Still, it feels nice to sit on some real furniture. And look—new jewelry." She held out her ankle to reveal a black monitor.

Tobias was a pleasant-looking man with a short, stout frame, receding dark-gray hair, and round wire-framed glasses. He looked solid and dependable, and Alex felt a small measure of relief when she saw him.

He patted Lidia's shoulder. "Just keep on the straight and narrow. That will make my job a lot easier. Because trust me, I'm going to be fighting these charges."

Lidia sighed. "You've already done so much. Thank you."

"By the way, do you have an alibi for the time of death? If you do, we can nip the police's suspicions in the bud now." He gazed at Lidia expectantly.

Lidia ran a hand through her air, her face sagging with exhaustion. "I'm afraid not, Tobias. At least not one that I can share."

He shot her a concerned look and rubbed his chin. "Well then, that makes things a bit more challenging." But then he smiled. "No matter, we'll discuss it more once you've gotten some rest."

Alex stared at her aunt, wondering where she'd been when Randy was murdered. After Winston left, Alex knelt by her aunt's side. "Now that you're home, we can figure out what actually happened to Randy Bennett."

"Aleksandra. I have to say something first." Lidia reached for her hand and pulled her closer. "I am so sorry for the way I spoke to you last week when we were in the back room together. I had a bad feeling about Randy's death. There's a dark cloud hanging over all of us right now, and—" She shook her head. "There's no excuse. You were trying to be kind, and I responded with anger."

Alex's throat tightened, and she squeezed Lidia's hand back. She was touched that her aunt had remembered, and grateful that she had apologized. "I know, your famous temper. But it's okay."

"It's not. All weekend I thought about how glad I was that you were here to help my girls while I was gone, and that I had been unkind to you. I'm sorry." Her beautiful face appeared to have aged while she was in the holding cell, and Alex's heart hurt to see the strain this was causing.

"I've spent the weekend doing some thinking, too. Can you think of anyone—anyone at all—who would have wanted to kill Randy Bennett?"

Lidia shook her head. "That's the question I keep asking myself. But I can't name a single person who would want to hurt Randy. We weren't even close—not anymore. I haven't been a part of his life in ages, and he's not a part of mine. Why in the world would I kill him?"

"I understand." Alex reached down to kiss her aunt on the cheek. "I'm going to fix this, *Ciocia*. You'll see. Just leave it to me."

* * *

"Have you seen this trash?" Alex said to Minka and Kamila. They were in Alex's room, lying across her bed. "Here. It's Pepper's blog. You've got to read this for yourself." She handed over her phone.

Local businessman Randolph Bennett was found dead in his home on Wednesday morning. By Friday evening, Bellamy Bay P.D. had arrested their culprit: Lidia Sobieski. Ms. Sobieski is well known for her encyclopedic knowledge of plants. Sadly, all of that knowledge may have come in handy if she poisoned Mr. Bennett.

The Sobieski family is rather notorious. Some interesting rumors have followed them, and while normally this writer wouldn't pay any attention to such gossip, it's worth noting that instead of dying out, these same tales have haunted each generation of Sobieski women. There must be some truth to the stories, right?

The journal of none other than Captain John Bellamy gives us a detailed account of the Sobieskis, and it's quite fascinating. Their story involves love affairs, magic—and even murder. That's right, legend has it the Sobieskis have killed before. This entire puzzle will be set down piece-by-piece in detail very soon on this blog. Don't forget to subscribe so that you can read it first.

Minka frowned and handed back the cell. "I see Pepper's been making the most of our family's tragedy. How decent of her."

"Just Pepper being Pepper." Kamila rolled languidly onto her back and yawned. Judging by the dark circles under her eyes, she hadn't been sleeping well. "Our family is one of her favorite subjects. This is nothing new."

Alex wasn't inclined to be as gracious toward Pepper as her cousins were. What was Pepper's fixation with the Sobieskis about? "Doesn't this bother you? Even a little?"

"I guess so. I'm not sure what her interest in our family is. I think her own family history isn't exciting enough or something, so she's always digging into our past." She shrugged. "I'm really tired." Minka crawled off the bed. "I've got to get some sleep. I want to open Botanika tomorrow, to keep things running like usual. I can't even think about Pepper and her stupid blog." With that, Minka slumped off toward her own bedroom. "Wake me before dinner."

"Yeah, I'm with Minka," Kamila said. "I'm going to take a nap in my old bedroom and then maybe I'll get riled up, but now?" She yawned, and that was answer enough.

Alex was left alone in her room with Athena, who was snoring beside the bed. She closed the door and positioned her pillows against the headboard. Maybe Minka and Kamila weren't bothered by Pepper, but it bugged the heck out of her. She'd always had a protective streak, and she'd be darned if Pepper was going to spread this absurd gossip about her family. The best thing to do was to get the police looking in the right direction: away from Lidia. But where to start on the matter of Randy Bennett's murder?

She did a quick Google search on her phone and pulled up a few articles. Randy Bennett had been a real-estate developer, so many of the online photos showed him at ribbon cuttings holding a giant pair of scissors. Only one caught her interest, something about a land dispute that might have been heading to court.

She jotted a few notes, then stretched and rose. Her limbs were heavy from fatigue, but she'd never been one to nap. She tucked her notebook under an arm and walked downstairs to the kitchen, followed closely by Athena. Lidia was opening and closing the cabinets and mumbling to herself.

"Smells like someone's been baking," Alex said, before spotting a plate of *pączki*—Polish doughnuts—on the wooden top of the breakfast bar. Her face broke out into a grateful smile. "I tell ya, freshly baked treats from the motherland never gets old."

Lidia smiled over her shoulder. "Help yourself. I'm just reviewing the damage those lovely police officers did while they were searching my house." She flung a tall cabinet wide open to gesture at the towers of pots and pans. "Look at this. Were they raised in barns?"

Alex bit her lip. She'd actually been the one who'd tried to straighten up that cabinet. She didn't think it looked *that* bad. "How about if I make us some tea? Then I'll help you organize that pantry the way you like it."

"You're sweet." Lidia closed the doors again and stepped away. "But there's no need to clean it now. I want to have something to do for the next however many months, since they took all of my herbs away." She lowered herself onto a chair at the breakfast bar, looking withered. "I'm a prisoner in my own house."

"But hopefully not for long." Alex smiled sympathetically and reached for two mugs. "How about lavender tea?"

"Sounds perfect."

Alex put the kettle on the stove, scooping fragrant leaves into the teapot. When the tea was ready, she set a steaming mug in front of her aunt.

Lidia took a raspberry *pączki* and set it on a small plate. Then she pushed it toward Alex. "Raspberry is your favorite."

Alex was touched she remembered. "Yes it is."

"Those raspberries grow wild in the backyard," Lidia said, helping herself to a strawberry doughnut and taking a bite. "Better than the food I had all weekend."

Alex opened her notebook and flipped to the right page. "Okay. So, for now, we're saying you don't have an alibi?" She glanced at her aunt, hoping not to upset her.

Lidia shot her an annoyed look. "You heard what I told Tobias, yes?"

Nodding, Alex swallowed against the tightness in her throat. Her aunt certainly wasn't making this easy. "Okay, so let's talk suspects." She positioned her pen. "I've heard that most murders are committed by those closest to the victims. Randy was going through a divorce and his wife Stephanie was at the scene. Do you know her?"

Lidia chewed before responding. "Yes, we went to college together. She was going to be an interior designer, but once Randy made his millions, she abandoned her dreams." She paused. "Perhaps that's unkind. Stephanie has a number of charitable interests and she's done a lot of good, I'm sure."

"Randy was a millionaire?" Alex thought back to the sallow, disheveled man.

"Many tens of times over," Lidia said solemnly. "He owned Bay Realty Corporation. From what I've heard, it's worth about a hundred million dollars."

Alex let out a low whistle. "So Stephanie Bennett had a reason to kill her husband before the divorce was final. Maybe a hundred million of them."

"They were married for a long time." Lidia hesitated before adding, "If you're wondering if I think Stephanie could be capable of killing Randy for money, then yes, I think it's possible."

Alex wrote *Suspect: Stephanie Bennett. Motive: $100 million.*

"This is delicate, but do you think that Stephanie might want to frame you for Randy's murder?"

Alex braced herself for an angry outburst, but Lidia's face revealed nothing. "Stephanie and I were not friendly. I suppose it's possible that she would see me as a convenient scapegoat."

A look of skepticism crossed Alex's face. "But that means Stephanie would have to know that Randy had purchased tea from Botanika, and she would have added deadly nightshade berries to the leaves."

"Right." Aunt Lidia pursed her lips. "Motive and opportunity."

Lidia's shoulders slumped. "It does seem unlikely, doesn't it."

Alex bit her lower lip, unsure of how to respond. Lidia was right: she was the most obvious suspect.

"Although, Stephanie won't get all of the money if they sell the company," Lidia continued after some thought. "Edwin Kenley was Randy's business partner. I assume he'd get around half. And I've heard around town that Edwin wanted to sell, while Randy refused." She raised her mug to her lips. "Edwin had a very minor stroke a couple of years ago and has wanted to retire since then."

Alex added his name to her list. "Do you know anything about him?"

"Edwin? Nothing much. He keeps to himself. We've never socialized."

"But he had reason to kill Randy, too. Randy refused to sell Bay Realty and Edwin wanted out. When we're talking about tens of millions of dollars . . ." Alex shook her head.

"Apparently the Carolina Shipping Company was very interested in buying the business as well." Lidia rubbed her chin thoughtfully. "That's Bronson Bellamy's company."

Alex wrote the name on her pad. "Bellamy. Any relation to Pepper?"

Lidia nodded. "Bronson is her father. And he's also our mayor." She made a face. "Like all things Bellamy, the CSC has dreams of world domination," she said with a smirk. "Bay Realty would be a nice addition to the portfolio."

"Does Pepper have anything to do with the CSC?" Alex asked.

"No, Pepper has never worked for her father. But Bronson buys her lots of nice things that she can't afford on a small-town journalist's salary." Lidia squinted at the notebook. "What else do you have on there? Any other suspects?"

"Yes." Alex turned the page so that her aunt could read it. "Tegan Wesley. She wanted to buy Bay Realty's land, and apparently there was a dispute—"

"No."

A gust of strong wind hit her from out of nowhere, and Alex nearly fell off her seat. She grabbed the edge of the counter top, catching herself just in time. "What was that?" The windows were all shut.

Now Lidia rose, her anger on full display. "Stay away from Tegan Wesley. If she catches you asking around about her—" Lidia lifted her plate and mug. "Alex, don't meddle in this. You're only going to make a bad situation much, much worse." She set her dishes in the sink. "Now, if you'll excuse me, I need to rest." With that, she swept out of the room.

Alex tapped her finger thoughtfully on the paper. A few days ago, her aunt's sudden outburst might have upset her, but now she saw it for what it was: fear. "*The lady doth protest too much, methinks,* Athena," she whispered, and circled the name *Tegan Wesley.*

She had just become suspect number one.

Chapter Eight

M inka and Alex opened Botanika on Tuesday and prepared for the worst. Alex envisioned hordes of nosy people crowding the shop aisles, wanting to know exactly how Lidia had poisoned Randy Bennett. Minka's posture was ramrod straight as she unlocked the front door, almost as if she were steadying herself for a battle. But half an hour into the opening, no one had entered the shop.

There were no shelves to straighten or floors to sweep. No product to restock. They stood with their backs pressed against the counter and watched the door. Plenty of people walked past the windows, and many even lingered to peer inside. But no one entered.

"This is a joke," Minka sulked. "We may as well close until the trial's over."

"It's only been half an hour," Alex said, glancing at the clock on the wall. But she worried that even loyal customers had become afraid to shop there. "How about if I go grab us some coffees? I need another eight hours of sleep or several cups of coffee before I'll feel functional today."

Minka agreed, and Alex hurried outside. Yes, she wanted a cup of coffee—desperately. More importantly, now was about the time that Jack would be in Coffee O'Clock, and she wanted to speak with him about the suspects on her list. Had he even considered them? As she rounded the corner of First and Main, she saw him, annoyingly handsome, opening the red door to the coffee shop. He saw her and paused. "Hello, Alex."

"Detective Frazier," she replied coolly.

He waited for her to walk up the steps. "How are you doing?"

The sincerity of his question caught her off guard. "Do you want the truth? Or do you want me to be polite?"

He smiled a little at that. "It's your answer, so you get to choose."

When they walked inside, Alex instantly felt curious stares. She tried to ignore them, but whispering followed. She caught fragments of sentences: ". . . niece . . ." ". . . poison . . ." ". . . tea . . ." She tugged at her clothing as the discomfort crawled over her body.

"I'm not doing too well, Jack," she said softly. "I think you've made a rush to judgment with my aunt and overlooked some major suspects."

"I understand," he replied. "But the evidence is pretty clear to me. There were poisonous berries in the tea Lidia gave the victim. How do you explain that?"

"Easy. Someone planted those berries."

Jack cocked his head at her. "Come on, now. Who would do that?"

"Exactly. That's the question you need to ask."

He didn't respond, because it was Alex's turn to place her order. She had become friendly with the barista, a college-age African American woman named Celeste with long, silky black hair and a flawless complexion similar in color to the latte she'd just poured. A few freckles covered the bridge of her nose. She turned sympathetically toward Alex. "How are you holding up?"

"Everyone knows, don't they?" Alex sighed and lowered her voice, conscious of Jack waiting in line behind her. "I've been better, but thanks for asking. How are your courses going?"

Celeste was in her last semester of a two-year MBA program at Bellamy College. She groaned at the question. "I've got another group project, which means I've got to babysit my teammates and make sure they're working."

Alex knew all about Celeste's classmates, many of whom were more interested in socializing than studying. "One day, they'll regret all the slacking off they did," she said.

She winked. "I figure its good practice for when I'm their boss."

Celeste was wearing a necklace of hand-painted beads in shades of purple flecked with gold. As Celeste reached for a coffee cup, Alex said, "That is a stunning piece of jewelry."

She had often admired Celeste's effortless understated style. She was the kind of person who wore simple, elegant clothes paired with funky jewelry and barely any makeup to accent her pretty features.

Celeste's hazel eyes brightened at the compliment, and she touched a hand to her throat. "Thank you. It was a gift."

"Lucky boy. Am I right?"

Celeste laughed, and when she moved, Alex caught a hint of her perfume. After her lesson with her aunt, Alex enjoyed breaking down perfumes into their notes and trying to identify them. The scent Celeste wore was elegant and subtle, like her. A top note of something floral . . . honeysuckle. The middle note was fruity—probably red apple—and the bottom note? Sweet and woodsy, it reminded Alex of fresh hay she'd smelled the last time she'd gone pumpkin picking.

"Not lucky boy, lucky *man*," she corrected with a grin. "Not like these college boys around here."

"Anyone I know?" Alex asked, but Celeste shook her head, suddenly busy fiddling with paper cups. "Someone in your MBA program?"

"Definitely not. He's older. I just wish we saw each other more. All he does is work."

Alex was getting the feeling there was much Celeste wasn't telling her about her new friend. "Is it serious?"

"Could be. We'll see. He wants to keep things quiet . . . he says it's because of his position in town. People will talk."

"Oh." Alex wasn't sure what to say. Sounded like her boyfriend was hiding something, and she hoped it wasn't a wife. Celeste was too nice a girl to be mixed up with a cheater, which is what her mystery guy sounded like, but Alex didn't feel comfortable giving her more advice. She wasn't her mother or even a friend. She was just a customer at the coffee shop.

Alex said her goodbyes, then stood off to the side to wait for Jack to order his black coffee. No bagel this time. When his drink was ready, he waved her over into a quiet corner, away from prying eyes.

"This is such a small town, you have to stay out of earshot," he explained. "Otherwise everything you say will end up on Pepper Bellamy's gossip blog."

A surge of gratitude flooded her chest at that small, considerate gesture. "Thank you."

"Don't mention it. I don't want to be quoted, either."

"And thank you for talking to me."

They were standing close together now in a small hall that led to restrooms and a kitchen, away from the tables of customers. His blue eyes softened. "You don't need to thank me, Alex. You're concerned for your aunt."

"Great. I'm glad you understand that. Will you hear me out, then?"

"I can promise I'll listen to your concerns; how's that?"

She wasn't going to nitpick. She knew she had a short window in which to make her point. "My aunt had no motive for killing Randy Bennett. What does she gain now that he's dead? Nothing. However"—Alex lowered her voice even more—"Stephanie Bennett will inherit half of his estate. They were in the middle of a divorce. Maybe she took a shortcut."

Jack folded back the lid on his coffee cup. "What else?"

"Edwin Kenley," Alex continued. "The business partner who is now free to sell the company. Or maybe one of the Bellamys. CSC is trying to buy Bennett's business. Did you know that?"

He shook his head as he scribbled something on his pad, then gestured for her to continue.

"But Bennett wouldn't sell to them. And then there's Tegan Wesley, who Randy Bennett had a land dispute with—"

"Tegan Wesley." Jack frowned. "What kind of land dispute?"

"I'm not—the details weren't clear."

"How many years ago?"

"Two."

"Was a lawsuit ever filed?"

"Not that I could find."

Jack held up a hand. "Then how can we assume that gives Mrs. Wesley a motive? Maybe they resolved the land dispute amicably."

Alex folded her arms. "Jack, I think—"

"Please listen." He went to touch her arm, but stopped himself. "The simplest answer is that Lidia put something in the vic's tea because she was angry with him. Maybe she didn't actually intend to kill him, but that's for a jury to decide. And she also can't account for her time when Bennett was killed." He released a deep breath. "Now, if we find compelling evidence to reconsider the case, or discover she has a rock-sold alibi, then yeah. Of course we'll reassess. But the witnesses who saw your aunt that day in the shop said they'd never seen anything like it. They said it was like the whole place was shaking."

Alex tried to look unconcerned. "She has a little bit of a temper—"

"And people with hot tempers can find themselves involved in murder investigations. Now," he said, stopping her as she opened her mouth to argue. "Like I said, I'm committed to getting this right, Alex. If there is concrete evidence we're overlooking, I need to know. But short of that?" He shook his head. "We've got the only person who makes sense."

She saw from the set of his jaw that he was not going to move off his position, but neither was she. "Then I guess I'll have to find that concrete evidence for you, won't I?"

He fought to remain stern, but a small smile escaped. "Again, I respect your concerns. But I hope you'll trust me when I say that we're taking this case very seriously and considering all angles. We don't need citizens to help."

"Got it."

Jack's posture relaxed upon her assurance. "I should get going." His eyes met hers and held her gaze. "Maybe I'll see you tomorrow?"

She struggled to keep the bright, phony smile on her face. "Maybe."

He walked out the door and down the steps, and once he was out of view, she finally exhaled. Jack was kidding himself if he thought she was going to wait for the police to find another suspect. Her father had been a detective, so she knew that once a suspect was arrested, the case was turned over to the prosecutors. The police didn't look for alternative killers. Jack Frazier had his murderer, and he was going to move on to other matters.

If there is concrete evidence we're overlooking, I need to know. A killer was loose in town, and Alex was going to find the evidence Jack needed to arrest that person.

Challenge accepted.

*   *   *

For the remainder of the day, sales at Botanika were discouraging, to say the least. Minka had never experienced such a downturn. "I don't understand. How can people think my mom would hurt anyone? She's devoted her life to helping others."

"You know what else really bothers me?" Alex said. "The person who killed Randy Bennett is somewhere out there, getting away with it."

Minka's eyes widened. "You're right. I've been so focused on Mom that I haven't even stopped to consider that there's a murderer on the loose in Bellamy Bay."

Alex reached for her cousin's hand. "They won't get away with it. Because I'm not going to allow that to happen."

She reviewed her list of suspects with Minka. Her cousin was well versed in town chatter and had plenty to say about Stephanie Bennett.

"She's as phony as they come," she declared without hesitation. "Don't get me wrong, she knows how to keep up appearances. She wears designer clothing and she heads all the right committees. But you can't trust her any further than you can throw her."

About Edwin Kenley? "All work and no play. I hope he takes vitamin D, because I can't imagine he ever sees the sun. He's a workaholic."

"So he's suspect number two," Alex said. "And next is Bronson Bellamy, who wanted to buy Bay Realty—"

Minka burst out laughing. "Oh, I'm sorry. It's not funny," she said, continuing to chuckle. "But it would really take the sparkle off Pepper's sports car if her dad was caught up in a murder." She wiped at her eyes. "But yes, Bronson Bellamy has dreams of owning everything in town. If he had a real-estate company, he'd grow the family's influence."

"Was there any bad blood between Randy and Bronson? I mean, besides Randy's decision not to sell the company."

Minka shrugged. "Not that I've heard."

Alex made a note to find out more. She looked at her cousin. "And suspect number four is Tegan Wesley."

Minka abruptly stopped laughing. "Tegan? Oh no." She actually glanced behind her shoulder to make sure they were alone in the shop.

"Your mom didn't like that I added her as a possible suspect, either."

"No, I wouldn't think so," Minka said. "The relationship between our families is complicated, to put it mildly." She frowned, chewing on her lower lip. "Tegan Wesley. I can't say that's impossible. I mean . . . maybe."

Now this was interesting. Alex stepped closer and lowered her voice, too. "What do you know about Tegan?"

"Just what I know about all of the Wesleys. That they're different from us. There's bad blood. Our families don't get along. Never have. Mom and Tegan are like oil and water."

"Is there enough bad blood that Tegan would poison Randy to frame your mom?"

"I don't know. I'd like to say absolutely not . . . but it could be her children, too. Dylan or Bryn."

"What do you know about them?"

Minka explained that Tegan was the CEO of Wesley, Inc., and had been since her husband died ten years before. Dylan and Bryn both held executive positions within the company. "I don't know either of them well. I don't care to know them, either. But they turn up at different events. Highbrow things like gallery showings and black-tie galas."

"What does the company do?"

Minka sighed, as if the question taxed her. "They buy up companies, do stuff to them, and then sell them. And then I heard they also develop properties—like they buy up whole small towns and city blocks in big cities."

Alex eyed her skeptically. "Really?" When Minka nodded, she glanced at the clock. It was nearly two, and she hadn't taken a lunch. "Minka, this has been helpful. Would you mind if I took a break?" She was already untying her apron.

"You're really going to investigate this, aren't you?" Minka gripped her cousin's wrist. "Listen, whatever you do with the Wesleys, you have to be careful. Promise me."

Alex couldn't help but grin. "There's no need to worry. I'm going to introduce myself and ask a few questions, that's all. Get to know them. What could they possibly do to me?"

But the fear in Minka's eyes was evident. "They're dangerous, Alex. You can't underestimate any of them. Promise me."

Alex grabbed her handbag and tried not to convey her growing irritation, but she was tired of her family's secrecy. "Minka, what could they possibly do to me?" She blurted out. "I'll be safe. I promise."

Minka hesitated before handing over her car keys. "Here. If you're hunting down the Wesleys, you're going to need these."

* * *

The corporate headquarters was located on the opposite end of town in a five-story structure with mirrored windows. The building wasn't impressive until she realized that the foundation was perched on a cliff overlooking the Atlantic. Her breath caught when she entered the brightly lit white marble lobby that offered sweeping views of the water and the Bellamy Bay lighthouse.

A man positioned behind a crescent-shaped white marble desk with the words *Wesley, Inc.* on the front observed her reaction with a smile. He carried himself with a posture that suggested a military background. "Spectacular, isn't it? That view makes my day every morning."

Alex was captivated. All she could see was smooth, blue water. "It's beautiful."

He grinned. "The Wesleys have the best of everything."

He was a striking man in his midtwenties with a bronzed complexion, close-cropped curly black hair, and a square jaw. "I assume you're here for the job interviews?"

Alex bit the inside of her cheek. She hadn't actually invented a pretense for the visit. She'd thought she'd simply introduce herself to the Wesleys and make small talk. After all, the families knew each other. But now that she'd seen the majestic space in which the Wesleys conducted their business, she realized one didn't simply wander into Wesley, Inc., headquarters to be neighborly.

"No, I was hoping to speak with someone about another matter. Unfortunately, I'm not able to stay." She glanced around the lobby, which was filled with young men and women in professional attire clutching leather binders and portfolios. "I, uh, didn't realize there would be such a wait."

"You should've seen it this morning." He chuckled. "It's a career fair. Only happens once in a blue moon."

"I'll bet." Alex glanced around her one more time before leaning across the counter and reading the name tag on his lapel. "Listen, Harrison. I'm wondering if Tegan Wesley is here?"

He shook his head. "No, ma'am, I'm afraid Mrs. Wesley isn't in. Did you want to leave a message?"

Did she? "No, I'm . . . an old friend of the family. I'll have to come back—"

Harrison glanced toward the far end of the lobby, where a man and woman had stepped off an elevator. "Mr. Wesley," he nodded. "And Ms. Wesley. Good afternoon."

For the second time since she'd entered the building, Alex's breath stopped. The man Harrison had addressed as Mr. Wesley was wearing a black suit perfectly tailored to his broad shoulders and tall, fit frame. Darkly attractive with short dark-brown hair, angular features, full lips, and strong eyebrows, he was tan even in early spring. He exuded self-assurance and power, and the room fell silent as he entered the lobby. At least, she thought it had. She couldn't be sure, because she was staring at him and his dark eyes were fixed right on hers. *Dylan Wesley.*

"Good afternoon, Harrison," Mr. Wesley replied, without turning his gaze from Alex.

Bryn was at Dylan's side, pretty and impeccably dressed. "Harrison," she said coolly. "Please send for the car."

Harrison instantly pressed a button. "Yes, ma'am."

But Dylan was still watching Alex with an intensity that made her heart race. "Go ahead. I'll catch up."

Bryn pursed her lips. "They're not going to wait forever, Dylan."

Alex could barely breathe. So this was Dylan Wesley? How had Minka neglected to mention that he looked like a movie star?

Dylan Wesley barely acknowledged his sister's concern. "They'll wait as long as I want them to."

She huffed. "Fine. I guess I'm going alone, then."

Dylan stepped closer to Alex, enveloping her in his cologne of spice and smoke. "I know you," he said, lowering his deep voice. "From long ago."

Her throat tightened and her face burned. "You—I—you must be mistaken—"

"I'm never mistaken." He was invading her space, towering over her and knitting his brow as he tried to place her face. "You're a Sobieski, aren't you?"

How had he known? The blood rushed to her cheeks. She started to deny it, but then Dylan continued, "Of course you are. You're Aleksandra." The corner of his mouth rose. "You used to summer in Bellamy Bay. We played in Lidia's garden." His eyes softened. "Don't you remember me?"

Images appeared in a flood. The shy, sentimental boy who had played with her on those lazy summer days and offered her a crown of flowers. They had turned her aunt's lush garden into a kingdom. He'd appear only when she was alone, which had caused her parents to brush him off as an imaginary friend, no matter how much she'd insisted he was real.

"You were my queen," he said, his voice going husky.

She felt as if her face were on fire. "And you were my king. That was you," she whispered. "I must have forgotten your name."

"I never gave you my real name." He chuckled. "I swore our driver to secrecy. If my mother had found out I was sneaking off . . ." His voice trailed, and he led her off to the side of the room. "So why are you here, if you aren't looking for me?" His brow furrowed. "You don't need a job, do you?"

She chuckled uncomfortably, pushing the oddly intimate memory away. "No, I don't." She searched for a tactful way to explain that she was simply spying on his family. She settled on explaining her own predicament. "You may have heard about my aunt."

"Yes, I'm afraid a lot of people are talking about it." A shadow crossed his face. "We should go somewhere more private to discuss this. Come with me."

Alex followed him into a waiting elevator. He pressed a button for the fifth floor, and they rode in silence until the doors opened again and he said, "After you." Then she followed him to an office at the end of the hall. The door said *Dylan Wesley / Chief Financial Officer.*

He swung open the heavy wooden door to reveal a corner suite with floor-to-ceiling windows that stared over the eternity of the ocean. "Can I get you anything to drink?" He gestured to a wet bar against the wall.

Alex held up a hand. "No, thank you."

"Then let's sit."

The decor of the office was surprisingly traditional, in contrast to the overall modern feel of the building. Dylan's office furnishings were stately dark ebony and burgundy leather, and he directed Alex to sit on a couch. The leather was smooth and cool beneath her legs. He chose a seat in a matching chair opposite her, a round wood table between them. "I was sorry to hear about Lidia's troubles," he began in his polished, prep-school voice with just a hint of elegant southern drawl. He unfastened the button on his suit jacket. "If there's anything we can do to help . . ."

Alex recalled her aunt's reaction at the mere mention of the Wesley name, and Minka's warning that the family was dangerous. Her shoulders tightened. "That's kind of you," she began carefully. "But our families don't get along. I don't think my aunt would accept your help."

"Then why are you here, Aleksandra?" His features took on a suspicious bent.

"Just Alex is fine," she said.

"All right, Alex. If you don't want my help, then what do you want?"

She folded her hands on her lap to still the nervous energy rushing though her body. "My aunt didn't kill anyone."

He flung one arm across the back of his chair and casually shrugged. "Then the police are wrong and they'll fix their mistake."

"I understand your mother had a dispute with Randy Bennett over some land. Do you know what that was about? Did it involve the land where Bay Realty Corporation is developing an apartment building?"

Understanding settled across his sharp features, but instead of being angry, Dylan smiled. "I see. You're a sleuth now, is that it?"

Alex's face boiled as he continued. "If so, you're in the wrong place. My mother is a pillar of society. She would never kill anyone, least of all Mr. Bennett."

"Of course you would say that," Alex replied. "But that wasn't my question. I asked you what you knew about this land dispute."

"Which one?" He crossed his arms over his chest as he studied her. "We've invested in several of their developments, and if you know anything about real estate, you know that it's never smooth sailing." He shrugged. "Land disputes are routine, I'm afraid. The lawyers deal with it. Although it's rare that anyone ends up dead." He grinned. "Frankly, it's all boring, and I try not to get involved."

Now Alex smiled. "You're the chief financial officer. How do you not get involved?"

"I open the coffers as needed. You'd be amazed at how many problems money can solve."

"Look. Someone ended Randy Bennett's life and went to a lot of trouble to frame my aunt. Your family hates mine for some reason—" She paused when Dylan began to chuckle. "What's funny?"

"You realize this isn't the first time a member of your family has killed anyone, right? Your great-great-grandmother killed my great-great-granduncle."

"That's not true." Alex declared reflexively.

"I'm afraid it is. There's a reason our families don't get along."

Her head was spinning. Pepper Bellamy had also said a member of her family had killed someone before, but Alex had dismissed it as absurd. Now she wondered if there was truth to the story after all.

"I don't subscribe to any of it, you understand," Dylan continued. "Ancestral animosity. Who has the energy to hold a grudge for something that happened over a hundred years ago?"

Dylan uncrossed his arms and leaned forward. "Yes, there are still some hard feelings in my family. But not enough to actually frame your aunt for murder. We have a thriving corporation and other interests in our lives. A fixation on revenge would be . . . alarming."

Alex's skin was on fire, so deep was her discomfort. How did she not know anything about her own family? How had Minka not prepared her for any of this? One thing was sure: before she went any further, she had to get to the root of this story. Otherwise she'd only be inviting more opportunity for someone to expose her ignorance the way Dylan just had.

She looked up, expecting to see Dylan gloating. He wasn't. "It is good to see you again, Aleksandra. I'd always wondered where you'd gone. We all heard when your mother drowned." His brow tightened. "I was very sorry to hear it."

She swallowed, unsure of what to do with either his kindness or her unfortunate attraction to him. The man was gorgeous. "Thank you," she said, and rose to her feet. "I should get going. You must be very busy."

He stood. "I try to never be too busy to see old friends." He placed a hand softly on the small of her back as he guided her to the door, sending a jolt of awareness through her body. "In fact, if you're in town for a while, I would love to see you again."

Was that an invitation? She didn't know how to respond. "I'm not sure how long I'm here," she replied truthfully. "And my *ciocia* needs me at Botanika—"

"Of course. You're very busy, too. But if you're in the neighborhood again, the invitation stands." He took her hand gently in his. "After all, you always welcomed me."

There went her breath again. He was an intense one, this Dylan Wesley. "It's nice to see you again, Dylan. I'll leave you to your meeting." She carefully withdrew her hand from his grasp. "I'll show myself out."

She headed to the elevator and pressed the button. Again, it was waiting for her. Slipping inside the chamber, she was relieved when the doors finally closed and she no longer felt Dylan's gaze on her back.

Chapter Nine

Alex left Wesley, Inc., and hurried across the parking lot to Minka's green hybrid sedan. For a long time, she sat in the car and stared out the windshield. She'd been disgusted to read Pepper Bellamy's blog posts about her aunt, but to find out that her great-great-grandmother had actually killed a man made her head hurt. What else was true in that blog? Was she going to find out next that the Sobieski women were actually witches?

She laughed to herself and turned the ignition. Of course they weren't witches. She came from a long line of women who were good with plants and herbal medicine, and in more superstitious times such women had been labeled witches. Maybe Captain Bellamy believed it with his whole heart, but that didn't make it true. But the murder? Now that was something verifiable, and there was obviously a very dark story around it if the Sobieskis and Wesleys were still feuding decades later.

"It's my family, too," she said as she pulled out of the parking space. "I deserve to know what happened."

Her father should have told her, but maybe he hadn't known, either. *Maybe it's my fault*, Alex reasoned. She could have done some research when she was older and at least uncovered the basics.

She felt silly, not knowing anything about her mother's family which obviously had very deep roots here in Bellamy Bay. Her father's family had immigrated from England around the turn of the century; no big secrets there. All she knew about her mother's side was that they had immigrated from Poland and settled into a small community in Bellamy Bay. Her mother had died too early to give her details, but man—Alex had missed some *major* details.

Once she reached Botanika, she charged inside and stomped right up to Minka. "You've been keeping things from me," she declared, and backpedaled when she saw the confusion on Minka's face. "Sorry. Not just you, I mean the collective you. The family. There are lots of things no one has told me."

Minka furrowed her brow. There was a fashion magazine spread out on the counter in front of her, a confirmation that business had not picked up that day. "Where is this coming from, Alex?"

She flung her purse and the car keys down on the counter. "I just had a conversation with Dylan Wesley. He told me that our great-great-grandmother murdered his great-great-granduncle and that's why our families hate each other." She folded her arms across her chest. "This seems like relevant information, considering you knew I was going to talk to the Wesleys. Is this the complicated history you didn't want to tell me about?"

Minka shrugged. "It was, like, a hundred years ago."

"But you should have warned me. I was caught completely off guard when Dylan mentioned it."

Minka glanced at the clock. "Four thirty," she said. "We haven't had a single customer today." She shut the magazine and took the car keys. "You want to go home?"

"Only if you're going to answer my questions once we're there." Alex reached for her purse. "Don't think I'm going to forget this."

"Oh, I know you won't. But my mom is the one who knows family history best." She smiled and set a hand on Alex's arm, urging her toward the door. "Let's go. Mom probably doesn't know what to do with herself, and Athena probably misses you."

But Lidia had found plenty to do on her first full day of house arrest. "I straightened up and did some baking," she announced when they entered.

In fact, Lidia had alphabetized her spice rack, grouped the food in the cabinet by type and purpose, organized and polished her pots and pans, and baked *sernik,* Polish cheesecake with drizzled chocolate topping, *makowiec,* a sweet poppy-seed roll, *piernik,* gingerbread, and peanut-butter dog cookies. "Athena has a new favorite treat," Lidia said, and lifted a small round cookie from a plate. "Athena, sit."

The German shepherd quickly sat at attention, already salivating. Alex shook her head as she watched Athena gobble up her cookie. If this happened every day, she'd have to put Athena on a diet by June. Heck, if she didn't keep up her daily jogs, she'd have to put *herself* on a diet. When she'd lived in New York, there'd been a Polish bakery located a few blocks from her apartment, but she'd never found the time to visit except around Christmas and Easter when she really craved some holiday pastries. With her aunt baking her childhood favorites on a daily basis, it would be a challenge to abstain from eating cake every day.

Kamila sat on a stool at the breakfast bar, looking shell-shocked. "I've tried to get her to calm down," she said. "But she won't stop moving."

"Are you ready for dinner?" Lidia asked as she headed to the stove. "I made some *borscht.*"

Minka held up a hand. "Not yet, Mom. Wow, you've been busy." She helped herself to a slice of cheesecake, promising to run an extra mile later.

"Yes, I'm determined to make the best of this." Lidia polished an imaginary spot on the marble counter with a dish towel. "I may take up knitting."

Alex, Kamila, and Minka exchanged a glance. "Great," Minka said. "But look, Alex was asking me some questions about our family."

"Like what?" Lidia folded up the dish towel neatly and set it beside the sink.

"Like about the thing with the Wesleys?" Minka said softly.

Lidia froze, her back to them. "What thing?"

Now Alex spoke up. "The thing where my great-great-grandmother killed their great-great-granduncle. I think I deserve to know what happened."

She waited for another one of Lidia's temper flares, but to her surprise, her aunt turned with a look of resignation on her face. "You're right. You do deserve to know." Lidia combed her fingers through her long black hair and gestured at the spread of baked goods on the breakfast bar. "Should we sit here? At least there's food. Maybe something to drink?"

Lidia bustled around the kitchen, grinding beans and finding clean mugs, while Alex joined Kamila, even though she had no appetite.

"How did you hear about this?" Lidia began, once the coffee was served.

Alex looked away briefly. "Pepper Bellamy has been saying things on her blog."

"I see." Lidia's mouth set into a straight line.

"We need to talk to Pepper," Kamila said as she broke off a piece of a muffin. "Do you want me to handle it? She's always been a little afraid of me."

But Lidia set her hand on her daughter's forearm. "Not now, love. One thing at a time. The thing is, Alex." Lidia took a deep breath. "There was a death long ago, but it's not what anyone thinks. And ever since you came back to Bellamy Bay, I've known this day would come, but I was waiting for the right time to tell you—" She lifted her hands in the air. "I guess I'll just say it. We're witches."

Alex laughed out loud. "Yeah. Pepper says that, too. She's ridiculous."

She waited for Lidia and her cousins to join her in the joke, but their faces remained somber. Minka gently bumped Alex's shoulder with her own and said, "No, Mom's serious. We're witches."

Alex glanced back and forth at each of the women, but their faces gave nothing away. She nodded slowly. "Oh. Interesting."

So her aunt and cousins imagined themselves to . . . have powers? She shifted in her seat. This conversation had taken a turn for the bizarre. Maybe it was time to think about sending out her résumé and moving on.

"I don't even like the term *witches*," Lidia continued. "We're so much more than that."

"Some of us are," Kamila said in a pointed tone. "Others of us choose to live a less complicated lifestyle."

"Sure," Alex agreed mechanically.

"Alex, it's true." Minka reached for Alex's left hand. "You remember what happened with your finger, right? You had that terrible cut, and then it vanished?"

Alex had been so distracted over the last few days that she hadn't even thought about the incident. She'd assumed . . . actually, she hadn't come up with any rational explanation. But now she was remembering all of that blood, and how unlikely it was that she would not have needed stitches after an injury like that, let alone a Band-Aid. "That—what did you do?"

"I healed you." Minka grinned. "Like I said, we're witches." She squeezed Alex's hand. "And you are, too."

"No." Alex shook her head. "I'm not a witch. Definitely not. I've never done anything magical in my life."

"All of the Sobieskis are magical," Lidia said. "It's in our DNA. You used to sit in the garden by the mermaid fountain and make the water leap for joy. Do you remember that?"

Alex pinched her leg. No, she wasn't dreaming, and she definitely did not recall that. "No way. I would remember something as amazing as that."

Lidia's smile fell. "It's all of that time living as a Mundane," she explained. "You've forgotten how to be magical."

Alex's vision swam for a moment, and she felt light-headed, as if she'd fall if she wasn't already sitting. "Mundane?"

"Mundane means nonmagical," Minka explained, then leaned forward on an elbow. "Mom, maybe you should start at the beginning. This is a lot of information for Alex to digest."

"Of course," Lidia agreed. "I'm just excited for you to finally learn the truth about yourself. Stay right there; I'll get the book."

Once Lidia left the room, Kamila rose and hastily picked up her plate and mug. "I'm out of here," she announced. "I want no part of this." She dropped her dishes into the dishwasher and left the room.

Alex watched her go. "What's that about?" she asked Minka. The television blared from the next room.

"Don't mind Kam," she said. "There are some Magicals who choose not to practice. She's one of them. She doesn't think Mom and I should practice, either."

When Lidia returned, she was holding a dusty book bound with soft, worn green leather. She glanced at Kamila's empty seat but didn't remark before setting the book on the table and opening to the first page. "Now. This is the family tree," she began, pointing to a list of names carefully written in ancient lettering. "Our family history begins in Poland in the sixteenth century. You remember the *Syrenka Warszawska*, the Mermaid of Warsaw, of course."

Alex hesitated to confess that she had no idea what her aunt was talking about, but if she wanted answers, she'd have to ask for them. "I don't. I'm sorry."

Lidia appeared crestfallen. "Oh, I thought for sure your father would have—that's fine," she continued. "The Mermaid of Warsaw is something of a legend in Poland, though of course we know it's true. A trio of fisherman noticed that whenever they went fishing, the waves were stronger than normal, their nets were always getting tangled, and their fish were set free. At night they watched the river and discovered a beautiful *syrena*, a mermaid, was the cause of their problems. They captured her, but she enchanted them with her singing and they set her free."

Alex thought back to Pepper's suggestion that she had enchanted Jack Frazier. That couldn't possibly be true . . . could it?

"But then a wealthy business owner trapped her, placed her in a prison with plans to profit from her uniqueness."

Minka made a face. "You mean he wanted to treat her like a freak show."

Lidia patted her daughter's leg. "A lesson we can all learn from. We have to always guard our secret lest others try to profit from our abilities." She turned back to her niece. "The fishermen heard her pleas for help and set her free. She was so grateful for their kindness that she vowed to use her magical abilities to protect the city and its people. Her image has been on the Warsaw coat of arms since the fourteenth century, and statues of her stand all over Warsaw with a shield and sword to represent her fierce protectiveness. She was apparently an impressive warrior when she wanted to be."

"Here," Minka said, reaching for her cell phone. "I'll show you." She searched online until she found an image and showed Alex the screen. "This is just one of many statues of her. This one is overlooking the Vistula River."

Alex looked at the photograph. The statue was intimidating in size, but the mermaid was beautiful and elegant, even as her arm rose above her holding a sword. "Impressive. We're descended from her?"

Minka nodded, fairly bursting with pride.

"And that's why the . . ." She gestured toward the mermaid fountain outside. "Fountain?" She almost laughed, except her throat was tight and dry. "Like an inside joke?"

"Not a joke," Lidia said carefully. "A reminder. Of who we are. *What* we are."

Alex mentally stumbled over the *what we are* response, but tried to think rationally. Tried to process the overwhelming information her family was giving her. She glanced at the photo on Minka's screen again, blinking until her vision stopped swimming. "What's with the sword and shield? That's not a part of any mermaid stories I've heard in the past."

Lidia laughed. "Apparently she had a gentle temperament and a kind heart, but she was certainly not the Little Mermaid, though some believe the two were sisters." Alex's eyes widened, but her aunt only waved her hand. "That's another story for another time. All you need to know is that she used her powers for good. She protected those who couldn't protect themselves."

"Yeah," Minka chimed in. "At the end of the day, that's what it's about. That's why we heal." Her face turned pink with excitement. "That's why we *help*. The age-old story of good prevailing over evil. Kamila likes to think she's not a part of this, but she's a cop, for goodness' sake. She has the urge to protect, too; she just does it in a Mundane way."

Alex gazed at her cousin, impressed by her passion for the family history. She was certainly enthusiastic about their heritage.

"The folklore is mistaken, though," Minka continued. "Because the mermaid didn't return to the sea. She fell in love with one of the fishermen that saved her." She grinned. "So that part is like the Danish folktale. She traded her life in the water for a life on land, and her agreement was to protect not just the city of Warsaw, but humans in general."

"What agreement?" Alex asked.

"With the Warsaw community," Lidia explained. "She was clever. When she chose to spend more time on land—whatever that looked like, we're not sure—she knew life could be dangerous. Becoming a protector for others meant she was protected herself." Lidia turned a page in the old book. "The Warsaw community knew she was a mermaid, but she was so valuable to them as a healer that if anyone made trouble for her, the others would work together to keep her and her family safe."

"She's the first magical Sobieski," Minka said. "She's the reason we have these . . . abilities. Apparently, she had several daughters, and they were able to switch between human and mermaid form. Eventually they all left Poland to start new lives where they could live as humans and settled in other areas—the British Isles, Asia, the Americas, Africa. Many countries and cultures have folktales related to mermaids. And their children, like our ancestor that helped found Bellamy Bay, lost the ability to transform into mermaids." She wiggled her bottom in her seat with a grin. "No fish tails."

"Here, you can read it for yourself sometime," Lidia said as she turned the yellowed pages of the book. "Dozens and dozens of pages tracing our family history, all the way to the present day. Around here"—she pointed to a name and date from the end of the seventeenth century—"our family began to immigrate to the colonies. Had they remained in Poland, they may have experienced something like the Doruchów witch trials. What we do can be very dangerous." She turned to a point later in the book, where someone had drawn a map in ink. "We settled in Bellamy Bay—or the area, at least. It didn't become Bellamy Bay until years later. But the Sobieski men made a good living as fishermen—shrimpers, mostly—and the Sobieski women became renowned as healers."

"Our ancestors delivered healthy babies and saved many people from infectious diseases like malaria, the yellow fever, and smallpox," Minka said, brimming with pride. "This town thrived because of them."

"It's true," Lidia agreed. "Even though the town is named after the Bellamys, the Sobieskis are the reason that family settled here. You can read about it in journals from that time. Townspeople report that their children were on the brink of death until one of our ancestors intervened, or that someone was kicked by a horse but survived because a Sobieski cleaned the wounds and set the broken bones."

Alex was transfixed by the tale and their sincerity. They believed this history, and so did people like Pepper Bellamy. Was it possibly true? "So we have healing powers?"

"Exactly. We're water witches, for lack of a better term," Lidia replied. "We can manipulate water—anything with moisture, really. But we can also harness the power of nature, especially the elements of rain, snow—"

"Air," Minka added, with a nod toward her mother. "That's how Mom picked up Randy Bennett that time, because there's water in air."

Alex remembered feeling a gust of wind each time Lidia's vicious temper appeared. "The jars on the shelves rattled," she said. "Even the windows seemed to shake."

"Oh yeah," Minka said. "Mom creates a vortex when she's angry."

Lidia took the charges in stride and reached for a serving of gingerbread. "I'm working on my temper. But yes, we can heal," Lidia continued. "And we take our ancestor's pledge to protect humans very seriously, only using our powers for good."

"Before you ask," Minka said, "no, we can't bring people back from the dead. People used to get angry at the Sobieskis because they couldn't do that."

"That's why some started calling us witches, ironically enough," Lidia explained. "They were angry and wanted to hurt our ancestors, who they had perceived as denying them help. And with all of the terrible baggage that comes with that word—the trials and burning innocent women—calling the Sobieski women witches put a target on their backs. And I still disagree with using that label, by the way. Minka tells me I need to embrace it."

"We can't fight it, so we try to own it," she said.

Thoughts swirled in Alex's head. Minka pushed the plate of sliced poppy-seed roll toward her. "You look like you could use some cake."

Absently, Alex placed a slice on a dish. She was still trying to understand. "So our great-great-grandmother . . . she was a bad witch?"

"Oh, right, I was getting there," Lidia said. "No sweetie, she wasn't bad at all. She was practicing self-defense, and it went terribly wrong."

"The Wesleys are magic, too," Minka said. "You have to explain that, Mom."

"Yes, yes. After the Sobieskis arrived from Warsaw, the area began to prosper and other mermaid families followed, including the Wesleys. Of course, back then they were Wasilewskis."

"Wait." Alex set her elbows on the table and rested her head in her hands. This was dizzying. "Are we related to the Wesleys?"

"Technically, all mermaids are related, but it would be something like first cousins twenty times removed. Not worth mentioning," Lidia said, again gesturing to the book. "But what happened long ago was that Jakub Wesley fell in love with Zofia Sobieski, your great-great-grandmother. Or perhaps he fell in love with the idea of combining two very powerful families, I don't know. But Zofia was in love with someone else, a Mundane."

"The Sobieski women have always loved Mundanes," said Minka.

"Right. So Jakub fell in love with Zofia, and when she didn't return his affection, he became aggressive. He held her down and tried to force an enchanted ring on her finger, and she panicked and used her magic to force him away." Lidia sighed. "In her fear, she miscast her magic. Jakub died of a brain aneurysm, and the

Wesley family has always blamed our family for that and demanded an apology."

"But that's not right," Alex said. "She was only protecting herself."

"Now you understand," Minka said. "This has been going on for decades. The Wesleys think Zofia murdered Jakub, and we believe Jakub had it coming."

"Minka," Lidia warned.

"You know it's true." Minka sat back in the stool like a sulky teenager. "According to history, Jakub Wesley was the worst."

They must have had this discussion before, considering the way Lidia looked to the ceiling. "Both families feel strongly that their ancestor was wronged. But Zofia went on to marry the love of her life. They had a beautiful little girl, and that was your great-grandmother."

Alex plucked at her food. She was too preoccupied to actually eat. The story was great, but how could any of this actually be true? She folded her hands and looked at the women around her. "Okay, you say we're witches. Prove it."

"You want a parlor trick?" Lidia slid off her stool. "Watch this."

She retrieved a glass from the cabinet, set it on the counter, and turned on the faucet above the sink. At first the water fell into the sink as usual, but then Lidia's eyebrow cocked. Suddenly the water from the faucet arched and fell neatly into the drinking glass. "There," Lidia said, and shut off the faucet again. "That's a basic one."

Alex's mouth hung open. "Oh my gosh . . ."

Minka squeezed Alex's arm. "We can control thoughts, too," she said eagerly. "And read minds."

"What?" Alex whipped her head from her cousin to her aunt.

"Now Minka," Lidia said. "I think poor Alex is overwhelmed as it is."

But her cousin leaned over to whisper, "I'll teach you how to do it later."

Alex stared at her hands. Was she actually capable of working this kind of magic herself? She'd never accomplished anything like it, and wouldn't know where to begin. She stared at Lidia, seeing her differently. "What about my mother? Was she also magical?"

Her aunt's face brightened at the question. "Oh yes. Bianca was the most powerful of our kind to be born in generations. A force to be reckoned with."

Alex frowned. If her mother had been so powerful, then how come she had never seen any of that magic? Surely she would have remembered something like that. As if reading her thoughts, Minka reached up to stroke Alex's hair affectionately and say, "Your father didn't like magic. He asked her not to use it, and she agreed."

Alex froze in her seat. "You mean Dad knew about all of this?"

"Yes, Robert knew all of it," Lidia confirmed. "And he wasn't comfortable with any of it. He said he couldn't marry a witch, so your mother stopped practicing."

"They loved each other," Alex replied, feeling an ache unfurling in her chest. "Mom would have done anything for him, and he would've done anything for her." But she didn't like that her father had asked her mother to hide a part of herself. "He must have had his reasons for asking her to stop," she added, quick to defend him.

Lidia set her warm hand across Alex's. "Your father was a wonderful man. He was a true gentleman who raised a gorgeous, intelligent daughter."

Tears formed in Alex's eyes. "Thank you, *Ciocia*."

"We were always sad that he stayed away from us after your mother—after the accident," Lidia continued. "I'd hoped that one day he would change his mind."

Alex thought a moment. "But if she was descended from mermaids, how could she have drowned?"

Lidia grimaced. "I've wondered that a million times myself," she said softly. "Your mother was a strong swimmer who could stay underwater even longer than I ever could. I can't explain her death, and I struggled with it for ages."

She squeezed Alex's hand. "I've waited for so long to tell you the truth, though I would never have chosen to tell you like this, in the context of . . . this unfortunate event."

The murder, Alex thought. She turned her face toward the window and saw some gray clouds gathering. She'd always believed there was something soothing about the rain, and right now she would have welcomed a downpour. Alex brought her attention back to her aunt and cousins. "So Randy Bennett wasn't being bizarre when he came to Botanika looking for a potion. You infuse your products with magic, don't you?" No wonder customers saw remarkable results.

"Some of them, yes." Lidia nodded. "Of course, herbal remedies work and can be a powerful medicine, but Zofia Sobieski deserves all the credit. She began selling teas and salves many, many years ago. Disguising it as a business helped her avoid the occasional witch hunter who came to Bellamy Bay. Botanika continues that tradition."

"Witch hunters," Alex gasped. "Those are real?"

"Very real and very scary," Minka replied ominously.

"So basically our family is involved in magic laundering," Lidia continued. "The store is a legitimate front that allows us to practice our healing powers."

A stretch of silence covered the women, and Alex had the sense that they were all waiting for her to say something in response to all she'd just learned. But Alex felt disoriented, like her world had just shifted beneath her. Mermaids and witches? If what her family said was true, then everything was different. Magic existed, *and* she had the ability to practice it. How could that be, when Alex had spent her life believing in facts and evidence?

Her father had been the most practical man she'd ever met. His job as a police detective required a dedication to facts. He didn't make assumptions, he didn't rush to judgment, and he didn't believe in magic. "There's no such thing," he would tell her when she asked. The Tooth Fairy hadn't come to her house, and neither had Santa or the Easter Bunny. When her dad had said there were no fairies or witches and that Halloween was only for fun, she'd believed him. The thing was, her father had known *for a fact* that magic existed in the world.

All of her life, he'd been lying to her.

She pushed back from the breakfast bar and stood on uncertain feet. This was all so very confusing, and there was only one way she knew to sort out a cluttered mind.

"I'm going to go for a run, if you don't mind," she said quietly. "I need to do some thinking, and I'd like to get out before the rain starts." She snapped her fingers at Athena, who instantly jumped to her feet.

"You can just push the raindrops away from you," Minka said. "I do it all the time. If you go for a walk, I'll join you."

"Thank you," Alex said. "But I need to be alone. With Athena, of course," she added. The dog cocked her head at the sound of her name.

"I understand." Minka gave her a big hug.

Now Lidia stood and walked over to the refrigerator. "Take as long as you need, love. It's a lot to process. And when you come back, I'll have a hot bowl of soup waiting."

"Thank you," Alex said.

"I know it's overwhelming, but it must feel good, right?" Minka said. "I mean, to finally know who you are?"

Alex nodded, but she'd already thought she knew who she was. Now she wasn't so sure.

Chapter Ten

It was Alex's father who'd taught her to run. "Running is life support," he'd explained. "When you feel good, you run. When you feel bad, you run. Confused, sad, stressed—you take it out on the road and you leave it there." He'd been an avid runner himself, often leaving before dawn to get his miles in. This was how he dealt with his grief after her mother died and the many pressures at work.

Alex had never appreciated the example he'd set until she reached high school and felt the pressure to achieve. Suddenly everything in her life was about getting into college and what looked good on a transcript or an application. To deal with that stress, some of her friends had turned to alcohol. Alex, the daughter of a police detective, didn't think she'd have a prayer if her father caught her drinking underage.

As a law enforcer, her father had learned to use mediation to alleviate the symptoms of stress. He'd tried to get her to practice *stilling her mind*, as he called it, and she'd grudgingly tried it once. She must've done it wrong, because it hadn't worked. She'd fallen asleep and woken up more anxious than ever about her test that day.

But she did enjoy the physicality of exercising. So she'd taken her father's advice and become a runner. Amazingly, it worked.

Running had gotten Alex through high school, college, business school, and a professional career in risk management. Now she left the house on Cypress Lane with Athena at her side, away from stories of mermaids and witches and toward the ocean, eager to leave her confusion on the road. The air was cold and damp, the gray clouds overhead threatening to burst any moment, and Alex pushed herself until her legs began to burn.

She jumped off the uneven cement sidewalk and onto the asphalt, her breath heavy in her ears. Away from the house, she could almost pretend the conversation had never happened at all. She could almost outrun it. Then a thought would creep in—the cut on her finger vanishing, the vivid image of her mother released by the perfume, the tap water leaping in an arc into a drinking glass—and Alex would pick up speed. She hit the boardwalk at a sprint, desperate to return to a comfortable place in her mind again.

How could this be?

Alex sprinted until her legs felt like lead. She came to a rest near a wooden bench that looked out over an empty beach, and Athena paused, wagging her tail and waiting expectantly. The waves crashed against the shore, and for a moment, Alex stood still just to watch them. She'd always loved the water.

Water witch.

The words came to her as if on a breeze. Could she actually move water? Alex glanced around, but the boardwalk was empty. She decided she would try to move the ocean water in an arc, just the way Lidia had moved the water from the faucet. Lidia had made it seem so easy.

"All right," she whispered, and pointed a finger at the ocean. "Move."

She waited for a change, but the ocean waves continued to crash against the shore just as they had before. Maybe it took more fingers? She directed all ten of her fingers at the water, forming two big claws.

"Come on, move," she whispered.

Nada.

"Well, shoot."

It was a silly thought, anyway. Why in the world would she think any of what Lidia had said was true? Mermaids? Alex chuckled to herself. She'd gotten swept up in an interesting story, but it was more legend than anything else. Rumors and gossip, nothing more. Obviously she couldn't move water. The idea was absurd.

That was when Alex noticed a little red plastic bucket that a child had forgotten. It was poking out of some of the sea grass growing in thick bunches beside the boardwalk, and it looked like it had been there for some time. Alex jogged to retrieve it, lifting the bucket by the yellow plastic handle. The lip was chipped, but otherwise it was intact.

Maybe moving the ocean was a little ambitious for a newbie, she reasoned. Maybe she needed to practice on something much smaller. She found a path to the water and scurried down, her heart picking up pace as she grew more excited. *What if . . . ?* She couldn't finish the thought. The possibilities were exciting enough.

Alex stepped into the edge of the water without stopping to kick off her running shoes. A wave crashed around her ankles, soaking her legs. It didn't matter. She crouched to snatch some water in the red bucket and hurried back up to the boardwalk, her shoes squirting water with each step. Nearby, Athena dug a hole in the sand.

"Okay, let's try this again," she whispered as she set the bucket on the seat of the bench. What had Lidia done? Pointed a finger? Alex shut her eyes and tried to recall the image. No, she hadn't pointed or moved her hands. All she'd done was look at the faucet and the water had moved.

Alex gathered a breath and stared at the little puddle of water in the child's red bucket. There was a clump of sand on the bottom. "Okay, water. Swirl."

She narrowed her gaze, imagining lasers shooting from her eyeballs, because that was what it would look like on television. The water was perfectly glasslike, the sand still clumped solidly at the edge.

"Move, water," she urged, and then, with a hint of desperation, "Come on, please?"

Nothing.

"I give up."

But then it happened. A tiny vortex began at the bottom of the bucket. It picked up the sand and pulled it around and around, twirling faster and faster until every drop of water was consumed by the vortex and the sand had turned the water brown. Alex's eyes widened.

She'd moved water. It was true; she was magical. "I can make smoothies with my mind," she gasped. Athena barked and bounded toward her, leaping up on her hind legs. "I did it, Athena." The dog rolled around happily on her back.

Alex heard footsteps pounding on the boardwalk. The bucket overturned itself, spilling its contents on the ground. Another runner was approaching. It was Jack. He looked like he was running from something, too, but his serious face relaxed when their eyes met. "I'm beginning to think you're following me, Alex," he said breathlessly as he slowed to a stop.

She smiled. "I was here first."

"Then I guess I'm following you."

He was wearing an old gray sweat shirt that said *N.Y.P.D.* in navy print and black shorts. She admired his lean, muscular legs as he bent to greet Athena. "Apparently we're the only people who think they can beat the rain," he said, and pointed back to the empty boardwalk. He took a moment to slow his breathing. "Though it's probably not a good idea for anyone to see us talking here. Twice in one day."

Alex shrugged. "We're just two runners, out for a run."

"Still." His gaze fell to her shoes. "Your feet are wet."

She glanced down at the puddle her shoes had left around her. "Yeah, I was going to try to run on the sand, but a wave grabbed me."

He looked out over the water. "Look, I've been thinking about what you said, about your concerns with your aunt. I want you to know that I take them seriously."

She waited for him to say something more. "But . . . ?"

"If there's something you know that you're not telling me, I have to know what it is. I know you were in Botanika when the victim was there. You saw what happened. If there's some factual basis for you believing Lidia didn't hurt him, I want you to come down to the station to make a statement."

That was a terrible idea. After all, she'd seen her aunt lift Randy Bennett into the air, hold him against the wall, drop him, and then retrieve the tea that had allegedly poisoned him from the back room. She'd only be confirming the witness statements that had led to Lidia's arrest in the first place. "I don't have any additional information. I just know my aunt, that's all. She would never kill anyone. She's made her living healing people."

With magic. Magic that Alex had, too.

Alex tried to look weighed down; she really did. But at that moment she was so elated at the thought that she'd just moved water that she was struggling. Unfortunately, that only seemed to encouraged Jack's suspicions.

"I've been a police detective for years now. I've interrogated a lot of witnesses, and I've gotten pretty good at reading people. I can tell when someone's hiding something."

Alex had heard all of this before. "Let me guess. . . you can always tell when someone is lying?" She affected a bored expression. "It's in their eyes, their mannerisms, their gestures?"

His eyebrows lifted in surprise. "How did you—"

"My dad was a police detective, remember. He reminded me a million times a day how he could tell when I was lying." She smirked. "He was actually pretty good. I never got away with feeding my vegetables to the dog."

Jack frowned. "Okay, I guess that line won't work on you, then."

"Sorry to disappoint."

She was trying to shrug off his critical gaze, but Jack apparently wasn't in the mood for levity. "There's something going on, Alex," Jack finally said. "I don't know what it is, but I know that something is off."

I am a water witch, Alex thought gleefully while attempting to look nonchalant. Judging by Jack's frown, she was failing to deceive this man whose only job was to detect lies. "I told you, I don't have any additional information." A raindrop fell on her cheek. "I should wrap up my run. Besides, you're right. It would look bad if people caught us talking twice in one day."

She clicked her tongue at Athena, and they both turned and began running back to Lidia's house, leaving Jack standing alone on the boardwalk.

*   *   *

"I did it!" Alex announced when she opened the front door. The rain had picked up on the run home, and she was drenched, but she didn't care. "I did it. I moved water."

Minka entered the foyer and clapped her hands. "Congratulations. Oh, wet dog. One sec." She fled the room but returned quickly, carrying a bath towel. Athena panted while Minka dried her off. "I'm so excited to have someone else to practice magic with. Kam wants nothing to do with any of it."

"It was incredible," Alex gushed. "I found a bucket, filled it with water, and swirled it around. All I did was focus on it. Is it really that simple?"

"It's as natural as breathing." She laughed while Athena shook herself off and trotted away.

"Though the bucket did fall over. I didn't mean for that to happen."

"There is a technique you can use to maintain control. Don't worry, I can help you." Minka gripped Alex's shoulders. "This is so great. You know, we have a Mermaid Festival here in town every summer, and now that you know the truth, you can come to the private parties and network with the other Magicals in the area." Her eyes shone with excitement. "Magical parties are to die for."

Alex smiled. "It's all true. I can barely believe it, but it's true." She looked down at the floor and noticed a puddle collecting at her feet. "I don't want to ruin the floor. I'll go get showered."

"Mom's getting dinner ready. It'll be about fifteen minutes."

"Great."

Alex bounded upstairs and into her room. Her head was still buzzing as she grabbed a pair of jogging pants and a sweat shirt to change into. She headed into the bathroom and turned the hot water on. As she undressed, she reflected on the interaction with Jack. Man, how feelings could change on a dime. Alex couldn't get him to crack a smile, let alone enchant him. A sadness whirled in her chest at the unfairness of it. She hadn't done anything wrong.

She treated herself to an indulgent shower. She was chilled from the downpour, and the hot water turned her skin bright pink. She dressed and was towel-drying her hair in her bedroom when her cell phone chirped. Alex touched the screen and saw that she had a voice mail.

She sat on the edge of the bed finger-combing her hair while she waited for the voice mail to connect. Finally the message came through. "Hey Alex. This is Carter Hawthorne."

Her heart skipped. Carter Hawthorne was one of her former clients. The CEO of Barber Industries, he was aristocratically handsome and from an old-money family. Known to be a jet-set-ter and a partier, he was also an astute businessman. He must've heard she'd left the firm.

Why in the world would he be calling her now? She swallowed and picked up her phone as the message continued. "I heard that you left Johnson, Lovitz, Ream & Cannon, and I was sorry to hear that. All of us were. You've been our senior consultant for years now." Alex smiled at the compliment and breathed easier. "So here's the thing," Carter continued. "We have an opening at Barber for a director of operational risk management. You'd be in charge of—pretty much everything. There'd be some international travel, but you'd work right here in Manhattan. Right down the hall from me. I—well, you've been here a million times. You know where we are." He chuckled. "Anyway, think about it. Whatever your salary was, we'll pay you more. Full benefits, of course. Give me a call when you have a chance. Talk to you later."

Alex's cheeks blazed as she saved the voice mail. Well. She'd landed a job with her favorite client on the same day she'd learned she was descended from mermaids. She set the phone down on the bed, too overwhelmed to know how to proceed with the generous offer. This day would be difficult to top.

She danced down the stairs humming happily and twirled into the kitchen with a flourish. She froze when she saw the looks on Lidia's, Minka's, and Kamila's faces. "What happened?"

Minka slid her phone across the breakfast bar with a scowl. "It's Pepper. She's on a roll."

Alex picked up the screen and read the headline of the article. *Water Witches Live Among Us.* Her jaw tightened. "All right," she said. "So tell me, how exactly do we stop this?"

Chapter Eleven

The next morning, Alex left Botanika wearing jeans, purple boots and carrying an umbrella. She'd planned to visit Pepper after lunch, but once again the shop was empty. There was no reason to delay.

Yesterday, Pepper Bellamy had written a brief teaser in her blog:

> *You guys, I have proof positive that water witches—descended from mermaids—live among us.*
>
> *Bellamy Bay was the setting for a tale of seduction, murder, and witchcraft. This complicated story may sound incredible, but I have proof that it happened. I intend to show you that magic surrounds us, and that it presents a clear danger. It may be time to consider how to protect ourselves. Stay tuned . . .*

* * *

"What is this proof?" Lidia had asked the night before, her cheeks drained of color. "Did either of you use your magic in public?"

Minka wrinkled her nose. "No, of course not."

"Mom, no way," Kamila said. "You know how I feel about magic."

But Lidia's brow creased with worry. "She's always made these threats before, but if she has proof?" Her eyes grew dark. "That may mean she's going to mention names. I don't know what we'll do. She's going to attract witch hunters. She can get someone killed."

"Killed?" Alex echoed, suddenly sobered. She had never before thought about what witch hunters might do, or considered that she or her family members could be targets.

"There are at least two kinds. Those motivated to eradicate our kind from the earth—those are the ones you commonly hear about in history, with witch hunts and witch trials. The Puritanicals, religious zealots who believe we all practice black magic." She rolled her eyes. "And then there are those you've probably never heard about, those who believe they can profit from our abilities. The Traders. They literally hunt us down for body parts or our blood and sell them to the highest bidder."

Bile rose up and down Alex's throat, and she bowed her head until the queasiness left her. She'd heard enough. Pepper had to be stopped from publishing more on her blog.

And so Alex had become the Sobieski assigned to reining in Pepper Bellamy before someone was hurt, or worse. "I'm an unknown," she'd reasoned. "Pepper won't expect me, and she won't know how to deal with me."

Once again, she'd found herself in the position of protector without knowing how to go about protecting anyone, but there was no choice. If Pepper had actual evidence of someone practicing their magic—video, or even audio—Alex had to find a way to make sure that evidence was never released. But mere feet from Pepper's door, Alex didn't have a plan other than to knock and be charming.

Pepper lived on Magnolia Street. Located a few blocks from Main Street, it was a historic section of town where stately, townhouses in pastel shades of green, blue, purple, and pink populated a street lined with fragrant magnolia trees. Alex could touch the first-floor windows of any house on the street by reaching her arm out from the sidewalk, but being set back only a few yards from the road wasn't the only feature that distinguished the area from the more modern sections of town. Wrought-iron fences and lampposts decorated each tiny patch of yard, all bursting with flowers and giving the area a photogenic appeal that made it a favorite for tourists. During Christmas, the homes were extravagantly decorated and opened up for public tours in which the owners served hot chocolate and holiday pastries.

Pepper's home was a sherbet yellow with a large black door, matching shutters, and a brick chimney. A small brass plaque beside the door stated that the house had been built in 1770 and was originally used for commercial purposes, with the owner living on the top two floors. The home was unique for having an extensive side garden and a still-standing structure in the back, originally used as a warehouse. The property was well kept and lovely, and Alex knew it had cost a pretty penny. This part of town was highly desirable, and Pepper had boasted about her family's wealth. A local journalist and gossip blogger would need a healthy trust fund to pay this mortgage.

She tapped the silver knocker. To her surprise, the door was unlatched and swung right open. Alex peeked into the interior. "Pepper? Hello?"

She'd seen Pepper's BMW parked on the curb, so she assumed the reporter was home, but she didn't hear any sounds coming from inside the house. Alex stepped back to look through one of the front windows. Pepper either had extraordinary taste or a fabulous interior designer. The space was bright, even in the rainy daylight, with white built-in bookcases, white leather furniture accented with soft, gray throw pillows, and large windows overlooking the backyard.

Beautiful, but no sign of Pepper. Alex was moving to leave when something caught her eye. A large vase, broken into two pieces, lay in the middle of the floor.

She frowned, leaning in closer to the window to examine the rest of the room. That's when she saw it. Pillows tossed on the floor. Books pulled from a shelf and scattered. An overturned lamp. Something was very wrong.

Alex pounded on the door again. "Pepper?" she called. She set a foot inside. "Pepper, it's Alex Daniels. Are you okay?" She waited. There was no response.

She glanced behind her. No one was on the street. Quickly, she slipped inside and shut the door behind her.

Electricity filled the air, like the feeling before lightning struck. The skin on her arms exploded into goose bumps. The house smelled like a thunderstorm at the beach. She took another step and saw chaos. A runner in the hall, askew. Open cabinet doors. Broken glass on the kitchen floor.

"Pepper?" Alex barely recognized her own anxious voice. "Is anyone here?"

She entered the kitchen. A broken bowl lay like a shattered eggshell on the floor. She pulled a sharp knife from the butcher block and proceeded through the house on tiptoe, opening doors and checking shadows. Something was terribly wrong. The deeper she crept into the home, the more signs she saw that Pepper had been running from someone. But there was no one on the first floor. Alex turned her gaze to the staircase, her heart in her throat. No. She couldn't do this. She couldn't go upstairs.

But what if Pepper was in danger?

Alex held her breath and took a step on the first stair. She kept her back to the wall and the knife pointed outward. Two steps, then three, then four. She was choking on fear by the time she reached the landing. Silence. Three rooms. She surveyed each, finding no one. She exhaled.

But the office was a disaster—an overturned desk, books tossed all over the floor. Clothes were strewn across the bed and sticking out of open dresser drawers. The third room, which contained only a few cardboard boxes, appeared to have been untouched. Pepper was gone.

Alex pulled her cell phone from her pocket and called Jack. He picked up on the third ring. "Alex?"

"Jack," she gasped. "I'm at Pepper Bellamy's house. She's missing, and it looks like something's very wrong."

"What? Why are you there?"

"I—I wanted to talk to her," Alex stammered. "Can you please come? She may be in danger." She gave the address.

"I'll be right there."

She disconnected the call and wrapped her arms around herself. She was still clutching the knife, but she wasn't about to let it go. She rushed down the stairs and out the front door to wait for the police on the front steps. Who would have entered Pepper's house, and why? All she was doing was writing about Randy Bennett's murder and teasing her readers with a story about water witches. As far as Alex knew, that included the Sobieskis and the Wesleys—

Alex's hands went cold. She had come to speak with Pepper on behalf of the Sobieskis. Maybe someone had come from the Wesleys, and they'd gotten to Pepper first.

The Wesleys aren't like us. They're dangerous.

Some of the bookcases had been emptied. Captain Bellamy's journal—where was it?

Alex sprinted into the house and up the stairs to Pepper's office. It was likely she had kept all of her work materials there, and in fact her laptop was still open. Alex tore through the books scattered on the floor. Most of them were modern—dictionaries and style guides, a few reference materials. An old journal would have been easy to spot, and it was definitely not mixed up in this clutter. Alex's gaze turned to the computer screen. A cursor was still blinking. Pepper had been working on a story. Alex read the screen.

There is a war between two notable families, both of them with powers beyond our comprehension. According to the journal, they have always been at odds. The night before Randy Bennett was murdered, I followed Lidia Sobieski from Botanika to a house in the exclusive community the Peninsula. I parked my vehicle down the road and hid in a bush, but what I saw was astounding. Lidia confronted Tegan Wesley. As they exchanged words, the wind picked up and—I swear this is true—Tegan radiated sparks from her fingertips. How many times have we heard people in Bellamy Bay gossip about Lidia's famous temper, and how it seems like she can make the earth shake? Apparently when Tegan is angry, she can set fire.

The writing stopped there. Now she remembered that Lidia had left Botanika in a hurry the night before Randy Bennett's death, claiming she had a meeting. Pepper had followed her?

Alex scrolled down the screen, and what she saw next made her heart stop. Pepper had embedded a video. With a trembling finger, Alex pressed play. The quality of the video was grainy, so it must have been taken on her cell phone from a distance, but the image was clear enough to stall her breath. Lidia and Tegan were standing at a distance, arguing. As their conflict escalated, a violent wind whipped at their hair. Then, Tegan's fingertips sprayed an arc of sparks.

Alex heard a car door open and close, and she looked back at the laptop, realizing she couldn't allow anyone to see this story. Without thinking, she deleted the file, realizing too late that she might have just tampered with evidence. She cursed under her breath, and a sheen of sweat began on her forehead. She could go to jail for this.

There were steps in the entry downstairs. "Hello?"

It was Jack's voice. Alex was shaky with guilt over snooping through Pepper's things, but she couldn't get caught. This was a family matter, nothing more. She swept her fingerprints off the keyboard with a cloth Pepper kept on her desk to wipe down her screen.

"Hello? Alex?" Jack was walking up the stairs.

"Up here," she called. "I, uh, thought I heard something."

She glanced around. The room was a mess, and she definitely looked like she had been snooping. The optics were not good at all. *I am so going to jail.* But when Jack appeared in the doorway, she tried to appear natural. "Hey. How are you?"

No, that was not natural, judging from the suspicious frown on Jack's face. He pointed to the knife she was gripping in her fist. "What's going on here?"

"Oh. This?" She casually glanced at the weapon in her hand and forced a smile. "Self-protection. But now that you're here . . ." She set it down on the only clean surface of Pepper's disordered desk.

Jack's frown deepened. "You want to tell me how you wound up in Pepper's house? Did you break in?"

"Of course not. The front door was open."

"And you just walked in?" He folded his muscular arms across his chest.

"No. Well, yes," Alex admitted, "but only because I was worried about Pepper. The downstairs was a screw up and the door was open, so—" She flung her arms out helplessly. "It looked like there was a struggle. And she's missing, so my instincts were right."

She followed his gaze around the messy room. "This could be a crime scene," he said. "And you were up here touching things and doing who knows what else."

The comment stung, accurate as it was. "I'm the one who called you here. Why are you talking to me that way?"

"Because you may have compromised our investigation."

His coldness gutted her. She'd actually liked Jack, and she'd trusted him. "Why are you treating me like I'm a suspect?"

His blue eyes narrowed, no sign of those adorable dimples whatsoever. "Alex, everyone knows that Pepper has been covering your aunt's arrest for the local newspaper. Just like we all know she's doing some research into your family history, and while it sounds like garbage to me"—he held up his hands—"we both know that Lidia is touchy."

Now it was Alex's turn to be suspicious. "Touchy? What's that supposed to mean?"

"She's a private person, and a little on the eccentric side, if I'm being honest. She must be pretty angry reading the news every day and seeing Pepper's fixation on her."

Alex couldn't believe this. How was it possible that no matter what, Jack was committed to the idea that Lidia was a cold-blooded murderer? "Lidia had nothing to do with this. She couldn't have. She's on house arrest."

"She is," he said softly. "But you're not."

Alex's eyes smarted as if she'd been slapped in the face. "Wow, Jack," she gasped. "Wow." She nearly stumbled across the floor as she headed to the door. "I'll leave you to your work. You'll need to process the scene, and I wouldn't want to ruin anything else."

She brushed past him, torn between heartache and rage. She gripped the banister, her knees weak as two more police officers entered the house. One of them pointed at her. "Miss. We're going to need a statement."

She nodded mutely and continued down the stairs. Beside the front door was a wooden key rack, empty except for a single dangling key. Alex froze. The car keys were gone, but Pepper's BMW was still parked on the street. Panic seized her throat. Was she still in the car?

She jogged past the police officers, went back to the street where the car was, and peered inside. The keys were lying on the driver's seat. But that didn't make any sense. Why would the keys be locked inside, unless . . . *Was Pepper in the trunk?* She didn't stop to think about fingerprints and crime-scene evidence as she yanked the driver's side door open. An image of her mother came to mind, drowning, gasping for air, and she knew she couldn't let that happen. She beat on the window, calling the woman's name. And then she heard a low moaning sound. She followed the sound to the back of the car and slapped the trunk.

"Pepper, are you in there?" She waited a moment and heard another soft mewling sound. She went back to the passenger's door and kicked it in a panic, wondering if Pepper was in danger of losing air.

She suddenly felt strong arms pull her away from the car, and struggled against the restraint. "She's in there, I have to save her."

"Who's in there?" Jack said, his breath coming fast as if he'd been running, and he turned her around to face him. "Pepper?"

Nodding, Alex took a few deep breaths. She showed him the key and told him about the sounds she'd heard.

Jack called for a policeman, who hustled over. They spoke for a moment, and the officer retrieved a baton from his utility belt and handed it to him. Keeping it collapsed, Jack aimed it at the lower corner of the window and punched through the window. Shards of glass flew through the air as Jack reached inside, grabbed the keys, and unlocked the trunk.

Alex ran to his side, and breathed a sigh of relief when they both saw Pepper curled into a ball, lying on her side, face devoid of all color and eyes wide with fear.

"Pepper."

Once again, Alex sensed an electricity in the air, but the energy dissipated almost at once. Pepper sat up as if she'd been napping. "What—where am I?" She was wearing a bathrobe and her hair was damp, presumably from her shower that morning.

Alex exhaled. She was relieved beyond words. "You're okay? What happened to you?"

Pepper struggled to focus her eyes, but she didn't appear injured. "I don't—know."

Jack wrapped an arm around her and helped her climb out of the trunk.

When she was able to stand, she clutched her robe tightly around her, and Alex touched her hand. "Whatever happened, you're safe now."

Thank goodness.

* * *

Pepper didn't remember a thing. She couldn't explain the disorder in her house or how she had wound up in the trunk of her car wearing only a bathrobe. Alex stood by, gnawing on her thumbnail, while Jack spoke to Pepper, who was now sitting in her living room. "Do you remember anything about this morning? Your laptop was open on your desk. Do you recall what you were working on?"

Pepper blinked, and her fingers sought her temples. "I'm sorry. I don't remember anything."

"Do you mind if I check you for injuries?" Jack asked.

"No, go ahead."

Jack rose and gently touched her head, checking for blood. "Does this hurt?"

"No."

He moved his hands to her neck, shoulders, arms, and legs, but there was nothing. No wounds, no bumps, no soreness—only memory loss. Jack nodded at his colleagues. "Call an ambulance. She needs to be evaluated." He turned back to Pepper. "I think you need to go to the hospital for some tests, Miss Bellamy. I'd almost feel better about your memory loss if I could see a bump, but because I don't, you should rule out other problems."

Pepper swallowed and appeared concerned for the first time. The fog in her head must be lifting, Alex thought. "Do you want me to go to the hospital with you, Pepper? Or is there someone I should call?"

Pepper's gaze wavered as she turned to Alex. "Alex." She leaned forward in confusion. "Why are you here?"

"I just—stopped by to talk to you about some things," Alex said. She didn't want to say anything in front of Jack, who was following her every move. "I'm the one who found you here," she added. She deserved at least a little credit for that.

"Oh." Pepper frowned as she struggled to piece the information together. "What were we going to talk about?"

Oh boy, Alex thought. Did Pepper really not remember all of the things she'd been writing about the Sobieskis? She chewed on her lower lip as she considered how to answer Pepper's question. "You told me about some research you were doing. Do you remember? Something about a journal?"

Pepper blinked a few times and shook her head. "What journal? I'm sorry, I . . . I don't remember anything about that." She glanced down at her hands. "Can someone call my mom? Maybe she can meet me at the hospital."

Jack nodded. "We'll take care of that. And the ambulance will be here any minute, Alex. You don't need to stay." His tone was stern.

Alex forced a smile. "Yes. Seems like you've got everything under control. Pepper, I'm glad you're safe. I'll see you later." She began to walk away.

"Wait." Jack caught up with her and touched her shoulder. "About what happened back in the house . . . it looked strange, with you walking around with a knife and Pepper missing. I hope you understand."

His expression was contrite, but Alex wasn't having it. "You said a lot of things and made a lot of assumptions."

"I know, but come on, Alex. You were standing in her office."

"Is this an apology, Jack? It's difficult to tell."

He straightened his posture, his eyes looking as sad as she felt. Their friendship had begun with so much promise—how had everything gone wrong? Alex shrugged off her raincoat and flung it over one arm. The sun was peeking through the clouds, and she was getting warm. But Jack stood watching her with his hands on his waist, not moving and not speaking.

"What?" she finally said in exasperation. He appeared as if he had something more to say, but she didn't have the time. She waited only a few seconds before giving up. "I'm not a criminal," she said, hoping to find Jack the friend, not Jack the detective. "Maybe someday you'll realize that."

But the hard planes of his face didn't soften. "Just be careful."

"Yeah. You too," she said coolly, and headed back down the gravel driveway to the sidewalk.

* * *

Later that day, Alex and Minka sat on the back counter at Botanika to talk about what had happened to Pepper. Another day with zero customers, and they were beginning to accept the possibility that this might be the new normal.

"She forgot everything, Minka," Alex said. "How is that even possible?"

Minka scrolled on her cell phone. "Holy cow. Her blog posts are gone, too."

"You're kidding me." Alex reached for the phone. Sure enough, all posts since Lidia's arrest had vanished. "How does this happen?"

"It's definitely magic," Minka said. "And not a good kind."

Alex handed the cell back to Minka. "I don't know whether to be disgusted or relieved that the family is safe—at least for now."

Minka's face was drawn, her eyes troubled. "Make no mistake, this was a brutal attack on Pepper. The women in our family don't erase memories." She shook her head angrily. "It's not right."

Alex had to agree. She'd witnessed the confusion and fear in Pepper's eyes. "You should've seen her place. Someone tore it apart. Pepper won't feel safe in her own home. You know," she said, thinking back to the moment she'd entered the cottage, "there was an energy in the air. Like electricity or something."

Minka nodded. "That's what it feels like when someone's been practicing the craft. The air is charged with magic, only Mundanes don't know that. I'll bet you interrupted them."

"It was the Wesleys, wasn't it?" The thought that Alex had almost come upon whoever had attacked Pepper sent shivers up her spine. "There was something on her computer, too. She'd been in the middle of disclosing an altercation between your mom and Tegan on the night Randy was murdered. I wonder if the person who hurt Pepper had intended to erase that blog post, too. Until I walked in."

"An altercation?" Minka clutched Alex's wrist. "What kind? What happened?"

Alex explained that Pepper had followed Lidia to the Peninsula on the night Randy Bennett was murdered. "She saw your mom and Tegan exchanging words, and Tegan was shooting sparks. I take it that means she was angry."

"Oh, that's nothing unusual." Minka waved a hand, seeming relieved. "Tegan always does that when Mom's around. But it's bad that Pepper saw it."

"It's worse than that," Alex said. "She took a video."

Minka swore. "That could've been very serious. No wonder someone erased her memories." She threaded her fingers through her hair. "That was too close."

"Do you know what your mom and Tegan were doing out there?"

Minka reflected for a moment but then shook her head. "I don't, sorry. You'd have to ask Mom."

That sounded like a dead end to Alex, considering how tight-lipped Lidia was. But she set that aside for now. Something was nagging her about the attack on Pepper. Something wasn't adding up. "What bothers me is, Pepper didn't just forget about the argument between your mom and Tegan. She also seems to have forgotten about Captain Bellamy's journal."

"What exactly did she forget?"

"Everything," Alex replied. "Its contents, even its existence—" Suddenly, it made sense. "What if there's something in that journal that someone wants to hide?"

"But why?" Minka creased her forehead. "What could Captain Bellamy have written that would be relevant to anyone today? From what I can tell, he was simply a gossip. Like great-great-grandfather, like great-great-granddaughter," she said with a wry grin.

Alex couldn't answer that question either, but she knew one thing for certain. "We have to find that journal, Minka. We have to know who attacked Pepper, and why."

And she knew exactly who to ask.

Chapter Twelve

When Dylan Wesley had invited Alex to stop by again, she hadn't known whether he was being serious or merely polite. But now that Pepper Bellamy had been attacked, Alex didn't care. She needed answers, and he was going to give them. She walked right into Wesley, Inc., headquarters on Tuesday afternoon and informed the unflappable Harrison that she would like to see Mr. Wesley.

Harrison lifted a phone. "Is he expecting you?"

Alex paused for a beat before proceeding with the lie. "Yes."

He raised an eyebrow in suspicion but didn't say more. She stood off to one side while Harrison called what sounded like Dylan's assistant. While she waited, Alex considered plan B. If Dylan refused to see her, she could dash to the elevator and go up herself. She knew where his office was. Or she could find a stairwell and sneak up that way. Or she could wait in the parking lot—

"Mr. Wesley will be right down," Harrison said as he set down the phone.

Huh. He'd actually meant what he'd said. Alex was stunned. "Th-thank you," she stammered.

"Of course. Would you like to have a seat?"

Harrison gestured to some couches surrounding a glass table, but Alex declined. "I'll stand. Thank you."

She heard the click of high heels and turned to see Bryn approaching in a perfectly tailored suit. Her milky skin was luminous and her patrician features were arrestingly beautiful. She carried herself as if she knew it.

"What do you want?" she demanded. "You're the reason Dylan was late to our meeting yesterday." She paused to give Alex a disapproving once-over. "Who are you, anyway?"

Flustered by the woman's apparent disdain for her, Alex forced a smile nonetheless. "Alex. Daniels."

The woman pushed her lips into a pout. "Well, Alex Daniels, I'm Bryn Wesley. Are you looking for a job or something? Why are you here again?"

"I'm Lidia Sobieski's niece," Alex replied. "I came here yesterday to introduce myself."

"Sobieski." Bryn's eyes widened and then narrowed. "You have a lot of nerve. Dylan was late to the meeting, and we almost lost an account because of you."

Alex's heart thumped in her chest, but she tried to maintain her cool. She'd done nothing wrong. "I never asked Dylan to be late for me."

"So? Why are you here again? Wait, don't tell me." Bryn smiled cruelly. "You want us to help out your little candle shop?" She batted her long, dark eyelashes. "Is business bad? Do you need a cash infusion?"

"Of course not. I just want to talk."

"Are you sure? I've heard business is bad since your aunt was arrested for murder. I'm afraid our multimillion-dollar company isn't able to invest in your little Etsy shop. So see? I've saved us all some time."

"Bryn, that's enough," Dylan's voice boomed as he approached from the elevators. Alex hadn't heard him coming, but he must have overheard part of the exchange, because he looked furious. "I'm sure you have something better to do."

Bryn's voice sounded syrupy sweet, even as her eyes flashed with anger. "I was just saying hello."

Alex watched the woman stalk to the elevator. "Your sister seems pleasant."

"She's nice for a viper. Sorry about all of that." Dylan chuckled. "I guess I should speak with her about manners. I love her, but honestly, she and I don't always get along either."

"Why not?"

He shrugged. "Politics, mostly. My mother is going to retire one day, and Bryn wants a larger role in the business. And she deserves one. She's smart. Driven. She's been instrumental to the company's success."

"Sounds like she'll get a promotion, then."

"Yes," he said slowly. "But the promotion she wants is to lead the company, and my mother is more inclined to choose a certain CFO for that position." He winked. "Therefore, Bryn doesn't care for said CFO, older brother or not."

Alex returned his smile. "Now I understand."

Dylan was dressed casually in pressed khakis and a slim-fitted blue silk shirt. He had forgone the tie and left the top button of his shirt open. "It's good to see you again, Alex."

"You too." He was disarming, but he might have just come from attacking Pepper that morning. Alex resisted his charm. "I was hoping we could speak somewhere private."

A flash of surprise crossed his face. "Right down to business, are we? Would you mind if we used a conference room? I have a meeting in my office at the moment."

"You—you took time out of a meeting? For me?"

"I thought it must be important if you were coming by on such short notice. Come, the conference room is this way."

He led her past the lobby and through a door that required a key card to open. The corridor they entered was eerily silent, but there were no offices here. They stopped at a gray door that Dylan opened into a conference room with one wall made entirely of windows. Alex admired the view of the lighthouse and the green blooming on the surrounding hills.

"Do people actually get work done in a room like this?" She gestured to the stunning vista.

Dylan smiled. "Unfortunately, every office in this building comes with amazing views." He chuckled. "It was purposely designed that way." He pulled a leather seat from the sleek black table and offered it to Alex.

"Thank you."

"Now," Dylan said as he pulled out another chair beside hers, "what did you want to discuss?"

Alex folded her hands on the table. "First, I should tell you that I've learned more about our families since we spoke yesterday. I know that our families have . . . powers."

The hint of a smile appeared on his face. "I was surprised you'd forgotten. The way you used to make the water in Lidia's fountain jump—"

Alex rolled her eyes, not wanting to hear more about the apparently magically gifted child she'd been. "Yes, so I've heard."

"Your designs were elaborate," he said. "Arches, swirls, these loopy things—" He gave her a gentle smile. "Someone must've removed those memories for you."

The breath caught in Alex's throat. She'd never considered that possibility. Who would've done such a thing? Her mother, at her father's request? She tried to suppress the disturbing thought, but she was rattled. She took a deep breath and focused on the man watching her. "Look, I know you're busy, so I'll get to the point. Something happened today, and I need to know if the Wesleys had anything to do with it."

He listened as Alex explained that someone had attacked Pepper and erased her memories of Captain John Bellamy's journal. Dylan shook his head slightly. "Why would anyone do that? Pepper's a nuisance, but she's harmless."

"That's why I'm here," she replied. "There are only a few people who could—and would—erase Pepper's memory and steal that journal, and it wasn't a Sobieski."

Dylan clenched his jaw. "So we're back to that again? You think my family had something to do with this?"

"You tell me," Alex replied. "You're the one who called your own sister a viper."

"Only because she has an edge. But that doesn't mean . . ." He leaned back in his chair. "I work closely with my mother and sister. Nothing would happen without my knowledge. I don't know what you've heard, but we don't encourage violence."

"I'm asking for your help, Dylan. If the Wesleys weren't involved, then who was?"

He stared out the window. "I don't know. But I'll get to the bottom of it."

*   *   *

By Thursday, customers were returning to Botanika. Yes, they entered furtively, found what they needed, and left right away, but it was a start.

"What can I say?" Minka said. "The products work, and when they run out, they'll return for more." Minka tore a forgotten receipt from the cash register and tossed it into the trash. "We'll be okay." This was the most optimistic Alex had seen her cousin in a week.

Now that Lidia was under house arrest, Alex was busy trying to learn the family trade. Fortunately, Minka was already familiar with her mother's techniques and products and was able to fill in while Lidia was home. If Alex had been left alone in the back room, she feared she'd accidentally have set something on fire.

"If business picks up again, we're both going to be busy making more products. I understand herbs," Alex said as she set a textbook on natural remedies down on the counter. "But how do you infuse the products with magic?"

"It's hard to explain," Minka said, and scrunched her nose as she tried to find the right words. "It's the same way you do anything. You intend to do it and it happens."

This was not helpful, though Alex knew Minka was trying her best. The night before, Alex had gone to the mermaid fountain and attempted to move the water. Instead, Minka had found her scolding the water and threatening to allow it to go dry if it didn't obey her.

"That's not going to work," Minka had said gently, leading Alex to a bench. "There is a certain state of mind you have to find, sort of like tuning to a radio station. Once you find the frequency, you can do anything."

"Dylan Wesley said I did this all the time as a kid," Alex replied, sulking. "Why can't I do it now?"

"It's easier when you're a child, before you hear people you trust telling you that magic isn't real."

Alex thought immediately of her father and the great pains he had taken to tell her there was no such thing as magic. She'd always assumed he was just being practical.

"But I don't remember any of it," she whispered, sinking her head into her hands. "I don't remember the magic at all. Dylan thought someone had erased my memories . . ." She looked at her cousin questioningly.

"I don't know anything about that." Minka set a hand on Alex's shoulder. "But you were young; we all forget some things from childhood. And of course, you were told magic doesn't exist, and that's what you came to believe. Now." She lifted Alex's chin. "Watch."

Minka put on a remarkable show, making the fountain bubble and the water dance. All of that without lifting a finger or uttering a word. "You try," she said.

"All right. Tell me how," Alex countered.

But explaining magic was beyond Minka's abilities. "I can't tell you how, exactly. It's just practice. Our family motto is, 'Power comes with practice.'" She patted Alex's knee reassuringly. "So, practice."

Alex took a deep breath and focused on the water in the fountain. *Just jump*, she pleaded silently. *Please, please, please.* "Nothing. See? I told you, I need more help than that." Alex rose from the bench. "When I really try, nothing happens—"

And in a flash, the water leapt right at them both, soaking their clothes. "Oh." Minka laughed. "That's cold."

That had ended Alex's lesson on water magic for the evening, and she'd retreated to her room to take a very nonmagical bath. But the fact remained that if Alex was going to be useful at Botanika, she had no choice but to learn how to harness her abilities. "If I don't figure this stuff out," she said to Minka, "I might end up hurting someone."

Now Minka frowned. "How do you think you would hurt someone?"

"I don't know." Alex waved her arms as her anxiety grew. "I could make a perfume that turns a person into a skunk. There are any number of ways I could fail." She paused as her cousin dissolved into laughter. "What's so funny?"

Minka leaned one arm on the counter for support. "I'm sorry, it's not—I understand. I do. But none of that is going to happen. Part of your power lies in amplifying the materials we use. They're going to work well simply because you made them."

*   *   *

Alex was studying the finer details of essential oils when the bell on the front door chimed and Dylan Wesley appeared at the entrance. He walked confidently toward her, his expression serious. "Alex. I was wondering if you would like to have a cup of coffee."

Before she could respond, Minka gestured at the empty store and replied, "Dylan? We're working here. Alex can't just run off."

He nodded at her. "Hello, Minka. I apologize for any inconvenience, but this is important."

The women exchanged a glance, and Alex felt Minka's thoughts gently prodding her mind. *You don't have to go, you know.*

I'll be fine, Alex responded telepathically. She turned to look at Dylan, wondering if he could hear their thoughts, if he knew they were having a conversation about him. But he appeared unbothered, with his hands shoved deep into the pockets of his pants.

"Would you mind?" Alex said, this time aloud. "I promise we'll be brief. Right, Dylan?"

"Of course."

With that, Minka sighed. "All right. As long as it's quick. I don't want to be caught alone in the afternoon crush."

There had not been an afternoon crush since Lidia's arrest, but Dylan didn't need to know that. When he turned away, Minka whispered, "Be careful."

Alex gave her a tiny smile and squeezed her hand. She met Dylan at the front of the shop. "Coffee O' Clock is a block away," Alex said as they stepped outside. "Let's go there."

"Sounds good."

She tried to read him as they walked in silence, but Dylan wasn't giving much away. He was confident and aloof, per usual. Again he was dressed casually in dark jeans and a pullover V-neck shirt, but he still managed to look polished. He must have felt her eyes on him, because he glanced over at her and smiled, but his gaze remained icy.

"Are you having a nice day so far?" he asked.

"Lovely," she said, copying his bland tone. "And you?"

"Better now."

Alex laughed out loud. "You are charming, Mr. Wesley."

He lifted the corner of his mouth in a smile as they came up on the coffee shop. "I'm not the enchantress, Ms. Daniels."

After the morning rush, the coffee shop was almost empty and there was no line. Celeste was behind the counter, this time wearing her hair in a long, loose braid that she had flung romantically over one shoulder. She greeted Dylan with a flirtatious wink. "Good afternoon, Mr. Wesley. How's my favorite CFO doing?"

He grinned. "I'm just fine, Celeste. And I'll have the usual."

She flashed him another megawatt smile. "Right away, sir."

Trying not to laugh, Alex noticed that Celeste's southern drawl was more pronounced when she flirted. Or was that simply the southern belle in her showing?

The barista turned to Alex, her eyes lighting up. "Hey, you." The usual for you and Minka?" She was already reaching for a to-go coffee cup.

"Actually, nothing for Minka today. I'll take a chai latte. For here." She looked at Dylan. "And I'm paying for his."

His smile was indulgent. "I invited you, Alex. It's my treat."

Alex swallowed. She didn't trust Dylan and she didn't want to feel indebted to him. But then he said, "No strings attached. I promise." He held up his right hand as if taking an oath.

She nodded. "All right. Thank you. Why don't you grab us a table? I'll bring the drinks over."

He bowed slightly. "As you wish."

Amused, she watched him for a moment, wondering if all the men in Bellamy Bay were this courtly. His old-fashioned manners seemed almost antiquated, and yet she found them very appealing.

When Dylan settled into a corner table, Alex turned back to Celeste with a grin. "Your favorite CFO, huh?"

Celeste giggled. "Just laying the groundwork for a job after I graduate. I interned at his company last semester. It's either that, work at the military base nearby, at Carolina Shipping, or move away to a bigger city." She set out a cup-and-saucer set and began working the espresso machine. "I have a few limited opportunities to use my MBA in Bellamy Bay, but I'd prefer to work at Wesley, Inc. And my mother would be very happy if I didn't move away."

"I get it. Makes sense. You and your mother are close?"

When the espresso machine sent out a puff of steam, Celeste retrieved a slice of lemon from the refrigerated cabinet behind her and placed it on the saucer. "The closest. We've always had a great relationship. I couldn't imagine my life without—" Her eyes widened. "Oh, Alex, I'm so sorry. I know what happened to your mother—and I—I'm being so insensitive. I—"

"Don't worry about it. It's fine. If my mother had lived, we would've had the same relationship. Don't apologize for that."

The barista's face was flushed with embarrassment, and Alex could tell by the way she moved that she was flustered. Poor girl; she hadn't meant anything by the comment, and Alex understood that. She wanted to distract Celeste before she dropped a mug or something, and when the pretty gold-and-diamond earrings she wore caught the sunlight streaming in from the front window, Alex knew just what to say. Smiling, she gestured toward her ear. "Another gift?"

Celeste touched an earlobe. "Oh, this?"

Alex relaxed when she saw a smile return to the young woman's face.

Celeste nodded. "What can I say, he likes to spoil me. But honestly, I worry that it's his way of making sure I stay happy and quiet about our relationship."

Alex took a moment to consider her words. "Be careful, Celeste. If it's true love, you shouldn't have to hide it."

Emotion flickered in Celeste's eyes before she pasted a smile on her face, and Alex wondered if she'd overstepped. But Celeste looked unbothered by the comment. "One minute." She picked up the espresso, rounded the corner, and hand-delivered it to Dylan.

Alex watched the exchange with some amusement, hoping that Celeste got the job she wanted at Wesley, Inc. Dylan gave her cash for the drinks, winked, and told her to keep the change.

When Celeste returned, she seemed to have forgotten all about the awkward moment between them. "So, how's your aunt doing?"

"Keeping busy. The house is sparkling and we're eating well."

This time Celeste's smile was genuine. "I'm happy to hear it. You know, your aunt and my mother are good friends. Miss Lidia was always coming over for coffee when I was growing up." She chuckled. "I remember thinking their conversations about herbal remedies were *so* boring."

The scents of cinnamon and cardamom wafted around Alex, comforting and relaxing her as the tea Celeste prepared began to steep. But it didn't completely relieve the pressure in her chest, that tight ball of anxiety that had appeared the moment she'd seen Dylan in the shop.

"And then they'd go into my mother's craft room, their heads together, whispering and making tonics and such. Of course, I think it's cool now. I mix my own herbal tea blends sometimes too. It's one of the reasons I wanted to work here. I love coffee and tea," she enthused.

"That's great," Alex replied, slightly distracted as she glanced over at Dylan, who was checking his phone. *What does he want to talk about?*

"Sometimes I think that's why my boyfriend is with me," she giggled. "For my tea blends. I make this great calming blend with holy basil and valerian. It's his go-to relaxation aid after a stressful day of work."

Alex nodded, her thoughts and worries still on Dylan. "What's so stressful about his work?"

Celeste shrugged, her eyes becoming guarded. "I don't want to go into details, but he's been working on some sort of deal, and the other party refused to budge in their position. It's been really upsetting for him." An exasperated huff escaped her lips. "I wish I could help him with this. I wish there was a tea or some sort of potion I could make for him that would magically fix everything for him." She snapped her fingers. "Poof, problem solved." But then the disturbed look on her face passed and she grinned. "But we both know there's no such thing as magic."

At her last word, Alex stared at her. "What did you just say?"

But Celeste only laughed. "It's nothing. Just me ranting. Sorry about that; not very professional of me." She pushed a steaming mug toward her. "Your chai's ready."

Dylan was seated at a small table by the window. As she approached, he rose and pulled out a chair for her.

"Thank you for the tea."

"It's my pleasure." Dylan waited for her to sit before taking his own seat. Then he said, "You don't trust me."

He was right, but she'd hoped she wasn't being so obvious. Then the realization struck that he could be reading her mind. She shifted in her chair, self-conscious. "That's not true," she said carefully, and left it at that.

"It is, but I hope to change that. Are you in town for long?"

Alex's thoughts went to the job offer she'd just received at Barber Industries. She hadn't called Carter back yet. She planned to accept—after all, it wasn't every day that an opportunity like that came along. But she was reluctant to leave before she set things right for her aunt and cousins. Once this situation was resolved, she'd be on her way.

"Maybe a few weeks," she replied. "I'm not certain."

He leaned forward and lowered his voice. "You asked me about the matter with Pepper Bellamy."

"The attack, yes." She didn't want to downplay the gravity of the incident. "Did you learn something?"

"In fact, I did."

He took a slow sip of his espresso before answering. He set the white ceramic cup down on the saucer. "So. It turns out you were correct. A family member visited Pepper yesterday and took the journal."

"Visited?" Alex echoed. "That person *assaulted* Pepper."

"Oh, come on." Dylan leaned back in his seat. "She's physically fine, Alex. And no one is going to change that. Look," he said, cutting her off as she began to object. "I'm not defending this conduct. It was wrong. But you need to know that it's over. I spoke to that person and reminded them that this was out of line. It's not something that anyone needs to bring to the Council, all right?"

"The Council?" she whispered. "What is that?"

Now Dylan looked up at the exposed beams on the ceiling and said, "I keep forgetting you don't know how any of this works. The Council is the oversight board, that's all."

"Oversight for what?"

He gestured between the two of them. "People like us. And given our surroundings, that's all either of us should say about it."

Alex slowly nodded. "All right." She moved her tea to the side so she could lean closer. "But Dylan, I think that's unfair. You come in here and tell me one of your family members attacked someone, but you took care of it so I should let it go? And are you going to tell me who it was? Your mother? Your sister?"

"You don't need to know who did it. What's important is that the situation has been handled."

"Well, whoever did it needs to be punished." Alex leaned forward, her cheeks warming with anger. "There should be consequences for their actions."

He leaned forward, lowering his voice. "What kind of consequence are you looking for, exactly? Do you want to call the police?

Tell them someone erased Pepper Bellamy's memories with magic? If you make that call, please promise you'll let me listen in." He shook his head, still amused. "I'm not laughing at you. There are only a few of us around here, and we've all lived with this . . . knowledge. And then you grow up with Mundanes, and—sorry, Alex. It's kind of cute."

She gritted her teeth. "And that's kind of condescending, Dylan."

"I don't mean it, I swear." He set a hand over hers, but she withdrew from the contact. "Fine. Fair enough," he said. "Look, I'm not a bad guy. A family member made a mistake with Pepper, but that person had nothing to do with Bennett's murder. These are unrelated things."

"Really?" She lifted her chin. "Prove it. Get me that journal."

He rubbed at his jaw as he considered the request. "It's not that easy."

"It seems like it should be that easy."

He shot her a dark look but didn't respond.

She could tell that Dylan was unaccustomed to people pushing back against him. What was it like, she wondered, to work at the top of a powerful company that shared your name? Probably pretty nice.

"Dylan," she said, mustering some sweetness, "I want to believe you. But I barely know you, and you've admitted that a member of your family was responsible for attacking Pepper and stealing the journal. How can I trust you when you tell me this same family member had nothing to do with Randy Bennett's murder? Pepper was reporting on that murder."

He leaned forward, his dark eyes sparkling with mischief. "Why don't you join me at a party tomorrow night. It's a charity auction at our home. You can meet my mother and sister and see for yourself that they're not murderers. You want to believe me?" He shrugged. "You can get to know us."

"I don't know—"

Dylan slid his chair closer. "Just say yes," he whispered, his fingers landing softly on her wrist. "Just give me a chance to prove it to you."

And Alex, her head blurry from the contact, instantly said, "Yes."

Chapter Thirteen

Alex closed Botanika so Minka could leave early. Her poor cousin hadn't even taken a lunch break. Besides, after her coffee with Dylan, Alex needed some time alone to reflect. After she locked the doors, she swept the floors and thought about what she knew. Someone had killed Randy Bennett and framed Lidia. Someone—a member of the Wesley family—had attacked Pepper Bellamy and stolen her great-great-grandfather's journal. Dylan swore the two events weren't connected, but Alex suspected they were. She just couldn't prove it . . . yet. Now that she had an invitation to the Wesley estate, this was her chance to find that journal.

Her cell rang and a name flashed across the screen. *Carter Hawthorne.* Alex's stomach clenched, but she had been avoiding him long enough. "Hello, this is Alex."

"Alex," came the energetic reply. "It's Carter. So good to hear from you."

"You too," she said, and smiled. It was nice to hear from an old friend.

"Listen, I don't know if you got my message, but all of us were just shocked to hear you'd left. I assume it was messy."

She wasn't about to explain that she'd been passed over for promotion. That would be mortifying. "Yes, it got a little ugly there," she confessed. "I'm better now."

"Glad to hear it. You haven't gone anywhere else, have you?"

"No, not yet. I'm visiting some family in North Carolina. Bellamy Bay. Do you know it?"

"I've heard of the Outer Banks."

Alex chuckled. "Further south."

"Then no, I don't know it." She could hear the grin in his voice. "Is it nice? I'm due a vacation; maybe I should come down sometime."

"Yes, very," Alex said. *Aside from the occasional murder.* "I should've called you back sooner, but I've been distracted with some, uh, family issues. But I want you to know that I appreciate your offer and I'm very interested in working for Barber Industries. I just . . . I can't give you a definite answer yet. Because of the family things."

"You don't know how happy that makes me, Alex. Not your family problems, of course. Sorry." Carter laughed. "We'd love to have you on board, so you take the time you need, okay? What would you say—give me a call in two weeks to let me know what you think? We'll hold the position open for you."

"Wow," Alex gasped. "That's very generous, Carter."

"I learned long ago that it's worth waiting to find the right person for the position. So, two weeks?"

"Thank you. Yes, we'll talk in two weeks."

They disconnected the call. Alex locked up the shop and began the walk home.

A bracing wind brushed right through her, bringing her back to the present. No, first things first. The job offer at Barber was attractive, but she couldn't leave town until she knew that the charges against her aunt had been dropped and the killer had been locked up. Family first.

Alex opened the door to the Queen Anne. "Hello?" she called.

Athena ran into the foyer and whimpered at her feet, ears down, her entire body wagging with happiness. "Hey, sweet girl," Alex cooed as she bent to pet her. "How was your day?" Athena yelped and lifted her front legs into the air, overcome with joy. "Everyone deserves to have someone who loves them this much," Alex said with a laugh, and gave Athena a good scratch on her shoulders.

Lidia, Minka, and Kamila were sitting in the living room, deep in conversation. "I'm afraid the cat's out of the bag, Kamila. We can't undo—" Lidia paused when she noticed Alex. "Hello. We were just talking about you."

Alex noticed the tight set of Kamila's shoulders. "What's going on?"

Minka grabbed a large blue throw pillow and took a seat on the floor. "We were just saying how happy we are that you're a part of this family." She gave her sister a meaningful look. "In every possible way."

Alex noticed that Minka's voice was unusually cheery, even for her. She glanced at her other cousin, feeling like she was missing something. Kamila remained withdrawn. While the conversation continued around her, Kamila moved to the floor to scratch Athena behind the ears.

"There's so much more to teach you. So much history to share," Lidia added with a smile, her voice soft with emotion. "I just wish your mother was here."

"If Aunt Bianca was here, she wouldn't want Alex learning anything and certainly not practicing anything!"

The outburst came from Kamila. Her cheeks were flushed, and her eyes glistened with anger as she turned toward her mother and sister. "Have either of you stopped to think about that? What you're doing isn't loving. It's dangerous and irresponsible."

With that, Kamila rose to her feet and stormed out of the house into the back gardens, shutting the door firmly behind her. Alex looked between her aunt and cousin, who were sitting in stunned silence. Then she stood. "I'll check on her. I have to take Athena out, anyway."

She found Kamila sitting on a wooden bench beside the fountain, her hands buried in the sleeves of her sweat shirt. "I'm not angry at you," she said as Alex approached. "I shouldn't have yelled like that."

Alex took a seat on the marble bench across from Kamila. "What did you mean when you said my mom didn't want me to know about magic?"

Being older, Kamila had known her mother well. She must have more memories from that time, Alex reasoned.

Kamila avoided Alex's gaze, but reached out toward Athena as the dog sniffed the base of the fountain. "I don't know what Mom told you, but it wasn't your father's fault that you forgot about magic," she began. "He wasn't the one who didn't want to raise you as a Magical. Not at first. It was your mom. She's the one who had a problem with the lifestyle." Kamila leaned her elbows on her knees. "I just get angry that my mom and sister are bringing you into this world when your parents were so against it."

Alex moved to sit beside Kamila. "Tell me what you know. I want to understand."

Kamila kicked at a pebble and frowned at the bricks at their feet. "She had a moral objection to magic. She was the first

Magical I ever heard of doing that. Rejecting magic and choosing to live as a Mundane, I mean. I stopped practicing magic because of her, but it wasn't always that way," she clarified. "*Ciocia* Bianca could practice magic with the best of them. From what I understand and remember, she was very powerful. But something happened that made her stop."

The hair on the back of Alex's neck rose. "What happened?"

"I don't know," she admitted. "Maybe it was nothing. But I remember her having these big arguments with my parents about how it's unethical to practice magic in this world, and how we don't understand what the long-term effects can be."

"Is that why you don't practice?"

"Yeah," Kamila said. "I stopped when I was a teenager. And I wish my mom and sister would stop. They've convinced themselves that what they're doing is harmless because it's so-called good magic. But there's no such thing, Alex. Magic is magic, and it comes with a cost. It tears apart families. And I've seen it ruin people. Look at the Wesleys. You think Tegan was always like that?" Kamila wiped at her eyes, which had gone glossy with unshed tears. "Mom said that when she was younger, she was different, happier. But now? She's cold. Heartless. She does nothing without the explicit purpose of gaining something from it. In fact, I've heard she only married into the Wesley family because she thought they possessed the *Warsaw Tarcza*, the Warsaw Shield. All she wants is to accumulate power."

"What's the Warsaw Shield?"

"It doesn't exist anymore, as far as I know," Kamila explained. "It was forged by mermen under the Baltic Sea, and it was supposed to make anyone who wielded it invincible to both Mundane weapons and our magic. The Mermaid of Warsaw—our ancestor—used it to protect the city. One of the Wesleys stole it from our family, but before we could get it back, it was destroyed by a fire set by witch hunters. The Wesleys claimed to have found it in the rubble and hidden it away somewhere, but no one believes that." She waved a hand. "Who knows what's actually true?"

Alex mulled over this information. She had just learned about magic, but there was so much she didn't know. "So, is magic bad?"

"It feels great at first, don't get me wrong. But over time, the power we feel when practicing corrupts us." She positioned her body to look Alex in the eye. "You see Mom's temper, don't you? Those flashes of pure, violent rage? It drove our father away." Kamila's voice caught on her words. "And she's only getting worse, and right before our eyes."

Alex sighed, vaguely recalling Minka and Kamila's father. A fun uncle who was always smiling and giving her candy when she visited. But then one summer, he just wasn't around anymore. A divorce, she'd heard her parents whispering one night. He'd had enough and left without a backward glance. She'd never heard her cousins discuss their father, and she felt strongly that now was not the time to ask questions.

She glanced around the garden filled with beautiful flowers, medicinal plants, and healthy fruits and vegetables, and she knew that her aunt was good, even with her temper. "Your mom only uses her magic to heal. How can that be bad?"

"That's not bad in itself," Kamila conceded. "But it's like . . . have you heard of a God complex? Sometimes doctors get it."

"Sure. They believe they're powerful. Invincible, even."

"The same thing happens with Magicals," she said. "You cure a cold. Then you cure someone's eczema. Then you enhance a couple's fertility. A Magical can start to feel like she's got power over life itself, like she's justified in choosing whether a Mundane lives, suffers, or dies."

Something about her cousin's words gave Alex pause. She had observed that since Randy Bennett's murder, Kamila had been keeping her distance from the family. "Do you think your mother has reached that point?" she whispered. "Do you think she actually killed Randy Bennett?"

A flash of pain crossed Kamila's face, and her voice wavered. "She practices magic and her temper is out of control. She hated him." Tears began to fall down her face. "How can I be certain she didn't?"

"Kam, I was there when Randy came into the shop last Monday." Alex took her cousin's hand. "Your mom didn't have time to poison the tea she gave him from the back room. She only went there because the jar on the shop floor was empty. We all had dinner together on Monday night, so we know she didn't leave the house. And she didn't go to Randy's house on Tuesday night, when he died, either. Pepper Bellamy followed Lidia right after work to some kind of meeting with Tegan Wesley. They had an argument and it was all captured on video."

Kamila was deep in thought. "Edwin Kenley asked the police to run a check because Randy hadn't shown up to an important dinner meeting on Tuesday night. Probably because he was already dead at dinnertime."

"Right. And that means your mom wouldn't have had the opportunity to poison him. She was working in the shop all day Tuesday, and she went to a meeting directly after work." She squeezed Kamila's hand. "It wasn't magic that killed him. These were old-fashioned poison berries that someone had to drop into his tea. She didn't do it."

Slowly, Kamila nodded. "Okay. You're right." She drew a breath before her face crumbled into a sob. "I'm just relieved," she told Alex, who'd pulled her into a hug. "I thought for sure . . ."

Alex swallowed. "I understand."

The door to the house opened, and Minka appeared and glanced around the yard. Once she spotted them, she walked over quickly. "Is everything all right? Mom and I were getting worried. Oh." She stopped when she noticed that Kamila was upset. "Why are you crying?"

Kamila wiped her cheeks with her fingertips and gathered her breath. "You know how I feel about practicing magic, and now you're bringing Alex into it. And I'm worried about Mom."

Minka sat on the other side of her sister and wrapped an arm around her shoulders. "I know you hate magic. But lots of what worries you hasn't even been proven. It's all theory, not fact. Mom and I are careful not to let it corrupt us, okay?"

Alex had to admit, if you gave Minka a poufy white dress and a glittery wand, she'd practically be Glenda the Good Witch.

But Kamila tightened her lips and looked away without responding. Alex was relieved to hear Minka say that Kamila's objections to magic were based only on theory. She was excited to explore her abilities, and she wasn't worried about somehow becoming corrupted by her own powers. Her cousin meant well, but Alex didn't see any evidence that Minka or Lidia was suffering from a God complex.

"Kam," Alex said, "is there any way that you can talk to Jack about looking at other suspects? He won't listen to a word I say."

"Can't. The prosecutors built an ethical wall around me," Kam said. "If I got Jack to look in another direction, the prosecution would be tainted and the killer would walk."

Alex could imagine that scenario. If Kamila influenced Jack to look at another suspect in order to help her mother avoid jail, any decent defense attorney would eat the Bellamy Bay PD for breakfast. "So if you helped Jack to find another suspect—the real killer—your involvement would create enough reasonable doubt to get that killer out of serving jail time."

"Exactly," Kamila said. "If the defense attorney caught a whiff of my input, they would tell the jury that I was only trying to help my mom, and that I planted evidence or something, and that she was the real guilty party all along. Then we'd be right back here, with someone getting away with murder. So the best thing for everyone is for me to stay out of it, as grueling as that is."

Alex had always admired her cousin, but now she saw a new facet of her strength. "You're a person of principle," Alex remarked. If her mom had been falsely accused of murder, she didn't know if she could have been so restrained.

"I believe in justice, and I believe in process," Kamila replied matter-of-factly. "I've gotten to know Jack better, and he's a good detective. I know that he will set this right. It's only a matter of time."

Minka rested her head on her sister's shoulder. "You have such a good heart, even if we don't agree on everything."

Kamila returned the compliment with a hug. "I'm sorry I got angry. I just worry."

"I know you do. But if I ever went *dark*, became a practitioner of black magic, I'd quit cold turkey. You have my permission in advance to stage an intervention."

Kamila smiled but maintained a look of skepticism. Alex decided to change the subject. "I have something to tell you, but you have to promise not to tell your mom."

In a low voice, she detailed her meeting with Dylan earlier that afternoon and explained that a member of his family was responsible for erasing Pepper's memories and stealing Captain Bellamy's journal. "I understand why they would erase her memories and blog posts, but why steal the journal? Even if Captain Bellamy called us water witches, no one would believe him." Alex leaned closer. "There's something more in that journal. I want to know what it is, and I'm going to find out."

"How?" asked Minka.

"Dylan invited me to a charity auction at his home tomorrow night. I'm going to try to find that journal."

Her cousins grew serious. "I don't suppose we could persuade you to reconsider?" Kamila said quietly.

Alex shook her head. "Nope. Sorry."

The sisters exchanged a worried glance. "The Wesleys really are trouble," Minka said. "Mom's not kidding. And they don't like our family, so that's a double threat to you."

Kamila shook her head and rose to her feet. "I can't be involved in this. I love you, Alex, and I don't want to see you get hurt. I wish you'd let this investigation of yours go and trust the police."

"Are the police currently investigating other suspects?"

Kamila hung her head. "No."

"Then I don't have any choice. I understand if you can't help, but I've got to try."

Kamila sighed, "I should get going home. I'll see you both tomorrow." With that, she returned to the house.

Once they were alone, Minka scooted over to sit closer to Alex. "Please be careful."

"I promise."

"I'm going to teach you a trick for guarding your thoughts, too. We respect each other's privacy in this family, but I don't trust Dylan one bit."

"That's a good idea," Alex agreed. "I have a feeling he was eavesdropping on my thoughts today."

"I wouldn't doubt it." Minka kicked her heels against the fountain. "You know, we could also create a guidance spell for this investigation. I don't know why I didn't think of that sooner. It's just that I don't use them that often—"

"A guidance spell?" Alex sat bolt upright. "That's a thing too?" Eyes sparkling with excitement, Minka nodded.

"Brilliant. Let's do that now."

She began to stand, but Minka grabbed her hand and pulled her back down. "Not so fast, Sherlock. If we're going to do a guidance spell, I need something that Randy Bennett touched or owned. Otherwise it won't work."

"You're kidding." Alex rolled her eyes. "How in the world am I supposed to get that?"

"No one said it would be easy." Minka smiled. "But I have faith in you."

Alex would have to think about how to go about getting something Randy had touched. For now, though, she had to think about how to protect herself from the Wesleys. "All right. Tell me how to guard my thoughts."

Chapter Fourteen

On Friday night, Alex was grateful for safety pins. This emerald-green cocktail dress had always been one of her favorites: sexy without giving too much away, elegant without being stuffy. She loved the organza straps across the shoulders and the way the body of the dress clung before falling into a gentle A-line at the waist.

"That should do it," Minka said as she pushed the fabric into place and secured a final pin.

Alex studied her reflection in the standing mirror and did a little twirl, feeling like a child playing dress-up. "Minka, your pinning skills are unparalleled."

Her cousin curtsied before dropping the safety pins into the palm of her hand. "You know I'm walking on thin ice here," she reminded Alex. "Mom would not approve of you going to the Wesleys' place tonight."

"So I've heard," Alex replied.

They had been through this a hundred times, but Alex no longer cared. She was a grown woman who could do what she wanted. Alex turned to face her cousin. "Do I look okay?"

Minka grinned. "Are you sure you don't have a crush on Dylan?"

Alex moved away before Minka had the chance to see her blush. "I have to look presentable. You know that."

But Alex knew she looked more than presentable. Her dark eyebrows were freshly arched, her makeup was flawless, and her hair was pulled into a fishtail braid that had taken Alex ages to get perfectly loose and deliberately messy. The final touch was a spell for silence that Minka had put on Alex's thoughts to make them unreadable for the evening. She'd tried to teach Alex how to guard them herself, but she hadn't quite mastered it.

"You look like a movie star," Minka said. "Now go find that journal."

Alex mock-saluted her before sneaking down the stairs and slipping out the door before her aunt noticed. She entered Dylan's address into her phone and backed Minka's car out of the drive-way and into the road. The directions took her on a scenic coastal road that gradually led to the Peninsula. Water glinted on either side of the road and the sun was just setting, turning the sky a dreamy mixture of creamy white, orange, pink, and purple. She could get used to that view.

She'd been referring to the Wesley house as an estate, but now as she approached, she realized it was more of a compound. After the car passed through the wrought-iron gates, the imposing gothic structure rose into view as if emerging from the ocean below. The dramatic pitched roofline and pillars commanded attention and evaporated Alex's confidence. What, exactly, was she messing with here?

She pulled around the circular driveway and stopped the car beside waiting valets in formal black dress. One opened her door while another assisted her out of the car and escorted her to the wide steps of the mansion. Inside, guests in formal wear lingered and chatted, sounding like an enormous flock of geese. The men were sharply dressed in tuxedoes while the women glittered in diamonds and gemstones. She was captivated by the enormous five-tiered crystal chandelier that dangled in the foyer beside a winding staircase. Alex clutched her handbag as she walked across the travertine floor. She had been to fancy cocktail parties before, but this was way out of her league.

Before she could freak out and retreat to her car, the crowd parted and Dylan entered her view, his dark eyes fixed on hers. He was arresting in his black tuxedo, and heads turned as he passed. Instantly, her stomach roiled with nervous energy. Was she really going to pull this off and find that journal? At least her thoughts were hidden for the evening.

"Aleksandra." He lifted her hand and bowed to kiss it, keeping his gaze on her the entire time. "You are breathtaking."

"I could say the same about you," she whispered, and blushed. "This house is incredible. It's unlike anything I've ever seen."

Dylan smiled and righted himself again, keeping her hand in his. "The Gothic style is a bit gloomy to me, but the house is large enough that we can all live here and maintain our privacy."

"Your family must have lived here for hundreds of years."

"About a hundred," he replied. "The house my ancestors built burned down, unfortunately. They purchased this one from some robber baron." He gestured toward the interior of the home. "Come. I'll show you around."

He set his hand against the small of her back and led her into the crowd. Alex braced herself to nudge her way through, but somehow the partygoers parted for them, turning their heads, smiling and nodding as they passed. Dylan radiated authority. Alex had to admit that being in the presence of someone so powerful was intoxicating. Maybe there was something to Kamila's theory that power quickly went to a person's head. "Where are we going?"

"I want to introduce you to your hostess."

They climbed a small flight of stairs to a landing that overlooked the crowd below. Here was an elegant woman dressed in a draping black dress that sparkled when she moved. Her dark hair was pulled into a chignon and her diamond chandelier earrings caught the light as she turned. Alex recognized her at once as Tegan Wesley. Her porcelain skin called attention to the intensity of her chilly blue gaze. She reminded Alex of a wolf.

"Mother," Dylan said, "do you remember Aleksandra Daniels? She's Bianca Sobieski's daughter."

Tegan bared her teeth in a small smile. "You look exactly like your mother," she said, and set a cool hand on Alex's bare wrist. Her own shone with silver bands and precious gemstones. "Tell me, how is Lidia?"

Alex studied Tegan, wondering how she intended that question. At best, Tegan Wesley took pleasure in the thought of her nemesis rotting under house arrest. At worst, Tegan was pleased that she'd framed Lidia for the murder of Randy Bennett.

"She's doing about as well as you could expect, under the circumstances," Alex replied carefully. "I've heard a lot about you, Mrs. Wesley. It's nice to meet you."

Tegan must have been exquisitely beautiful when she was younger. As it was, she was in her sixties and still a stunning woman. Maybe not a wolf. A reptile? Something cold and unfeeling, and with a capacity for . . . murder? A chill went up Alex's spine. Yes, she felt confident the woman before her could kill without blinking an icy-blue eye.

"You haven't been around here in a long time," Tegan observed. "We weren't sure what happened to you." She kept her fingers gripped on Alex's wrist.

"Yes, it's been a long time," she agreed. She gestured to the room below. "What an event."

Tegan allowed Alex her arm back. She turned to her son. "I assume you are doing introductions. You will find Bryn down there somewhere, probably drinking too much and flirting with some trust fund degenerate instead of networking like she's supposed to."

His smile tightened. "Mother."

"At least my son is reliable."

Alex took a breath. "I want to express my condolences. About Randy Bennett."

Tegan turned towards her. "Randy Bennett?"

"You knew him, didn't you?" Alex explained. "I remember reading something about a real-estate matter. Didn't you sell him some land?"

Tegan's lips curled into the unfriendliest of smiles. "You are mistaken. I never sold that man any land."

Alex feigned confusion. "I must have been thinking of something else. Oh, right." She snapped her fingers. "It was a dispute about some land. A lawsuit, correct?" Her heart was pounding.

Tegan's eyes flashed a warning, but she remained outwardly calm. "Yes. Now I remember. There was a disagreement about some property. A minor thing, really. I'm surprised you would bring that up."

This piqued Dylan's interest. "What was this, Mother?"

"It doesn't matter," she said, and waved her hand as if shooing a fly. "It was resolved. But I didn't know Randy, no. Only in passing. Our lawyers handled the entire thing."

"Was this the same land that Bellamy Bay Realty is building apartments on?"

Tegan gestured down at the crowd. "If you're so interested in Mr. Bennett's affairs, his wife Stephanie is right there, in the blue dress. She's generously donated a week at their place in Hilton Head for the auction. Poor pet. She just lost her husband and she's putting on such a brave face."

Alex followed Tegan's eyes and located Stephanie Bennett in the sea of formal wear, standing beside Edwin Kenley. She was laughing at something Edwin had said as she clutched his arm affectionately. She didn't look too choked up to Alex.

"If anyone should be receiving your condolences," Tegan said, "it's Stephanie."

Alex smiled politely. "I'll be sure to offer them."

Tegan set a hand on her son's arm. "Dylan, why don't you get us a cocktail?"

He turned to Alex with a grin. "Would you mind if I snuck away for a moment?"

Yes, she would mind. She was terrified at the thought of being left alone with Tegan, who looked like she might snap Alex's neck without warning. "Of course not. I'll have a glass of white wine, please."

"And I know my mother will want a whiskey neat. I'll be back in a few." He winked at Alex before heading back down the stairs.

Once they were alone, Tegan pulled Alex aside. "I don't know what you're up to, but I don't like it."

Alex blinked innocently. "I'm not up to anything. Dylan invited me here—"

"I'm aware of my son's weaknesses," she replied, leaning in closer until Alex was enveloped in a cloud of her expensive perfume, a heady scent of jasmine, topped by notes of herbal green tea and ending with something dark and rich like leather or tobacco. "He's full of opinions, and he thinks it's time for the Wesleys and Sobieskis to set aside our differences."

Alex shrugged. "I lived my entire life without knowing anything about the conflict between our families. And you only married into the Wesley family," Alex noted. "Don't you agree that this feud has gone on long enough?"

The wine-colored ruby in the center of Tegan's necklace caught the light. "I didn't grow up with the last name Wesley, true. But my late husband and I were distant cousins, and now I'm head of Wesley, Inc." She smiled coolly. "Any enemy of the Wesleys is an enemy of mine."

"The Sobieskis have nothing to do with Wesley, Inc.," Alex said, meeting Tegan's eyes. "We have our own business and we don't have any ill will."

"You seem like a well-meaning girl. But it's complicated between our families, and you really don't know what you're talking about. There are some unresolved matters that must be dealt with."

The two women stood silently side by side, watching the crowd. "I understand you're looking into the murder," Tegan said quietly. "What have you found?"

"Not much," Alex replied. She wasn't about to disclose that the Wesleys were acting increasingly suspect. "A not-yet-divorced wife who will inherit half the company. A business partner who wanted to sell but couldn't because Randy Bennett wouldn't allow it."

"I'm sure your list of suspects doesn't end there." Tegan lifted her upper lip in a sneer. "You can play amateur detective all you want. Just keep your nose out of my family's business."

* * *

A little later, Dylan led Alex onto the patio. She shivered as the cool spring air hit her bare arms. "Thanks. It was getting a little warm in there."

The patio wasn't nearly as crowded as the inside of the mansion, but the area was hardly private. Several propane fires were blazing in stone containers and giving off enough heat to keep the guests comfortable. Dylan walked Alex to a darkened corner beside the stone wall that closed off the patio area. Alex admired the way the moonlight illuminated the expansive estate.

He leaned his elbows against the top of the wall. "My mom can be a little intense. What did she say to you?"

When Dylan had returned with drinks, Alex had nearly thrown herself into his arms. Then she'd fanned herself and mentioned how stuffy the air was, desperate to get as far away as possible from Tegan.

"Was it that obvious?" Alex laughed uncomfortably.

"Kind of." Dylan smiled.

He was such a friendly contrast to his brittle mother, but Alex caught herself before she said any more. For all she knew, the two were playing good cop, bad cop, and Dylan was manipulating her into giving something away. "She made it clear that she doesn't like the Sobieskis, that's all."

"Sorry about that. It's the old generation. They're fixated on family history."

"Your sister doesn't like us, either," Alex blurted out.

"True, but she takes her cues from our mother." He looked down at the slate at their feet. "These things take time to smooth over."

"I'm thinking about two hundred years. We're halfway there." Alex took a generous gulp of her wine.

She eyed her companion. He was suited to darkness. Somehow the way the moonlight hit his face made him even more attractive.

"I appreciate you playing the diplomat," she said. "Unfortunately, I'm not convinced that your family members wouldn't be eager to frame my aunt for murder."

Dylan didn't reply except to smile.

She was suddenly light-headed, but maybe it was the wine.

"It's a beautiful night. Dance with me." He lifted the almost empty glass out of her hand and set it on the top of the wall.

"I'm a terrible dancer," she protested. "I can't tell the difference between a tango and a waltz." This was not true. She was a great dancer, but she didn't want to dance with Dylan. She didn't want to lean in close to him, his hand on the small of her back as he enveloped her in his scent . . .

Still, she allowed herself to be led to an open area. He wrapped a hand around her waist and held her other hand at his shoulder.

"All you have to do is follow my lead," he whispered.

He was intoxicating, and as they danced together, she was weightless. He moved her around the patio to the sound of the quartet playing inside the house, only a sliver of moonlight separating them. "You dance beautifully, Aleksandra." His lips touched her ear as he spoke, sending a shiver across her skin.

This was unlike anything she'd ever experienced. Alex had been attracted to men and she'd had relationships, but she'd never felt this dizzying rush before. Dylan moved her in the moonlight, and she lost all sense of herself, aware of only his powerful frame. She sighed as the pleasure of the moment enveloped her. Dancing with Dylan was nothing short of magical.

Magic.

The thought jolted her from her trance. Dylan was a Magical. Was he trying to enchant her?

She stopped moving and stepped away from him. "That's enough," she said.

As she pulled away, her senses returned. She was here, on the Wesleys' patio, and the Wesleys were murder suspects. She shouldn't dance with him. She smoothed her hands over her dress as if brushing off the remnants of his spell. "I told you, I'm not a good dancer."

Dylan's brow creased. "You seemed like you were enjoying yourself."

She reached for her wineglass with a shaky hand. What had just happened to her? Whatever it was, she couldn't allow it to happen again. She downed the remains of her wine and showed him the empty glass. "I'm going to get some more."

Always the gentleman, he extended his arm to her. "Allow me—"

"No." The word came out more sharply than she'd intended. "Sorry. It's fine. You're one of the hosts. I'm sure you have something else to do other than get me drinks all night. Besides, I'd like to mingle."

He bowed politely. "Whatever you wish."

Alex was trying to make light of the situation, but judging from Dylan's downcast expression, she was failing. He was hurt, or confused. Or—she reminded herself—disappointed that she'd foiled him. Because whatever had transpired between them had been powerful, and she didn't trust it for a second.

She tried her best to smile disarmingly. "I'll catch up with you later. I'm just going to have a walk around."

She entered the house and headed straight for the bar, her head still reeling from the effects of whatever Dylan had just done to her. "Just a water, please. Extra ice." She needed her inhibitions if she was going to fend off any more spells.

"Cabernet."

Alex did a double take at the sound of the smoky voice beside her. It was Stephanie Bennett. Her hair was a high-maintenance shade of blonde, and her tanned skin was suspiciously free of lines. In her early fifties, Stephanie was a beauty with deep-set eyes and a pert upturned nose.

She caught Alex's stare as they waited for their drinks. "Have we met before?"

"S-sorry," Alex stammered. "I don't think so. I'm Alex Daniels."

Judging from Stephanie's blank expression, the name was unfamiliar. "Nice to meet you. I'm Stephanie."

"Bennett, right?" Alex said too eagerly. She took a breath. "My aunt is Lydia Sobieski."

Stephanie's deep-blue eyes hardened. "Oh." She glanced away.

The bartender set their respective drinks on the edge of the bar, and the women grabbed their glasses.

"I'm very sorry for your loss." Alex tried to recover, but the moment was irredeemably awkward. "Randy—Mr. Bennett . . . I met him only once. But he seemed nice."

"Nice?" She arched an eyebrow. "My husband was larger than life. That's what drew people to him, his charisma. He loved his business and all the wealth that came with it. He gave to charity when he needed a tax deduction, and he was good to me when it suited his purposes." The edge of her mouth trembled with tightly controlled anger. "But he wasn't nice."

Alex swallowed. She was failing at making friends that evening. "He sounds like he was complicated."

"He was," Stephanie conceded as she swirled her wine. "And his death has been complicated, too. I feel like I've aged ten years in the past week."

"Do you have family in town? To help?"

"No, actually. We never had children, and my brother lives in Hong Kong—"

She stopped as Edwin pulled up beside her and set his hand possessively on her elbow. He had thinning ash-brown hair flecked with gray and a round baby face. "Steph, I wanted to tell you—" Once he noticed Alex, his dark eyes regarded her with suspicion. "Hello."

She smiled. "Hi. I'm Alex."

"Edwin Kenley." His handshake was firm, but his hand was soft and wet.

Stephanie set a hand on Edwin's forearm. "Ed was Randy's business partner and a dear friend," she explained. In a flash of self-consciousness, Stephanie let go of Edwin's arm and embraced the bulb of her wineglass with two hands. "Alex is Lidia's niece," she said, almost through clenched teeth.

This statement only heightened Edwin's protective instincts. "Oh?" He stepped between Stephanie and Alex. "I'm surprised to see you here, given . . ."

Given the relationship between the Sobieskis and the Wesleys? Or given the fact that Lidia had just been arrested for murder? Edwin had the sense to stop himself from saying more, but the damage was done. Alex's skin grew hot, and she clutched her glass of ice water tightly against her sternum.

Edwin turned to one side as a man in a black tuxedo approached. He was short and powerfully built, with short russet-colored hair, graying at the sides, tanned weathered skin that was mostly freckled, and round friendly features, including shrewd green eyes that seemed to take everything in at once.

"Stephanie," Edwin said, "you know Mayor Bellamy."

"Of course, we've met many times," the man boomed, and kissed Stephanie on the cheek. "How are you holding up, my dear? I'm sorry for your loss."

"I'm all right," she said breathily. "Thank you for your kindness. The flowers you sent to the funeral home were simply gorgeous."

He covered her hand with his own. "I loved Randy, I really did."

"He was a special man, wasn't he?" Stephanie said.

"That he was," Bronson agreed, shifting in his expensive black loafers. He noticed Alex for the first time. "I'm afraid we haven't met. Mayor Bronson Bellamy."

"Alex Daniels." She accepted his firm handshake, letting him pump her hand furiously a few time, and then glanced nervously at Stephanie. She probably wouldn't appreciate her next question, but who knew when she'd see the mayor again. "Mayor Bronson, I've heard you were very upset about the negotiations to purchase Bellamy Bay Realty. Or the lack thereof?"

His eyebrows shot up in surprise. "No, of course I wasn't upset. Surprised, perhaps. Randy and I were friends and friendly business competitors. But I certainly didn't take it personally. Sometimes I want what I want and I don't like to take no for an answer." His laugh fell flat as his eyes swept the room. He looked like he wanted to be anywhere but here answering her questions.

To Alex he looked guilty . . . of something.

He clasped Stephanie's hand in both of his. "And I was relieved to learn the police made a quick arrest. Our police department is small but top-notch."

Edwin gave Alex an angry look. "If you don't mind, Ms. Daniels, we have some business matters to discuss."

"Of course. I was just leaving, actually. I'm here with someone, but I seem to have lost him." She forced an awkward laugh. "I should probably go see what he's up to. Nice to meet you all."

"Likewise." Edwin's tone was flat as he turned Stephanie away.

Well, that was great, Alex thought. It wasn't every day she managed to offend someone with her very presence. The crowd of guests was overwhelming, and she couldn't make out Dylan's dark figure anywhere. Tegan was no longer at her post on the stair landing, either. The charity auction might be beginning soon, so they could be distracted, Alex thought. It seemed the perfect time to do some searching for Captain Bellamy's journal.

She made her way through the crowd in the great hall and entered yet another hall full of people. The mansion was expansive. Alex walked along the wall, pausing here and there to admire the artwork. The Wesleys had great taste and had filled the home with a range of work in classic styles. She recognized a painting of water lilies by Monet and a group of ballerinas by Degas. Priceless works of art simply hanging on the walls.

Alex scurried to the far end of the hall, where the crowd had dissipated. She froze. Security guards blocked the entry to the rest of the house. She bit the inside of her cheek as she tried to muster a reason for entering the residence. Then she lifted her chin and began to walk through the doorway as if she owned the place.

It didn't work.

"Miss." One of the beefy security guards physically stopped her exit. "The event is limited to the great halls."

Alex blinked. "I was just—looking for Dylan," she said.

"Dylan Wesley?"

"Yes. He's my date."

One guard turned to the other. They both had earpieces. When the other guard moved, she saw his holster. "Did Dylan come this way?"

"I didn't see him." The second guard kept his eyes fixed on the crowd.

"I'm sorry, miss, but he's not here. You're going to have to turn back."

Shoot. Wasn't Alex supposed to be irresistible to men? She'd have to ask Minka how that worked, exactly. In the meantime, she had a small vial of Violet in her handbag. Alex calmly stepped to one side of the guard, opened her bag, and took a moment to spritz some of the perfume on herself, recalling that Lidia had said this made a woman irresistible. As she sent a spray of the perfume into the air, Alex imagined herself as the kind of woman a man couldn't say no to, hoping to amplify the spell already in place.

She set the bottle back into her handbag and looked up. One of the security guards had moved to the side of the room to speak with someone who was getting too close to a piece of art. The security guard who remained was watching her every movement. She smiled as she approached again. Amazingly, he smiled back. "I don't suppose there's a ladies' room through there?" she asked sweetly. "The other ones are so crowded."

Now the guard grinned and leaned closer to whisper, "Through the door and down the hall to the right. But don't tell anyone I let you through."

"It's our secret." She winked and gave him a little pat on the shoulder just before slipping past. *Thank you, Ciocia Lidia.*

She couldn't believe anyone lived in this museum of a structure. This hallway was wider than Lidia's living room and seemed to stretch on for miles. The Gothic architecture was cold and ornate, with elaborate stone archways that led down other hallways or into open rooms. Alex didn't venture far before she found something spectacular: a pillared entry opening to a round library stacked floor to second story with books. A leather couch and two chairs gathered in front of the massive fieldstone fireplace that sat empty in the center of the far wall. Elaborate Turkish rugs added warmth, and the ceiling was capped by glass. Moonlight gave the room an otherworldly glow. For a moment, Alex stood in breathless admiration of the most beautiful library she'd ever seen.

This would be a great place to hide an old journal.

Down the hall, she heard the hum of voices and music, but the library was quiet enough that she noticed her own breath. She crept down the stone steps that led to the floor and stood agape at the stacks of books. There were thousands of titles here—where would she begin looking?

Alex took a turn around the room, running her fingers along the spines. The titles closest to the door were mostly hardcovers with shiny dust jackets. It wouldn't be there, or among the large art history collection, or the books of folklore and mythology. But the books around the fireplace were delicate, and many appeared to be first editions. An old journal could sit there for a long time without being noticed.

Alex's heart beat harder as time passed. The library stacks were enormous. To search them adequately, she'd have to climb the ladder, check each and every title—it would take hours. "Darn it." She stepped back from the shelves and set her hands on her hips. "All of this for nothing."

And that's when she saw something: a single misplaced book in a perfectly ordered library, hastily flung on top of a row of leather-bound novels. She stood on her toes and stretched her arm as far as it would go, but her fingernails only reached the very corner. She held her breath and took a tentative step onto the bottom shelf. One careless move and the books could come crashing down on her. She paused to test the shelf's strength, but it held her weight. Pressing her foot down, she launched herself just high enough to swat at the book. It inched forward. Once again, she jumped up. This time, she got it.

She landed on the floor, her fingers trembling as she opened the brown leather book. There was no title on the cover and the pages were yellowed and brittle. Alex turned the cover slowly, her heart thundering in her ears. On the inside front cover in tight scrawl, someone had written, *Capt. John Bellamy.*

Alex grinned. "Bingo."

Chapter Fifteen

Alex paused only a moment to thumb through Captain Bellamy's journal. Her palms were damp and her pulse throbbed in her throat as she hurried away from the bookcase. The journal was too large to slip inside her clutch, but with all the commotion in the hall, she doubted anyone would notice her walking out with an old leather book. She would just tuck it under her arm—

Something kicked Alex's foot from underneath her, and she tumbled to the stone floor. Her clutch fell beside her, but when she lifted her head, she didn't see the journal. She crawled on her hands and knees, searching for it. "Oh no, oh no," she whispered to herself. Cursing her luck, she stood again.

The journal was hovering in midair.

Alex reached for it, but the book flew out of her reach and into the hallway. She peered into the darkness, but couldn't sense anyone. And then someone stepped out of the shadows and into the moonlight. It was Bryn. The journal sank into her waiting hand. "This doesn't belong to you," she sneered.

Alex took a moment to straighten her dress and brush herself off after her fall. "It doesn't belong to you either, Bryn," she said. "But I don't need to tell you that."

"Oh, please." Bryn rolled her eyes to the heavens as she walked down the steps. She was dressed in a figure-hugging black dress and stiletto heels, but her skin was luminescent in the dim light. "You were about to sneak this out of my house, and you have the nerve to lecture me about stealing."

"At least I didn't attack anyone." She stepped closer and narrowed her eyes. "You hurt Pepper and stole that journal."

"And scrubbed her phone to delete that video she took." Bryn shrugged. "So what? Any Magical would have done the same to protect their secrets. Before you get all high and mighty, you might stop and consider that I protected your family's secrets, too. You're welcome." She let go of the journal, and it floated over Alex's head and back into place on the shelf.

Alex clenched her fists tightly at her side. "Did you kill Randy Bennett, Bryn? Is there something in that journal that would implicate you?"

"Don't you talk about anything else?"

"Answer my question."

"I don't have to." Bryn's eyes drilled holes through Alex. "Are you here because you like my brother? Or because you think one of us killed that man?"

Alex had never been a good liar, but she no longer knew how to answer that question. Dylan was handsome, yes. She enjoyed his company and he made her feel an attraction, a visceral magnetism she'd never felt before. That scared her. But what truly terrified her was that Dylan was not just a Wesley, but a potential murderer—and a Magical one at that. How could she be sure anything between them was real? "I—I like Dylan," she stammered.

Bryn's lip curled. "Yeah. Now you're lying to me." She folded her arms. "I told him you were no good. I warned him about dating a Sobieski. But you know Dylan; he wants to think the best of people. But I was right."

Now it was Alex's turn to feel disgust. "We're not dating. Come on—"

"You're trying to hurt my family, and I won't let that happen." She pointed a long index finger at the center of Alex's chest. "You've been warned."

Alex stood stunned for a moment, unable to process what had just happened. It was over. She'd failed to recover the journal, and she had failed to learn more about Randy Bennett's murder. If anything, she'd only put herself on the radar of some very nasty people. Alex pushed past Bryn, leaving her standing in the center of the library. She had to leave.

She moved quickly back toward the hallway, picking up her pace once she reached the darkness. She was not safe here, and every shadow set her nerves on fire. She was running as she rounded the corner and entered the hall.

Several steps in, she saw Dylan. He was talking to a guest. Alex barely glanced in their direction before she took off toward the entrance.

"Alex, wait." Dylan caught her before she ran past him. "What happened? You look like you've seen a ghost."

Even in the comfort of his strong hands, she was trembling. "It's nothing," she said through chattering teeth. "I don't feel well, that's all."

"What's wrong? Are you sick? What can I do?"

"N-nothing. It's nothing." She eased herself out of his grasp. "I'm going to go home and lie down."

"You're panicked." His dark eyes softened. "You can't drive in this condition. I'll take you myself—"

"No." She didn't mean for the word to come out so sharply. "No, I mean, you have so many guests here. And I'll be fine, really. I think I ate something that didn't agree with me, that's all."

Dylan sighed. "You won't let me help you." He took a step back. "I'll respect your wishes."

The genuine sadness on his face turned guilt in her chest. She had used him to try to find Captain Bellamy's journal. He kept showing kindness, and she kept pushing him aside. "Dylan, I had a nice time tonight. Thank you for inviting me."

"My pleasure." His face was inscrutable. "The roads heading out of the Peninsula are narrow and dark. Drive safely, Alex."

* * *

Alex was relieved to get back into the car and speed away from the Wesley estate. She still had chills on her arms from her confrontation with Bryn.

"Just fantastic, Alex," she mumbled to herself. "Way to make a bad situation worse."

As the estate faded from view in the rearview mirror, she breathed easier, but she couldn't stop thinking about Bryn's threats.

"It's nothing," she told herself. "Bryn is full of hot air. She won't actually hurt you." Lidia was a Magical, and so were Minka and Kamila. They would keep Alex safe.

She drove along the Peninsula, down a dark, narrow road that turned sharply at times. She tapped the brakes to round a corner, cursing the lack of streetlamps. This part of town—the Peninsula, a few acres of land that jutted into the ocean—was purposely undeveloped, with a single long road that looped around the area. Here there were only million-dollar oceanfront homes.

The rest was protected habitat for the various birds and animals that lived there.

And while the area was beautiful in its unspoiled splendor by day, by night it was downright spooky. The road Alex drove on began to head back to the mainland, a narrow stretch where she could see dark water on either side of her. She gripped the steering wheel and focused on the patch illuminated by her headlights. She didn't have much farther to go, but she couldn't get there soon enough.

Just as she began to round another turn, the hair on her neck stood on end. Suddenly, there was a deafening bang and the car jolted to the right. Another bang sent the car violently back to the left. Alex fought to keep the vehicle from crashing straight through the guardrail and into the water, but the steering wheel was nearly useless. She heard the grinding of asphalt. The car shook, lurching from side to side in an uncontrolled skid. She held her breath to keep from screaming as she wrestled with the wheel, jerking it back as the vehicle headed toward sand, beach grass, and then the water. Finally, Alex gained control of her steering wheel, and she pulled to the bank. She put the car in park and sat shaking. Her breath came in sobs. How was she still alive?

She stepped out and immediately saw the cause of the problem: all four of her tires had blown. Even in the darkness, she could make out chunks of rubber scattered on the road. Alex drew a shaky breath, but she couldn't stop hyperventilating. For the second time, she caught the unique scent of sea salt, ozone, and wet sand in the air—the scent that lingered after lightning struck, mixed with the smells of the beach.

Magic.

This was no accident.

She scrambled back in the car to find her cell phone. Her clumsy fingers tried twice to call Jack, but she was shaking so hard that she kept hitting the wrong buttons. Finally she reached him.

"Jack, I need help. I think someone tried to kill me." Just saying the words out loud dispelled the shock and sent tears streaming down her cheeks. "Please hurry."

"I need to know if you're safe right now. Are you alone?" Jack's voice was a practiced calm. "I'm on my way, but it's important for you to get to a safe location."

"I'm safe," she said. "I'm on the Peninsula, near the mainland. I'm on the side of the road."

"Okay, good. I'm leaving now. Tell me what happened."

She heard a door close and his car engine roar to life. She took a shaky breath. "All four of my tires blew at once. I came from a party at the Wesleys' house, and—I think someone did something to the car while I was there."

"I'm going to be there in about five minutes. Do you want to keep talking?"

The sound of his voice was so comforting. "Yes," she whispered. "Please don't hang up."

"I wouldn't think of it," Jack said gently.

They didn't speak much while Jack drove to her location. He asked Alex about her day—other than almost dying—and made small talk about some television show he'd been watching. She didn't care. The conversation made her feel like she wasn't sitting alone on a dark stretch of roadway in a busted car.

"Minka's going to be so angry with me," she whispered as Jack pulled up in a black Jeep Wrangler.

"Why?" he asked as he stepped out of his SUV and turned on a flashlight. "This wasn't your fault, and insurance should cover it."

How could Alex explain that she felt responsible? Her aunt and cousins had told her not to screw up with the Wesleys, and she'd gone ahead and done it anyway. Now someone wanted to scare her—or worse. And so it was all her fault that Minka's car was a wreck.

"It's kind of a long story," she said, finally disconnecting their phone call and stepping out of the car. "I made the wrong person angry."

Jack frowned as he turned the light toward the bottom of the vehicle. "These tires look like they exploded." He shone the beam down the road. "There are pieces all over the place."

The stink of burned rubber was overwhelming the scent of magic that Alex had detected immediately after she pulled over.

"They did explode," she said. "I couldn't control the car. I—I thought I was going to die." She was trying to be strong, but now that Jack was here, she felt safe enough to let go.

"Alex." He wrapped an arm around her and pulled her closer. "You're safe now. If someone is trying to hurt you, I'm going to hunt them down. That's a promise."

She felt herself relaxing against his chest. He was right, she was safe now. Jack wasn't some weird Magical who could make books float or erase her memories. He was blissfully normal. No wonder the Sobieski women had fallen in love with Mundanes. They were a respite from the dangers of the magical world.

Alex eased her arms up around Jack's torso, like clutching a tree in the tempest. "Thank you, Jack," she whispered against his chest.

"You're shaking." He brought her closer. "I have a blanket in the car. You may be experiencing some shock. I'll go get it—"

"No. Please, don't leave me." She tightened her grip on him. She had always prided herself on being tough and an independent woman, but she just couldn't be that person right now.

Jack smoothed his hand down her back, and they stood there for a moment. She could hear the steady strum of his heart through his shirt. "I'm going to call someone to tow your car to the shop. I'll have one of my officers inspect it for signs of tampering."

"They won't find anything."

He pulled back to study her. "Why do you say that?"

Alex released her hold on him and folded her arms across her chest as a cool breeze rushed past. "Nothing. Just a feeling."

"Do you know who might have done this?"

Alex nodded slowly. "Yes. One of the Wesleys. They murdered Randy Bennett, they attacked Pepper Bellamy, and now they're trying to kill me." She shivered as she remembered Dylan's parting words.

Drive safely, Alex.

Jack shut his eyes briefly. "Pepper is fine. She was checked out at the hospital. The doctor thinks she may have done it for the attention. She's been referred to outpatient therapy."

Alex frowned. "An incident where she trashed her house, then locked herself in her trunk?"

He shrugged. "Stranger things have happened. You'd be surprised what people can do under stress." Curiosity glinted in his eyes. "Why do you keep insisting I investigate the Wesley family?"

"Because their family hates mine. It's retribution for something that happened a long time ago—" She stopped when she saw the discomfort on Jack's face. To him, she sounded irrational. "Forget it. I know what you're going to say. I need to find evidence, right?"

He stepped in front of her so that she couldn't avoid his gaze. "I want you to leave the evidence-finding to the police, is that clear? If you're correct and someone tried to hurt you—well, I don't want it to happen again."

"But the police aren't looking in the right place," she insisted. "You have your suspect already. Case closed."

"Maybe not." Jack gestured to the Prius. "If we comb the car and find evidence of a crime, it could lead our investigation in a different direction."

But Alex already knew that the police wouldn't find anything on the car, just as they'd come up empty when they'd investigated Pepper's house. It was too easy to blame the incident on faulty tires. A chill swept down her spine. Her family was all alone in this.

A squad car approached and pulled over to the side of the road. Jack waved to the officer. "Do you need a ride home?" he asked Alex.

She gestured to her car. "Yeah. Kind of."

"Stupid question," Jack said with a smile. "Come on. I'll take you."

* * *

Alex had never felt so relieved to be home. Athena ran circles around her legs with her ears down, whimpering with happiness. She took a moment to give the sweet dog a hug and a scratch on the belly before she entered the living room. Lidia and Minka were reading, but they closed their books as soon as Alex approached.

"Alex," her aunt called out. "I'm so glad you're home. I had a bad feeling."

Alex unbraided her hair and slipped off her heels. Athena grabbed a shoe and walked over to her bed to sit with it.

"I should've listened to you both," she said, feeling sheepish. "You were right. The Wesleys are nothing but trouble."

She proceeded to tell them about the evening, about how cold Tegan had been, how Dylan had placed her under some spell, and how Bryn had threatened her. "And then when I was driving home, all four of my tires blew out almost simultaneously. I'm so sorry, Minka," she added. "I'll pay to replace them."

"Don't worry about that now," her cousin said. "I'm just glad you're safe. Thank goodness."

Alex winced when she looked at Lidia, who had sat quietly during the story. "*Ciocia* Lidia, I'm sorry. I shouldn't have gone. I understand if you're mad at me—"

"Mad?" Lidia's brows rose. "No. I'm not mad. Not at you. But that family has gone too far." She jumped to her feet, and a light wind swirled in the living room. "I'm going to raise this with the Council."

This was the second time she'd heard talk of the Council. "What exactly is that?"

"They hear complaints and set standards," Minka explained. "Like how much black-magic practice is acceptable."

"We're permitted to use up to ten percent," Lidia said. "The Council recognizes that there are times when one needs to protect oneself, and of course when we get angry, it can just happen." She glanced down guiltily. "But the Wesleys are different. They are notorious for using far too much black magic."

"Mom is the chair of the local Council chapter," Minka said, "but Tegan feels entitled to that position. As if they needed any more gasoline on the fire between them."

Alex thought back to the night Randy Bennett had been murdered, and how Pepper Bellamy had witnessed a heated exchange between Lidia and Tegan. "By any chance, did the Council just meet?"

"Last week," Lidia replied, and then smiled ironically. "The night Randy died, in fact. Which gives me no alibi at all. What am I supposed to tell those Mundane detectives—that I couldn't have poisoned Randy because I was leading a meeting of witches?"

Alex groaned. "So that explains why you were so tight-lipped about your alibi." Sighing, she ran a hand through her hair. "And Tegan was there, too. You were arguing. Pepper followed you and saw actual sparks flying."

"Tegan is negligent about displaying her magic when she's angry," Lidia spat. Then, when she caught Minka's questioning gaze, she sighed. "And I suppose I can work on that, too."

"How long did the meeting last that night?" Alex asked.

Lidia thought back. "Later than usual. I'd have to check the minutes for the exact time, but we didn't adjourn until around two in the morning."

"And Tegan was there all night?"

Her aunt rolled her eyes. "Tegan was the reason we were there. We were discussing a change to the black-magic policy, reducing it to only eight percent. A change of two measly points, and she went ballistic."

If Lidia had left Botanika directly after work on Tuesday and gone to the meeting, she wouldn't have had time to visit Randy and poison his tea. Of course, if Tegan had worked all day on Tuesday and then spent the night at the same meeting, then she had an alibi as well.

"Did Tegan leave at any time during the meeting?"

Her aunt gave her a knowing look. "Leave long enough to kill Randy, you mean?" She shook her head. "As much as I'd like to find out who did this, I don't think Tegan had the opportunity."

"Right. It's not like she can be in two places at one time."

"Well . . ." Lidia gazed thoughtfully at her niece. "There is a spell . . . one of those spells for trouble, but it requires a lot of energy and dark magic. And if Tegan had cast that particular spell on that night, there's no way she would've had the stamina to throw the spectacular tantrum we all witnessed."

So her aunt was Tegan's alibi, and Tegan . . . She looked around the room at her family, suddenly excited. "Would Tegan vouch for your whereabouts at the time of the murder, substituting the purpose of the meeting with something . . . more Mundane than a Council meeting?"

Minka and Kamila made faces, while Lidia snorted out a most unladylike laugh. "That witch would rather see me hang than exonerate me from anything." She shook her head. "Tegan Wesley wouldn't help me out of a parking ticket."

Alex's face fell. "Okay . . . " So, she should cross Tegan off her list? She didn't feel quite ready to do that just yet, but she'd put her on the back burner for now. That left Bryn and Dylan. "By any chance, did you say anything to Tegan about Randy visiting Botanika on Monday?" Otherwise, how would the Wesleys have known how to poison him?

"She didn't have to," Minka answered. "Pepper was there, remember? She wrote up a little note on her blog about Mom going berserk on a customer. She didn't mention names, but she dropped enough clues that anyone who read it would know who she was talking about."

Alex rubbed her fingers across her tightening forehead. Her temples throbbed. "I think I should get to bed."

"Minka," Lidia said, "we have to teach Alex more about her powers. This has gotten very serious. She has to learn how to defend herself against the Wesleys."

"I agree, Mom," Minka replied. "You want me to do that? I'll use the fountain. It's perfect for practicing."

"If you use the fountain, you'll have to teach her yourself," she said, and gestured to her ankle bracelet. "I'm a prisoner in here."

Minka touched Alex on the arm. "You should get some rest. Being the victim of black magic will drain your energy if you don't know how to protect yourself against it. I think it's best that we start working on your skills after a good night's sleep."

Alex's limbs were so heavy that she couldn't possibly have argued otherwise. "Sounds good."

"Come on, I'll walk you upstairs."

Minka and Alex left the room with Athena in tow, carrying Alex's high heel gently in her mouth. When they arrived at her bedroom, Minka pulled some jars out of a basket and set them on the dresser. "Use the lavender cream tonight and the citrus and sage in the morning," she instructed. "You'll feel back to normal by breakfast time."

"And if I don't?" Alex grinned.

Minka shook her head gravely. "Black-magic hangover. Trust me, you don't want to go there."

She turned down the sheets on the bed while Alex removed her jewelry. "Thank you for taking such good care of me, Minka. I never would have believed that people like the Wesleys existed. But now I understand."

"We've got to get our hands on something Randy owned so that we can cast a guidance spell. Then we'll know exactly who did this."

"I'll work on it," Alex promised. "I met Stephanie tonight. Maybe I'll make up an excuse to visit her."

"Maybe Monday," Minka agreed. "Give it a few days so you don't look too eager. There's something else." Minka sat on the bed. "When you mentioned that Dylan put a spell on you—what exactly did you mean?"

"Oh." Alex whirled around, angry still as she thought back to the dance in the moonlight. "We were out on the patio, under the moon. It's hard to explain it, but there was this feeling that came over me, like there was nothing else in the world. Blissful?" Alex sighed. "But it was magic, I know it was. I've literally never felt anything like it."

"Yeah." Minka hesitated. "But actually, only women can enchant men. It doesn't work the other way. It's a power specific to mermaids, and it only works on Mundanes. So, I just thought you should know that."

Alex froze as she tried to process that information, but Minka kept talking, "Dylan doesn't even practice magic, last I knew. He's like Kamila, one of those Magicals who don't want anything to do with their powers, so . . ." She let her thought trail. "I'm just saying. He didn't cast an enchantment spell on you. It's not possible, and he wouldn't even try."

"So he didn't put a spell on me?" Alex flung herself back on the bed next to her cousin, still wearing her party dress. "I don't understand."

Minka smiled. "I think you do." She patted her leg. "You just don't like what it means."

Chapter Sixteen

Like the Wesleys, Stephanie Bennett lived on the Peninsula. Despite Alex's reluctance to return to the location of her accident, Minka urged her to pay her a visit on Monday afternoon.

"Kamila says she's been cleared to empty Randy's things out of the house they shared, and apparently she's been bringing some boxes to her house. If you can manage to snatch something he owned, I can perform a guidance spell."

Alex agreed to visit Stephanie. The sooner she found the killer, the sooner she could leave Bellamy Bay and start over at a great new job in New York City. Hopefully there was minimal witchcraft there.

She took Lidia's sedan and arrived at a stately brick colonial just after lunchtime. Stephanie had the trunk of her black Porsche SUV open, and she was carrying large cardboard boxes into the house. She paused to stare as Alex pulled beside the curb. "What are you doing here?" she asked when Alex stepped out of the car.

Alex smiled because the universe had handed her a reason for stopping. "I saw you struggling with those boxes. Would you like a hand?"

"No," Stephanie snapped. But when Alex crossed onto the driveway undeterred, she reconsidered. "Okay, fine. These are kind of heavy."

"They looked it." Alex pulled a box from the trunk. Yeesh, it must have weighed fifty pounds. "Where do you want these?"

"In the house." Stephanie dropped the box she was carrying at her feet and unlocked the front door. "It's all of Randy's stuff. I have to go through it." Her blonde hair was pulled into a ponytail, and she was dressed in an oversized blue denim shirt and white cotton capris. She blew a loose tendril of hair out of her face and held the front door open for Alex. "I should've hired someone."

Alex went into the house, finding herself in a large foyer. The house was humble in comparison to the Wesleys' place, but far from small. The term McMansion came to mind. Stephanie pointed to a side room. "You can just put it in there."

There were piles of cardboard boxes stacked in the room Stephanie had gestured to, all marked similarly. *Randy's clothes. Randy's shoes. Randy's junk.* Stephanie entered and set her box on top of the one Alex had just dropped. "You probably think it's callous," she said. "Me cleaning out his stuff like this, so soon after . . . But we were getting a divorce. He was already missing from my life."

Stephanie paused and stood with her hands on her hips as she surveyed the inventory. Then her face crumpled and she began to sob.

"Oh." Alex rushed to her side. "Stephanie. I'm sorry. This must be very difficult."

Stephanie covered her face with her hands, shaking with the force of her tears as Alex rubbed her arm. "I can't believe he's gone. There were so many things I would have changed."

"Of course," Alex said. "Death has a way of giving us perspective on what matters."

With a shuddering breath, Stephanie lifted her head again and wiped off her cheeks. "Enough of that," she said after a moment, regaining her calm again. "What's done is done." She shot Alex a critical stare. "I don't even know you. And your aunt killed my husband. Why are you here?"

Alex tried not to be shaken by the widow's sudden turn. "I wanted to offer my support, that's all. When we met at the Wesleys' party the other night, you said you didn't have any family around here. I know what that's like. My dad raised me on his own, and until about two weeks ago, I hadn't seen my aunt and cousins in twenty years." She tried to smile in the face of Stephanie's glare. "Do you want any more help with the boxes?"

Stephanie looked as if she was about to say no again, but then thought better of it. "Okay. But let's do it quickly."

As Stephanie led the way out of the house, Alex noticed an open shoebox filled with trinkets and labeled *Randy's crap*. Inside she spotted jeweled watches and class rings—was this what passed for garbage in Stephanie's world? She was just about to paw through the box when Stephanie moved in the doorway. "I'm going to grab a drink. You want a whiskey?"

Alex put up a hand. "None for me, thanks."

"Why don't you go ahead to the car? Don't wait for me."

And so Alex finished emptying the Porsche while Stephanie sat on a box labeled *Randy's books* and nursed her drink. When Alex had planted the final box in the room, Stephanie's eyes were glassy.

"I did love him, you know. We were trying to work things out. We might have even stayed married if he'd been able to leave his mistress." She threw her head back and finished her drink. "Men. Am I right?" Her smile was feeble.

Wow, did Stephanie display a spectrum of emotions. But her feelings toward her husband seemed complicated, especially if she hadn't wanted to get divorced. Would she have killed him over jealousy?

"You knew he was cheating on you?" Alex asked, feeling like she was crossing into dangerous territory.

But Stephanie smiled. "Wives know these things. He was spending extra time getting ready in the morning, wearing a new cologne, going out for more 'business dinners.'" She made air quotes. "More travel. Suddenly he was a stranger. It's like I had no idea who he was."

"Do you know who his mistress was?"

"Of course not," she snorted. "Most likely some young girl looking for a sugar daddy. We couldn't have children. It was devastating to both of us. I've always wondered if he strayed to try his luck with someone else." She went to take another drink. Finding her tumbler empty, Stephanie stared sadly at the bottom of the glass. "But I loved him. I'm a fool."

Randy had purchased a bottle of Violet when he was at Botanika. He'd called it *something pretty* for his *something pretty*. Now Alex saw firsthand how deeply Randy's behavior had hurt his wife. "Stephanie, did Randy happen to buy you a bottle of perfume before he . . . died?"

Her eyes flashed. "No. Did he buy his girlfriend something? He did, didn't he? No, wait." She shook her head. "Don't tell me. I gave my life to that man—"

She jumped to her feet. Without warning, she kicked the box she'd been sitting on and screamed. Alex backed away, knocking over the box of trinkets—the "crap." The contents scattered across the floor.

"Sorry," she muttered, and hurried to pick up the mess.

Stephanie stopped kicking and turned her anger to Alex. "Did you come here just to rub it in my face that my husband was seeing someone else? Did you come here to hurt me?" She pointed to the door. "I want you out. Now."

Alex gestured to the clutter on the ground. "I will, but let me pick this up—"

"Get out," Stephanie shrieked.

She didn't need to say it again. Alex ran out the door and to her car. Once she was safely inside, she locked the doors in case Stephanie decided to follow her. Then she opened her fist. She'd managed to grab a gold cuff link marked with the initials *RB*.

Despite everything, Alex smiled.

* * *

They were waiting until midnight to cast the guidance spell. After casting accidental guidance spells of her own, Alex knew they worked just fine in the middle of the day, but Minka insisted on waiting, and Alex couldn't do this alone.

"The stronger the moon, the better," Minka had explained. "It enhances our powers."

Alex passed the time impatiently, watching television with Lidia with one eye on the clock. Finally, at a quarter to twelve, while Alex was reading in her bedroom, Minka poked her head through the doorway and said, "Okay. You ready?"

Alex reached into her pocket and retrieved the cuff link. "Ready."

"Let's do this."

As she rolled off the bed, Athena looked up from her spot on the floor, blinking her eyes. Then she stretched and followed Alex into Minka's room, where Minka was reaching for a wooden box at the top of her closet.

"This is like three hundred years old," she said as she handed it to Alex. "So don't drop it."

Alex unlatched the lid. Inside was a crystal bowl set in blue silk lining. The bowl was surprisingly heavy and etched with strange marks that resembled hieroglyphs. "Are these letters of some kind?"

"It's mermaid language, I think," Minka said. "That's what Mom says, but it's not like anyone can confirm it." She lifted the bowl out of Alex's hands. "Come on, we're going outside."

Athena nuzzled Alex's hand. "I know, girl. It's bedtime," she said soothingly. "But this is important." The German shepherd must have been convinced, because she walked beside Alex as they followed Minka into the backyard.

"I love that Mom has this fountain. You really need water that's been charged by a full moon if you're going to get a clear answer." Minka gazed at the sky and smiled. "And we're in luck." She dipped the edge of the bowl into the pool of the fountain and then set the bowl on the bench. "The item, my dear."

Alex dropped the cuff link into Minka's open palm.

"Are we sure it's Randy's?" She squinted at the gold in the bright moonlight. "A guidance spell like this is hard to get right—"

"*Now* you tell me," Alex said. "Do you realize what I had to go through to get this cuff link?"

"You have a better idea?" Minka cocked her head.

"Well, it has his initials on it, and it was in a box labeled *Randy's crap*."

"That's good enough for me." Minka dropped the cuff link into the crystal bowl.

"Can you teach me how to do this?" Alex asked. "It would be good to know how to do this kind of thing on purpose."

"Oh, right. Okay, I'm going to drop the cuff link into the water first. Now. It's important to get into the right mind-set. That means clearing your mind of everything except for the question you have, got it? No thinking about your grocery list or how your dog needs a bath."

Alex looked at Athena, who smiled and thumped her tail. "All right."

"Here, let's hold hands. Like I was saying, this is tricky, but if we try it together, we might get somewhere."

Alex gripped her cousin's hand, focusing intently on her question: *who killed Randy Bennett?*

A full moon reflected in the still surface of the water in the crystal bowl, along with a wisp of a cloud. Then the water began to vibrate.

"Here it is," Minka whispered, and tightened her grasp on Alex's hand. Alex was too scared to breathe lest she screw up the entire spell.

They observed tiny ripples coursing through the bowl. The moon vanished as the clear water turned cloudy. Then a dark image took shape. "It's a Magical," Minka said.

"How do you know?"

"Because they're all shadow. They won't allow us to see them, which means they knew we would try." Minka's eyes narrowed. "A Magical killed him, all right. And they don't feel remorse. There's a dark energy around. This person is using a cloaking spell, disguising themselves."

"Disguise? Like how?"

"It's murky, but this is a Magical pretending to be something or someone they're not. Could be a Magical disguising themselves as a Mundane." Minka dragged a finger through the bowl, breaking the image in half. "What I know is that a cloaking spell is one of the spells for trouble. The Council says there is no legitimate reason to use it."

"What's a spell for trouble? I think I heard *Ciocia* Lidia mention it earlier."

"It's the Council's formal list of banned spells. Spells for trouble are enchantments no one needs unless they're up to no good—unless they're practicing black magic. The cloaking spell is one of them." A dark look crossed Minka's face. "This person is extremely dangerous. We're talking about someone who doesn't hesitate to practice black magic, to use their powers for bad." The image had vanished.

Alex's heart was pounding. *Dark energy. Extremely dangerous. Black magic.* None of these were the answers she'd hoped for. "So we're looking for a Magical. A Wesley?"

"I don't know." Minka picked the cuff link out of the water before she poured the contents of the bowl into the fountain. "This is bad." She handed the cuff link back to Alex. "I guess part of me was hoping it was a Mundane. We can handle a Mundane, but a Magical?"

"But are we sure the guidance spell was correct? Randy wasn't killed by magic."

"That's just to avoid the Council's scrutiny," Minka said. "If he had been killed by magic, they would've opened their own investigation. The guidance spell is never wrong."

Her cousin was already walking back toward the house. Alex snapped her fingers at Athena, who jumped up to follow them. "Wait. What are we supposed to do now?"

But Minka was walking ahead as if she hadn't even heard her. Alex sprung ahead to grab her shoulder, halting her cousin's retreat. "Now what?"

She had never seen anything like the fear she saw in Minka's wide, blue eyes. She was clutching the crystal bowl against her chest like a shield. "I can't answer that question. This is a person who killed once and won't hesitate to do it again. If you pursue this, you're in grave danger."

Alex flung her hands wide. "And if I don't pursue this, your mom will go to jail for something she didn't do!"

"Mom may go to jail anyway. I don't want to lose you, too."

Alex softened. "You're not going to lose me," she whispered, even though she knew she couldn't make that promise. "Let's think about this. How can we continue to investigate without being so obvious?"

Minka bit her lower lip and glanced back toward the fountain. "I just keep thinking that it's too bad Pepper has lost interest in the case. It would be good to have her on our side."

"I wanted to know what she'd found in Captain Bellamy's journal. I'm not sure we'll ever know the truth now."

Minka twirled a lock of hair around her fingers as she thought. Suddenly she froze. "What if we give Pepper some of her memories back?"

"We can do that?"

"To an extent. Memories erased by magic aren't gone forever; they're just rendered inaccessible. But if we remind Pepper of what's already there, maybe she can get something back."

Without warning, Minka sprinted back toward the fountain. Alex followed at a jog. "I thought we liked that our secrets were safe? I don't want Pepper printing all of that gossip about our family again."

Minka dipped the crystal bowl into the fountain. "I don't either. That's why we have to be very careful about how we do this. We're going to raise suspicion about the Wesleys, that's all. If there's something already there, she's going to keep digging until she remembers it again." She set the bowl on the bench again. "It's like when you forget a person's name. It bothers you until you figure it out."

"But how do we know she won't remember seeing your mom and Tegan arguing?"

"Even if she did, she no longer has the video on her phone. I'm confident Bryn deleted that."

Alex nodded. "You're right, she mentioned that she had scrubbed the phone."

"So even if she remembers that she thought we were water witches, that's a far cry from having actual proof."

Alex's eyes were burning with fatigue, and she yawned. "All right. So, now we cast a spell in this water and Pepper will get some of her memories back?"

"Oh no," Minka said. "She has to drink this water in order for the spell to work."

Alex groaned so loudly that Athena nuzzled her side in alarm. "How are we supposed to get her to drink that? Is it even clean?" She wrinkled her nose.

"It's enchanted water. It's clean," Minka assured her. "Here's what you're going to do. Tomorrow you're going to meet Pepper for coffee—"

"Yeah, right."

"And you're going to give her the thought that she's thirsty for water. Then you'll give her some of this to drink, and *bam*. Memories start to come back."

Alex crossed her arms. This was sounding like an impossible task.

"Trust me, it's not impossible," Minka said.

"How did you—?"

"I heard your thoughts," Minka explained. "They're actually really loud. We have to work on that. The Wesleys can probably hear you thinking from a mile away." She picked up the crystal bowl, careful not to spill its contents.

Alex's face heated with embarrassment. No wonder the Wesleys didn't care for her. "Now that you mention it, I think I heard Jack's thoughts right before he asked me out. I heard a male voice say, *Ask her out already*."

Minka shook her head knowingly. "Mundanes are so obvious sometimes."

"It was weird that I heard that voice, but it didn't freak me out, you know? I've always been able to guess at what people were thinking, just been very intuitive . . . I wonder if I was hearing thoughts without realizing it?"

Maybe," Minka said brightly, squeezing Alex's hand. "*But* putting a thought in someone's head is different from reading their thoughts,"

Alex massaged her temples, trying to process it all. "You mean, if we can transmit thoughts to someone, we're not simply mind readers. We're telepathic?"

Yes," Minka said. "We can pass thoughts to each other when we want to, and often we can influence Mundanes to act in certain ways. But it's not like we can make them do our bidding or anything. You're new at this," Minka continued, "but Pepper is impressionable, so suggesting that she's thirsty isn't a biggie. You can handle it."

Alex fluttered her lips. "Except that I have no idea how to be telepathic."

"Power comes with practice. And remember that magic is as natural as breathing." Minka put her hands on Alex's shoulders. "All you have to do is clear your mind and focus on what it is you want. In this case, just tell Pepper that she's thirsty."

Alex felt uncertain that anything magical was that easy, but she nodded nevertheless. She could at least give it a try. "And I'll practice making my thoughts quieter."

Minka dropped her hands. "It's more complicated than that," she admitted, picking up the crystal bowl. "You have to construct a wall to guard your mind. Mundanes just walk around thinking whatever they want, and most of it is really boring and not worth listening to. But Magicals have to be careful." She paused. "I'll give you some more strategies."

They walked back into the house, tiptoeing so as not to wake Lidia. Minka found a bottle of water in the refrigerator, opened it, and poured a little into Athena's water bowl. She replaced the amount she'd emptied with the enchanted water in the crystal bowl. Then she capped it and handed it to Alex. "Your mission, if you choose to accept it."

Alex gripped the cold plastic bottle in her hands. "I guess there's no going back now, is there?"

Minka smirked. "You're way past the point of no return."

Chapter Seventeen

Two weeks after the murder, Botanika was back in business. Alex blamed it on a combination of limited attention spans and minimal news coverage, thanks to Bryn's assault on Pepper. Alex hated to admit that Bryn was right and that the attack had actually benefited both of their families, but she couldn't deny that there had been a definite uptick in business since the previous week. So on the day that she was going to find Pepper and coax back some of her memories, Alex had cold feet. "What if this backfires and she starts writing about how terrible the Sobieskis are again?"

"She can't, because she doesn't have the journal," Minka reasoned. "That's where she was getting her information from. Could we land in the spotlight again? Yes. But if we're going to find the person who killed Randy, we could use Pepper's help. She's relentless. What's the other choice?"

None. There simply wasn't one.

Alex excused herself from the shop floor midmorning to call the *Bellamy Bay Bugler* and ask to speak with Pepper.

"I'm afraid she's not due in until later," the receptionist replied. "Is this for a story?"

"Yes, actually. I have a tip for her." Really, what was one more lie? "I can't speak with anyone else. It has to be Pepper, and unfortunately I don't have her cell."

"Oh, I can give you her work number," the woman said cheerfully. "If she's not at her desk, it will ring her cell. Tell me when you're ready."

Alex reached for a pen and paper. "Go ahead."

She wrote down the number, thanked the woman for her helpfulness, and disconnected the call. Then she dialed Pepper's number.

The call was picked up on the second ring. "This is Alex Daniels. From Botanika?"

"Yes, I know who you are." There was a stretch of silence.

"I was wondering how you're feeling?"

"Fine," came the tight reply.

"I mean, since the thing at your house—"

"It's fine." There was a stretch of silence. "Do you have a tip or something for me?"

"Maybe," Alex hedged.

"I'm at the coffee shop if you want to talk, but I have a meeting later today—"

"I'll be right there," Alex said.

"Great." Pepper sounded like she meant the opposite. Then she disconnected the call.

Undeterred by the reporter's rudeness, Alex grabbed her handbag. "I'm meeting with Pepper," she told Minka as she headed out the door.

Minka shimmied her shoulders in excitement. "Good luck."

As she exited the shop, Alex patted her handbag to make sure the water bottle was still there. It was. A knot formed in her stomach. She was going to try this telepathy thing and hope for the best.

The coffee shop was filled with customers, but Alex found Pepper immediately. Her bright-red hair, styled into a jaunty topknot, was like a beacon in the dining area. Alex waved to her before heading to the counter and ordering a regular coffee. As she walked over to the empty seat across from Pepper, the journalist remarked, "That was quick."

Alex slid her oversize ceramic coffee mug and saucer on the table and pulled out the chair. "I work around the corner, and it was my break." She added a splash of cream to her coffee. "I've been worried about you since last week. Have you been feeling okay?"

Pepper's closed her laptop, sighing. "I feel... off kilter," she admitted. "Just off. The doctors put me through all of these tests, but no one can find anything. I can't remember what I was doing that day." She massaged her forehead. "I don't know why I was in the car, or where I was going. And my doctor implied that I might have emotional issues." She shot Alex a look of disbelief. "Like I'd be so upset that I'd lock myself in my own trunk." She laughed. "I'm totally fine, but I have to go see a counselor and discuss how I'm feeling." Her eyes met Alex's gaze. "I should thank you. You kind of saved my life."

"Please don't mention it. I'm just happy you're safe."

"You're happy? I'm mortified that people saw me like that." She lowered her voice. "Please tell me I wasn't exposed in any way. I mean, my bathrobe covered me, right?"

Alex nodded. "I promise. No one saw anything."

"Oh, thank goodness." She slumped back in her seat. "I've had this anxiety about it; you have no idea."

"I can imagine."

"It's nice that you're checking up." Pepper smiled weakly and wrapped her fingers around her mug. "Jack Frazier was nice enough to follow up with me, too. I mean, it's nothing. I know you two are kind of seeing each other." She looked at Alex expectantly.

"Jack and I are only friends," she replied, drinking her coffee. "Dating him is out of the question, considering he arrested Lidia. He's much too professional for that, and I'm not sure I want to be friends with someone who believes my aunt is a murderer."

Relief crossed Pepper's face. "Right, that makes sense."

"I don't even want to date anyone right now," Alex continued. "I'm not certain how much longer I'm going to be in town. I have a job offer in New York—well." She waved a hand. "Enough about me."

Pepper put her laptop into the messenger bag on the floor. "You know, I don't have anything against your aunt, right? I have to cover the crime. It's my job. I don't think Lidia did it, either," she continued. "I mean, I did at first. Everyone did. But I feel like . . . it doesn't make sense. And I can't quite put my finger on why."

"I've noticed you haven't updated your blog lately."

A shadow crossed Pepper's face. "It's funny you say that. I have this weird feeling like I was working on something else, but I can't remember the specifics and I can't find my notes. But I always take notes," she emphasized. "I have this feeling that I was working on something and that it was important." She shrugged. "Maybe it was just a dream."

"Maybe," Alex agreed slowly. "Or maybe it has something to do with your memory loss."

"They can't find anything. No lesions, no bruises. It wasn't a stroke, thank goodness."

"That's a relief." Alex turned to the window and pretended to look off into the distance. "Something keeps bothering me, too, Pepper. How come the police didn't look at Stephanie Bennett? She's going to inherit tens of millions of dollars now. She wouldn't have gotten that much if Randy had died after the divorce was finalized."

"Tell me about it." She leaned closer. "It's usually the spouse, and statistically speaking, women prefer poison."

Alex nodded. "I've heard the same. And she had a key to his house and everything. She could've easily snuck in to poison his tea."

Pepper flashed her eyebrows and took another sip of her coffee. "I've heard that this poisoning was unlike anything the coroner had ever seen. It was bad."

Alex thought back to the guidance spell as a thought occurred to her. Could Stephanie be a Magical? And using one of those spells for trouble to cloak her abilities? She'd have to ask her family. "That's . . . terrifying."

"I know, right?" Pepper shook her head. "Such a shame. She finished the rest of her beverage and set the mug down again. Alex took a breath and decided it was now or never. *You're thirsty. You need to drink something.*

Pepper licked her lips and frowned. "I think I'm going to get another coffee."

Oh no, that wasn't what she'd intended. She focused all of her energy and tried again. *You're thirsty for water.* This time, Pepper rose to her feet. "Actually, I'll get a water. I've been drinking too much coffee."

It had worked! Alex was nearly giddy. "Don't bother. I have one." She reached into her bag. When Pepper looked at her oddly, Alex laughed. "It's good water. And free. Here." She pretended to break the seal on the cap and set it in the center of the table. "It's important to stay hydrated."

Pepper eyed her warily, then smiled. "Okay. Thank you."

She lowered herself into her seat again and reached for the bottle. Alex bit her lip as Pepper took a long, slow drink of water, finishing half the bottle. "Wow. I guess I was thirsty. You're right, that's good water." Pepper read the label. It was a generic water bottle from the local grocery store. "I'll have to remember this kind. I usually go for the fancy ones." She capped the bottle again and set it to the side. "What were we talking about?"

"Stephanie Bennett," Alex said. "How she might have poisoned the tea."

"Right." But Pepper hesitated before she leaned over to pull a notebook and pen out of her messenger. "What do you think of the Wesleys, though? Do you think one of them had it out for Bennett?"

Alex frowned like the thought had never occurred to her. "The Wesleys? Why do you think they would do something like that?"

Pepper blinked at the table, fighting to access her memories. "I don't . . . it's a feeling I have. She dropped her pen in frustration. "I hate this. I feel like there's something I'm missing. Like it's right in front of me but I can't see it."

Alex set her hand over Pepper's. She had always felt terrible about the attack, and now that she saw the effect it was having on the journalist, her heart hurt. This was one of those ethical situations Kamila had alluded to, and the reason she didn't practice.

"Be patient with yourself, Pepper. You're a great reporter, and I know you're going to pull it all together."

Pepper gave Alex an assessing look. "Most people don't like me, whether it's because I'm a Bellamy, because my dad's the mayor, we're rich . . ." She shrugged "Who can know? I think it's mostly because of my job." She grinned with pride. "They see me and think of all the ways I'm about to uncover their secrets and ruin their lives." She leaned in close. "They're afraid of me, because I have power," she chuckled.

The knot in Alex's stomach hardened as she realized Pepper appeared to enjoy being disliked and feared. Her throat tightened, and she wondered how she could ever keep her family's secrets from this woman. She tried to smile at Pepper as she swallowed the lump in her throat, but she felt like she'd only accomplished a slight twitch of the lips.

"But you're different. You're not afraid of me. You must not have anything to hide." She gave Alex a plaintive look. "I'm glad we had coffee today."

Alex bit her lip, unsure how to respond. She didn't fear Pepper exactly, but the journalist did had the power to ruin her family and their business with just a few words, so she was concerned— no, *worried* was probably a better word. And oh, she had something to hide all right, and the last thing she needed was a nosy reporter with a chip on her shoulder digging into their past, a past she was known to be obsessed with.

On the other hand, she was using Pepper to get information, which made her no better and caused her stomach to knot up with anxiety. From a strategic point of view, it was probably better to keep Pepper close and on good terms so that if the blogger ever did find something on her family, Alex would be in a position to run interference. Easier to do that as friends, and Pepper, oddly enough, seemed to be extending an olive branch of sorts. She'd be a fool not to take it, and so she decided to return Pepper's smile. "I'm glad we had coffee too."

"But now I've gotta run." Pepper hurriedly packed up her belongings. "There's something about that family—the Wesleys—that's bothering me. And I'm going to go find Tegan."

"No!" Alex jumped to her feet without thinking. She'd hoped that Pepper would remember what was in that journal, not that she'd actually pursue the Wesleys. She didn't want Pepper to get hurt. "I mean, you're investigating a murder suspect," she said softly, lowering herself back into her seat. "Can you take someone with you, at least? Do you want me to go?"

"I always take a can of mace with me," Pepper assured her as she typed into her phone. "And I let a colleague at work know where I'm going, how long I'll be there, and when I should be back. Just as a precaution."

"And meet somewhere public," Alex added quickly, genuinely concerned for her safety. "You just never know."

"I'll be safe, I promise."

Pepper paused, her eyes glinting with mischief. "Is this what it feels like to have a friend?"

Swallowing nervously, Alex smiled at her. "I'm just a worrier, a professional worrier, actually." She told Pepper what she did for a living. "I basically determine risks and then identify ways to reduce them."

The journalist gave her an appraising look. "Interesting."

Alex sat back in her chair. "Could you let me know if you learn anything? I'll promise to do the same for you."

"Of course."

Alex watched Pepper leave the coffee shop with the same self-confidence she'd seen the first time she'd entered Botanika. This was a woman on a mission.

She carried her mug and saucer to a black bin beside the trash where dirty dishes were collected. She stopped. In the back, mixed with the aromas of baked biscuits and ground coffee, were the unmistakable scents of violet blossoms and raspberries.

Violet.

There was only one person in this area, a young woman sharing a table with a laptop and a stack of college textbooks. Alex approached her with a friendly smile. "Hello. I couldn't help but notice your perfume."

The young woman looked up. "Mine?"

"Yes." Alex kept her tone gentle. "It's Violet, isn't it? It suits you."

She was very pretty, with a heart-shaped face, shoulder-length light brown hair, and wide-set brown eyes. Alex had meant the compliment to be disarming, but she became alarmed when the young woman's eyes filled with tears. "It was a gift," she said softly. "My boyfriend gave it to me just before he died."

"Oh no." Without asking permission, Alex slid into the empty chair across from her. "I didn't mean to upset you. I just know that fragrance."

The woman pulled a stack of tissues from her handbag and wiped her nose and eyes. "It's not your fault. You couldn't have known."

Alex couldn't believe her good fortune—or rather, the young woman's misfortune. Stephanie had mentioned that Randy Bennett had a mistress, and he'd purchased a bottle of Violet for her right before his death. What were the chances that a different man had purchased the same bottle of perfume before dying? She lowered her voice to a whisper and said, "Was your boyfriend Randy Bennett?"

Now the woman's eyes widened in sheer panic. "No. Why would you—he had a wife." But she shifted her gaze around in a way that told Alex she was covering the truth.

"It's okay," Alex assured her. "I'm not here to judge you."

With that, the woman's face dissolved into tears again. "I can't—I'm not . . . "No one knows—*knew*—about us. I've been holding it in, grieving alone ever since—" She blinked back fresh tears. "I'm sorry."

"You don't need to apologize to me," Alex said. "Really. I understand."

She looked relieved. "How did you know about us?"

"I work at Botanika. He bought that perfume there. And I'm sorry for your loss. It's obvious you cared about him."

"He knew how much I loved that shop. We were in love," she explained.

Alex set her handbag on her lap, settling in for a longer conversation. "My name is Alex Daniels."

"Jenna Hoffman. Nice to meet you." She closed her laptop and reached for her tea.

"How long had you and Randy been seeing each other?"

"About a year." She wrapped her hands around the mug and pulled it closer to her chest. "I know, it was wrong for us to date. I felt terribly guilty at the beginning, and I tried to break things off. But he told me he and his wife were separated. She was seeing someone else, too." She took a sip of her tea. "I don't know. I told myself that if she was seeing someone else, it was okay. Funny how we justify things." She gave a pained smile.

Alex leaned closer and lowered her voice. "Jenna, was it true that Randy and Stephanie were trying to get back together?"

Her chin quivered. "He said Stephanie wanted to reconcile, but he didn't. We were going to get married as soon as the divorce was finalized."

This pretty young woman wanted to marry Randy Bennett? He had to have been more than thirty years older than her, and the years had not been kind to him. She could understand why Randy would have been infatuated with Jenna, but Alex was surprised that Jenna had returned his feelings. She also wondered if what Jenna had said was true, that Stephanie had wanted to remain married to Randy but he wanted a divorce. Stephanie had made it sound as if they both wanted to patch the relationship, although she had admitted that Randy wouldn't leave his girlfriend.

Jenna blew her nose into a tissue. "I don't understand why that horrible woman would want to kill him. Why would anyone? He was so funny and generous. He was the best person I knew."

The best person she knew? Alex thought back to the disheveled, unshaven man who'd entered Botanika begging for a potion. *It's true what they say,* she thought. *Love is blind.*

"Jenna, you should know that Lidia Sobieski is my aunt, and I'm certain she had nothing to do with Randy's death."

"You think the police were wrong?"

"I do. Lidia and Randy weren't friends, but she had no reason to hurt him."

Jenna nodded slowly. "I thought it seemed strange. He'd never mentioned Lidia, not even when I talked about how much I loved her shop." She exhaled. "Actually, I feel a little better if she wasn't involved. I didn't mean what I said about her being horrible. She was nice to me whenever I went to Botanika." She balled the tissue in her fist. "Are the police looking for another killer? At Stephanie, maybe?"

"They may be open to the possibility," Alex replied evasively. She pointed to the college textbooks. "You're in school?"

"Yes. Graduate school. Although I'm really behind on my schoolwork. I work two jobs, and I've been a bundle of nerves since Randy died." Jenna reached for her books. "I can't drop out, though. My student loans would come due, and how in the world would I pay them? Randy was going to help me find a job after I graduated. Now I don't know what I'm going to do."

Two jobs, student loans, and help getting a great job? That explained why someone as young and vibrant as Jenna would be interested in Randy. He would've provided financial security for her.

"I'm lucky the Wesleys are so kind," Jenna continued. "They've allowed me to cut back the hours on my internship. I told them someone in my family died." She paused. "Do you think that's wrong?"

Now this was interesting. "No. It's understandable." Alex set her elbows on the table and leaned closer. "You intern at Wesley, Inc.?"

Jenna nodded. "Yes. They're amazing."

"What do you do there?"

"Not much lately," she said. "But mostly I've been working on acquisitions. I research companies they might want to buy and put together a proposal. It's kind of boring unless you're into that stuff."

Alex smiled. "And it sounds like you're into it."

"I am. And it's perfect. I'm getting my MBA so I can do this type of work after I graduate."

Alex glanced around the shop for Celeste. She was also getting her MBA. Maybe she knew Jenna and could answer a few questions? But the barista was busy managing a long line of customers, tendrils of her hair escaping her ponytail. She caught Alex's eye and waved.

Jenna took a sip of her tea. "The Wesleys almost never have job openings. But I can hope . . ."

And she also interned at Wesley, like Celeste, Alex mused. She definitely had to speak with Celeste about the college student. Alex focused on Jenna, who was still talking about Wesley, Inc., employment opportunities.

Jenna shuffled her books around the table. "I've heard rumors that Tegan is retiring soon. If that's true, they're going to need some new résumés. Mine's already on file."

"So you think Tegan's retirement will create openings at the company?"

"Probably. If Dylan gets Tegan's job, then someone else would take his place, and so on," she reasoned. "They promote from within the company, which is great, don't get me wrong." She rested her chin on her hand. "But I'm getting out of school with a lot of loans. I can't afford to work my way up from the mail room."

As a business school graduate, Alex understood only too well how student loans could limit a person's career options. "And so that's why Randy was going to help you to get a good-paying position?"

"Right. Of course now . . ." Her voice trailed and her nose reddened. "I tell myself one day at a time, you know?"

"That's the only thing you can do when you lose someone you love," Alex said gently.

"You sound like you've been there, too."

"My dad died a few months ago. And my mom died when I was young."

Jenna tilted her head. "I'm so sorry."

"Thank you." She set a hand over Jenna's. "But if there's one thing I know, it's that we can get through this. One day you're going to look back and be amazed at how strong you are."

Jenna took a quivering breath and nodded silently. "Does it stop hurting?"

"No," Alex said. "But it stops hurting so intensely."

She glanced at the clock on the wall, which was shaped like a white ceramic mug of coffee. She'd been away from Botanika for long enough. "I should get back," Alex said. "It was nice to speak with you, Jenna."

The young woman smiled. "You too. I hope we see each other again."

"Why don't you stop by the shop sometime? I can even show you how we make that perfume you're wearing."

A look of gratitude softened Jenna's face. "I would love that. Do you have any of that Sweet Dreams balm? It sounds weird, but I have the soundest sleep when I use it."

"We have tons of it," Alex assured her. "I can even give you a discount."

* * *

After Jenna left, Alex made her way to the counter. Celeste was wiping sweat from her brow, but she grinned when she saw Alex.

"Hey, you."

"Hey, yourself." Alex settled onto a stool at the bar. "It was a madhouse in here for a while, wasn't it?"

"Yeah." Celeste nodded, grabbing a towel and wiping down the area in front of Alex. "That always happens when someone goes on break." She laughed, then nodded toward the dining area. "Everything okay? You seemed deep in thought with that other customer."

"About her . . ." Alex planted her elbows on the counter and leaned forward. "Her name is Jenna. She's in the same MBA program as you and interns at Wesley, Inc. What can you tell me about her?"

Celeste's eyes widened. "Really? I've seen her in here a few times, but never at school or at Wesley when I was there."

"Could be something . . . or nothing," Alex mused.

"Probably nothing," Celeste added. "There are about a thousand students in the MBA program. I suppose I can't know them all." She laughed.

"Right." Alex stood. "Okay then. I best be going. Don't work too hard."

As Alex left the café and stepped onto the sidewalk, a deep sadness for Jenna welled inside her. She felt sorry for the young woman, and she didn't see what she would have had to gain from murdering Randy. Jenna wouldn't inherit any money. To the contrary, she'd lost the possibility of an imminent wedding and a better job after graduate school. But if Jenna was telling the truth, it only made Stephanie more of a suspect in Alex's mind. If Jenna had nothing to gain from Randy's death, then it was equally true that Stephanie had nothing to lose.

Chapter Eighteen

When Alex and Minka came home that evening, Athena greeted them at the door with her leash in her mouth.

"I think she wants a walk," Minka observed with a grin.

"If only there was some way she could tell me." Alex laughed. "Okay, girl. Give me a minute to change."

Alex took her dog on a run away from downtown, back toward a quieter area of Bellamy Bay. When they hit the boardwalk by the beach, Alex let Athena off her leash so she could run after seagulls without pulling Alex into the vegetation. The beach was deserted except for a few gulls that landed in the sand, took a few steps, and took off again. Athena took a moment to roll around in the sand and pause with her legs up in the air. Then she flipped onto her stomach, barked at nothing, and continued running beside Alex.

"You keep things interesting, sweet girl."

Alex and Athena were approaching the part of town where the tourists stayed, a neighborhood of bed-and-breakfasts and a motel that faced the water. Tourist season was approaching, and after Memorial Day, Alex wouldn't be able to allow Athena to run on the beach at all, let alone without a leash.

After Memorial Day. Was Alex even going to be in town for another five weeks? Now that she was running along the water with Athena playing happily at her side, Alex didn't know that she wanted to leave. Since coming to Bellamy Bay, everything had felt different. Everything *was* different. She had learned the truth about her family and their powers—how could she return to Mundane life again?

Athena was venturing close to the waves, looking for a drink. Alex called her, and the dog sped up the beach and sat at her feet, tongue hanging out the side of her mouth. "I think that's enough of that, miss," Alex joked as she snapped the leash back on her collar. "If you drank that water, we'd both be very unhappy with the results."

They walked a few more feet to a dog-and-human water fountain on the side of the path. Alex stepped on a lever, and fresh water emptied into a metal sink at the bottom. Athena lapped at it eagerly.

While she was waiting for the dog to finish, Alex admired a white Victorian house called the Seaside, a quaint bed-and-breakfast. The structure was charming, with its wide front porch and antique lamppost marking the brick path to the entrance. A large brass pineapple decorated the door. Athena had just started pawing at the bowl and splashing when a couple emerged from the inn, holding hands. They paused on the porch to enjoy a long kiss. Alex did a double take. Could it be? Then the couple looked right out at the water, leaving no doubt as to their identity.

Stephanie Bennett and Edwin Kenley.

Alex crouched down and hoped they wouldn't see her. She'd thought they'd been awfully cozy at the Wesleys' charity event, but now she knew for sure that they were an item. How long had this been going on? Was Edwin the "other man" that Randy had used to justify having his own side relationship?

She waited while they walked around to the parking lot behind the inn. Once they were out of sight, Alex tugged Athena's leash. "Come on, sweetie. Run's over."

* * *

Lidia had finished knitting a long fluffy white scarf and had started on a matching cap. When Alex and Athena came in, she held up her work proudly. "It's going to be perfect for the winter months. Who wants it?"

"Oh, wow." Alex nodded politely, indicating she'd take it. It would certainly help keep her warm in the winter if she returned to New York. "It's beautiful." She unhooked Athena's leash and hung it up on a coatrack. Athena did a sweep of the downstairs, stopping to say a quick hello to Minka, Lidia, and Kamila. Then she plopped herself down on her favorite spot on the living room rug and sighed happily.

Minka giggled. "She had a good run?"

"I let her go off leash for a little while. It's one of the perks of owning a police academy dropout: she listens when I call."

The women were enjoying sweet iced teas and talking about their days. Kamila reached down to scratch Athena's back. "Aw, good girl," she cooed. "Too soft to be a police officer." Athena dutifully showed her belly.

"And how was your day, Alex?" Lidia asked.

Alex laughed, even though little of her day had been funny. She simply didn't know where to begin. "It was interesting," she said. "And I'm glad you asked."

She pulled up a large pillow and sat on the floor. Then she spent the next half hour relaying the day's events in detail. She told the women about the guidance spell Minka had cast the night before, and the enchanted water she'd served to Pepper. She stole a guilty glimpse at Kamila, but her cousin didn't appear angry or surprised. "Someone's going to need to keep an eye on Pepper now that she's digging into the Wesley family," Alex said. "Is there anything we can do to protect her?"

Kamila groaned. "You don't know her like we do. She was horrible in school. Arrogant, mean, always thinking everyone was jealous of her." She shook her head. "It's no surprise no one likes her, and you want to help her?"

Alex gave her cousin a hopeful look. "But she's helping us."

"You know what I think? Pepper Bellamy uses her position as a news reporter to get back at all the people she thinks disliked her when we were kids. She's power hungry."

"Even so, she may be integral in clearing your mother's good name."

Kamila rolled her eyes. "I won't like it, but I'll keep an eye on her. I don't live far from her house. I'll check in periodically and drive by her office, make sure there's no magic in the air."

"The Wesleys won't touch her if Kam's around," Minka said. "Even if she doesn't practice magic, she can spot it. If she catches them messing with a Mundane, she'll haul them in front of the Council for a shackle spell."

There was so much to learn about this hidden world in Bellamy Bay. "What does a shackle spell do?" Alex asked.

"It's the most severe form of punishment for a Magical," Lidia explained. "It renders their magic inaccessible. Sometimes the Magical forgets they ever had abilities."

"The Wesleys won't risk it," Kamila said. "Don't worry."

The heaviness in Alex's chest lightened. "Perfect. Thank you."

Then she told them about Jenna, and finally about her discovery that Stephanie and Edwin were very much a romantic item.

Minka fussed with some pillow tassels she worked out the possibilities. "Why would Stephanie want to reunite with Randy if she's seeing Edwin?" she asked aloud.

"She was going to lose a lot of money in the divorce," Kamila replied. "Randy owned sixty percent of Bay Realty. It could come down to money, not love."

"Maybe she really did love Randy and had regrets about the affair," Alex suggested. "But if I'm being cynical, she may have wanted to slow down the divorce proceedings for some reason, and talking about reuniting could do that. We know Edwin wants to sell the company. What if she was trying to influence Randy to sell so that she and Edwin could make a new life together?"

"So you think she might have tried to work out their marriage only as a favor to her boyfriend?" Minka frowned. "Man, that's cold."

Lidia set down the hat she was knitting and leaned forward in her chair. "How do we know they were trying to work things out? Stephanie could have been lying to throw suspicion elsewhere."

"We know because Jenna said the same thing as Stephanie," Alex explained. "They both said that Stephanie wanted to remain married to Randy, but ultimately he wouldn't leave Jenna." She jabbed her index finger into her palm for emphasis. "Stephanie had every reason to kill Randy. Now she has his sixty percent of the company and Edwin has the other forty. If they get married, they're each much wealthier than they were before Randy died."

"So Edwin had motive, too," Kamila noted.

"But it couldn't be Edwin," Minka said. "The guidance spell revealed that a Magical killed Randy."

"But we've already established that someone we know could be masquerading as a Mundane. Edwin is still a suspect," Alex pointed out.

Lidia snorted out a laugh. "That boring little man doesn't have a magical bone in his body. I'd wager the shop on that."

"But we can't discount him just yet, right?"

"I suppose," Lidia finally said.

"What about Stephanie Bennett as a Magical?" Alex turned to Lidia. "She has more motive than anyone else."

"If she is, she's not registered." A serious look crossed Lidia's face as she considered the discussion. "All Magicals are required to register with the Council. Is it possible some don't? Yes. Unfortunately, we don't have a litmus test. Unless she's shown her powers, no one would be able to tell."

"I never practice," Kamila explained to Alex. "If I moved somewhere else and didn't register with the local council, they would never know."

Alex laughed drily. "Yeah, that's what I did. Except unintentionally."

"Unregistered Magicals are a real threat," Lidia continued somberly. "If they don't comply with registration requirements, then they are probably not complying with Council safety regulations, either."

"And there's no . . . witch radar?" She laughed at the term. "No way to just know someone is a Magical without them saying anything?"

Kamila rolled her eyes. "Yeah, there is, kind of. If someone has recently practiced magic, you can smell it on them."

Magic had a smell? Alex almost laughed at the idea. "What does it smell like?" She chuckled. "Rainbows and unicorns?"

Lidia gave her a serious look. "No. Ozone mostly, the smell of electricity in the air. You'll recognize it as the scent in the air after a good rain. But the smell of magic has terroir, just like wine or coffee. It takes on the smell of its environment. If you're in the mountains, it may smell like pine trees, if you're at the beach . . . sea salt, for example."

"Yeah," Minka chimed in. " The scent can be masked, though. Anything stronger can hide it—perfume, car exhaust, cooking food . . . On the other hand, if you decide to really embrace . . . our heritage, your sense of smell will rival Athena's."

Kamila laughed. "Yeah, it's not common knowledge, but fish—and mermaids—have highly developed taste and olfactory systems, so once you begin practicing magic, you'll see your ability to smell increase."

"All true," Lidia interjected. "However, a very experienced witch can completely hide the scent if they're willing to use black magic to mask it." Lidia shook her head. "But it takes a toll on the health."

Alex took a moment to process all the information. It was a lot, and she still wasn't sure she understood everything. "Considering all of our suspects, the person who benefits most from his death is Stephanie."

"She must be an unregistered Magical," Minka said. "It makes sense. Would she have a reason to frame you, Mom?"

The silence stretched for so long that Alex wondered if Lidia had heard Minka's question. Lidia's face darkened, and she folded her arms into her chest. Finally, she spoke. "Yes, I believe she would."

The three women waited quietly for Lidia to continue. Alex held her breath, not wanting to miss a word. "I have done some things I'm not proud of," Lidia began. "I've kept it to myself for years, but it's time to come clean.

"Randy, Stephanie, and I all went to Bellamy College together, and we were very friendly. Stephanie and I were sorority sisters. Randy and Stephanie were an item, but Randy and I were always flirting. He was much cuter then." She smiled at the memory. "And then in senior year, Randy and Stephanie broke up. I kissed him one night, one thing led to another . . . we started dating. We didn't even hide it from Stephanie. I didn't care. I thought I was in love." She tucked her long hair behind one ear, suddenly looking much younger as she thought back to that time. "But we weren't in love, not really. And then when I was tired of him, I dumped him."

"Holy cow." Minka's jaw dropped. "That's cold."

Lidia winced. "That's not even the half of it. Randy and Stephanie reunited immediately, but she never forgave me. Our friendship was over. I never understood why she blamed me but not Randy. It takes two." She shook her head. "But I take responsibility for my actions. We were both wrong."

"Is that why you and Randy didn't get along? Because of bad blood between you and Stephanie?" Kamila asked.

"Not exactly. Randy was furious with me for breaking up with him. He went around telling everyone that I was a witch." Lidia reached up a hand to rub the tension from her temples. "I must have said some things to him. I don't actually remember. But I do know it didn't take long for the witch hunter to come."

Nausea roiled in Alex's stomach, and she wondered what type of witch hunter had come calling. She recalled her aunt telling her there were two kinds, the Puritanicals and the Traders.

Her aunt looked at her with despondent eyes. *He was a Puritanical. He only wanted to destroy our kind.*

Alex realized her aunt had heard her thoughts and telepathed her response. She looked around the room, realizing her cousins had heard the answer too. They locked eyes, and a feeling of sadness, heavy and dark, wrapped around them.

The three women waited intently while Lidia struggled to continue. Her eyes brimmed with tears and her chin quivered. "The witch hunter caught wind of the rumors that Randy had been spreading. But he got the name wrong, because he went after my aunt. Lilianna Sobieski, not Lidia." A tear streaked down one cheek. "He murdered her. Brutally. A jury said he was insane, and he'll be in an institution for the rest of his life, but all of us in the family knew he was a witch hunter. He knew exactly what he was doing."

"Oh, Mom." Minka sat on the arm of the sofa beside her and rubbed her back. "That's so terrible."

"My uncle and cousins moved far away. I hated myself for a long, long time. I couldn't eat or sleep, I was sick with guilt. Then I realized something." Lidia's face changed as she relived the memories, taking on a tortured appearance. "My cousins lost their mother, but it should have been *me*. By spreading those rumors, Randy sent the witch hunter. He's the one who said my name. He'd put us all in danger, and he knew it."

"Had you shown him your magic?" Kamila asked softly. "Did he know for certain that you were a Magical?"

"Oh yes, he knew," Lidia said, her face growing red as she continued. "He had become fond of my teas during college. Randy used to be an athlete, believe it or not. He'd get injured playing rugby, and then I'd give him a tea so he'd be back to perfect for the next game, just like that." She snapped her fingers. "I gave him teas to help retain information before exams, to heal colds, for good luck. But after my aunt died, I vowed that he would pay. I thought for years about what I would do to punish him for causing her death. And when I decided on the perfect revenge, I took action."

Alex's breath stuck in her lungs, but Minka voiced her question. "Did you kill him?"

"No," Lidia replied. Alex and her cousins released a collective breath. "But only because that would've been too quick."

Alex sneaked a look at Kamila. She'd been right about the ethical morass of practicing magic. She stared at her aunt, trying to hide her horror. God complex, much?

Lidia gave her a reassuring smile that didn't quite do the job for Alex, continuing her story. "Randy was fascinated with the idea of having the perfect life. He wanted the beautiful wife and the big house, but most of all, he wanted children. Maybe it had something to do with him being an only child, but he wanted a huge family. Lots of sons to carry on his name and legacy and business." Lidia lowered her voice to a whisper. "I made sure he never had them."

Kamila glared at her mother. "You made him sterile, didn't you?"

"That was one aspect, yes," she confessed. "I cast one dark-magic spell. That's all it took. If he and Stephanie tried fertility treatments, those would fail. And if they ever applied to adopt, they would be turned away."

Alex set her head in her hands and stared at her own feet. She recalled Randy's desperate words to her aunt in the shop. *Haven't you punished me enough?* "He knew, didn't he?"

Lidia nodded, slowly. "He came to me for help once, and I told him that what was happening was his own fault. I reasoned that if I was going to be tortured for the rest of my life, he should be, too."

"And Stephanie?" Alex said. "Did she know?"

"If she did, that would give her a good reason to take her own revenge, wouldn't it?" Lidia smiled painfully. "But she may not have known anything until recently. If she is a Magical, then she could have counteracted my magic at some point. She didn't." Lidia absently stroked the knot of soft yarn in her basket. "I'm not proud of any of this. I'd give anything to take it all back. But I can't. So I look at this"—she gestured to her ankle monitor—"as a form of punishment for my bad conduct. I may not be guilty of Randy's murder, but I'm not innocent, girls. Not by a long shot."

The air in the room had grown heavy and warm, almost stifling. The four women sat quietly, each of them lost in her own thoughts. Alex stroked Athena's soft ears and watched them twitch at the contact. Dogs were so much simpler than people.

"I've got to talk with Detective Frazier about Stephanie," Kamila finally said. "He needs to know that you two have a history."

"I thought you said that you weren't allowed to talk about this at work," Minka said.

"Let me speak with him," Alex said. When the women looked at her in surprise, she explained, "You don't want anyone at work to call your ethics into question, Kamila. And you said it yourself: you can't touch this case."

Kamila hesitated for a moment but then nodded. "Okay. You're right. But someone needs to say something." She pointed to Lidia. "Stephanie must've recently discovered what Mom did."

Her jaw clenched as she gazed at her mother. "She had every reason to frame Mom."

"But you can't say that Mom prevented Randy and Stephanie from having children," Minka said. "No Mundane will understand that."

"I'll just encourage him to take a closer look," Alex said. "If she's guilty, he'll find something."

Minka grew quiet. She had wrapped her arms around herself tightly and was staring at the floor.

"Minka?" Alex asked. "Are you okay?"

She glanced up, her expressional uncharacteristically somber. "Just whatever you do, be careful, Alex."

She didn't need to say anything more. Alex understood. If Stephanie Bennett had killed her husband, that meant she was an unregistered Magical. And if she was a Magical, one that didn't adhere to the rules of the Council, she was a deadly one.

Chapter Nineteen

The next morning, Pepper burst through the doors of Botanika in a cloud of grapefruit, basil, and vanilla. "Girl." She dashed over to Alex's side. "Have I got a scoop for you."

Alex was stacking soaps into a pyramid, and she grinned at Pepper's enthusiasm. "What's going on?"

"Tegan Wesley, that's what." Pepper stuck out her hip. "I went to visit her yesterday after our talk, remember?"

Alex nodded.

"Well, that woman is something else. She was so rude to me." She picked up a bar of soap and held it to her nose. "Yum. Smells like coconut." She took another deeper breath. "Makes me think of the beach, for sure."

"That's the idea," Alex grinned, knowing the soap was enchanted with the essence of the beach: the warmth of the sun, relaxing breezes, and clean fresh vibrations. It would also conjure happy memories of the beach if the customer had any.

"What does it do?"

"It's made with coconut oil, so it's moisturizing, but it also has sand from our very own Bellamy Bay beach to help with exfoliation and sea salt for a detoxification effect."

Pepper's eyes widened in interest. "I'll buy a few. Makes me think of going to the beach with my parents when I was little. Funny, I haven't thought of those trips in ages." Pepper grabbed a couple more. "So anyway, I asked her where she was the night of Bennett's murder, and she wouldn't tell me."

Of course not, Alex thought. *Because Tegan was at the Council meeting the night Randy was killed, and that's top secret.* But she listened intently as Pepper continued.

"Then I asked her about this land dispute with him, and she was furious."

Alex winced just imagining the conversation. "Yikes."

"Her face turned red, and I thought for sure she was going to start foaming at the mouth. Then she told me—get this—that I should keep my nose out of her family affairs and stick to writing fluff pieces." Pepper's eyes flashed. "Can you imagine? I don't write fluff. I'm an investigative reporter."

Alex set a hand reassuringly on Pepper's wrist. "You're a heck of a reporter, Pepper. Don't listen to her."

"I won't," she replied, and lifted her chin. "In fact, I'm more suspicious than ever. She's covering something, I swear it. Oh, wait. She had a message for you."

"Me?"

"Hold on, I want to get it right." She pulled her notebook out of her bag and flipped through it. "She said, 'Next time Alex wants to borrow a book from our library, tell her it's polite to ask first.'"

Alex's face went hot. "Noted," she said.

"I assume that's between you two." Pepper set the notebook back in her bag. "I'm just the messenger."

Minka had been right: Pepper was relentless once she sunk her teeth into a story. Alex liked having Pepper on her side, but even if Kamila was going to be watching her, she couldn't stand by idly and allow Pepper to put herself in harm's way. The Wesleys were like hornets: dangerous when provoked. "You know, I think it's a shame that no one has investigated Stephanie Bennett," she began. "She had more reason than anyone to kill Randy."

"She's going to be a very wealthy woman," Pepper said solemnly. "A source tells me the ink is drying on a lucrative deal to sell Bellamy Bay Realty."

"Already?" Alex gasped. If that didn't reveal a crystal-clear motive for murder, she didn't know what did.

"Yes," Pepper continued. "The whole company and the building, too. It's going to some company named Neptune Investments. I checked the secretary of state's website, but I can't find much. It's a company within a company within a company. Legit shady," she concluded with a flick of her hair.

"What about your family's company?"

Pepper paused. "What about them?"

"Weren't they the highest bidder before Bennett died?" Alex carefully placed a thick bar of soap at the top of the display pyramid. "Would they set up a shell company for the purchase?"

Pepper tipped her head to one side as she considered this. "Funny you mention it. My father is very tight-lipped about business, but he cares about public perception." Lines formed between her arched brows. "He might worry about what it would look like if CSC bought the company so soon after Bennett's death."

"That's understandable," Alex said. "Even if Edwin Kenley is eager to sell, people might talk about the timing." Despite his polite talk at the party, Bronson Bellamy had made it clear to the press that Randy Bennett had stood in the way of the sale to CSC.

Swooping in to close the deal mere days after Bennett's murder seemed tacky.

Alex could practically see Pepper wrestling with that idea as she stared down at her designer heels. But to Alex, Bronson Bellamy's decision to set up a difficult-to-trace company in an effort to avoid public scrutiny was natural. Bronson was a politician, after all.

Alex realized that this might be a way to get Pepper out of harm's way. If she was researching Neptune Investments, she wouldn't be bothering the Wesleys. "We should find out who Neptune Investments is, don't you think?"

The bell on the door chimed. Jenna entered and waved excitedly to Alex. She was dressed in skinny jeans, espadrilles, and a frilly apricot-colored blouse with capped sleeves . "I took you up on your invitation," she said. "I hope you don't mind."

"Of course I don't mind," Alex said, and took her hand. "Pepper, this is Jenna Hoffman. We met at the coffee shop yesterday."

"Hello," Jenna said shyly. "I told Alex how much I love Botanika, and she was nice enough to offer to show me around."

"Nice to meet you," Pepper said, but it was clear she was still thinking about Neptune Investments.

"You know, I was actually wondering if you have a job opening." Jenna's eyes were wide as she took in the numerous shelves of salves, ointments, teas, tonics, and candles. She finally focused on Alex. "My internship is almost over and my boss is cutting my hours. I have a lot of retail experience and I love your products."

Minka must have overheard, because she came running from the back of the shop.

"When can you start?" she asked Jenna. "If I don't get more inventory ready before Memorial Day weekend, we'll never catch up. Summer's our busiest time and Alex has been busy, uh, running errands." The cousins shared a glance. "If we have someone watching the floor, I could get something done."

Jenna's face brightened. "I don't have class today."

"She's getting her MBA," Alex explained to Minka.

"You're hired," Minka declared. "Come on, I'll show you around."

"Oh, okay." Jenna laughed lightly and stuck a hand into her bag. "I brought a résumé and some references—"

"Perfect. I'll call them later. We can really use the help." Minka ushered Jenna toward the back of the shop. "I'll show you where you can put your stuff."

Alex laughed as Jenna glanced over her shoulder with a big smile. "We'll chat later," Alex assured her. "Minka will keep you very busy." She turned back to Pepper, who was frowning. "Everything okay?"

"I was thinking about what you said. I need to know who is behind Neptune Investments."

"Can you ask your father?"

"He wouldn't tell me," Pepper replied. "Not if he was trying to conceal the company's identity. For some reason, he thinks I have a big mouth." She batted her eyelashes innocently.

Alex couldn't suppress a grin.

"I'm going to hit the library and do some research there, try to figure this out," Pepper continued. "But Stephanie is definitely next on my list. She was at the coffee shop just now. I should've asked her some questions there."

Alex tried not to look too excited. "She's there? Now?"

"Yeah, but I'm not going back. I'd rather talk to her when I know some more." She held up several bars of soap. "Can I buy these?"

Alex rang Pepper up, and once again they promised to keep each other informed. Minka was showing Jenna the teas, pointing to a chart that explained the different ingredients.

Once Pepper left the shop, Minka smiled coyly. "So, you're friends now?"

Alex laughed. "Not exactly. More a case of keeping your friends close and your enemies closer. But it's paying off." Alex was already untying her apron. "She just told me that a certain someone is at the coffee shop. I've got to get to her before she leaves."

Minka took a step backward. "Who are you talking about?"

Stephanie, Alex mouthed. She didn't want Jenna to overhear her talking about Randy's wife.

"Alex," Minka warned.

"I'll be careful, don't worry." She folded up her apron and stuck it behind the counter. She whispered, "Stephanie's not going to do anything to me in broad daylight with witnesses all over. She wouldn't dare."

She took off toward Coffee O'Clock at nearly a sprint. "Please be there, please be there," she whispered as she took the cement steps into the coffee shop two at a time. She pulled open the door and instantly saw Stephanie sitting at a table in the back, reading a book. Stephanie was wearing a flowery sundress and sling-backs, and her legs were bare—fitting for the warm spring day.

She marched in and headed straight over to Stephanie. Magical or not, Alex was furious that the woman thought she was going to get away with murder. "Stephanie, we need to talk."

She looked up from her book in alarm but composed herself quickly. "I have nothing to say to you," she snapped. "And if you're here to harass me, you'd better leave."

"Mind if I sit?" Alex pulled out the chair across the table. "The grieving-widow performance you gave the other day at your house was a good one. You're quite an actress, I'll give you that."

Stephanie eyed her. "I don't have any idea what you're talking about."

"Come on. I saw you and Edwin leaving that bed-and-breakfast yesterday. You told me how upset you were that Randy had a girlfriend, but you were seeing someone, too. Randy's business partner."

Her blue eyes scanned the shop nervously; then she leaned forward to hiss, "So what? We were in the middle of a divorce. Our marriage was failing."

"Then why did you tell me you were trying to work it out?"

"I don't owe you an explanation." Stephanie's voice echoed across the room, and patrons stopped to look.

Alex lowered her voice and held up her hands. "There's no need to make a scene."

"I'm not making a scene." Stephanie closed her eyes, visibly fighting for control. When she opened them again, she appeared calmer. "My husband left our marriage years ago. Woman after woman, night after night. He humiliated me. And yes, I discovered that Edwin and I had a lot in common. We were both victims of Randy's enormous ego. It's like he was unable to think of anyone but himself." She balled her fists in her lap. "But Edwin is different. He's sweet and he's faithful. I did love Randy. I gave my life to him, and I'm still devastated that he didn't feel the same way." Her jaw tightened and she looked down. "I don't know why I'm telling you this. It makes no difference now that Randy's dead."

Alex leaned in. "It makes a big difference if you killed him."

Stephanie blanched. Her mouth opened and closed, but no sound emerged. Alex thought she might begin shouting again, but her blue eyes narrowed into daggers and her cheeks flushed with rage. "I should sue you for even suggesting that."

"You know you hate my aunt Lidia. And you hated your cheating husband, too. So you decided to take care of them both at the same time."

"Yes, I despise your aunt," she spat out. "But I have nothing more to say about that. I didn't kill my husband, and if you continue to harass me, I'm going to contact the police."

"Too late," a deep voice said from behind her.

Alex turned around to see Jack approaching their table with a disapproving glare. "Is everything all right here?"

Alex groaned. "Just fantastic."

Stephanie shoved her novel forcefully into her bag. "I finished bringing Randy's clothes to the thrift shop, and I was looking forward to just having a quiet cup of coffee. You ruined that." She zipped her bag with bravado and skidded her chair backward on the wood floor. "Yes, I wanted to be with Edwin. Are you happy now? He's a better man than Randy ever was. And I'm not sorry Randy's dead. But that doesn't mean I killed him." With that, she stormed out of the coffee shop, her nose high in the air.

Jack watched her leave and then lifted his brows at Alex. "You okay? Things seemed a little tense."

"We were only talking," she scowled. "Everything's fine."

Jack pulled up the chair Stephanie had just abandoned. "Alex, the last time I saw you, you'd blown four tires. And now I see Stephanie Bennett announcing that she's not sorry her husband's dead, and something about a lover—"

"Edwin," Alex said. "Randy's partner."

Jack stopped to massage his forehead. "Yes. Of course." He sighed. "And here I thought small-town murder would be simple after working in New York City."

"Rookie mistake." Alex folded her hands on the table.

"My point is, either trouble's following you or you're looking for it. I tend to think it's the latter."

"You saw how upset Stephanie was, right? I thought she might slug me for a minute there."

"Most people don't like being accused of murder. In my experience, they don't take it well."

Around them, the shop had returned to normal. The smell of fresh-ground coffee beans wafted through the space, and the room was filled with the sounds of chatter. Alex turned her head and caught Celeste watching her and Jack as she knocked coffee grounds into the trash. The barista's eyebrows raised in question, but Alex only looked away, suddenly embarrassed by her own conduct.

"Alex, what are you doing here?" Jack spread his hands wide. "Why are you bothering a woman who just lost her husband?"

"I'm trying to solve this crime," she said earnestly. "My aunt had no reason to kill Randy. But you heard Stephanie. She's not sorry her husband is dead."

Jack nodded. "Yes. The entire town heard that."

"She's getting sixty percent of the company and all of their marital assets. I'm sure Randy had a life insurance policy, too." Alex counted the reasons on her fingers. "She's in love with Edwin Kenley, Randy's business partner. And now that Randy is dead, the two of them own the entire company, which is worth one hundred million dollars, Jack. And from what I hear, they've already found a buyer."

His expression was serious as he listened to her argument. "It's a lot of money," he agreed.

"It's more money than either of them would have ever seen if Randy Bennett hadn't suddenly died. And you know what else? Stephanie hates my aunt. Ask anyone in here." She waved an arm around the room. "They all heard her say it. She had every reason to frame her for murder. And she's probably the one who tried to send me off the Peninsula, too."

Jack eyed her. "We didn't find anything on your car. No signs of tampering."

"So you're telling me we'll never know who did it?" Even if she'd been correct, she was disappointed.

"It could have been a defect in the tires. If you want, we could send you the report and you can speak with the manufacturer—"

She knew that wouldn't go anywhere. There had been nothing wrong with those tires, design-wise. But she didn't want to have a lengthy conversation with Jack about it. "Yeah, that sounds good. In the meantime"—she edged closer to Jack—"what are you going to do about the fact that Stephanie Bennett murdered her husband but my aunt is under house arrest?"

He returned her steady gaze and said, "New evidence in the case, coupled with the information you've just shared, convinces me I need to investigate this further."

Relief surged in her chest. She'd done it. When Jack stood, Alex jumped up and gave him a hug. "Thank you, Jack. I knew I could count on you."

She only realized what she'd done when his body stiffened. Quickly, she released her arms and backed away, but the moment was officially weird.

"Sorry," she mumbled. "I got a little carried away."

He looked visibly torn as he looked from her to the patrons around the coffee shop. She thought she could hear his thoughts. *Small town. Gossip. Bias. Ethical violations.* The words were almost whispered in her mind, but she had no doubt that Jack was screaming in his.

"Wait. You said new evidence?"

"We finally had the opportunity to review all the security footage in the area."

"And?"

"And"—he leaned forward—"seems like Edwin Kenley paid his business partner a visit a few hours before he died."

"What?" She slapped a hand over her mouth and looked around the café, hoping no one had heard her. "You're kidding me," she said in a whisper.

He nodded. "We got him on a neighbor's security cam knocking on the door with an envelope in his hand. They worked together and it's probably nothing, but I'll look into it. He stayed about thirty minutes and then left. Bennett walked him to the door, so we know he was alive when he left."

"But if he put something in his tea and Randy drank it later . . ." She couldn't hide the excitement bubbling in her chest. They were one step closer to freeing her aunt. She wanted to wrap her arms around Jack and squeeze him tight again, but she restrained herself this time. They still had to cross all their *t*'s and dot all their *i*'s. There was another suspect on her list that needed investigating. I'm so grateful that you're looking into this, Jack . . . but there is one more thing I'd like for you to do." She rushed on when she saw his eyebrow arch in warning. "Just ask Bronson Bellamy what he was doing when the murder happened, and if anyone can corroborate his whereabouts."

His eyes widened, and he leaned toward her. "You want me to ask the mayor of Bellamy Bay if he killed someone?"

Sighing, she tried to look apologetic, but she really needed to know if the mayor had an alibi. "Yes."

He gave her a look of warning. "Careful, Alex," he said quietly. "Your questions are going to annoy the wrong people, and I don't want to get a call that you've been seriously injured or worse. You're chasing after a cold-blooded killer. Even the best people get desperate when they're cornered."

She swallowed. He was right; she'd been making some enemies. But now that Jack was going to investigate Stephanie and Edwin, Alex could stop her own sleuthing. "I'm done. I promise."

But Jack's expression soured. "I've heard that before. I don't want to hear promises. I just want you to be safe, got it?"

He meant well, but the hard tone of his voice stung. Clearly her investigation had struck a nerve. Maybe Jack really did care about her more than he was letting on. "Got it."

He gave her upper arm an affectionate squeeze before heading to the counter to give Celeste his order. Alex avoided the curious glances that followed her out of the coffee shop. She walked to a small park organized around a large mermaid fountain. She gazed at the structure and suppressed a laugh: another mermaid fountain? It seemed the water witches of Bellamy Bay were hiding in plain sight.

When the water was running, four bronze mermaids held shells that sprayed water out of their openings into the center of the pool. The park was empty. She sat on a bench and pulled her phone from her purse. Apologies were in order.

She hadn't heard from or spoken to Dylan since that nightmare of a party, but now she felt guilty about the way she'd treated him and how she'd sneaked around the Wesleys' library. She'd thought Captain Bellamy's journal would lead her to the killer, but perhaps she'd drawn connections that weren't there and embarrassed herself in the process. She was eager to help her aunt, but Alex had to consider whether she'd gone too far. Nervously, she found his phone number in her contacts list and waited to see if he would pick up. The phone had barely rung when he answered.

"It's Alex Daniels." She had forgotten to plan what to say, and now she stood, pacing to get her brain working again. "How are you?"

"I'm well," he replied, his voice guarded. "I was actually going to call you. Your car is finished. Minka's car, really."

Alex was speechless. How in the world would he know that? "I own some body shops in the area," Dylan explained. "It's an investment I made a few years ago."

"Oh. I had no idea."

He chuckled. "There's probably a lot about me you don't know." He softened his voice. "I was concerned when I heard about your accident. Are you all right?"

Her chest tingled at his concern, but now that Jack was onto Stephanie and Edwin, the issue would be resolved. Stephanie was a Magical and she was in cahoots with Edwin, plain and simple. Once she was arrested, the Council would place a shackle spell on her, Edwin would go to jail, and Alex wouldn't fear any more attacks. "Yes, thank you. Look, I'm calling you because you're right, there's a lot about you I don't know, and I unfairly judged you. I want to apologize for that."

"I accept your apology, and I hope you'll consider having dinner with me again. Just you and me, no crowds. My place?"

"I do hate crowds." Alex smiled.

"So what do you say? Tomorrow night?"

Alex hesitated. Was this a date? No, this was just two friends meeting for a meal. And that was the truth. Even so, she wondered why her stomach suddenly filled with butterflies. "That sounds lovely," she grinned, realizing that she really, really wanted to see him again.

"I'll pick you up at Lidia's."

"No," she said, a bit too firmly, and then lightened her tone. Even if the Wesleys weren't responsible for Randy's death, there was still plenty of bad blood between the families, and Alex didn't need the additional drama. "Why don't we meet somewhere else? On the beach? In front of the Seaside Bed and Breakfast?"

To her relief, Dylan understood. "I'll be there. And when you arrive here, your car will be waiting."

After they disconnected the call, Alex headed back to Botanika. All in all, she felt great. It was only a matter of time before Jack dropped the charges against Lidia, and Dylan didn't hate her. She was smiling as she opened the door to the herbal apothecary. "Hey, Minka. How's Jenna's first day going?"

She froze one step into the shop.

Bryn was standing in the middle of the floor, her brilliant blue eyes practically glowing. "There you are," she hissed. "We need to talk."

She was wearing a pinstriped skirt suit and high heels, and her hair was pulled into a severe knot. As usual, Bryn looked poised, stunning, and pissed off.

Alex caught sight of Minka alone at the back counter, looking shaken. "Where's Jenna?"

Her voice was weak. "She ran out to get us doughnuts. Her treat. She wanted to do something nice for us since we gave her a job."

Alex was sick and tired of Dylan's sister being a bully. "What do you want, Bryn?" she asked, lacing her voice with boredom.

"You've got a lot of nerve," she spat. "I erased all of Pepper's memories about that journal. So why is she messing with my family again? I know you sent her. You're obsessed with my family."

Alex scoffed. "I don't control Pepper Bellamy. But if she's asking questions, I suggest you answer them. She's relentless."

Bryn's crimson lips twisted into a sneer. "She's bothering my mother, just like you did. I have a low tolerance for that."

Alex returned her glare. "And I have a low tolerance for your attitude, Bryn. You should leave."

Bryn raised an eyebrow. "You have no idea who you're messing with. Or what I'm capable of." With that, she brushed past Alex and strutted for the door, pausing to point at the ceiling. "You should get that fixed."

Alex followed her gaze. "Get what fixed?"

There was a sound like a gunshot. Alex shrieked and ducked behind a table. But it wasn't a gun. Water poured through the ceiling. Minka yelped in surprise, and Alex stared in shock as the water spilled right onto a display of soaps. Bath bombs fizzed on the floor, turning the water into a rainbow-colored stream.

Bryn smiled. "Sounds like a pipe burst." And with that, she walked out the door.

Chapter Twenty

Minka found a large brown wastebasket in the back room and Alex found a mop.

"Unbelievable," Minka grumbled as she tossed the melted soaps into the trash. "All of this work is gone."

She'd been able to stop the water with a flick of her wrist, but that still left a broken pipe and plenty of damage to the shop. They'd called a plumber and posted a sign on the door explaining the unexpected closure.

Poor Jenna had returned with a box of baked goodies only to hear that the shop was closed for the rest of the day. "It's just a fluke," Alex had assured her. "We'll be back in business tomorrow."

Jenna offered to help clean, but Minka told her to take the rest of the afternoon off.

"I really like her," Minka confided to Alex as they cleaned. "She picks things up quickly."

"She loves that lavender-and-lemon balm your mom makes. The one for sweet dreams," Alex said.

"That's good to know. I'm going to make her a basket of products to take home and try. I'll be sure to include that one."

Minka paused. "I feel terrible that Bryn pulled this on her first day."

"It's not your fault." Alex dragged the mop across the floor, but it was like trying to soak up a lake. "And we're going to get everything done, don't worry. Even if we have to come in early and leave late. And did I mention that Jack is going to be looking at Stephanie Bennett and Edwin Kenley now? The mayor too. Your mom may be back at the shop sooner than you realize."

Minka's eyes brightened. "Oh, that would be so wonderful. I miss having her here. No offense, Alex," she added.

"None taken at all."

"Don't even bother with the mop. We're water witches, remember?" Minka swept a pile of soaps into the trash and pushed the receptacle aside. "We can command water. Come here. I'll show you how it's done."

Minka went into the back room and came back with a bucket. She set it on its side, away from the edge of the water. "You just have to tell it where to go," she explained. "If there's no magic around, water will follow the rules of nature and physics. But if there's a witch . . ."

She pointed to the water, and immediately it formed a stream and ran straight into the bucket. When it was full, Minka turned the bucket upright again. "This is going to take forever," she mused. The water sloshed around her shoes as she walked.

"Why don't we move the water outside?" Alex suggested. "Cut out the bucket entirely."

"Excellent idea. You want to try it? Just clear your mind and focus."

Alex rubbed her hands together. Clearing her mind was easier said than done. She closed her eyes and took a few deep breaths.

When she opened her eyes again, she focused her gaze on the water. Pointing to it, she whispered, "Go outside."

The bright colors on the surface of the water rippled and danced. Then they arched in the direction of the doorway, almost as if they were showing the way out. The water collected and ran in a single, gentle stream under the crack in the shop door. Alex grinned. "It works."

"Nicely done. You're a natural."

With a rush of confidence, the water picked up speed. The current bumped against the door in a pileup as every droplet hurried to obey Alex's command. The two women stood side by side, watching as the water between the floorboards gathered to join the running stream. Within minutes, the floor was bone-dry.

"Whew. That was hard," Minka joked, and checked the time on the cell phone in her back pocket. "The plumber isn't coming until four, right?"

"That's what they said, yeah."

Minka fluttered her lips. "We can't open until that pipe is fixed, but you don't need to stick around if you don't want to."

Alex was torn. She wanted to track down Edwin and ask him about the pending Neptune Investments deal, but she didn't want to be unfair to Minka. "I don't want to leave you here all by yourself."

Minka waved a hand. "Don't worry about me. I have a romance novel and a dark-chocolate bar. And I know you're going to run off to interview a suspect, so you don't need to tell me."

Alex bit her lower lip. "My thoughts are loud, aren't they?"

"Deafening." Minka gave Alex a hug. "Be careful. I mean it when I say that I'm fond of you and I don't want to lose you again."

Alex tightened their embrace. "You can read my thoughts. Do they sound mad at you?"

She laughed. "I've heard worse."

*　*　*

Alex didn't have a car, so she called a taxi to take her to Edwin Kenley's office. The drive took so long that she feared he'd entered the wrong address into his GPS. How could they possibly still be in the same town? And when the car stopped in front of a gracious, white colonial, Alex knew there had been a mistake. "This can't be right," she said. "It looks like someone lives here."

"Fifteen Seashell Way?" he asked. "This is the place."

That's when she noticed the unobtrusive wooden sign staked beside the driveway that advertised Bay Realty. "Oh, you're right. It doesn't look like a business, does it?"

"No miss, it sure doesn't."

She closed the door to the cab and stepped out onto the driveway. No wonder it had taken them so long to reach this property. The winding roads had led them to the very top of Bellamy Bay. From here she had a view of the arc of the bay itself, the cluster of homes and businesses comprising downtown, and the mansions on the Peninsula. The land was isolated because it was surrounded by the Captain John Bellamy Homestead Nature Preserve, which made this spot especially peaceful. Alex spotted the Wesley, Inc., headquarters sparkling like a quarter in the sunshine off in the distance. She'd thought the view from that building was breathtaking, but this was even better. This was where one would go to see everything that was happening in town.

The building itself was stately, traditional architecture. Alex took a moment to admire the clean lines and the symmetry of the structure, from the generous windows to the large pillars. The lawn was flawlessly clipped and already a lush green. Bright tulips brought hues of red and yellow to the flower beds. Standing on the front porch, she peeked into a window and saw the receptionist raising a mug of something to her lips as she stared at her screen. The woman looked up, and Alex quickly pressed herself against the side of the building.

She needed to get inside and up the stairs to see Edwin without anyone stopping her. Closing her eyes, she took a deep breath and visualized the receptionist's body filling with liquid, so much so that she was about to have an accident if she didn't go to the bathroom right now. *Go to the bathroom. You need to go really bad.* Alex peered into the window again. To her delight, the woman stood up, clutching her torso, and ran down the hall.

With the coast clear, Alex confidently entered the office, buoyed by her successful use of magic, and took in her surroundings. She found a directory on the wall indicating that Edwin's office was upstairs. Alex froze when she saw three employees gathered at the top of the stairs, talking. She glanced down at her jeans and T-shirt, cringing. She definitely didn't fit in here. *Here goes nothing,* she thought as she ascended the stairs. As she approached the trio, Alex lifted her chin and focused her thoughts. *Ignore my clothes. I look like I belong here. Ask me how you can help me.*

A woman smiled. "Can I help you find someone? You look lost."

"Yes, I'm looking for Mr. Kenley."

She pointed to the end of the hall. "Down and to the right. He has the big corner office. You can't miss it."

Alex thanked her and continued on her way. *Yes!* She was finally getting the hang of it. If she could've jumped into the air and clicked her heels, she would've. Instead, she thought about what she would say to Edwin when she found him.

When she approached his office, she discovered the door was conveniently open. He was standing in front of a shelf, book in hand. He whirled around when she knocked on the door, and the pleasant look on his face quickly went ugly. "Who let you in?"

She put on an easy smile and stuck a thumb over her shoulder. "There wasn't anyone at the front desk. Do you have a couple minutes, Mr. Kenley?"

He was taller than her, but thin and hunched from years of bending over a desk. Physically, Alex didn't fear him, but she didn't like the way he looked at her at all. His eyes hardened. "Funny. I was just thinking about you." He gestured toward his office and waited for her to enter before he closed the door. "Have a seat."

He walked behind a rather modest L-shaped desk and sat down himself. "Stephanie just called me in a panic. The police showed up at her house, asking questions about Randy's death. This came after you cornered her in a crowded coffee shop and accused her of poisoning him in front of half the town."

She fought to retain her composure, but she was secretly elated that Jack had already been to Stephanie's house. *He said he would and he is following through*, she thought. *Because Jack is a straight shooter who does what he says he will do.* "I'm not sure what you're implying, Mr. Kenley," she said cautiously. "The police would only investigate Stephanie if they had a reason." *And they're about to investigate you*, she thought with a measure of enjoyment.

"They already arrested Lidia." His face reddened, and a fat blue vein in his forehead swelled. "What kinds of rumors have you been spreading?"

"No rumors. On the contrary, I'm trying to get the facts of this case straight. For example, I'd like to know who is behind Neptune Investments, and why are you and Stephanie selling this business to them so soon after Randy's death?"

A shadow crossed his face, and his snarl relaxed. "Neptune Investments? Is that what this is about?"

"The timing is a little suspicious, don't you think?" Alex might be provoking a cobra, but she continued anyway. "Tacky at best."

But Edwin appeared relieved that the sale of the company was at the root of her suspicions. "We haven't signed anything. We've only been in discussions. And in fact, Randy and I were speaking with Neptune about the sale before he—" He paused. "Passed away. Stephanie is only agreeing to continue negotiations, nothing more."

"So there's no purchase-and-sale agreement?"

He shook his head. "None whatsoever. And if that's the reason the police are after Stephanie . . ." Edwin shrugged. "Then we'll table the whole thing. Six months. A year. Whatever is the appropriate mourning period in this stupid town." He nearly spat the words. "And then we're getting married and moving out of here. I can't wait." The color in his cheeks had returned to normal and the vein had receded, but his irritation was palpable.

"You don't like Bellamy Bay?" Alex asked.

He choked out a laugh. "No, I don't. In fact, I hate it. Everyone needs to know everything about you. It's not the kind of place where you can blend in and simply be who you are." He turned his chair to look out the window, keeping his profile to Alex. "Randy and I met years ago. I was working as an architect in a firm in Raleigh, designing office buildings. He had this great piece of land that he said he wanted to build an empire on."

Edwin chuckled. "Randy had a way of pulling people into his vision. Next thing I knew, we were designing this very office together and I'd become his chief architect. I agreed to hold forty percent of the company. It seemed fair, considering all the money Randy invested. Big mistake." His face grew serious. "You know what I got for all of my hard work and sacrifice? A stroke. My doctor said that if I don't change my lifestyle, I will die young. And when I told Randy I wanted out, he wouldn't agree to sell. He didn't care about me. He didn't care about anyone but himself."

Alex studied him, noting again the vein pulsating in the center of his forehead. Did Edwin have a temper? "Couldn't you have sold your interest to him?"

"Not for what I could sell it to a company like Neptune for." Edwin turned back to face her. "They drove up the price beyond my wildest dreams. They said they would beat any offer, and they did, and then some."

Alex whistled. "Wow. Did they tell you why they wanted this company so badly?"

"They see tremendous growth potential. We've established ourselves as the leading name in luxury coastal properties in the Southeast. Neptune wants to expand."

That kind of ambition sounded like what she'd come to expect from the Bellamys. They had named a town and a prestigious college after themselves, so why wouldn't they want to spread their influence?

"Randy and I never wanted to move beyond this region," Edwin continued. "This was what we wanted."

"What the two of you built is very impressive."

"I have a team of talented architects and a set of proven design systems. Randy has me to thank for our company's success," he said bitterly. "But he wouldn't sell. The price didn't matter. My opinion didn't matter. For Randy, nothing was enough."

She swallowed hard. Betrayal was a great motivation for murder. Was she staring into the eyes of Randy's murderer? She smiled nervously at him. "Does Stephanie want to sell to Neptune?"

"Yeah, she does." Then, realizing that he'd just given Stephanie motive to murder her husband, he said, "She wants a fresh start, now that Randy's gone. Stephanie doesn't know how to run this business, and she doesn't care to learn. She's talked about living in this building once the company is sold, but as much as it looks like a home, it's really not." He smiled sadly. "Clever design, don't you think?"

"I thought you were selling the land with the business?" Pepper had said the land was part of the deal.

"No way. This is the best piece of real estate in Bellamy Bay." He shook his head. "It's too late, anyway. We've submitted an application to build an apartment building on the northern edge of the lot. Our long-term plans include offices and restaurants. Mixuse. It's my design," Edwin added. "It's going to be spectacular."

"Assuming the plans are approved," she noted.

"They will be. I have Mayor Bellamy's support. The zoning commission will do whatever he tells them to."

Alex recalled Edwin schmoozing with Bronson Bellamy at the charity auction. She smiled politely. Maybe Bronson and Edwin were in on this together? And Stephanie? Her temples began to pound at the possibilities. "It sounds like you have it all figured out."

He folded his hands on his desk and leaned forward. "I don't know you, Alex. I don't know why you're fixating on Stephanie for this crime, but she's innocent."

It's not just Stephanie that looks good for this crime. It's you too.

She wanted to ask him point blank what he'd been doing at Randy Bennett's house the night he died, but she knew she should wait and let Jack do it. She decided to try another strategy. "Tell me, does Stephanie take any interest in the supernatural?"

"Strange question." Edwin was watching her with interest now. "No, on the contrary, it was Randy who was superstitious."

Alex narrowed her eyes, trying to assess his manner and gestures. Trying to spot the signs that he was lying. "By superstitious, do you mean he believed in good and bad luck?"

"Why?"

His voice was guarded, but Alex smiled disarmingly. "He came into Botanika to purchase Good Luck tea, that's all."

"That's because he was obsessed with Lidia," Edwin blurted out. "He had this idea that she was out to get him. Every time something bad happened—someone scratched his car or we lost a client, anything—he'd do something weird to counteract it."

Sitting back in her chair, Alex felt disappointment seize her. She had the sense that he was telling the truth. "Like what?"

"Ridiculous things, like throwing salt over his shoulder or carrying a rabbit's foot or crystals. He'd get agitated if a black cat crossed his path, and he was a bundle of nerves on Friday the thirteenth. It was a joke around the office, except he didn't laugh. One night after a few drinks, he confided that Lidia had magical powers and that she was out to get him. That she practiced witchcraft." His gaze didn't stray from hers. "Was Randy right? Does Lidia believe herself to be a witch?"

Edwin didn't appear to have any inkling of Lidia's true powers—or of Stephanie's, for that matter. He considered this to be a matter of paranoia. "Of course Lidia doesn't have anything to do with black cats or Friday the thirteenth," Alex said lightly. "But if Stephanie knew about Randy's so-called obsession with Lidia hurting him, doesn't it make sense that she'd frame her for his murder?"

Edwin raised an eyebrow. "Lots of people knew about Randy's fears, myself included. Do you think I poisoned him?"

And there it was. Her opening. "I don't know what to think, honestly. But I've heard you were seen on security footage visiting Randy the night he was killed." She held her breath, wondering if he was about to reveal himself as the murderer, or try to attack her, or . . .

But no. He sat calmly in his seat with a slight look of distaste directed at her. "I knew that would come out eventually. Actually, I'm relieved." He gave her a sickly smile. "Apparently I was the last person to see him alive."

"Yeah. And?"

"And I was delivering papers. That's it."

"Paperwork related to Neptune Investments?"

He rolled his eyes. "This again?"

She pushed on. "From what I understand, it's a company within a company. Do you know who owns it?"

He chuckled. "I let my lawyers handle that. As long as their cash is good, what do I care?"

"Well, I care." She grabbed a pen and a sticky note from his desk and wrote down her cell phone number. "I'm trying to clear my aunt's name. Call me if you think of anything that could help her. Please."

He shot her a bored look. "I doubt I'll—" Edwin suddenly stopped and stared at something behind Alex. She followed his gaze. The receptionist was standing in the doorway, a look of confusion on her face.

"Sir?" the receptionist interrupted. "The police are here to see you. They told me it was urgent."

Edwin rose as Jack entered the room.

"Mr. Kenley?" Jack said, before noticing Alex. "What are you doing here?" He sounded exasperated.

"Talking." Alex stood and put on her most innocent smile. "We met at a charity event last week, so I stopped by to say hello."

A muscle on Jack's jawline moved. "Alex, can I speak with you?"

"Detective," Edwin said, "what's all of this about?"

"I have a few questions for you, Mr. Kenley. Nothing that should take too long. But first I need to speak with Ms. Daniels for a moment."

Jack led Alex out of the office and back into a private area off the hallway. When he was certain they were alone, he whispered, "What are you doing? I thought I told you to let me handle this."

"I know," she said, "but I had some questions for Edwin too."

Jack closed his eyes and pinched the bridge of his nose. "Stephanie Bennett is a dead end. We checked her alibi. She was out of town at a spa the days before Randy died. She returned to town the morning we found him dead. She may have had motive to kill her husband, but she didn't have opportunity."

Alex stared at him. "That's not possible. Of course Stephanie killed him. She's the only one—"

"She didn't." Jack's voice commanded her attention. "You have to let this go. We were able to eliminate her in a matter of minutes. She gave us receipts for spa treatments and names of witnesses."

What about one of those spells for trouble? she wanted to ask him. But how crazy would she sound, explaining to him that Stephanie might be an unregistered Magical with the ability to be in two places at one time . . . probably? Desperate, Alex grabbed his arms. "But you arrested the wrong person."

"I should also tell you that I made a discreet inquiry into the mayor's schedule with his assistant." He paused for effect. "He was two towns over at a mayors' retreat on creating more green spaces in the community. The meeting was taped for one of the local public-access channels." He gave her a concerned look. "He didn't do it either."

"Okay, I get it. The mayor's innocent; I can totally buy that. But Stephanie's different. She has a reason to frame Lidia, a reason to kill her husband, there's an affair, and she may be—" She stopped short of saying the word *Magical*. He needed context, but she just couldn't. She huffed in exasperation.

"She may be . . . what?" When Alex didn't speak, he smiled gently at her. "Look, I understand you want to believe that your aunt is innocent, but the evidence suggests otherwise." He gently twisted his arms out of her grip. "Allow me to do my job without civilian interference."

"What about Edwin? He just told me he was the last person to see Randy before he died."

"You know, I regret telling you about the footage now." He shook his head wearily. "I will talk to him about it, but you have to let this go."

"I know, but his alibi is so weak."

"Alex, leave it alone."

"But—"

He held up a hand to silence her. "No buts."

Her throat tightened. This was so unfair. She had to learn more about those spells for trouble. How had Stephanie pulled this off? And how was Edwin involved? Everyone knew it was always the spouse. And in this case, the spouse had an accomplice. An accomplice with motive. She shot Jack a frustrated look. She was not letting this go. Not when she was this fired up. Not when she was this close to figuring it all out. "There's something we're missing."

Jack sighed. "Just stay out of my case, okay, Alex?"

She lifted her chin. "I'm afraid I can't make any promises. Not so long as my aunt is under house arrest while the real killer goes free."

Jack clenched his jaw. "Then you'd better be careful about interfering with the investigation. I don't treat that kindly."

"I can't interfere in an investigation you're not conducting, Detective."

She turned before he could say anything to stop her. Even if he had, she wouldn't have listened. Edwin was standing in the doorway to his office, watching the exchange. Their eyes met. Alex lowered her head and walked toward the exit.

Chapter
Twenty-One

That evening, Alex took off her shoes and walked on the beach. She would be meeting Dylan soon, but she'd left early to clear her head. Walking on the beach was only second to running on the beach for the best way to clear her mind. The sand was cool and the wind off the water whipped the hem of her dress around her legs, but she was too absorbed by her own thoughts to give it much thought.

Yesterday she'd been so hopeful about Jack investigating Stephanie, but that had been short-lived. Now that he was convinced Stephanie had an alibi, Alex was back to square one. The Magical element was a complication. Alex couldn't explain to Jack that Stephanie had somehow used her powers to create an alibi so that she could poison her husband. She had to find something a Mundane would understand.

She sat on the sand, drawing her knees close to her chest. The skin on her legs was pocked with gooseflesh. As she watched the sun hovering above the horizon, Alex ached for her mother. This was where she had vanished under the waves, never to surface again. The police had said she was caught in an undertow and pulled out to sea, but Alex had prayed each night that she would see her mother at the breakfast table. All she wanted was to wake up from the nightmare.

She'd often thought about the things she would have done with her mother had she lived, like shop for prom dresses and talk about her boyfriends. Now she knew there was so much more they would have done together. Her mother could have taught her about magic and how to operate within this confusing world. She could have sent her out prepared for the challenges she'd face. Maybe then, Alex would know how to help her family out of this situation.

"I miss you, Mom," she whispered.

Alex swirled shapes in the sand and wiped them away again, drawing hearts over and over, as if the images could seep into the water and bring her back.

She checked the time on her phone and saw a series of texts from Pepper. All of her research on Neptune Investments had come up empty. *This is a company that wants privacy*, she wrote. *It's not even a domestic corporation.* An international company wanted to purchase Bay Realty? Who owned that company? Was it Bronson Bellamy? Or someone else?

Or perhaps the sale of Bennett's company—like his divorce—had nothing to do with the reason he was murdered. She'd operated from a series of assumptions, but Alex had to face the fact that she might be wrong. There might be something she was missing entirely.

She rose to her feet and brushed the sand off her legs and dress. Now she wondered if she'd dressed too nicely for her dinner with Dylan, or not nicely enough. She was wearing a blue cocktail dress and carrying heels, but she didn't know what to expect. Dylan had mentioned they would have dinner at his house, but did that mean they were going to be making spaghetti in the kitchen together? Or was he imagining a four-course meal by candlelight?

Her stomach turned with nerves. What if Bryn was there? Or—heaven help her—Tegan? She'd felt braver about smoothing over tensions before this moment.

The water was receding. Alex hadn't noticed, but the tide had been moving out, and quickly. Only puddles remained where the waves had lapped minutes before.

Alex approached the area, wondering if the low tide would reveal any sea glass. Suddenly her heart began to race and the air was filled with electricity. She gasped as the water mounted in the distance, forming an enormous wall. She couldn't stop staring at the water, almost mesmerized by the sight before her.

Her feet felt glued to the sand, and her attention focused on the water. It was almost hypnotic. Multiple shades of blue swirled together, climbing toward the sky. It was beautiful. It was frightening. *It's a tidal wave*, she realized with a start. With a scream, she took off in a sprint for the boardwalk, but she was too far from the stairs—she'd never make it in time. She looked over her shoulder.

The wave had to be twenty feet high, and it was coming right at her.

There was no time to get to higher ground. She wrapped her arms around a boulder and willed her muscles to hold on. A bone-chilling wave slammed her against the rock. Her body rose and floated away from shore. Alex tried to scream. She was pushed below the icy surface. Desperately she clawed at the black water. It held her down, drawing her deeper. *Not like this*, she thought. *Not like my mother.* Her lungs burned. She tumbled deeper into the darkness. Alex no longer knew which way was up, or how far she was from shore. Something hard knocked against her leg, sending shards of pain. She screamed and took in a lungful of water.

Not like this.

The water released its hold and flung her violently down onto the sand. The waves receded again, leaving her on her hands and knees, choking as she struggled to regain her breath.

"Alex," a voice called from far away, but she didn't reply. She was staring at the pool of blood gathering at her legs.

Someone lifted her. "I've got you. Come on."

Numbly, she allowed herself to be moved, too tired and stunned to fight. It was Dylan. He was carrying her away from the water. No, he was carrying her *through* the water, which had parted like the Red Sea in the Bible to reveal a passageway back to shore. "There's a path," she whispered, and pointed at the dry sand beneath them.

"I made it," he said. "You were about to drown."

"Oh." She rested her head against his shoulder. She was so tired, and her chest was heavy.

Dylan carried her over the sand and up the stairs to the boardwalk. Once they reached safety, he eased her onto a bench. "Alex, look at me."

She struggled to focus her eyes on him.

"Bleeding," she whispered.

A burst of white flashed across her vision. Fire in her face. Her cheekbone was probably fractured. Her lungs wouldn't work the right way. She coughed up a mouthful of salt water.

"Let me help you."

He set his hands on her arms and went very still. Her nerves tingled under his touch. The energy gathered until it burned, flaming across her body.

"What are you doing?" Terror squeezed her voice.

His dark eyes met hers. "I'm healing you."

Alex ground her teeth, helpless against the pain of energy coursing in her veins. "It hurts," she gasped, screwing her eyes closed.

"Stay with me, Alex." His voice was distant but soothing. "Look at me." Somehow Dylan was calm as he burned her from the inside out. She held his steady gaze. "That's right," he said. "Just keep your eyes on me."

The pain surged faster now, traveling in waves up her body. Suddenly Alex's lungs lightened. She leaned to one side and coughed, releasing what seemed like buckets of water. Her cheek was hot and tight, and her leg felt like it was being stitched together from the inside. She groaned. "Stop. It hurts too much."

Instantly, the pain ended. Alex fell to her side. "Alex." Dylan lifted her face to look in her eyes. "Talk to me. Please. Tell me I got here in time."

She inhaled a sharp, frosty breath that felt bottomless. Her lungs were clear. She touched a hand to her cheekbone, but it felt normal. There was no hint of the wound on her leg.

"You saved me," she gasped. Overcome, she flung her arms around his shoulders as tears slid down her cheeks. "I thought for sure I was going to die. M-my mother drowned there." Was this what her mother had experienced?

Dylan smoothed his hand down her hair and held her tightly. "I know, darling. But you're safe. Did I miss anything?" He pulled back and studied her battered figure, which actually didn't feel quite so battered anymore. She felt almost euphoric. "Your cheek is better, but your face will be tender for a few days. The artery in your leg is closed again."

"Artery?" She glanced down. Blood covered her dress, but there was no sign of a cut on her leg. Then she saw Dylan's blood-soaked white shirt and gasped. "Are you—did you—"

He glanced down. "No, that's from you. That wound on your leg alone would've killed you. You would've bled out. What hit you out there? No, never mind," he shook his head. "It doesn't matter." Dylan sat back on his heels and grasped his head in his hands. "Someone just sent a giant wave after you. If you can't protect yourself, stay away from the water."

Alex looked down at the ground. "I'm glad you were here."

"You're lucky I was here. You would've died." He gestured out to the water as his voice rose in anger. "Parting the ocean is basic magic for our kind, Alex. Do you really know nothing about this?"

"I guess not." She shivered as a gust of wind hit her body. Her skin was ice and her teeth were chattering, but the tear that rolled down her cheek was hot. "I don't know why you're yelling at me. I didn't do anything wrong."

He took a breath. His face softened, and he set a hand on her knee. "You're right, I'm sorry." She noticed for the first time that he was wearing a suit. He peeled off his coat and wrapped it around her shoulders. "Come on. Let's get you out of here."

Alex held up a bare foot. "I lost my shoes. She looked back over the water. "They were designer, too."

"I'll bring you back to your aunt's home, and you can get another pair of shoes."

"No, I don't want my family to panic. I'll just go barefoot."

"That's the most ridiculous thing I've heard today." He rose to his feet. "Give me a minute."

She sat on the bench and waited while Dylan walked back down the stairs to the water. A gentle wave hit the shore. He bent down to pick up something from the sand and lifted his hand in the air to show her.

She grinned as he bounded up the stairs and proudly presented her shoes to her. "Your heels, madam."

"How did you do that?" She picked a strand of seaweed out of one toe and scooped some mud out of the other.

"I asked," he said, and offered his hand to her. "You'd be surprised at what's possible when you ask the ocean. She's very generous."

"She?" Alex leaned her back against the bench. "The ocean is a woman?"

"The ocean has a feminine energy." He gazed at the body of water thoughtfully. "All life came from the ocean," he said as he took to one knee. "Some of us more recently than others." He helped her foot into one wet shoe.

Alex glanced back over the water. "That water has taken a lot from me," she replied, her throat thickening with emotion. "I don't trust it. I don't trust *her*."

Dylan eased on her other shoe. "Sometimes people misuse the ocean. But she means no harm. You should talk to her sometime." He reached out a hand to help her to her feet.

She hadn't gone swimming in the ocean since her mother's death. To Alex, the water loomed like a constant threat, and the tidal wave had not changed her mind. "Maybe."

Alex gripped his hand as he led her to his car. To her dismay, he was driving a very shiny red sports car. "Well, that certainly makes a statement."

"Does it?" He gazed at the car for a moment. "I guess. I hope it says fun."

She glanced at the back of the car. *Maserati.* She raised her eyebrows but said nothing.

"Picked it up last week. It's a sweet ride for the summer, don't you think?"

"Sure. But . . ." She worried that her wet bottom was about to ruin the leather seats. "I'm soaking wet. Maybe you should use your powers to dry me off?"

He shook his head. "I only use magic in life-saving situations. It's where I choose to draw the line."

Alex sighed. "Then I hope you have towels in there."

But Dylan just smiled. "Don't worry, I've never minded water."

* * *

The car drove like a dream, hugging the turns on the coastal roads like they were nothing at all. Alex stole a glance at the man behind the wheel. He had probably ruined his clothes while rescuing her, and he would certainly have to do something about the puddles she was leaving on the seats, and yet he was cheerful.

"Why are you being so nice to me?"

He did a double take. "Are you kidding?"

"You barely know me and you're driving me around in your new sports car, saving my life. Why?"

"The first time I saw you, I was ten years old and being driven to piano lessons. I told myself, if you were still playing in the garden when I returned, I'd ask my driver, Simmons, to stop so I could meet you." He looked down at his feet in an uncharacteristically shy manner, and Alex, oddly touched by the gesture, suddenly recalled him doing it often when they were younger. "You were there," he grinned. "And I made Simmons stop. I met you. And we played together. And twice a week on my way back from music lessons, we explored your aunt's gardens together."

He chuckled, and Alex though she saw a slight blush under his sun-kissed complexion. "I had a major crush on you back then."

He looked at her directly, his gaze searching her own. "I still like you, Alex. Is that so hard to believe?"

Now that shut her up. She sat back in her seat, unable to answer that question. She knew that men found her attractive. But she couldn't dispel the fear that he was up to something. She'd witnessed Dylan practicing magic, parting the water, expelling the fluid from her lungs, and calling her shoes to the shore. What if he'd been the one who'd sent the tidal wave in the first place? What if this had all been some elaborate scheme to win her trust? What if he had conspired with a member of his family to murder Randy Bennett? She mulled this over, grateful that she had gotten better at guarding her thoughts.

The Wesley estate appeared the same as it had when she'd pulled in last week, but somehow less intimidating. It was an old, Gothic stone house, nothing more, she thought as Dylan pulled around the circular driveway. As promised, Minka's car was waiting.

"Thank you for fixing the car," Alex said. "Insurance should cover most of it, and I told Minka I'd take care of the deductible—"

He held up a hand to stop her. "There are no charges for the tires or any of the repairs," he said. "It was scratched up, but I had the shop give it a fresh coat of paint. Same color. I hope your cousin doesn't mind." He smiled uncertainly.

Minka would be excited her insurance rate wouldn't be rising. "I can't imagine she would be upset." Alex touched his forearm. A flash of heat ran up her hand. She pulled away.

Dylan opened his car door. "Would you like to come in?"

She glanced down at her wet clothing and laughed. "I think our dinner is ruined."

"I could at least give you some towels before you go. I'll light a fire and get you something warm to drink."

The thought of sitting in front of warm dancing flames was enticing. Besides, this was her chance to get back into the Wesley library. Now that she knew Stephanie had been out of town when Randy was poisoned, she was back to considering other possibilities. Maybe she could sneak away and get her hands on Captain Bellamy's journal, after all—if for no reason but to rule out her suspicion that something in the journal was connected to the murder. "That sounds great, Dylan."

He came around to open her door and held out a hand to help her out, but her feet were bare again. Her shoes had shrunk from the water and she'd taken them off in the car. She winced as her weight pressed into the gravel.

"May I pick you up?" Dylan asked.

Alex considered the distance from the vehicle to the front door. Grudgingly, she nodded. "Sure. I don't think my feet can make it."

He reached down to lift her legs and carried her to the front door as if she weighed nothing at all. "We're sure getting to know each other, aren't we?" Alex cracked.

Dylan set her down gently on the marble. "I don't mind, do you?"

Her throat tightened and she shook her head.

He smiled. "Come on, let's get you warm."

He led her to a bathroom and gave her a stack of fluffy towels before leaving her alone. Alex wrapped the towels around her shoulders, luxuriating in the feel of the softly scented cotton. Once she was a little drier, she hung the wet towels on a rack and went to find Dylan. As promised, he was in front of a stone fireplace in a small side room, lighting a fire. Judging by the desk and the shelves of books, the room was primarily used as a study, but the leather chairs in front of the fire looked inviting. Alex grinned at Dylan's focus as he struck a match and waited for the kindling to catch. "Were you a Boy Scout?"

"For about a year," he quipped. "I asked our butler to make you a tea, but we can make it a hot toddy if you'd prefer."

"Better not; I'm driving." She sat on the rug and leaned her back against a chair. The kindling snapped and threw sparks as the flames caught. "Thanks again, Dylan."

He sat beside her. "For what? The towels? I don't do the laundry, so it makes no difference."

She laughed lightly. "No. I mean, yes, for the towels. But also for saving my life, and for taking care of Minka's car, and for finding my shoes." She noticed that he'd set them directly in front of the fire to dry them out. "You're . . . thoughtful." *And distractingly handsome.*

He'd changed out of his bloody shirt into a clean one, and this time he'd put on jeans instead of dress pants. As they watched the flames catch, Alex looked idly at a stack of documents on the desk. Her breath caught in her throat. The brown accordion file was marked with the name *Neptune Investments*. The Wesleys were behind Neptune Investments? Not Bronson Bellamy after all?

She'd barely digested this discovery when Dylan said, "This is my favorite room in the house."

"It's pretty."

Alex had to get him out of here. She had to sift through those files and figure out what he was up to. If she could get Dylan to leave the room. . . Alex focused on sending a thought to Dylan's mind. *Go check on the tea.*

He kept his profile to her. "Don't do that."

Startled, she looked at him. "Do what?"

Now he turned his dark eyes toward hers, and even in the dim firelight she saw disappointment. "Manipulate me with your thoughts. Friends don't do that to each other."

She swallowed, embarrassed by her feeble attempts. There was no point in lying. "How did you know?"

"My mother taught me how to block thought manipulation when I was a child. It's basic protection." He eased his back against the bottom of the couch. "And your thoughts are loud."

Alex's cheeks flushed in embarrassment. She'd thought she'd improved her guarding skills. What else had he heard her thinking about?

"A lot," he replied to her unspoken question. "You're suspicious of me. I can't do anything to change that except to be honest with you. So go ahead, Alex. Ask me what you want to know. Be honest with me for a change."

She flinched. He was right; she was being deceitful now, and had been during the course of their relationship. "Are you behind Neptune Investments?"

"I've invested most of my personal fortune. I'm behind a lot of companies," he replied simply. "And yes, Neptune is one of them." He set his head back against the cushion of the couch. "There's nothing suspicious about it. Bay Realty is a strong business and they're looking to sell. I'm trying to buy it."

"You're willing to pay more than it's worth. Why?"

The side of his mouth curled upward. "I get what I want, Alex. By any means necessary." He allowed the words to hang between them for a moment.

By any means necessary? Did that include murder?

He looked at her again, his sadness evident, and she realized once again that he'd heard her thoughts.

"It's a great company, and it's one my mother has been eyeing for a long time. If I get that for her, she'll head up Bay Realty and leave Wesley, Inc., in my capable hands." He frowned. "But Edwin called me yesterday and informed me that the deal is off. He said that people were sniffing around, making more of the transaction than it is."

He didn't need to say any more. Alex's throat tightened and she stared down at her feet. "It *is* kind of suspicious," she grumbled. "I mean, Randy Bennett's body is barely cold."

The fire was roaring now. A man in a butler's uniform entered silently with a tray of tea and scones.

"It's past teatime," Dylan explained, "but I thought you might be hungry."

Alex was too uncomfortable to eat, but she accepted a cup of tea and held it between her fingers. "Thank you."

He thanked the butler quietly and waited for him to exit the room. "So, what's with this journal you're so fixated on? Oh, don't look surprised," he said when she turned to him. "You snuck into the library during the charity auction. Bryn told me all about it." His jaw tightened. "She's always said that you're using me. It looks like she's right."

Ouch. "Dylan, I'm not—"

He held up a hand. "We're being honest with each other, remember? So I don't want to hear a defense, but I do want to know why you want Captain Bellamy's book. You only accepted my invitation tonight so that you could try to get it again."

"That's not true! I wasn't even thinking about that journal when you invited me here." Alex kept her focus on the fire. "But Bryn stole it from Pepper Bellamy. It should be returned. I was going to bring it back."

"The *truth*, Alex."

"Stop listening to my thoughts," she snapped. "I thought friends didn't do things like that to each other? Or are you only pretending to be my friend?"

A flush of red crawled up his neck. "How can I help but hear them when you're practically shouting?"

"You have a choice." Alex's voice trembled, but she couldn't help it. She was hurt that he'd spy on her. "You've been listening in on my thoughts this entire time. You didn't have to."

He drew a deep breath. "Your family should teach you how to protect yourself from people like me."

Her stomach clenched. *People like me?* What did that mean? Magicals? Or people capable of murder? She slid a furtive look his way, wondering if he'd heard her thoughts. He was nice, but there was something dangerous about him too, simmering underneath. Contained. But only because he wanted it to be.

They sat in silence. Dylan might have just saved her life, but Alex no longer trusted him.

"Why do you want the journal?" He turned toward her.

She gripped her teacup tighter. "I think there may be something in there that will lead me to the person who killed Randy Bennett."

"Based on what?"

"Based on the lengths your sister went to in order to stop Pepper from publishing information from that journal." When Alex saw Dylan's jaw clench, she added, "You told me to be honest, remember?"

The room felt chilly despite the roaring flames. The man did know how to get a fire going.

"Why in the world would my sister murder him?"

"I can't answer that," Alex admitted. "I would need to see the journal in order to know for sure."

He sat for a moment before suddenly rising and leaving the room.

He was gone for so long that Alex resolved to show herself out. With a sigh, she set her teacup down on the silver tray and grabbed her high heels. They were finally dry, but they would never look right again. She had pulled them on and resigned herself to throwing them out once she got home when Dylan reentered the room, carrying the book.

He held it out to her. "You want the journal? Here you go." When Alex hesitated, he said, "You were going to steal it. This is the better way, don't you think?"

She took the old leather journal in her hands and ran her fingers over the cover. "Dylan, I'm—"

"Don't." He stepped back to allow her a clear exit to the hallway. "I don't agree with my sister's methods for taking this, but I do agree with her reasons. Some secrets need to be protected, and what she did helped many families, yours included. So if you take it, I only ask that you not give it back to Pepper. Do I have your word?"

"Yes. Of course."

He chuckled without humor. "Not *of course*, Alex. Not when you've been lying as much as you have."

"You don't get to throw stones," Alex replied. "You've been eavesdropping on my thoughts. But I'll give it back to you. I only want to read it."

He turned his back to her. "Your keys are in the car."

Alex proceeded out of the room. Just as she reached the hall, she heard Dylan's voice behind her. "Alex?"

She turned around and saw him standing in the doorway, his beautiful brown eyes brimmed with sadness. "Yes?"

"You should get yourself some magic lessons. I can't promise I'll always be around to save you from the water."

Chapter Twenty-Two

A lex told Lidia and Minka everything about her evening when she returned home that night. They listened, attentive but alarmed, as she explained how the tidal wave had almost drowned her.

"I would've died if Dylan hadn't been there."

Lidia inhaled deeply. "I always suspected he was a good man," she said. "I can't believe he practiced magic, but under the circumstances . . . I'm deeply grateful."

Somehow, her aunt's words only filled Alex with more shame. *A good man.* And Alex had used him to get what she wanted. Bryn had been right, and Alex had proven it. She couldn't bring herself to talk about the rest of the night and how he had confronted her. But she didn't have to. Her family had promised they would do their best to respect her privacy, but from the concern in Minka's eyes, she'd overheard a thought or two.

"Someone is trying to hurt you." Minka's curls bounced with the force of her words. "It's time that we taught you how to defend yourself."

"I couldn't agree more," Lidia said. "Come on, I'm going to show you all the defense spells."

And so for the rest of the evening, Lidia and Minka gave Alex lessons in self-defense, guarding thoughts, blocking wind, stopping waves, and parting water. When Alex was too tired to continue, Lidia decided that Minka would work alone the next day so Alex could spend her time practicing her new skills.

"Go out by the fountain and work until lunch," Lidia said. "I'm not going to be able to sleep at night until I know you are properly defended."

To Alex, her new skills were disappointing. She ordered a bathtub full of water to part and managed to keep it that way for only seconds at a time before the sides crashed back together again. When she tried it on the fountain, she was only slightly more successful. She couldn't imagine ever being skilled enough to actually part the Atlantic the way Dylan had. A chill rushed through her when she thought of the power he'd displayed the night before. Why would someone like him choose to live as a Mundane? Or was he not telling the truth about that choice and merely practicing magic when it was convenient?

She wasn't any better at guarding her thoughts, either, because the moment she walked into the house after practicing all morning by the fountain, Lidia said, "There's no reason to feel so discouraged. You'll get the hang of it."

"You're still able to hear my thoughts?"

"Like you're yelling from the rooftops," Lidia replied coolly.

"That's it. I'm giving up."

Athena sat eagerly at Alex's feet and waited for attention. Alex was only too happy to give her a scratch on the chest. "I won't ever be good at this," she continued. "I'm focusing my thoughts and clearing my mind, but nothing is working."

Her life was such a mess. Time to give up, take the high-paying job doing what she was good at, and pretend none of this had ever happened. "I need to accept that I'm never going to be good at this. I can't face a Magical who's had years of practice. There's no possible way for me to protect myself."

Lidia was mopping the kitchen tiles, which had become part of her daily routine. "Power comes with practice, Aleksandra. Don't forget that." She dipped the rag top of the mop into the bucket and squeezed it out again. "You're tired. You've been practicing all day."

"And I'm terrible at magic. I've always had a better knack for things."

Lidia arched a brow. "Your mother was the most powerful Magical in generations. You've got the genes. It's only a matter of unlearning everything you've been taught."

"*Ciocia* Lidia? There's something I need to tell you." She took a breath. "I have a job offer."

Lidia paused in midsweep. "Oh?"

"A good one. In New York," Alex said quietly. "And I'm going to accept it."

Her aunt eyed her silently, and Alex feared she was going to see her explode into another storm of anger. Beg her to stay. Create an earthquake in the house. Shatter a window. But none of the things she feared happened.

Lidia chuckled lightly. "I'm glad you finally told me. I know you've been thinking about the offer for a while."

Alex gasped. "You knew?" Recognition dawned, and she shook her head slowly. "You could hear my thoughts, and you didn't say anything. Minka and Kamila too?"

"It's fine," her aunt assured her with a gentle smile, even though her eyes were sad. "I'm happy for you—we all are. You deserve this."

A sob bubbled up from Alex's chest. As she covered her face with her hands, Athena whined and nudged at her elbow.

"Oh, Alex." Her aunt moved to her side and wrapped her in a hug. "Don't cry."

But how could she not? She was leaving Lidia still under house arrest for a murder she didn't commit. She was abandoning Minka and Kamila and running away to a brand-new life. How could she not feel terrible about that? "I've failed you," she said between her sobs. "I tried. I did, but—"

She couldn't finish. A Magical was trying to kill her, and she couldn't defend herself. She was leaving town in an act of self-preservation and selfishness. Jack was right, she needed to stop investigating. And Dylan was right, she had to stay away from the water, and that meant leaving Bellamy Bay.

But Lidia wouldn't hear of it. "Now you listen to me, Aleksandra," she said, pulling Alex's hands away from her face. "You didn't create this problem, and you don't have to solve it." "Everything will work out."

"How can you say that?"

Lidia shrugged. "Because the universe has a way of self-correcting. It always does. But you, you need to move on with your life. Stop worrying about fixing mine."

Alex swallowed. "I'm not going to be too far. Just New York."

Lidia pushed a tendril of hair out of Alex's face and sighed. "I'm so happy you came back to Bellamy Bay. I hope you will think of this as your second home."

"Of course I will, *Ciocia*."

She gave Alex a long, tight hug, finally releasing her with a sigh. "Even if you're not here, you can practice your magic. It should still work in New York." She winked before standing again and reaching for her mop. "Mark my words: one day, you'll get the hang of it, and when you do? It's like riding a bike."

Alex planned to stick to the basics. Sending thoughts could come in handy, as could moving water every now and then. Maybe she'd even employ the occasional guidance spell, but beyond that? She'd leave magic to those who were more skilled. And besides, if she practiced magic, it might bring her to the attention of other Magicals. And who needed that?

To her aunt, she simply said, "That's a good idea."

She snapped her fingers and headed upstairs, Athena at her side. She would call Carter Hawthorne and tell him her decision, of course, and then she should pack.

Alex's cell phone chirped in her back pocket. She was still deep in her thoughts when she pulled it out and squinted at the message. Someone who was not in her contacts had sent her a text. *Are you still looking into who killed Randy?*

The breath caught in her throat. She couldn't type fast enough. *Who is this?*

Edwin.

He was still typing. Before she could ask another question, he had sent another text. *Urgent we talk. About Neptune. You were right.*

Excitement rippled through her body. Right about what? But then she thought about the conversation she'd just had with her aunt, the decisions she'd made. No, she wouldn't get further involved. With a resolute heart she began tapping in her answer. *Sorry. Heading out of town. Call the police if you have more information.*

Alex knew her words sounded callous, but her meddling into the affairs of the locals of Bellamy Bay had resulted in absolutely nothing. So many times she'd thought she was onto something, and it had led her nowhere. Her aunt was still suspected of murder and she'd made herself a target for a psychopathic Magical. She flung the phone across the bed and rose to retrieve a suitcase from the closet. Lidia was right: she hadn't created these problems and they weren't hers to fix. Alex dropped the suitcase on the bed and unzipped it. She had just opened a dresser drawer when her cell chirped with another message. Alex sighed and reached over to check her phone.

I think I know who did it.

Her heart skipped. *Who?* She typed with shaking fingers. *Neptune?*

Alex held her breath, exhaling only when she saw the response.

They're coming to the office to talk. Now. I'll stall as long as I can.

Her heart sunk. Dylan. She grabbed her purse. *On my way.*

* * *

The ride to Bay Realty was probably beautiful, but Alex didn't notice. She gripped the steering wheel harder and floored the pedal, making the drive in record time.

Alex slowed her vehicle as she approached the beautiful white colonial. The parking lot was almost empty—it was Saturday, after all. But Stephanie's SUV was parked across the street, and Stephanie was still sitting in the driver's seat, slouched down as if she was trying to hide. Alex swore under her breath and ducked lower in her seat.

Too late. Stephanie rolled down her window, her face a mask of anger. "What are you doing here?"

277

Alex stopped her vehicle opposite Stephanie's. She attempted to look nonchalant. "Oh, hey Stephanie."

"Don't," she snapped. "What are you doing here? You haven't been in town long enough to be Edwin's mistress, so I know you're up to something else."

Alex pushed her sunglasses on top of her head. "What are you talking about?"

Stephanie's face crumpled into tears. She leaned her head back against the headrest. "I've been such a fool."

"Don't move." Alex turned the vehicle so that she was parked a few paces behind the SUV, got out, and walked toward Stephanie. "Tell me what happened," she said when she reached the driver's side door. Alex reached a hand through the window to touch her gently on the shoulder.

Stephanie gestured to the passenger seat. "Get in. Hurry. She'll see you."

Alex dutifully jogged over to the other side of the car and took a seat. "There now. Here, have a tissue." She'd pulled it from a box on the floor of the car.

The widow blew her nose loudly. Her eyes and nose were rimmed in red. *This isn't the first time she's cried today.*

"He's been cheating on me," she said in a thick voice. "For who knows how long. The snake." She wiped at the ring of mascara below her eyes. "I can't believe this is happening again. Why am I even telling you this? You just accused me of murdering my husband in a coffee shop."

Alex laughed uncomfortably. "But it turned out okay, right? I mean, the police said you have an alibi." *Even though you may know how to be in two places at once.*

Stephanie narrowed her gaze and gave Alex a hard stare. "You owe me an apology."

Alex pushed down a groan. The last thing she wanted to do was apologize to someone who might still in fact be the murderer. But she knew she wouldn't get more information from Stephanie unless she played along. She pasted a conciliatory smile on her face. "Fine. I'm sorry."

"Frankly, that's not good enough." She blew her nose into the tissue and tossed it into the back seat. Alex tried not to make a face. "I don't even care. *She's* in there now." She howled again. "Everything he said was a lie."

But Alex was still trying to wrap her head around this. Who could Edwin be dating? Her thoughts instantly went to Celeste and her mysterious boyfriend. The barista had mentioned something about a deal he'd been working on . . .

She closed her eyes and shook her head. She'd been so distracted thinking about Dylan; now she wished she'd paid more attention to what Celeste had shared with her. Alex had felt such a sense of relief when she'd discovered that Jenna was Randy Bennet's mistress. But now she worried. Was Celeste involved in this drama after all? "Stephanie, how do you know this? I thought you and Edwin were in love."

"I heard him talking to her this morning," she said, her voice a mixture of pain and anger. "He was telling her to calm down, all of this whispering. He made some excuse to me and left the house. I followed him here." She frowned at the office building. "And sure enough, she was there waiting."

"But . . . who is she?"

"I don't know." She glared at Alex as if she were the young woman herself. "I've heard him raving about some grad student he met. So clever, so polished, so professional." She mocked the compliments in a high voice. "He met her at a networking event. It *must* be her."

Alex followed her gaze to the building. "And they're in there now?"

She nodded. "Both of them."

Alex set a hand on Stephanie's forearm. "So? Do you want to go in? I'll come with you—"

But she pushed Alex away. "Shh. She's coming out. Get down."

They ducked, peeking out the driver's side window to watch a young woman in large mirrored aviator sunglasses, a fitted leather jacket that skimmed narrow hips, tight low-rise jeans, and high heels walking to a white sports car. Her face was hidden beneath the brim of a baseball cap, a long, dark ponytail sprouting out of the back of the hat. The car's alarm beeped as she unlocked the door and climbed in.

Stephanie whispered, "Is he still inside?"

"I haven't seen him come out," Alex replied.

The sports car sped out of the driveway, too fast for her to get a look at the license plate, and turned onto the road without stopping.

"Shoot," Alex whispered. "I couldn't see her face." She really hoped it wasn't Celeste. She liked her, and she seemed to have a good head on her shoulders—aside from her questionable taste in men, of course.

She turned to Stephanie, but the woman was already opening her door and muttering under her breath about all the things she was going to do once she got her hands on Edwin. Alex got out, too, and hurried after her, more concerned about stopping bloodshed than anything else. Stephanie marched quickly up the drive.

"Okay," Alex said, catching up with her. "Maybe we should take a few deep breaths—"

Stephanie shot her a drop-dead glare and pushed open the front door. "All right, maybe not," Alex muttered, and caught the door before Stephanie slammed it shut in her face.

Inside, the building was silent. Even for a beautiful Saturday afternoon, this seemed unusual to Alex. This was a multimillion-dollar company, after all—how could no one have work to do today? She had worked nearly every weekend since graduating from business school.

"Where is everyone?" she whispered as they mounted the staircase. It was too quiet to speak at a normal volume.

"It's Saturday," Stephanie replied. "The office is closed. But if you're a cheater like Edwin, Saturday is when you meet your college-aged girlfriend."

This was such an awkward situation—given that technically Stephanie was also a girlfriend who had been cheating on her husband with Edwin up until two weeks ago—but Alex knew better than to wade into that shark pool, and so she kept her lips sealed and her thoughts guarded to the best of her ability. Witch or not, Stephanie was scary when angry.

They turned the corner toward Edwin's office.

"Stephanie, listen. Whatever happens, you're going to be okay. We're going to confront him calmly without resorting to violence, and I'm going to be right next to you."

"You can go take a long walk off a short pier, for all I care," she replied. "This is between me and Edwin." She barged into his office. "Edwin. You lying son of a—"

She froze, one hand on the doorknob. Alex was giving them a respectful distance, but she peered around the corner out of curiosity.

"What's wrong?" she whispered.

But she saw right away. Edwin lay facedown on his desk. His face was hidden, but his hands hung limply. A handgun was at his feet.

"Oh no," Alex gasped.

Beside her, Stephanie released an ear-piercing scream.

*   *   *

Jack Frazier was even less amused to see Alex than Stephanie had been. "You've got to be kidding me," he said when he first set eyes on her in the foyer, far away from Edwin Kenley, who was most definitely dead. "Alex. What have I told you about staying out of trouble?"

Alex had urged Stephanie to wait for the police in the sitting area, and Stephanie now had her head between her knees while Alex rubbed her back.

"Jack," Alex said, not rising to meet his hostility. "Surely there must be more important things for you to focus on right now?"

He paused to deliver one last disapproving frown at her and then moved on. "I'm going to need statements from you. From both of you. Don't leave."

"Of course. We saw someone leaving. A young woman in a white sports car."

"Did you get a license plate?"

"No, but I can give you a description."

"First things first." He glanced up at the walkway that ran through the second story. "Is he upstairs?"

She nodded, and Jack gestured to the police officers. "Let's go."

She didn't warn him about the horrific scene. Edwin had died of a single shot to the head, but Alex and Stephanie hadn't heard a gunshot. It was possible the woman had used a silencer, or she'd used her magic to muffle the sound. Alex knew Stephanie wasn't the one responsible for Edwin's death. But if she wasn't responsible for killing Edwin, then she wasn't responsible for killing Randy, either. A sick feeling roiled in her stomach. She'd spent a lot of time focusing on the wrong person, and she also owed the grieving widow a big apology.

"Stephanie, I need to apologize to you. Again. This time, a real one. I'm so sorry for being so dramatic in the coffee shop, and for thinking that you killed your husband."

Stephanie sat up, keeping her elbows on her knees. She had been hyperventilating, and Alex had been the one to suggest putting her head between her knees. She didn't know whether that was real first aid or something she'd seen on television, but at least Stephanie was breathing easier.

"It doesn't matter," she said. "Nothing matters. Randy is gone, and now Edwin . . ." Her chin trembled. "It wasn't suicide. *She* killed him. Some young murdering monster is taking *everything* from me. *Suicide?*" She rolled her eyes. "As if he'd leave me by choice. He loved me." She let out a moan and dissolved into a fresh wave of tears.

And that was the other thing; Edwin had supposedly left a suicide note. All it said was, *I'm the one who killed Randy. I can't live with the guilt.* Alex knew it was fake, but she couldn't reveal to the police that the guidance spell had shown that a Magical had killed Randy. She set a hand over Stephanie's in a weak attempt to comfort her. "We have to find this girl. Do you know anything else about her?"

"This is a nightmare." Stephanie massaged her forehead while she thought. "I don't know anything." She clenched her fists. "She killed him. You saw her prance right out like nothing was wrong, right? I'm not imagining this."

"No, you're not imagining anything." Alex squeezed her hand.

Had the woman who walked out of the office looked like anyone she knew? They had been too far away to get a good look. She thought of the young women she'd met so far: Celeste, Bryn, and Jenna. But that meant nothing; Bellamy Bay was a college town, and there were hundreds of young women in the area who could've been Edwin's mistress. But she knew of one woman in particular who was probably dating a married man—Celeste. She had to find her, confront her, and make her come clean about who she was dating. And if it was Edwin? The thought stopped her cold. That meant Celeste was a Magical . . . and one who practiced black magic. She'd mentioned that her mother was friends with *Ciocia* Lidia. Were they both witches? Did they get together and do . . . witchy things?

She turned her attention back to Stephanie, her voice firm with resolve. "Don't you worry, we're going to find her. There must be video cameras around the building. The police won't stop until someone pays for this crime. This is a tourist town; they can't have a murderer running free, right?"

Stephanie's nod was almost imperceptible. "I have a headache." She closed her eyes.

Alex tried to remember her magic lessons with Minka, but they had barely scratched the surface of healing. Still, maybe it was worth a shot.

"My dad used to get headaches," she lied. "I know a trick for getting rid of them. Would you mind if I touched you?"

She closed her eyes, wincing at the pain. "No. Go ahead."

Alex moved so that she was facing Stephanie. She touched her fingertips to her temples, light as a feather. *Relax. Comfort.* She didn't know the magical words, but she knew the feeling. *Health.* Her fingertips tingled, but Alex tried not to get excited. Focus was essential in order for the spell to complete; Minka had taught her that. *As natural as breathing.* And all at once, Alex felt the very calm she was sending to Stephanie. Her mind loosened, her breath deepened, and she felt soothed.

Stephanie's eyes fluttered open. "Wow," she whispered. "What did you just do?"

Alex smiled and released her touch. "Just a little trick."

She touched her head. "I feel amazing. It's . . . wow."

Alex sat back down beside Stephanie. She felt great, too. This was what no one had ever told her: that magic done to others reflected back on the Magical. For the first time in ages, Alex's thoughts were crystal clear. Her path was finally visible.

"We're going to find her, Stephanie," she said softly. "She won't get away with this."

Chapter
Twenty-Three

After giving her statement to Jack, Alex called the coffee shop on her way home, hoping Celeste would answer the phone. She needed to confirm that she hadn't been dating Edwin. But a male voice said, "Coffee O'Clock. How may I help you?"

"May I speak with Celeste, please?"

"She's not working today."

The words were like a punch in the gut. "Do you—is there a way I can contact her? Is she at school?"

The man snorted. "I don't keep her schedule. But I think I heard she's taking a few days off. A trip or something. You wanna leave a message?"

A few days off? A sick feeling grew in the pit of her stomach. *Is she leaving town? Getting out of Dodge after killing two people? And what was her motive?* Alex declined politely and disconnected the call. As she drove, she tried talking herself out of her own suspicions. Celeste was seeing an older man, but that didn't mean she'd been dating Edwin. It couldn't be her. She was too sweet. Too nice. Alex would've picked up on something, sensed her evilness, her penchant for murder.

She almost laughed, except there was nothing funny about this situation. If Celeste was a Magical, she was probably using a spell for trouble and cloaking her abilities. Or maybe it was her perfume. Maybe that beautiful scent she wore hid the smell of magic.

But there was a silver lining. Edwin had professed to killing his business partner, which meant her aunt was off the hook. Forced admission or not, her aunt didn't deserve to be on house arrest for another single day. If Edwin's staged suicide was what set her free, Alex could sleep just fine. But that didn't mean she was finished. A killer was on the loose.

Alex was so distracted that she hit the curb as she pulled in front of her aunt's house. She ran inside without bothering to correct her poor parking job.

"Alex." Minka rushed into the foyer to hug her. "You poor thing. We just heard about Edwin."

She accepted the hug but needed to talk to her aunt about Celeste and her mother. Were they Magicals? What did she know about Celeste? Athena ran circles around the two of them joyfully. "Minka, where's your mother? I need to talk to her about—"

"Shh, I know." Minka linked her arm with Alex's. "Edwin didn't kill himself. We know that. But Tobias is here, so we have to, you know." She mimed locking her lips and tossing the key away.

Athena yelped. Alex reached down to greet her. "Sorry, Athena. Where are my manners?"

Kamila wandered in then, carrying a glass of water. "Hey, Alex," she said, and rubbed Alex's shoulder. "How're you holding up?" She held out the glass. "I thought you could use this."

"I think she might want something stronger than water," Minka said. "And I don't mean herbal tea."

"No, I'm fine." Alex took the glass. "Thank you both. I mean it."

"I'm just glad it's over," Kamila said, releasing a breath. "Tobias said that he'll be filing papers on Monday. All the charges will be dropped."

"A deathbed confession *is* compelling evidence," Minka added.

But it's not over, Alex wanted to say. *And I know who the murderer is. You guys are never going to guess.* Maybe Lidia was going to be freed, but there were now two dead bodies and still no murderer in custody. She took a sip of the ice-cold water to avoid saying anything out loud. Her cousins were right to be relieved. She had no business taking that from them.

"Come on," Kamila said, wrapping her arm around Alex's shoulder. "We're all in here, and Mom has cookies."

When they entered the living room, Lidia and Tobias were engaged in a serious tête-à-tête on the couch. They finished their discussion before standing to greet Alex.

"My dear." Lidia pulled her into an embrace. "What a terrible shock you must have had."

The comforting feel of her aunt's embrace settled around her, and she realized how tired she was. "It was awful." She turned to the attorney and held out a hand. "Hi, Tobias."

"Quite a lot of excitement for a Saturday." He was dressed for a day on the golf course in a white polo and khakis, but he looked genuinely pleased to be there. "I was just telling Lidia that Stephanie Bennett is about to be a very wealthy woman."

Alex's limbs were heavy with fatigue. "I guess," she said. Then she frowned. "Why is Stephanie going to be wealthy?"

"Edwin must have been planning this . . . act," Winston replied delicately. "He came into my office last week. Just after

Randy's funeral, it must've been. He wanted to change his will. Left everything to Stephanie." He shook his head as if he couldn't quite believe it. "Guilt makes people do strange things. That woman just made more money in the past two weeks than most people earn in a lifetime."

Lidia set a hand on Alex's forearm. "You look pale. Please, sit and relax."

Alex's knees weakened. She allowed herself to be led to a seat, but she couldn't relax.

"It's terribly tragic," Lidia said. "He seemed like such a gentle man. To think that he would hurt Randy . . ."

He didn't, Alex thought. *And he was killed by the same person who killed Randy.* By the look of surprise that Lidia gave her, she'd heard her thoughts clearly.

Alex turned her attention to Tobias. "Did Stephanie change her will?" He glanced away. "No, that's all right, Tobias. Never mind. I understand you're concerned about attorney-client privilege. But Edwin's will must be published with the probate court now that he's deceased."

"That's right. It's no longer privileged." He still appeared uneasy.

"But I'll bet she changed her will, too," Alex said. "They loved each other."

And that's why Alex didn't believe Edwin had been having an affair, like Stephanie feared. He wasn't a womanizer like Randy, although it was natural that someone who was used to having a cheating husband would fear that every partner would betray her. But Alex didn't think that was what had happened.

When Tobias and her aunt began talking again, she pulled out her phone and reread the texts Edwin had sent just before his death. He had been asking for help with Neptune Investments.

Had someone threatened Edwin on the phone call Stephanie overheard? Had the woman they'd seen leaving the office lured him under the guise of working out their differences when what she really intended to do was kill him?

Alex rubbed at her forehead. *Back to Dylan.* His hey-I'm-a-good-guy act had been just that. An act. He had to be involved; after all, Neptune Investments was his company and he was a Magical. She recalled Celeste's friendly manner with him at the coffee shop. Of course, she was friendly with all of the customers, but now Alex wondered if there was more to it. Were they working together? Maybe Dylan had put her up to dating Edwin so they could . . . what exactly?

Alex glanced at Minka, wondering if she could have a full-fledged telepathic conversation with her. Her cousin must've heard her, because she looked her way, and her response of *Sure* reverberated through Alex's mind. *What's up?*

Then she heard Kamila's thoughts. *Are you guys seriously going to do this now?* Alex stifled a laugh but composed her features and pretended to be listening to Tobias as he continued his conversation with her aunt. *Sorry, this is important. It's about Celeste; she works at the coffee shop. Do either of you know her beyond being a barista?*

Alex observed the smirk of Kamila's face and suppressed an eye roll. Her cousin was sarcastic even in her thoughts, Alex thought with a grin. She could hear the tone even telepathically.

Minka gave her sister a reproachful look. *Why?*

Is she a Magical? Alex couldn't stop herself from turning to look at Minka. *Does she practice black magic?*

At this, her aunt gave her a stern look before turning to smile at something Tobias had said. Could her aunt hear her too? *Yes, I can,* came the thought, louder than all of the others. *And it's very rude for you to be doing this while we have company. Can this wait?*

Alex bit her bottom lip. *Sorry, no it can't. I have reason to believe that—*

Celeste is registered, came the abrupt thought. *As is her mother. They're both rule-abiding and upstanding members of the Magical community. What's the problem?*

Alex couldn't hide the shock on her face. Celeste was a witch, too? She'd hoped she was wrong about Celeste. But now? How had she missed it? And why hadn't Celeste just told her? Sighing, she set down her water with a clink. Of course Celeste and Dylan were working together. *Laying down the groundwork, my behind.* Celeste was good; she had to give her that.

Tobias gave her a concerned look before taking another cookie from the dish. She really wished he'd leave. She needed to talk to her family in the normal way. She focused her thoughts on the attorney. *You're tired. Go home. Get up—*

Stop it, her aunt said, loud and clear.

Alex was afraid to look at her aunt's face, but she knew she'd find a scowl there. Swallowing hard, she nodded slightly. She realized she was exhausted, and her temples pounded.

Her aunt's words appeared in her mind, softer this time. *You're tired. Why don't you get some rest. Tobias will understand.*

That's a good idea, Ciocia. Alex smiled at her aunt for giving her the excuse she needed to leave.

She rose and stretched. "I think I'm going to rest for a little while before dinner. Tobias, it was nice to see you again."

"Likewise, Alex."

"Have a good rest," Lidia said.

Athena followed Alex up the stairs and into her bedroom. Once they were there, Alex turned off the lights, pulled the curtains closed, and shut the door. Her mind was full of facts, speculation, and theories. She needed some alone time to work through everything. She would try to meditate.

*   *   *

Smiling to herself, Alex lay on her bed and closed her eyes. It would please her father to know she was giving it another try. She tried to still her mind, but everything she knew whirled around inside her head at a frantic pace. She couldn't grab hold of one single idea, her thoughts were so chaotic.

She took deep, calming breaths until her mental churning slowed down. There were a few moments of darkness, no thought, and she went deeper into those moments, seeking guidance and clarity. Finally, she went so deep into her mind that she must've fallen asleep. Her eyes snapped open, and she had the sense that more time than she realized had passed. She also felt more refreshed.

Blinking away her fogginess, she sat up. And then she remembered the last image she'd seen in her mind before she fell asleep. *The journal.* Was there something in there that she'd missed? She looked over at Captain Bellamy's tattered old diary, which was still on her nightstand. She picked it up.

Alex had flipped through the old pages last night. John Bellamy had been as gossipy as his great-great-granddaughter, painstakingly chronicling town rumors and legends about the Sobieski and Wesley families and even drawing mermaids in the margins. One day Alex would go back through the journal with an eye toward learning more about her family, but for now she was looking for something else. She just didn't know what.

Unfortunately, aside from the gossip, Captain Bellamy was kind of dull. He grew corn, beans, and potatoes and kept some livestock, and he documented his farming efforts in detail. *Jakub said last frost has passed. We will begin planting in the morning.* Or, *Found pigs on Wesley farm. Repaired wall with stones found in cornfield.* Alex skimmed these entries again, feeling like maybe this journal had been a dead end after all.

She set the journal down. Maybe it was nothing; after all, she'd tried to meditate only to rest her mind, not to solve the case. The mental image of the journal probably meant nothing. Before Edwin called her, her plan had been to leave. She could do that now. Lidia was going to be set free. Let the police handle the rest. Isn't that what Jack wanted, anyway?

Her suitcase was still lying open on the bed. She opened her dresser drawers and grabbed clothing by the armful. She'd stay a couple more days at most.

Alex froze. That was it. That was what she'd been missing. She grabbed her phone and pulled up an Internet browser. She waited impatiently for the search to complete, and then there it was. "It was right in front of me."

All of the pieces fell into place. The Wesley family was all over Captain Bellamy's journal. Jakub Wesley helping him to plant. Pigs wandering into the Wesley yard. The families sharing their harvest. That means the Wesleys and the Bellamys had been neighbors. Friends. She recalled that the Captain John Bellamy Homestead Nature Preserve was located across the street from Bay Realty headquarters. A quick Internet search revealed that this land had once been John Bellamy's farmland. No one else had lived anywhere near that remote property. Therefore, the Wesleys' homestead must have been where Randy and Edwin's office now stood.

The land dispute Tegan had with Randy concerned the site of the Wesley homestead—the site of the home that had burned to the ground a hundred years ago. It must have, because Bay Realty was located on that very land. That's why Dylan had created Neptune Investments and had been willing to spend top dollar to buy the entire business. He wanted his ancestral land back. But why? Was it just sentimental value? Surely that couldn't be the motive for killing two people. Unless the Wesleys just had no regard for human life—for Mundane life?

Alex ran through the information she'd amassed on the case. With Randy out of the way, the property went to Stephanie and Edwin. Neither was interested in selling the property. He was going to sell the business and develop the real estate as an additional investment, and he'd just filed the application that would allow him to break ground. This was about the land. First Randy had been the problem, and he'd been removed. Then Edwin was in the way, and he'd been killed . . .

Now Stephanie Bennett was going to inherit the entire business, but she didn't want to sell the land, either. As Alex recalled, Edwin had said Stephanie wanted to sell the business but live on that property herself.

Alex's heart began to race. She knew for a fact that Stephanie wasn't an unregistered Magical. She'd had no part in either death. She was just a Mundane. The breath caught in Alex's throat. *A Mundane who is in grave danger.* And Celeste was leaving town, which meant she had one more murder on her list.

She raced out of the bedroom, Athena quick on her heels. She raced down the stairs, stumbling toward the bottom. "Minka, I need your car."

Her cousin entered the foyer with a *kolaczki* in her hand. "What's going on?"

"I need your car," Alex repeated. "It's an emergency."

"What?" She lowered her hand to feed the cookie to Athena, who was happy to gobble it up. "I'm going on a date in half an hour."

"Can he pick you up?"

"I guess so—"

"Great. Thank you."

Alex was in too much of a rush to explain. And Tobias was still eating cookies and drinking coffee with her aunt. She grabbed the car keys and raced out the door. She sped toward Stephanie's colonial on the other side of town.

Alex turned the corner onto Stephanie's street. She pulled into the driveway behind the Porsche, relieved that she was home. Now she had to convince Stephanie to get to safety—wherever that was. She hoped the woman would trust her. She rang the doorbell and waited while the chime echoed through the house. Stephanie's voice came over the intercom beside the door. "Hello?"

"Stephanie, it's Alex Daniels. Can I come in? It's urgent."

"Sure. Door's unlocked."

There wasn't a minute to spare. Alex pressed the door open and stepped inside. The house was quiet. "Where are you?"

"Upstairs. Come on up," her voice called from above.

Alex sniffed, and the hair on the back of her neck rose. There was magic in the air. *Guard your thoughts*, she reminded herself. Celeste was already here.

She mounted the carpeted stairs. Alex's heart was in her throat. She clutched the banister, white-knuckled.

"Stephanie?" she called into the silent hall. "Where are you?"

"Over here," rang out the cheerful reply. "I'm packing for a trip."

Alex paused at that. She was also leaving? It wasn't possible that she and Celeste were working together, was it? She had to admit that if they were, it was kind of brilliant and Stephanie deserved an Oscar for her acting abilities.

Moving slowly now, Alex went in the direction of the voice. She came upon an office. The door was partially closed. Alex tucked her cell into her back pocket to keep her hands free, just in case. With her foot, Alex nudged the door open, wondering once again if Stephanie was friend or foe. "Stephanie, we need to talk—"

But Stephanie wasn't able to talk. She was being held against the wall by what looked like glowing ropes of blue energy that crisscrossed her body like magical tape. She was a few feet off the ground, and even though she struggled against the restraints, she was trapped. She was also trying to scream, but she couldn't open her mouth. The same luminescent blue material covered the lower half of her face in a glowing gag. Stephanie's eyes were the only thing free to move, and they clearly transmitted her emotions. They were large with fear, her pupils dilated with panic. She looked from Alex to behind the door several times, as if she were trying to send her a message.

Too late, Alex figured out someone was hiding there, but she smelled them first. The fragrance of magic was strong—overpowering, really. It filled her nostrils, causing her to cough and her eyes to smart. But the scent meshed with notes of something else.

A flower? Honeysuckle? No . . . it was a fruit, a base note of something sweet and juicy. Alex gasped with the knowledge. She knew who the murderer was.

And then someone stepped out of the shadows.

Alex's breath hitched in her throat.

It was Jenna, and she was holding a gun.

Chapter
Twenty-Four

"Jenna," she whispered. "What are you doing here?"

And why did she smell magic? It was the strongest she'd ever experienced. Was someone else here? Or was Jenna a Magical, too? Unregistered and flying under everyone's radar? She was so confused.

"I could ask you the same thing. Except it's no secret you've been running around town sticking your nose into matters that are none of your concern. Now why would you do that?"

Alex studied the young woman, wondering at the change in her voice. Normally sweet and soft sounding, it had a hard edge to it and a nasty tone. Jenna had been acting the whole time . . . but why? She had nothing to gain by killing Randy and everything to lose.

Just then Alex felt a vibration against her skin. Her cell phone. Alex reached into her pocket, but a gust of wind knocked it out of her hand. It barreled across the room, hitting the wall.

"Oops, hope I didn't crack the screen." Jenna curled her lip. "Now why don't you settle in. No one's going anywhere." She gestured Alex further into the office using the gun. The room contained a beautiful wooden desk, built-in shelves filled with books, and not much else.

She twirled the gun in her hand with a laugh. "This is Stephanie's. Can you believe she tried to stop me with it?" Jenna set the gun down on the desk next to a stack of papers. "Such a shame about Edwin," she continued. "Randy got what he deserved. But Edwin was nice. Greedy, but nice. Stephanie and I were just talking. She's simply heartbroken over Edwin's death. Two men in a few weeks." Jenna shook her head. "No one will blame her for making a rash decision."

"Jenna." Alex nearly choked on her name. "Why are you here?"

"You haven't figured it out?" Jenna scoffed. "Stephanie has our land, and she won't give it back." She glared at the poor woman writhing on the wall. "It's not yours. I thought you understood that."

"But it's not yours either, Jenna," Alex said. "You're not a Wesley."

"Oh, right." Jenna grinned, and the scent of magic increased as a strong wind began to blow around her, giving her the appearance of being the actual eye of a storm. Jenna's hair whipped around her face, darkening in color before Alex's eyes. The contours of her heart-shaped faced stretching into more angles. All the while, she smiled knowingly, staring Alex straight in the eyes. Then the wind stopped. Jenna shook out her hair and smoothed it down. She patted her cheeks and touched her nose as if she was making sure everything was in place. "That's much better. Nothing like being in your own skin."

Alex gasped. Jenna had vanished, morphing into a completely different person.

"So you see, I actually *am* a Wesley," she purred.

"A spell for trouble." Alex murmured in amazement as she stared at Bryn. *It's real.* Bryn Wesley had used magic to turn herself into Jenna. "The cloaking spell. That's how you disguised yourself." Dylan had been right when he'd said his sister was nice for a viper.

Bryn's mouth dropped open. "I heard that!" With a fling of her arm, a gust of wind lifted Alex off the ground and smashed her back against the wall. Pain ripped through her shoulders and she heard a snap. Alex screamed as she hit the floor.

Bryn mock-winced. "That sounded bad. It's probably broken."

Alex gritted her teeth and clutched her broken shoulder. Her right arm was useless, and every movement sent fire through her muscles. When she spoke, she struggled to get the words out.

"You and your brother were in this together from the start." Alex felt sadness at the realization that Dylan had deceived her so completely. "I thought he was better than that."

"Ugh, don't get me started," Bryn spat. "Dylan. He's such a *Mundane*. I was shocked when he pulled you from that wave. Shocked, I tell you. I didn't think he even remembered how to do that . . . well. I'll finish you off in a minute."

Bryn rounded the desk and leaned against the front. "But no, he didn't know anything about this. Dylan is idealistic. He thinks anything can be negotiated and bought in the Mundane way. But he was wrong, wasn't he, Stephanie?" She glanced at the squirming woman stuck to the wall. "Randy wouldn't sell, so I took him out. I parked outside his house, waited for Edwin to leave, and then I paid him one last visit." She grinned. "We had tea together. It was kind of our thing."

"You weren't on the security footage," Alex pointed out. "How did you . . . Magic?"

"Ding, ding, ding. Give the girl a cookie. Yeah, I just made myself invisible for a few minutes. It's also a spell for trouble, but I think you know by now the Wesleys don't play by the rules."

"And Edwin?" Alex asked, hoping to keep her talking until she could figure out a way out of this situation.

"When Dylan reapproached the company, Edwin wasn't playing fair." She frowned. "He took the land off the table, said it wasn't for sale. I mean, no one actually wanted that stupid company. What we need is the *land*." She laughed in disbelief, stalking toward Alex until she was nearly on top of her. "Like anyone would pay one hundred million dollars for that real-estate company. It's only worth a quarter of that. Give me a break."

On the word *break*, Bryn pressed her fingers into Alex's broken shoulder. A red mist bloomed in front of Alex's eyes, and she screamed. "You have no idea how badly I wanted to get rid of you. Especially when you began looking for the journal," Bryn hissed. "But making it look like Stephanie killed you will work, too."

She gave one last push and Alex nearly lost consciousness, but she gritted her teeth, fought through the tears, and focused on her need to survive this moment.

Alex drew stuttering breaths and sat upright slowly, clasping her right arm to her side with her left hand. Could she actually heal herself without Bryn knowing? If Bryn found out, she might kill Alex outright.

"I don't get it," Alex said, buying time. "I understand that you want the land, but why go to these lengths? Why the urgency? Surely this could have been negotiated over time. Money's not an object for your family."

"Time is of the essence," Bryn said. "If Edwin hadn't filed those plans to develop the land, he would still be alive. That land can't be torn up by Mundanes. Do you have any idea what's under there?"

"How would I—" Alex paused. Something had clicked, or maybe she had heard Bryn's thoughts. "It's the Mermaid of

Warsaw's shield, isn't it?" From what Kamila had told her, the Warsaw Shield would make the owner invincible, giving the Wesleys unchecked power. "You think it's still on that land?"

"*Duh*," she snarled. "It was in the old house when it burned, but then no one could find it in the rubble."

"Maybe because it was never there," Alex replied. "Because it's just a fairy tale your ancestors made up and they never had it in the first place."

Bryn rolled her eyes. "The story in our family is that someone saved it from the fire and hid it from the witch hunter by burying it in the ground. But when it was safe to retrieve it, no one could remember where it was hidden." She grunted in frustration. "It's been lost for generations."

Alex watched her for a moment. "I believe you're actually telling the truth."

Bryn made a face. "Like I care what you believe. But even someone as Mundane as you can see what a tragedy it would be if that priceless part of our history was removed and carted off to some museum." A look of disgust twisted her features. "And Edwin was going to build his apartment building right over the place where our home used to stand. Someone had to intervene."

"But why frame my aunt?" Alex said. "You didn't have to do that."

"Yes I did, Alex," she replied with exaggerated patience. "Because your family still believes the shield belongs to them. Like I would do all of this work, get that land, and then leave Lidia free to come after us?" She scoffed. "No. I thought, let the Council do my work for me. Lidia gets convicted of murder and they slap a shackle spell on her. Perfect, right?" Bryn shook her head. "But then my mother pointed out that once we have the shield, we're untouchable. No more Council rules, no more worrying about black-magic percentages. We could do whatever we wanted."

"So Tegan knew about this?" Alex asked.

"Yes, I'm afraid she did, and I had her blessing. Her only advice to me was not to fail." A bitter look crossed her face. "Then you appeared, causing problems, raising questions—I have to admit, though, I was very surprised at how nice you were to poor little pathetic wimpy Jenna. Does it make you sad to know your kindness was wasted on a fake person?" Bryn frowned mockingly. "I don't want to make you sad, Alex. You were so darn *nice* to me in that coffee shop when you thought I was a crybaby mourning the loss of a disgusting sleazoid of a man. Then Minka gave me a job. I was touched." She chuckled. "You Sobieskis are something else.

"I was going to marry Randy as Jenna. I really was. Bryn was going to take a long trip to Paris while Jenna stayed around and married him. And then I was going to kill him after the ceremony so I'd get his property. Then Jenna would sell me the land before disappearing into thin air." She snapped her fingers.

She turned her glare on Stephanie. "But then Randy was talking about reconciling with his *wife*, and he gave me perfume as a consolation gift. Can you imagine? 'I'm sorry we're not getting married, but here's a bottle of perfume.'" She shook her head. "He had it coming. He'd planned to tell Stephanie he wanted her back, but she was at the spa. I hope that was restful, Stephanie. It sounds nice. Ill-timed but really, really lovely."

Stephanie's face creased in pain, but she still couldn't make a sound.

Alex closed her eyes to focus on healing her shoulder. A tingling sensation like nerves sparking rose through her right fingers and trembled up her arm. She ground her teeth together. The sensation of rapid healing was excruciating, and her eyes watered. She stopped, breathless. The pain was too much to continue. But now when she moved, her shoulder hurt considerably less.

"That's pretty low, Bryn," Alex began. "Even by Wesley standards. Were you having an affair with Randy *and* Edwin?" She looked at Stephanie, who was watching Bryn closely.

Maybe she could build up a gust of wind and send the gun flying into her own hands. But given her lack of control over her powers, the gun might accidentally go off, or fly in the wrong direction.

"Of course not." Bryn wrinkled her nose. "Randy was bad enough. No offense, Steph," she said with a nod. "I don't know how you stayed married to him. He was slimy. Edwin was a step up, so good for you. But no, I didn't have an affair with him. I tried to beguile Edwin, and I think I succeeded. Young graduate student, trying to negotiate a deal so she could impress her internship coordinator at Neptune Investments." She barked a laugh. "As if an intern would be given that responsibility. But Edwin ate it up, and me stroking his ego didn't hurt." She lifted a shoulder. "Men, you know?"

She stuck out her lower lip in a pout. "Sadly, it wasn't enough. So I killed him. I have to say, Alex." She turned back. "I thought I was handing you a gift by making Edwin confess to Randy's death. It was the least I could do to thank you for helping me in my time of fake need. Lidia would go free, everyone lives happily ever after . . ."

"Except Randy and Edwin," Alex said through a clenched jaw. "They won't live happily ever after."

"Right," Bryn nodded. "Or Stephanie here. She's got to go, too. Right after she signs a purchase-and-sale agreement for her interest in Bay Realty. Including the land." She looked at Stephanie. "Do you want to do that now?" She offered a polite hostess smile. "We may as well."

The blue bands holding Stephanie dissolved in clouds of blue sparks. She fell off the wall and crashed to the floor.

Alex started to jump up to run to her side, but the pain in her shoulder made her head spin. So much for healing. She sat back against the wall, clenching her jaw. "Are you okay?"

"She can't answer you, Einstein," Bryn said. "I sealed her mouth. Now Stephanie, I need you to sign some papers for me."

Alex watched helplessly as Stephanie stumbled to the desk and signed page after page. "It won't be valid without witnesses," Alex noted.

Bryn laughed. "Yeah, okay. You think I can't find someone to witness this after the fact? As long as I have her signature and her fingerprints on the papers."

When Stephanie was finished, she pushed the stack angrily over to Bryn. "One sec, I just need to check." She flipped casually through the pages. "You have to initial—oh no, I see it now. Great." She stacked the documents neatly. "Looks like all the paperwork is in order. I'll take this with me." She tucked the documents carefully into a manila envelope before filing them into a bag behind the desk. "I'm going to need you to write out a note, too. For the police. I'll dictate."

Stephanie's hand moved over the paper, but Alex knew that Bryn was controlling her by magic.

"'I'm lost without Edwin and Randy,'" Bryn dictated. "'At least the company will survive.'" Bryn checked the note and gave a satisfied nod. "That's perfect. Thank you for being so cooperative, Stephanie."

"You're not giving her a choice," Alex seethed.

"I'm trying to be nice," Bryn said in mock sotto voce. "Don't ruin this. Now, Stephanie, you're going to pick up that gun. Go ahead, now."

It was now or never, controlled magic or not. As Stephanie reached for the weapon, Alex focused her attention. *Come to me.* A strong breeze came out of nowhere and sent the gun flying toward the bookcase.

Bryn's gaze turned toward Alex, amused. "You want to make this interesting?" She couldn't suppress her laughter. "A magical girl fight?"

Alex cursed to herself. With a deep breath, she rolled onto her knees and launched herself toward the bookcase, her vision clouded by sparks of hot pain. As Alex reached out a hand to clasp the gun, Bryn kicked it out of reach. "Poor little witch. Too bad someone shackled your mother before she could teach you how to actually fight."

Alex froze, still stretched out on her left side. "What do you mean?"

"Oh, come on. I can't be telling you anything new." Bryn crouched lower. Stephanie was frozen by the desk, still restrained by magic. "Everyone knows that your mother was shackled when she drowned. She could practically command the ocean. How else do you explain it?"

Alex's eyes widened, and a fresh ache grew in the center of her chest. "But that means—"

"She was murdered," Bryn finished. "Lidia never told you? A Magical put a shackle spell on her and drowned her." She grunted an unladylike laugh. "I mean, the irony. A water witch drowning?" Her lips twisted into a sneer. "No offense, but I want to shake the hand of a witch powerful enough to defeat your mother. I heard she was fierce. The best." She sighed. "But you? You're just a nuisance."

But as Bryn began to focus her ice-blue eyes, Alex turned to the bookcase. *Strike*, she silently commanded a copy of the *Oxford English Dictionary*. Obediently, the book dropped onto Bryn's back, knocking her to the floor. "Ouch!"

Prodded by a surge of adrenaline, Alex fumbled toward the gun, her right arm limp at her side. Behind her, Bryn was already rising. *Knock her down*, she ordered a set of textbooks. One landed squarely against her back, but three others fell harmlessly to the ground.

"Enough of this amateur-hour shtick. What's next, pulling a rabbit out of a top hat?" Bryn thrust both hands forward, sending a hot gust of wind that knocked Alex's head against the large wooden desk. Her vision blurred. Alex blinked, seeing double. When she could see clearly, she was relieved that the gun was still lying on the floor and only inches away.

Alex sent the bookcase crashing down, but Bryn was too quick, and it missed hitting her by inches. But it distracted Bryn long enough to allow Alex to reach the gun. Fighting against the pain in her broken shoulder and tears welling in her eyes, Alex lifted the weapon in the air with her left hand and aimed it in Bryn's direction.

She'd gone shooting with her father a few times as a teenager. As a law enforcement officer, he'd thought it was important that his little girl know how to defend herself and handle a gun. Only she hadn't paid much attention to the lessons. Now she fervently wished she'd taken notes. However, she figured she could recall enough to shoot Bryn if it came down to it. She just really hoped it didn't.

"Tell me who shackled my mother," she demanded.

"Is that supposed to scare me?" Bryn tilted her head and pointed at the weapon.

"A bullet can kill you just like anyone else," Alex said. "Magical or not."

"I don't know who killed her." Bryn smirked. "I was barely out of diapers."

Bryn feinted to the right, then lurched forward, arms ready to fling another bone-shattering wind her way. Alex took a deep breath, held it, and then squeezed the trigger. She remembered to keep her eyes open and her arm steady. The gun fired with a spark and a loud bang.

Bryn held up a hand and tried to stop the bullet with her magic, and for a moment the bullet wavered in the air between them.

Alex focused everything she had on the bullet. *Hit her*, she commanded with all of the authority she could muster, and it slowly moved through the air, picking up speed as it closed in on her.

Bryn stared at the bullet, her eyes widening in shock as she realized that Alex's powers superseded her own. She released a blood-curdling scream as the bullet exploded into her arm.

Alex couldn't tell what hurt Bryn more: the pain of the bullet or the fact that she couldn't match Alex's power.

As Bryn clutched her right arm to her body, blood began to seep through her sleeve. She stared at the wound in her bicep, watching the blood drip out, and then she turned to Alex. "That was stupid," she growled.

She gazed down at her torn skin again and murmured something. Seconds later, Bryn turned her attention back to Alex. "I'm tired of you."

Alex didn't have to suffer Bryn's magic, and she didn't need Mundane weapons. She could block Bryn's power with her own.

As Bryn narrowed her gaze, Alex directed her focus on Bryn's neck. *You can't breathe.* With a shudder, Bryn's head flung back and she clutched at her throat. She turned in surprise and stared at Alex, who heard her thoughts clearly. *What do you think you're doing?*

"I'm stopping you," Alex replied calmly.

She kept her eyes fixed on Bryn, who was clawing at her neck. She felt a hum of power coursing through her veins, a rush of adrenaline unlike anything she'd ever experienced.

I am a water witch.

I am descended from the Mermaid of Warsaw.

She was powerful, a protector. She didn't wield a sword and shield like her ancestor, but she would not allow anyone to mess with the people she cared about. A sensation hummed through her body, a pulsating energy that came from protecting the weak. It suffused her whole being, and she knew she was fulfilling her purpose in a way she never had before. She searched the room for Stephanie and found her cowering behind her desk, suddenly released from Bryn's magic.

"You need to run, Stephanie. Now. Go get help."

Stephanie grabbed on to the rim of the desk but struggled to stand on her feet. "I can't. My legs. They feel so heavy."

Placing her attention on Stephanie must have weakened Alex's magical grip on Bryn. A gurgle escaped from Bryn's throat as a blast of wind struck Alex squarely in the face, knocking her against a wall.

"You baby witch," Bryn growled. "You think you're better than me?"

With a flick of her wrist, she lifted Alex off the ground and slammed her back against the wall again. Alex's scream echoed in her own ears as her newly healed shoulder, still tender and raw, was reinjured.

Footsteps hit the stairs outside the room. Minka turned the corner to see Alex's figure crumpled in the corner. "Oh no you don't, Bryn." She entered and lifted a hand, forcing Bryn to the floor. "Alex, can you heal yourself?"

She didn't think she could. Not again. Not in this moment. Healing magic hurt almost as much as the injury itself. "Minka. How did you know?" She righted herself, but couldn't stand.

Despite the seriousness of the moment, Minka smiled. "You butt-dialed me, girl."

"I must have called you when I checked to make sure my phone was in my pocket."

"I tried to call you back, but you didn't pick up." Minka shrugged. "It gave me a good excuse to leave my date early. He was kind of a dud. He's a Mundane. I don't know why I expected more. Maybe I should start dating Magicals. Anyway, now I have a long voice mail with Ms. Wesley here talking about how she killed everyone. Wonder what the Council will have to say about that? I'm guessing you're going to be put in a shackle spell and forced to live as a Mundane for a long, long time."

Bryn was on her knees, clawing at her throat.

Minka nodded to Alex. "Hold tight. The police should be here any minute."

Stephanie was watching them, awestruck. Alex gave a nod in her direction. "Minka? What do we do about you-know-who?"

Kamila charged into the room, weapon drawn. "What's going on?"

"It's Bryn Wesley," Minka said. "She killed Randy and Edwin and she was about to kill Stephanie."

"You can stop your magic," Kamila said, removing handcuffs from her belt. "No funny business, Bryn, got it? I haven't forgotten how to cast a spell." Kamila pulled Bryn's hands behind her back and snapped the cuffs into place. Bryn moaned in pain when her newly healed arm was moved but didn't resist.

"Stephanie saw us," Alex said, gesturing to the woman cowering in the corner. "She may need medical attention." *And her mind erased*, she telepathed to Minka.

"You first," Minka said.

Alex winced as Minka gazed at her shoulder. She placed a hand on it, and Alex screamed into the palm of her hand as the bone crunched back into place. The healing seared her nerves until half of her body felt on fire. Finally, mercifully, it was finished. Alex, damp with perspiration, sat for several minutes to gather her breath.

In the meantime, Minka approached Stephanie with a gentle smile. "You're safe now, Mrs. Bennett. Can we talk for a few minutes?"

More police officers barged into the office.

"It's all clear," Kamila said over her shoulder. "But you'll want to bag that gun on the floor, and we have a woman here who needs a doctor."

Jack entered the room as one of the officers called for an ambulance. "Alex Daniels," he said with a slight smile. "It's gotten to the point where I'm surprised when I *don't* see you at a crime scene." He crouched to meet her eyes. "Are you all right?"

He reached out to touch the shoulder that had just healed, but Alex instinctively stopped him. She gripped his hand, and he helped her to her feet. "I'm all right," she replied. "A little shaken. That's the woman who killed Randy Bennett *and* Edwin Kenley, and she was about to kill Stephanie, too. If you check that bag, you'll find a purchase-and-sale agreement she forced Stephanie to sign at gunpoint. I saw the whole thing."

Jack looked over at Stephanie. Minka was no doubt murmuring the spell that would make her forget all the magic she'd just witnessed. She winked when she caught Alex's gaze.

Jack set his hands on his waist. "Well. I think I may owe you an apology or three."

She smiled, heat rising to her cheeks. But she was proud of herself. Darn proud. "You made a mistake. You're human." *A Mundane*, she thought with a measure of affection.

He laughed at that and then nodded to Minka. "You two okay? Did she hurt you?"

"No, thankfully we're fine," Minka said. "And Detective, I want my mom to be released—"

Jack held up a hand to stop her. "That's priority number one, Ms. Sobieski. I've already initiated the paperwork."

Minka sighed happily and wrapped her arms around Alex. "I didn't know if it would ever happen, but . . . wow. You did it."

"*We* did it." Alex hugged her back.

She smiled. It felt good to win again.

Chapter Twenty-Five

Alex was grateful for quiet. The day after Bryn was arrested, she slept late and lingered over breakfast. If it had been up to her, she would've planted herself in front of the television all day. But Athena found her leash and dropped it at Alex's feet while she was scrolling on her cell, and Alex could've sworn she heard the dog think, *Run?*

"I'm too tired to run, Athena," she said as she clipped the leash onto her collar. "But how does a walk sound?" The German shepherd jumped to her feet and barked. Alex followed her to the door with a chuckle.

As much as she longed to relax, a walk would do her good. The matter with Bryn was scheduled to be raised at the Council the next night, and Alex would have to testify. As Minka explained, they were going to debate whether to place a shackle spell on Bryn as punishment for her role in the murders.

"If they do," Minka said, "she won't be practicing magic anymore."

But losing her powers was the least of Bryn's problems. Jack had said she would be charged with two counts of first-degree murder and one count of attempted murder, plus whatever else they could throw at her.

Alex and Athena walked to Coffee O'Clock. Through the large storefront windows, Alex saw Celeste working. Now she was so glad she hadn't confronted her and accused her of being a murderer. But she still had questions. Like, why hadn't she told Alex she was a Magical, for starters. She attached her dog's leash to a bike rack before entering the shop, and waited in a short line for her turn to order.

Celeste's jaw dropped when she saw her. "Alex! Are you all right? I leave town for a romantic getaway in Asheville and the world goes topsy-turvy. What happened? Ever since I returned, everyone's been talking about what happened with Bryn."

Alex glanced around the shop, suddenly self-conscious. Sure enough, customers were watching her and whispering. She leaned closer to Celeste. "What are they saying? What do they know?"

She shook her head. "Everyone thinks Bryn just went berserk. There's a story about her floating around saying she was overworked, obsessed with her job, and she had a breakdown or something, and—"

"And killed two people?" Alex laughed. "Who's buying that?"

Celeste shrugged. "Not many, but it's the Wesleys, and they have their ways, you know? I heard through the grapevine that her family's trying to get her sent to a mental health facility instead of prison."

Alex groaned. So that's how the Wesleys were going to work this—like Bryn was temporarily insane. And after a long stay at a cushy facility, she'd be back and more vicious than ever. *Just great.*

"Let me make something special for you. It's on the house." Alex nodded, and Celeste reached for a large ceramic mug and set it on the counter. "There should be some perks for doing battle with Bryn." Celeste gave Alex a knowing look. "She's strong. But I'm guessing you're stronger." She turned her back to Alex and opened a cabinet, searching for ingredients.

Alex wasn't sure how to take that comment. She stared at the back of Celeste's head, watching her high ponytail swing back and forth as she selected a glass bottle of syrup and a jar of spice. Was she saying she was stronger in an emotional sense? Physically stronger? Or stronger in her magical powers?

I mean it in all ways, came the response.

Startled, Alex gasped.

Celeste had just sent her thoughts to her. She turned around with a grin before setting the items down. "How about we go a little crazy? I feel like you deserve something extra this morning." When Alex didn't answer, Celeste went to the refrigerator and returned with a container of freshly made whipped cream.

Eyes wide, Alex leaned over the counter and lowered her voice. "Why didn't you tell me?"

"Because," she said patiently as she poured a light-golden brew into the cup and then sprinkled cinnamon into it. "Before you came to town, Minka told me they'd decided as a family not to share the family history with you." She stirred the spice around the coffee for a moment and then squirted a clear syrup tinged with purple into the mug. "At least not yet. If you decided to stick around, then they'd reconsider. How was I to know they changed their mind? Of course, when I heard through the Magical grapevine that you'd squared off with Bryn in a battle of wits and powers"—she laughed—"I figured you knew." She finished the beverage off with a heaping spoonful of local honey.

Alex stared at her as she spooned whipped cream into the drink. "Why would my family agree not to tell me about my heritage? It's a huge secret to keep."

Celeste pushed the drink toward her. "I think they were trying to honor your mother's request." She lowered her voice to a whisper. "Minka said she wanted you to live as a Mundane." She cleared her throat. "So that's how I treated you, just like I treat everyone. Coffee with a smile."

Alex blushed as she thought about her idea that Celeste had been working with Dylan. "So, I guess you really want a job at Wesley, Inc., huh?"

Celeste frowned. "Of course. Why would you—"

"It's nothing. Forget it. But I am dying to know something . . . who are you dating?"

Celeste's eyes widened in surprise. "You want to know who my boyfriend is? Why?"

"When all of this stuff was going on, I kept running into men who had mistresses, and I worried that—"

Celeste burst into laughter. She covered her mouth with her hands, her eyes watering with tears. "You thought I'd—that I would . . ." She stifled another giggle. "I would never be so stupid. I know my worth, and that's why I was so bothered about keeping Jasper's secret."

"Jasper," Alex repeated.

Celeste placed a hand on her hip. "My mom didn't put you up to this, did she?"

Alex laughed, raising her hands in mock surrender. "No. I promise."

"All right." Celeste glanced around the shop and leaned an elbow on the counter. "He's a professor at the college. I never took one of his classes, so that wasn't the conflict, but we did meet on campus at an art showing . . . and we hit it off. We tried to ignore how we felt. I mean, I didn't want to get him in trouble, and of course, he didn't want to lose his job. But he's really into me, and I *so* dig him."

She looked like she was about to swoon, and Alex couldn't help but laugh.

"My mother has met him." She paused. "And she doesn't hate him." She laughed. "But she doesn't like him either. She thinks he's too old for me, but I've always been mature for my age, and it's only a ten-year difference." She shrugged. "We didn't start dating until this spring, but we need to keep it quiet until he puts in his notice. That's what he's been working on for the last semester— a proposal to curate a new exhibit at the history museum in town."

So that was the deal that had frustrated her, the one she had wished she could fix with magic. Alex nodded, relieved.

"And he just got word this week that not only do they accept his proposal, but they want him to become director of the museum—apparently there's a vacancy. In a few weeks we can stop sneaking around like we have something to be ashamed of."

"That's great. Even though he probably is too old for you," Alex said with raised eyebrows. "I'm happy for you both." She picked up her cup and sipped her drink. "Oh my God, this is delicious. What are those flavors . . ." She took another taste and then sniffed the aroma lifting from the beverage. "French lavender? Honey?"

Celeste nodded. "And cinnamon. It's good, right? It's my favorite coffee drink for the spring. It's even better served cold."

"Let's make this my new daily order, okay?"

"You got it. Just ask for"—she waved her hand with a flourish— "Spring in Paris."

Alex stuffed a few bills into the tips cup. "I better go. Athena's waiting for me. Have a great day, Celeste."

"You too."

Alex went outside and released Athena from her stay. As they continued their walk, Alex inhaled the sweet, light spring air. *Forget spring in Paris; spring in Bellamy Bay is amazing.* She hadn't felt this unburdened in a long time.

She was deep in thought when a sleek black limousine pulled up beside her. The tinted window rolled down, revealing a familiar face. Dylan Wesley.

He smiled. "Alex. Do you have a minute?"

Her body stiffened. "Leave me alone, Dylan." She gestured to Athena. "I have a dog to walk."

"She can come in, too."

Alex cocked her head. "You realize your sister tried to kill me? She broke my shoulder in two places."

"And you shot her," Dylan said calmly. "And now she's sitting in a jail cell. She can't hurt you."

"That's not my point. Your family has tried to send my car into the water and drown me. Can you blame me for keeping a distance?"

"It's important that we speak."

"Why should I listen?" Alex glared at him. "Since when do the Wesleys care about telling the truth?" But when she looked at his dark eyes, she believed his sincerity.

"Please. It will only be a minute."

"Fine. You have exactly one minute."

He rolled up the window, but not before Alex heard someone inside snap, "Dylan, you know dogs are not allowed in the limo." When Dylan opened the door, she was surprised to see Tegan. Athena paused at the entrance and growled at Tegan, before Dylan gestured for them to enter.

"It's fine," he assured them.

Alex and Athena entered and took a seat by the door. Alex stared at Tegan, perfectly poised with her hair in an elegant chignon. Her pantsuit was clearly couture.

Dylan looked appealing as ever in a soft yellow short-sleeved polo and stone-colored chinos. There was a stretch of silence as the three eyed each other, waiting for someone to speak.

Finally Tegan cleared her throat. "I understand that my daughter has been a source of some . . . trouble of late."

"Trouble?" Alex snorted. "She murdered two people, if that's what you mean. And yeah, I'd say that's a problem."

"Alex, on behalf of our family, I want to extend a sincere apology," Dylan said, ever the diplomat. "What happened with Bryn was inexcusable. And I'm ashamed that she would carry out such atrocities in our name. We understand there's a Council meeting tomorrow to deal with that, and we know you will be called to testify. We hope we can count on your cooperation."

Alex balked. "My cooperation?"

"Yes," Dylan continued. "Bryn will be punished for her actions, and rightfully so. But there's no need to bring anyone else into the picture. Do you understand?"

"Not really."

Dylan glanced sidelong at his mother, who rolled her eyes. "We're telling you that there's no need to mention that anyone else might have known what Bryn was doing."

"Meaning you?" Alex said.

"Let's not name names," Tegan replied. "Bryn acted alone. She's always been a willful child. Brilliant but willful. Let her take the blame."

"Bryn will be punished before the Council and in the Mundane courts," Dylan said. "We just need your . . . discretion."

"What is there to be discrete about?"

"This is so tedious." Tegan sighed. "He's talking about the truce, Alex. Our ancestors signed one decades ago. We don't want your family to think this is grounds for a brand-new witchy war. Got it?"

Dylan turned to Alex. "Can we count on you?"

Stiffly, she nodded. "Sure. Whatever." She wasn't interested in creating more drama between the families. She only wanted Bryn to pay for her crimes. "But you're both to leave my family alone. If you don't, I'm going straight to the Council. Got it?"

Dylan and Tegan exchanged a glance before he said, "Yes, ma'am."

"Super." Alex opened the limo door. "Come on, Athena."

"Wait." Dylan followed her and Athena onto the sidewalk and closed the limo door behind them. "Alex, I owe you a personal apology." Pain crossed his face. "Bryn sent the tidal wave, but the car . . . I'm responsible."

It took Alex a moment before the realization struck. "You're the one who blew up the car tires? You could have killed me!"

She took a step back. When Dylan reached out to stop her, Athena darted between them, her hair raised and a low growl in her throat. He lowered his hand. "You never would have gone into the water. I know how to direct my powers for strategic results. But yes, I wanted to scare you. Scare you off this investigative kick you were on. I was protecting my family, but I was also protecting you."

"How in the world were you protecting me?"

He glanced over his shoulder at the limo and sighed. "My family has a zero tolerance for . . . anyone who gets in their way. I didn't want you to end up as collateral damage."

"So you admit it, you knew what your sister was up to."

"No," he said, his voice firm. "I knew my sister was up to *something*, but I didn't know what. She and I don't see eye to eye on how we manage the family business, and if there's anything to do with magic, I'm always the last to find out."

"But you just said you knew I was in danger."

"I knew you were causing Bryn problems, and I knew if you didn't stop, she'd figure out a way to neutralize you. I didn't want that to happen." He lowered his voice. "I care about you. I always have."

Alex's legs trembled as she took a step back. "I thought I could trust you," she whispered. "I thought you didn't practice magic."

"Sometimes I can't help myself." He winced and looked away. "Sometimes magic is the best and fastest way to address challenges."

"So, you're no different from Bryn. Maybe you draw the line at murder, I don't know. But you're willing to do whatever it takes to get whatever you want. Right?"

He stared at her, the lines of his face hardening. "I don't know what the right thing to say is here."

"That's because there is no right thing to say. No words to fix this." Alex touched a hand to her head. She felt dizzy. Her family was right. She was better off staying far away from the Wesleys.

She had fond memories of them as children playing in the garden together. Despite the animosity between their families, deep down Alex had hoped she'd found an ally in Dylan. The realization that he had betrayed her in such a terrible way brought tears to her eyes. "I should go."

He took her hand in his, and once again she felt a surge of energy arc between them. "I protected you from Bryn," he said. "I pulled you from the water and I fixed the car. I'm trying to make up for my mistakes." His touch—his mere presence—was intoxicating. "I feel something whenever you're around, Aleksandra. I always have . . . And I know you feel it, too. I promise, I'm *trying* to be a good guy."

He smiled, but she withdrew her hand. "That's the problem, Dylan. You have to *try* to be good."

The words hung between.

His gaze fell to the ground. "If you ever have a change of heart. . ."

Her throat was tight as she nodded and turned away. There was nothing else to say.

* * *

That afternoon, spring was in full bloom. Alex, Lidia, Minka, and Kamila gathered around the fountain in the backyard to drink iced tea and enjoy the sunshine. The trees were bursting with flowers and the sky was brilliant. Alex thought this was one of those impossibly beautiful spring days.

"Another perfect day in Bellamy Bay," Minka announced. She was wearing shorts and a spaghetti-strapped top, trying to get a start on her tan.

Lidia inhaled the sweet, fragrant air and smiled. "I will never, ever take sitting outside for granted again."

Alex admired the tall pink rosebush Stephanie Bennett had delivered. It was still in a bucket, but only until they decided where to plant it in the garden. Stephanie had spent the night in the hospital after Bryn's attack, suffering from severe dehydration and a depletion of electrolytes. But once she was released, she had carried the rosebush up the walkway herself. When

Alex had run out to greet her, she'd set the plant down to give Alex a long hug.

"You saved me from that awful woman. I can't ever thank you enough."

"It was nothing."

"No, it wasn't. Everyone in town is talking about how you just happened to stop by for a visit and ended up preventing a brutal attack. You're a hero." She'd stepped back from the embrace, keeping her hands on Alex's arms as she looked her in the eye. "I will never forget what you did for me. I don't have the first idea how to repay you, but I thought something beautiful for your garden was a start."

Stephanie didn't remember anything about the magic she'd witnessed. All she knew was that Bryn had barged into her house and forced her at gunpoint to sign a purchase-and-sale agreement and write a fake suicide note. Then, Alex had saved her.

"I hope you'll think of me when these roses bloom," Stephanie had said. "Pink is for gratitude, and I'll be forever grateful to you for saving my life."

Now as the family sat around the mermaid fountain, Kamila elbowed Alex playfully in the ribs. "You're quiet today. You must be thinking about Detective Frazier."

Alex was horrified to hear herself actually giggle. But yes, she *had* been thinking about Jack.

"I'm happy we're giving it another try," she said. "That's all."

"He'd be a fool not to want to go out with you," Minka said.

Alex didn't think of it that way. Jack was a nice guy who didn't play games. When he'd asked her last night if she'd be open to having dinner with him, she'd thought *she'd* be a fool to say no.

Athena walked over then and rested her head on Alex's lap. The dog must have sensed something, because she hadn't strayed from Alex's side. Alex stroked her soft cheek. She'd always been grateful for Athena, but today she was extra grateful for the comfort her furry guardian provided.

And Athena was happy here. She loved chasing birds around the yard and running along the beach. Bellamy Bay was the perfect spot for her, and Alex had decided on their walk that morning that spring was the time to make a new start. That's why she was going to politely decline Carter Hawthorne's generous job offer. She planned to tell him that her family needed her.

But this was only half the truth, because Alex needed her family, too. For ages she'd longed for a missing piece of her life, but her aunt and cousins had filled that hole. But even they, with all of their unconditional love and support, could not replace her mother.

My mother. Bryn's words about her drowning had been weighing heavily on Alex. Had someone in the Magical community actually killed her? Or had Bryn said that to upset Alex in the moment? Regardless, Alex couldn't leave now, not when that question was unanswered.

And there was still the matter of the Warsaw Shield, and whether it was actually located on the Bay Realty land. Alex, Minka, and Lidia had vowed to inform the Council of the possibility because they couldn't risk having it fall into the wrong hands. Alex couldn't leave town with that matter unresolved, either.

She just hoped her family would allow her to stay.

"I have something to say," Alex began, and took a glimpse at the women surrounding her. "*Ciocia* Lidia, you already know I had a job offer in New York. Minka and Kamila, I didn't mention it because . . . well, there were other things going on, and the truth is, I wasn't sure I was going to take it."

She took a deep breath. "But after giving it some thought, I think that job is wrong for me. I don't want to spend another moment thinking about how risky life can be, and the ways in which I can mitigate the dangers I face. I have the sense that my mother would not want that for me."

She pushed back the tears that welled in her eyes every time she thought of her mother. "I like being here in Bellamy Bay with all of you. I enjoy helping people, healing people . . . making soap and herbal remedies." She reached over to pet Athena's back. "So I'm wondering if it would be all right if I stay. I promise I'll earn my keep, help out at Botanika—"

She couldn't finish her sentence because Minka had wrapped her arms so tightly around her chest. "I'm so happy you want to stay."

"Minka," Kamila said, "I don't think she can breathe."

"Sorry." Minka released her grip, but her happiness was evident in her brilliant smile.

"Of course you can stay for as long as you'd like," Lidia said as she pulled Alex into a softer embrace. "There is plenty of room, and we could use some help at the shop for the summer."

"Yeah, I heard that new girl you hired didn't work out so well," Kamila said, deadpan, and took a sip of her iced tea. But then she grinned. "That's what happens when you don't check references first."

"Ugh. Please don't ever mention Bryn again," Minka said. "She's powerful. She masked her magic and made me think she was someone else entirely." She shook her head in disbelief. "My witch radar is usually pretty strong."

"You need to practice more," her mother added, before turning to Alex. "You are always welcome in our home and as long as you like. Bellamy Bay is where you belong, too."

"Thank you all," Alex said. "For everything. You've made me and Athena feel at home. I'm not sure I've ever felt that way before."

"Alex, you're family," said Kamila. "We love you."

"And you'll really love this," Alex said, inching forward on the bench. "The practice is paying off."

With barely a blink, she sent a shot of water straight into the air. It danced in a little loop before landing right next to Athena. The dog leaped to her feet and barked at nothing, her tail wagging. The women broke out in laughter, which only excited Athena more. "You've caught on quickly," Kamila said.

"A natural if I ever saw one, just like your mother." Lidia patted her on the knee.

"We'll make a witch of you yet," Minka agreed.

Alex smiled and leaned back on her seat. Her skin was warm; her heart was warm. Today, her life was perfectly magical.

Acknowledgments

I wish to thank Chelsey and Matt, for taking a chance on a mystery based on mermaids.

I am grateful to Jenny, Melissa, Ashley and the rest of the Crooked Lane Books team for their support and assistance in publishing this story.

And I wish to thank Crystal and the BookSparks team for assisting me in finding the audience for this series.